NIGHTINGALE, SING

KARSTEN KNIGHT

North Palm Beach Library

PRAISE FOR WILDEFIRE BY KARSTEN KNIGHT, AVAILABLE NOW FROM SIMON & SCHUSTER

"In an era when the young adult paranormal and urban fantasy field is blessed with an abundance of great stories and storytellers, WILDEFIRE is an exceptional standout."

-San Diego Union-Tribune

"Knight has created a novel quite different from the coming-of-age/paranormal-teen reads that have glutted the market recently. Ash is a wry and interesting protagonist and the romance and gritty, violent action scenes are compelling."

-School Library Journal

"Knight's debut novel is an edgy twist on the magical boarding school theme. It's a fun, well-written, and engaging read with a last-sentence twist."

-Publisher's Weekly

"There's introspection here as well as sizzling sexuality, but the novel's strong narrative thrust relies on action, from violent brawls and accidents to encounters with terrifying, supernatural creatures in the redwood forest. A promising first novel."

-Booklist

"Knight has written a riveting, original multicultural fantasy. Teens will quickly devour this story and will be relieved to know a sequel is on its way."

-VOYA

NIGHTINGALE, SING.
Text copyright © 2016 by Karsten Knight.
All rights reserved, including reproduction in whole or in part in any form.
First edition: March 2016
www.karstenknightbooks.com

This book is a work of fiction. References to real events, people, and locales, past or present, are used fictitiously. All other elements are products of the author's imagination.

The text for this book is set in Garamond, Cinzel, and Trattatello.
Cover image: "Between the Waves" by Ivan Konstantinovich Aivazovsky.

"The tree of liberty must be refreshed from time to time with the blood of patriots and tyrants."
-Thomas Jefferson, 1787

THE SERENGETI SAPPHIRE
BOSTON, MASSACHUSETTS

WITHIN THE HALLOWED GREEN WALLS OF FENWAY PARK, forty thousand Red Sox fans rose to their feet. They held their collective breath as a monstrous hit from Gabriel Carrera climbed higher, higher, until the tiny white meteor began its descent toward the right-field fence. When the baseball sailed just clear of the foul pole, the explosive cheers from the stadium could be heard as far away as the Charles River.

Three blocks east, Jack Tides fled through the dark community gardens. With a postcard clutched in one hand and a knife in the other, he was trying to get to a mailbox before the men in the black van found him.

Nox's boys were coming to kill him tonight.

In the darkness, Jack blindly smashed into a lawn chair and nearly skewered himself on his own blade as he fell. He landed hard in a zucchini patch and briefly lay there dazed, listening to the sounds of the Boston night, searching for any traces of his pursuers. For now, he could only hear the distant commotion from Fenway and the occasional car rushing down Park Drive.

That didn't mean they weren't still out there.

If it were anyone else after him, Jack might make a run for the stadium. After all, who would dare execute him in front of thousands of witnesses?

But this was Horace Nox, the nightclub owner, the gangster, the one man in Boston you did *not* fuck with.

And Jack had stolen from him the one thing he treasured most.

1

Jack gazed off in the direction of Back Bay, where the imposing fifty-two-story Prudential Tower loomed over the tree line. If he made a run for a populated area, like downtown or the stadium, they'd gun him down just the same. If he went to the police, Nox had men on his payroll there, too. And if he tried to hide in the gardens until morning …

He heard the hounds.

There were two of them, barking with feral delight. He could imagine them straining at their leashes, snouts low to the ground as they dragged one of Nox's men ever closer. They must have picked up his trail where he'd escaped from the museum.

From the sound of it, they'd converge on him in less than a minute.

It was now or never. Jack picked himself up off the dirt and sprinted through the gardens, jumping over makeshift wooden fences, ducking under trellises, and trampling any crops in his way. He clambered up the hillside, and when he stumbled out from between the trees onto Park Drive, that's when he saw it:

A mailbox. A beacon of hope, its blue paint flaking off in chips, in front of an aging brick apartment building.

Jack took off across the street. A car blared its horn as it swerved to avoid him, but he thundered on, until at last, with a trembling hand, he dropped the crumpled postcard down the mailbox's gullet.

The metal mouth snapped shut with a resounding clang as it swallowed his little sister's last chance for survival.

Jack turned back to the road as a taxi came around the bend. He tucked his knife into the waistband of his jeans and waved frantically from the curbside, but the cab was already full with passengers and never even slowed.

Tires screeched behind Jack, as the familiar black van barreled down the street. He prayed that they'd mistake him for an innocent pedestrian, but it was too late—the van accelerated toward him. Jack turned on his heel and sprinted for the bridge.

As he took the corner, his lungs burned and he knew that even though he was giving it everything he had left, the van would catch up in seconds. The decisions he made now, during this short window while he was obscured from view by a cluster of trees, could mean the difference between life and death. So as he reached the crest of the stone bridge that passed over the marshy water of the Fens, he did the only thing he could think of.

He jumped off the bridge.

The fall was quick. One moment he was hurdling over the railing, barely clearing the stone lip. The next he flopped face-first into the murky river below.

As Jack resurfaced, he resisted the urge to gag on the foul-smelling waters, which reeked like a compost pile. He sought refuge beneath the bridge's arch as quietly as he could, keeping all but his head submerged in the cold, slimy stream. It wasn't a second too soon. The van came to an abrupt stop directly overhead. Not long after that, the barking of the dogs rose to a crescendo. Their handler silenced them with a gruff "Heel!" Jack could hear the click of their nails on the pavement as they milled about.

The van door slammed with unnecessary force. "How the hell did we lose Tides again?" the driver raved. Jack recognized his voice as belonging to Drumm, the former NFL-linebacker-turned-enforcer.

"He's a slippery bastard, for sure," said a man with a Southern drawl and a voice that sounded like the croak of a bullfrog—Pearce, the dog-handler. "The hounds'll pick up his scent soon enough. Where'd our gal Aries wander off to?"

"The hell if I know," Drumm replied. "That junkie creeps me out." He must have flicked his cigarette off the bridge, because the smoldering butt of it landed in the water a few feet from where Jack was concealed. It hissed before the embers died in the murk.

"All right, you circle around the Fens with the van until you spot Tides. I'll sweep toward Berklee to see if the boys pick up his stink again."

Moments later, the vehicle peeled away. The hounds resumed their barking, searching in frustration for the fugitive's scent.

Pressed against the bridge's stone underbelly, Jack waited until he judged that Nox's men must be far enough away. Then he cautiously edged out from his hiding place and scrambled up the embankment.

He never saw the wooden croquet mallet coming until it smashed into his knee.

With a sharp cry, he reached for his battered leg, but the mallet whipped around again. This time it collided with his cheekbone.

Jack dropped limply into the marsh waters. As he lay there, half-floating, he was momentarily confused as to which way was up and which way was down.

A figure stepped into view overhead. Jack's vision was still swimming from the blow to his face, but he could make out the silhouette:

A woman with ram's horns spiraling out of either side of her head.

The horned woman crouched closer, until Jack could see that she was no demon—in fact, she couldn't be much older than her early twenties. Her ram's horns were actually metal prostheses fastened to her skull somewhere beneath the nest of her spiked hair.

"You've been a bad boy, Jack Tides," Aries said in a husky Latin accent. She pressed the shaft of her croquet mallet into Jack's windpipe. He let out a hollow wheeze and grabbed ahold of the stick, trying to keep his head from being forced under the water. Was this it? Was he going to drown in the Fens, his last minute on earth spent choking on putrid water while his brain died from oxygen deprivation?

"Enough," Drumm growled from somewhere behind Aries. "Boss wants him alive ... for now."

Grudgingly, she relented and the two mercenaries hauled Jack up by his shoulders. He bellowed as his weight came down on his mangled knee. Next thing he knew, he was tossed like a dishrag into the back of a van. The Boston night disappeared behind the sliding door.

THE SEAPORT

It wasn't that Jack didn't fight back. But with his injured leg struggling to support his weight and his knife lost in the Fenway marsh, he proved a less than formidable opponent as Drumm and Aries forcibly removed him from the van. With each of them securing one of his elbows, they carried him down the dimly lit alley.

A second vehicle arrived behind the brick building—it was Pearce, whose Rhodesian ridgebacks barked feverishly in the cab of his pickup, smelling that their prey was near. Pearce's comb-over glistened with sweat, which he wiped off with two fingers and flicked contemptuously at Jack's face. Then he cast open the building's two massive cellar doors and Jack's captors dragged him down into a dank basement.

Aries slammed him onto a wooden table, holding him down while Drumm used a length of rope to tie him in place. Jack tried to wriggle free, but the taut cords had him pinned at the shoulders. He hadn't been sure where they were taking him while he was in the windowless van, but between the briny smell of the harbor and the muffled melody of a big band orchestra playing one story above them, he now realized exactly where he was.

He was beneath the Nightingale.

On the other side of the basement, the elevator droned an ominous "ding" and the doors parted.

Horace Nox had arrived.

Horror-struck, Jack picked his aching head as far off the table as he could to get a good look at the man. Jack had worked at the Nightingale for over a month before he'd even met Nox, at first only observing the gangster from afar as he walked around the nightclub like a god amongst men. But when word of Jack's bottomless knowledge of local New England history had gotten around—a seed that Jack had intentionally sowed himself—Nox had offered him a new job. "A promotion," he had called it. He needed Jack's historical expertise in solving a 150-year-old trail of riddles, scribbled on the pages of an antique Civil War journal. Riddles that, according to myth, would lead to an object of immeasurable value.

So Jack had helped him unearth the second riddle. Then the third, and the fourth, and the fifth.

The last time Jack had seen Nox was a week ago, when they'd followed the clues in the sixth riddle to Block Island. There, they'd excavated a chest from a bluff overlooking the ocean, only to find it completely empty.

Because twenty-four hours prior, unbeknownst to Nox, Jack had dug up the seventh riddle for himself.

Nox walked unhurriedly across the cellar floor, a half-empty glass of scotch in one hand. When he reached Jack, he noisily dragged a stool up beside the table and peered quietly down at his captive. Nox was the kind of man who, from a distance, seemed to be well-preserved for his age. His long, luxuriant hair had prematurely turned pewter, but his face was smooth, his blue eyes shrewd and arrogant in the way he took in the room.

He wore an expensive three-piece suit, crisply pressed and tailored to his muscular contours. Yes, from a distance he looked closer to eighteen than thirty.

But up this close, Jack could see where the illusion ended. Somewhere beneath the youthful, energetic veneer, there was a deep and penetrating sickness. Not just of the mind, but of the body as well. His vulpine face was pulled too tight, too thin, the angles of it harsh and exact, like the woodcut features of a ventriloquist dummy.

Horace Nox was dying.

Nox drained the last remnants of his drink in one long gulp, then tapped the glass with his manicured fingernail—*ting, ting, ting.* "Get me another Blood and Sand, Drumm," he said in his baritone rasp. Even his vocal cords seemed to be stretched to their limits, a victim of wartime shrapnel. A scar still bisected his Adam's apple.

His giant manservant obediently snatched the tumbler from Nox's hand and disappeared.

"You know," Nox said, finally addressing Jack, "in my line of business, you have to be paranoid. It's the only way to survive, really. Day in and day out, I find myself dealing with gamblers and gangsters and drug dealers"—He jerked his thumb back toward where Aries was polishing one of her ram's horns in front of a dirty mirror—"and disreputable sorts of all varieties. Yet of all the creeps on my payroll, I would have never guessed that you would be the one to steal from me." He let out an exasperated laugh. "You! My fucking busboy! The ungrateful history nerd who ripped me off after I gave him the opportunity of a lifetime. *You're* the one who took what was rightfully mine?"

"Opportunity of a lifetime?" Jack echoed. "Golly, Pop, thanks for the minimum wage job scrubbing your dishes and doing your homework."

Nox *tsk-tsked*. "We both know you didn't do this for the money."

"You know nothing about me, Horace."

"Is that so?" Nox snapped his fingers and Pearce handed him a folder. He licked his thumb and leafed through the papers inside. "Jack Tides," he read aloud. "Age: eighteen. Graduated valedictorian of Dorchester High School and is now a freshman at Boston University majoring in American studies." Nox placed a hand over his heart. "How patriotic of you."

As Nox continued reading, he paced around the table. "Son of Calista and Jack Tides Senior, who goes by 'Buck' amongst his associates. Calista is an immigrant by way of Cyprus, who worked her way through nursing school and has been employed at Children's Hospital for the last twenty years. Shortly after she came to America in the early nineties, she met and married your degenerate father. Buck is old-city Irish and was a subway car driver for many years, but is currently locked away at Cedar Junction Correctional, serving a fifteen-year sentence for armed robbery. Chance of early parole for good behavior: unlikely." Nox raised his eyebrows. "I guess the apple doesn't fall far from the thieving tree."

"Enough," Jack growled.

Nox pursed his lips. "Oh, I haven't even gotten to the juicy parts yet. You have two sisters. Sabra, seventeen, just started her senior year at Dorchester High." He laughed lecherously and punched Jack on the arm. "Irish Twins, huh, only a year apart? I guess Mom and Old Buck couldn't wait another minute to get back in the sack after you popped out."

In his mind, Jack pictured himself snapping free of his restraints and ripping Nox's malformed larynx right out of his throat.

"Sabra spends her evenings making a little extra cash as a pedicab driver in Boston, which means her report cards don't tend to live up to those of her overachieving brother. And finally, there's little Echo, age eight, who if I'm doing the math correctly, must have been conceived right before the Boston Police caught your father trying to roll over a warehouse—one of *my* warehouses, no less—with a semiautomatic. And according to my meticulous research ..." Nox dropped the file and leaned over Jack. "... your eight-year-old sister is currently at Children's Hospital in the oncology ward, being treated for stage-three Hodgkin's lymphoma."

Jack's eye brimmed with tears at the mention of Echo. "I said *enough*, you asshole."

Drumm returned with Nox's cocktail. Nox swilled the sanguine liquid around, ruminating. "I'm not a heartless bastard like you probably think. Hell, I get it. Your little sister's dying of cancer. So you worm your way into my organization. You give me the slip, you steal a page from the journal, and you take up the quest for yourself. You thought you could find the Serengeti Sapphire on your own and then use it to save Echo." Nox broke off into a vile, wet cough. He plucked a white handkerchief from the pocket of his suit jacket and hacked explosively into it. When the convulsions finally ceased, he held the cloth up for Jack to see. It was speckled with blood. "But illness affects all of us, Jack. The Sapphire is destined to save me, not Echo."

"She's just a kid, Horace," Jack pleaded, choking on the words. "She is everything to me. And she is *suffering*. You of all people know what it's like to waste away your childhood in constant agony." He desperately searched Nox's face for any sign that he was getting through to him. "So please, let's put all this behind us and work together. There's still time for us to give her the miracle that she deserves, before it's too late."

There was a strange glint in Nox's eye as he stared down into his drink, and Jack briefly hoped that he might have struck a chord. But then Nox asked, "Do you know what the difference

9

is between me and Echo?" He tapped the area over his heart. "I'm a fighter. A survivor. After thirty years battling my way back from death's threshold, I've earned my stripes. So I'll be damned if I'm going to just pass off my ticket to a healthy life to some toddling slum rat who doesn't have the guts not to give up."

That last part pushed Jack so far over the edge that his lips took on a life of their own. "Thirty years? All I see is the same cowering, sick little boy who never grew up—"

Jack was blindsided when Nox drilled a fist into his injured knee. His vision seared white. "Where is the seventh page of the journal?" Nox screamed into his face. "Where is it, you little maggot?" The gangster hammered Jack's mangled knee a second time, this time eliciting a pained scream from the boy. "I know you found it, so where is it? In the museum?"

Jack offered nothing. He would protect Echo until his last breath.

In a rage, Nox threw his drink across the room. It shattered against the stone wall. The kingpin stripped off his expensive coat and rolled up his sleeves, cuffing them at the elbows, exposing a tattoo across his wrist that read *aiséirí*—Gaelic for "resurrection."

Nox wound up like he was going to strike Jack again, this time across the face, but his hand stopped just shy. Instead, the gangster gave his men a single softly spoken order: "Funnel him."

Before Jack could make sense of this, Drumm forced the end of a plastic tube into his mouth. While Jack gagged, Aries uncapped a bottle of vodka and began to pour it into a funnel attached to the tube.

The alcohol hit Jack's mouth like a tidal wave of napalm. While his throat burned, he tried to push the tube out with his tongue, but it was jammed so tight that he was forced to swallow the booze to keep it out of his airway. His stomach turned from the onslaught. Right as Drumm removed the funnel at last, Jack vomited. He had to turn his head to keep from drowning in his own bile.

"Where is the journal page?" Nox screamed. When Jack gritted his teeth and shook his head in response, Nox motioned to his henchmen and the process repeated. Drumm had to pry open Jack's jaw to get the tube back in, but eventually he prevailed, and again the vodka flowed down his throat.

By the time the second round of torture was over, the alcohol had already bled into Jack's system. The room spun in lazy, uneven circles, and when he turned his head, there seemed to be a three-second delay before his body would obey the commands of his brain.

This time, Nox grabbed a handful of Jack's hair and forced the teenage boy to stare into his eyes. "Last chance, Tides," Nox seethed. "Where is the journal page?"

Jack brought his lips as close to Nox's ear as he could.

And then he whispered, "I used it … to wipe my ass."

Nox took a step away and sized up his prisoner. "He's not going to tell me," he said, his fury giving way to resignation. "If he wants to be a martyr, then let him die." From a tray in the back of the room, Nox produced a large syringe. A transparent liquid squirted out of the needle when he tapped the plunger. "Pure ethanol," he explained. "See, when your blood alcohol level rises above point-three percent, your body slowly begins to shut down. Severe motor impairment. Loss of bladder control. Irregularities in breathing and heartbeat. Unconsciousness. And death. Combined with the alcohol already in your system, this should put you right up around point-six percent."

Jack squirmed beneath the ropes, but Drumm and Pearce held him down by his shoulders. Nox handed the syringe to Aries. "I'm going to find that riddle, with or without your help,

Jack. Once I obtain the Serengeti Sapphire and am resurrected, I promise to send two bereavement cards to your mother. One for you and one for Echo."

With that, Nox turned and headed back for the elevator doors.

"What do you want us to do with him, boss?" Aries asked, twirling the syringe between her fingers.

"Once his heart stops, toss him out in front of a rival nightclub," Nox said. "Preferably the Mad Raven. Tonight he'll be just another college student who didn't know his limits and drank himself to death." The elevator doors closed, and Jack's last image of Nox was of him grinning softly and humming the tune *We'll Meet Again*.

Jack felt at once terrified and sluggish, as the vodka in his stomach continued to leach into his bloodstream. Maybe this wasn't such a bad way to die. Maybe he'd feel nothing.

He shut his eyes, crying softly, as Aries came toward him with the needle.

But behind his closed eyelids, he saw something else.

Poor Echo, laid up in her hospital bed, looking pale and gossamer as ever, her dimples growing smaller with each passing day. Sabra and his mother sitting by her bedside. All of them, staring at the hospital door, waiting for him to come.

They'd never know the lengths he had gone to try and save Echo.

He felt Drumm and Pearce relax their grip on his shoulders. He felt the needle bite into his skin.

And that's when he struck.

With every vestige of strength he had left, he flung open his arms and jerked his body upright. Though the vodka may have diminished his coordination, it hadn't sapped his brute strength. The rope burned intensely as it cut into his shoulders, but he felt its resistance suddenly give way.

The rope snapped.

Everyone was caught by surprise, and even Jack was shocked that it had worked. He ripped the syringe out of his leg before Aries had fully expelled its contents, flipped it around, and plunged it into Drumm's thigh. Jack could feel the metal tip slice through the man's mammoth quadriceps until it struck his femur bone. Drumm screamed and collapsed to the ground.

Aries, doped up on Blyss, was slow to react, and Jack seized her by her prosthetic horns. With a savage jerk down, he smashed her face into the table and she too crumpled to the cellar floor.

Pearce wrapped an arm around Jack's neck and squeezed. Jack threw his elbow back into the dog handler's gut to stun him. Pearce's grip didn't falter, so Jack kicked off on the table. The momentum carried the two of them to the floor, with Pearce on the bottom. Jack's weight came down hard on the man, and there was a crack that must have been Pearce's skull striking the cement. His hold on Jack slackened.

Jack could already hear Aries stirring on the opposite side of the table, and Drumm was rolling on the floor, clutching his bloody thigh and growling something about murder.

Jack knew that as the alcohol continued to seep into his bloodstream, he would soon lose consciousness. So with no other choice, he limped across the basement, hobbled up the steps, shouldered his way through the cellar doors, and stumbled out into the chilly October night.

He had to call Sabra before the darkness took him.

SABRA TIDES
Four Hours Earlier

I LOVED STALKING THIS PARTICULAR STREET CORNER, because the tourists migrated here in droves.

And tourists made for the easiest marks.

As I idly spun the bicycle pedals in reverse, I decided the corner of North and Congress was the Bermuda Triangle of oblivious Boston tourists. A hundred feet from where I had parked my pedicab stood Quincy Market, a regal building with stately columns guarding its front entrance. From the outside it looked like a courthouse, but inside was a crowded, deafening hall of fast-food vendors that vacuumed in hungry tourists and college students alike. They flocked here by the thousands to stuff their faces with "authentic North End pizza" and "New England's finest clam chowder." Basically any food that would simultaneously empty their wallets and clog their arteries. I loved and hated the market at the same time, a sentiment I shared with most native Bostonians.

While the other pedicab drivers tended to lurk in the vicinity of the baseball stadium, squabbling with each other over fares, I liked to wait here and prey on the post-dinner crowd, who were generally too full to waddle any farther.

Unfortunately, not everyone was keen to climb into the back of a pedicab. I pedaled up beside a middle-aged couple who were trying to flag down a taxi. "Hop right in," I instructed them. "Twenty dollars and I'll take you anywhere within a three-mile radius."

The husband eyed my neon green reflective vest and my pedicab, all with measured disgust. "What the hell are you riding, girl?"

"This?" I gestured from my seat to the three-person carriage in tow. "Well, you see, when a bicycle loves a stagecoach very much, and they decide to bring a child into the world …" No response from the couple. "It's a pedicab. Cheaper than a taxi, *and* you get some fresh air on this beautiful October night."

The wife drew her fox-fur coat tightly around her. "Beautiful night? It's fifty-five degrees and plummeting—hardly a heat wave."

At that moment, a cab swerved sharply into the curb and the couple piled impatiently into the back without another glance at me. "Do you know how many drunken college kids have probably puked in that backseat?" I yelled after them, but my words were lost in the slipstream as the taxi peeled away. "Vultures," I muttered.

"Vultures are not indigenous to Boston, Sabra," said a familiar, nasally voice. "Seagulls, yes. Vultures, no."

I hadn't even heard Rufus pull up alongside me. Between his gangly frame and the sandy hair and beard that poked out from under the brim of his helmet, he always reminded me of an overstuffed scarecrow. Rufus was my only real friend in the competitive pedicab driver community. That said, the guy was a total train wreck for somebody pushing thirty years old. By day, he ran a disreputable private detective agency out of a dingy flat above a butcher shop in Malden. Despite working two jobs, he still never made rent on time, most likely because he smoked away the lion's share of his profits.

I nodded to the empty backseat of Rufus's pedicab. "Slow night for you, too?"

"Damnable college kids," he muttered in his best elderly voice, while shaking his fist. "Willing to spend hundreds of

15

dollars on their parents' credit cards at the bar, yet unwilling to spend more than a two-dollar subway ride to get there."

"Says Boston's finest role model for healthy life choices," I added.

Instead of responding, Rufus tilted his head up, gazing off toward the five-hundred-foot-tall clock tower of the Boston Custom House. "Storm's coming," he said reflectively.

The sky was clear. I shook my head. "Rufus, I can't tell half the time if you're talking about the weather, or if you're so high that you think you're Nostradamus."

Rufus stroked his scraggly beard. "Perhaps both," he mused. "Perhaps both ..."

To my surprise, I felt the first raindrops speckle my vest. The sporadic rain soon gave way to a light shower. "I guess you're not such a shoddy weatherman after all," I said. I slid down from my seat and busied myself drawing the convertible top over the pedicab carriage. Not that it mattered—the rain meant we'd automatically lose all our business to the dirty-yet-dry interiors of the taxis queued up along Congress Street.

As I raised the plastic hood, Rufus studied me through the rain with his bloodshot eyes. "Why do you do this, Sabra?" he asked. It sounded like another one of his stoned, faux-philosophical questions, but there was a certain clarity about him as he leaned over the handlebars. "Don't get me wrong," he went on, "you're better company than any of those other Lance Armstrong wannabes we ride with. But I have to figure most teenage girls spend their Friday nights doing teenager-y things. You know, like playing in field hockey games, or walking aimlessly around the mall, or parking their Honda Civics at Make-Out Point for a little R&R."

I snorted. "This isn't the 1950s, Rufus. We're not throwing on poodle skirts and racing cars around Dead Man's Curve anymore. And have you ever been to my hometown? Dorchester isn't exactly suburban bliss."

"Point is," Rufus said, leaning over further, "you haul your butt into Boston six nights a week so that you can sit in the freezing rain, and if you're lucky, you schlep around a few fares, all for some shitty tips from stingy tourists. Why do you do it?"

I tugged at one of the wet ruby ringlets dangling out from under my helmet. I had a cookie jar chock full of reasons for the lifestyle I'd chosen, and I wasn't in self-denial about any of them. There were selfless motives, like being closer to my sister's hospital in case, God forbid, anything went wrong. There were selfish reasons, too, like how I craved background noise, the kind that my perpetually empty home failed to provide.

But I wasn't in the mood for a therapy session tonight. I shrugged. "I like the exercise."

I caught sight of a couple jogging hand-in-hand through the rain. While all the other families were rushing for cover and looking miserable, this twosome couldn't stop laughing. I pedaled up beside them and pointed to their Red Sox jerseys. "Headed to the big game?" I asked.

"If it doesn't get rained out first," the woman replied, turning her head up to the sky.

I nodded to the carriage. "All aboard. It's not like you're going to get any wetter at this point." The couple hesitated, gazing questioningly at each other, so I said, "I'll tell you what —if you hitch a ride with me, I'll have a talk with the clouds and make sure this pesky rain stops before Martinez throws the first pitch."

The couple caved. "Three miles is a long way to pedal in a downpour," said the man as he climbed in. Meanwhile, the woman fished through her purse until she found a crumpled twenty.

I waved off the money. "This ride's on me." I pulled away from the curb, my legs giving the pedals a little extra *oomph* to accommodate the added weight of my two passengers. "I'm headed in that direction anyway."

BOSTON CHILDREN'S HOSPITAL

On the seventh floor of Children's Hospital, my mother emerged from Echo's room right as I exited the elevator doors. With her red-going-on-gray hair pulled back in a bun, there was nothing to hide her disapproval as she eyed my soggy reflector vest and biking pants. She crossed her arms tightly over her bright blue scrubs. "Please tell me you weren't out there pedaling that monstrosity in the rain."

"No, I'm just breaking in my Halloween costume," I said. "I'm going as a sponge this year."

Mom sighed. "At least when the pneumonia sets in, you'll only be an elevator ride away from the ER."

I turned to the closed door of the hospital room. I could hear muffled voices, one of them male—Jack must have been visiting, too. "How's she doing?" I asked.

Mom lowered her voice. "Nausea's been getting the best of her. Her appetite hasn't reared its head since Tuesday. The hardest part is seeing the way she looks at food. I remember when she was in first grade and we'd take her to that pizza buffet. She was like a bottomless vortex."

Nostalgia only ended in tears, so I rubbed my mother's arm. "I'll kick it here with Echo until she falls asleep. If you happen to see any cute male candy stripers downstairs during your shift, send them on up."

Mom actually laughed. "For you or for Echo?" She shook her head as she walked away, heading for the elevators.

When I stepped into the room, Jack was seated on a stool at the foot of Echo's bed. He held a small hardcover book open in front of him, reading a passage from it in a lofty lilt, while Echo listened, fully enthralled.

"And so," Jack concluded, "after Arachne hung herself, Hera took pity on the young weaver. She anointed Arachne's corpse with a special juice and resurrected her—only not as a human, but as a spider. Arachne's descendants continue to live on as the spiders, or *arachnids,* that inhabit the world around us today, the same brilliant weavers as their ancient Greek ancestor." Jack snapped the book shut.

Echo rapturously applauded and offered me a sleepy smile. "Oh, Sabra—Jack brought the most wonderful book! You must read to me from it when he leaves."

I tried not to chuckle at the way Echo said "the most *wonderful* book." The more time my sister spent around Jack, the more she sounded like Anne of Green Gables.

I plucked the book out of Jack's hands and turned it over. The title emblazoned in gold letters on the leather cover read *Goddesses, Nymphs, and Dryads, Oh My: A Crash Course in Greek Mythology.*

Echo tried to sit upright, even though I could tell it took most of her strength to do so. Still, she gestured animatedly as she talked. "Jack brought that to show me where my name comes from. See, Echo was a handmaiden for Hera, the queen of the gods. And when the king of the gods, Zeus, wanted to—"

Jack cleared his throat. "When Zeus wanted to, uh, *hang out* with other women who weren't his wife."

"Yes!" Echo said. "When he wanted to get coffee with the other women, Echo would distract Hera by talking to her incessantly. But when Hera figured out what Echo was doing for her husband, she punished her by cursing her so that she could only repeat things that other people said. Then, one day, Echo was walking through the woods when she came across a boy named Nar ... Nars ..."

"Narcissus," Jack said helpfully.

"Yes! Narsissy was so in love with himself that when he caught his own reflection in the river, he couldn't take his eyes off it. He stared at it for so long that he eventually died of hunger." Echo abruptly closed her eyes tight in pain—another wave of nausea. I tried to hand her the bedpan, but she waved me off. "Can you finish the story, Jack?" she asked quietly.

Jack knelt on the other side of her bed. "Because Echo was in love with Narcissus, she withered away alongside him, pining after him, wasting away until only her voice remained. And that's why, sometimes, when you say something loudly in a cave, or a canyon, or an empty hall, you can hear her spirit repeating the last words you said right back at you—an echo."

Echo's eyes remained closed, but her grimace transformed back into a smile. Before long, her head relaxed against her pillow and her breath whistled through the gap in her two front teeth, the way it always did when she slept.

It was the most comforting sound I swear I'd ever heard.

When I was sure Echo was fast asleep, I raised an eyebrow at my brother. "Seriously?" I pointed to the book at the end of the bed. "What kind of smut have you been reading her?"

Jack sniffed with insult. "It's not smut. It's mythology."

"*Ancient* smut then," I amended. I put a hand to Echo's clammy forehead, checking her temperature. The last few rounds of treatment had claimed most of her hair, but one long wisp of her beautiful red bangs still defiantly clung to her head. It dangled out from under her green cap, curling into a question mark against her temple.

Jack jabbed a finger at the small television mounted to the wall. "It's no worse than any of that reality TV garbage you watch with her on Tuesday nights," he said. "Think of it as *The Real Housewives of Olympus*. Greek myths are just like … colorful fairytales."

I laughed dryly. "Fairytales with suicide, and murder, and booze, and gods fornicating with nymphs."

"What does 'fornicating' mean?" Echo had chosen that moment to stir from her slumber, her eyes blinking sleepily.

"Baking cookies," I replied, at the same time that Jack said, "Filing taxes."

He tucked the fleece blanket up around Echo's neck. "I have to get going now, kiddo. But I'm sure Sabra will be happy to read you more ancient smut when you're feeling up to it." As he stood up to leave, he glanced at his watch and I caught a disconcerting gravity in his eyes, something brooding that I'd missed while he was reading to Echo. When he realized I was studying him, he flashed me a smile that was unmistakably forced.

I followed Jack as far as the door, where I snagged him by the elbow. "Everything alright, Jack?"

"Yeah, fine," he said absently, almost by reflex. "Hey, so Dad's birthday is Sunday. You going to visit him?"

"Dunno," I replied. "What am I going to do, slide him a cupcake between the prison bars? The warden will probably cut it open anyway to make sure we didn't bake a shiv into it."

Jack feigned a laugh, but his eyes darted to his watch again. I punched him on the shoulder. "You got a hot Friday night date that we're keeping you from?"

"I have to make it over to the Museum of Fine Arts before it closes," he said. "This history course project is going to be the death of me."

Then he slipped out into the foyer. I watched his blurred outline through the opaque glass window, until I heard Echo speak behind me. "Sabra, will you read me another story?" she

21

asked weakly. "Just one more and I think I'll be able to fall asleep for good."

I plopped down at the foot of her bed and picked up the leather-bound book. Echo offered an encouraging smile, so I flipped to a random page and began to read. "There once was a king named Midas, and all that he touched would turn into gold ..."

LONG WHARF

I stood at the wharf railing, gazing out over the dark harbor waters. October had only begun, but I knew that winter was already well on its way into Boston. I could feel it in the extra bite in the wind coming off the sea. I could see it across the now empty Harborwalk, which normally bustled with visitors soaking up the sun and drinking margaritas during the warmer summer months.

Winter signaled more than the death of beach weather, though. In a matter of weeks, the pedicab business would go into hibernation as the temperatures continued to fall and the baseball season rolled to an end. With my bike parked in a garage for the long, temperamental New England winter, I would lose the one outlet that had carried me through the last six months.

The streets of Boston were my fortress, my escape when the weight of everything pressed down on me—the one place I could draw a deep breath when I felt as though I'd hit rock bottom.

But on days like this, when Echo seemed to be losing the fight against that bastard illness, I realized I hadn't really hit rock bottom yet at all.

There were fathoms of hell I had yet to experience, and might still before the year was even over.

My cell phone vibrated in the pocket of my bicycling pants —I had a nightly alarm set to remind me when it was time to catch the last train home out of South Station. It was only as I heard the ringtone, the *1812 Overture*, that I realized it was my brother calling.

I leaned on the Harborwalk railing and pressed the answer button. Before I could greet Jack, his voice anxiously spilled out through the speakerphone:

"*Sabra, you need to listen to me carefully. Before I lose consciousness.*"

My throat instantly constricted. I raised the phone closer to my ear. Jack's words were slurred and breathless, and I was having trouble hearing him. "Jack, what's going on? Why do you sound like you're drunk?"

"Listen," he repeated, and now I could hear something else —hard, uneven footsteps against concrete. Jack was running. "I did it for Echo. I thought … I thought I could save her. But he figured out what I was up to."

This time I froze. I had no idea what Jack was babbling about, but it made my hackles rise. Then there was the fact that Jack, the good egg of the bunch, had never touched a drop of alcohol in his life as far as I knew.

"Just tell me where you are," I urged him. "You can explain everything to me then."

There was a pause, and his footsteps slowed on the other end. Finally, he mumbled, "Seaport … You'll never make it … to me in time … before they do."

The Seaport? I directed my gaze across the water to the southeast, where the old piers jutted out into the harbor like broken teeth. It couldn't be more than a mile on foot to the Seaport district.

I took off running down the wharf, my feet slapping against the wooden boards. "I'm coming for you, Jack," I promised.

"No!" he half-slurred, half-growled into the phone. "I'm not important ... anymore. Only ... Echo is. You need to ... find the next journal page ... even after ... I'm gone."

"Listen to me, Jack: If someone is after you, you need to hide until I can find you. But please, stay on the phone with me. Stay conscious and *stay with me.*"

The receiver grew quiet once more, and at first I thought I'd lost him already to whatever poison was in his veins. But then Jack drew in a deep, resigned breath and said as clearly as he could:

"I sent you a postcard. Don't call the police and don't let them catch you. And tell Echo"—another labored breath—"tell her to *hold on.*"

The line went dead.

I cursed and picked up speed. I sprinted down the sidewalk as taxis zipped by me on Atlantic Avenue. Both of my frantic attempts to redial Jack went to voicemail.

Finally, I reached Seaport Boulevard and took a hard left onto the Moakley Bridge. Between the misty haze that lingered in the air from the earlier rain and the ghostly glow of the streetlights, the bridge looked ethereal at this time of night. In another hour, it would briefly fill up with patrons stumbling home from the waterfront bars, but for now, it remained nearly empty of any traffic.

Halfway across the bridge, I saw him.

To anyone else, he might have looked like a crazed man, but I could recognize my brother even through the thick shroud of sea mist. He was running with an exaggerated limp. I screamed out his name, and when he spotted me on the opposite sidewalk, he stumbled out into the street.

I intercepted him in the middle of the road, catching him by the shoulders right as he fell. While I cradled him, he blinked up at me, the light behind his eyes dimming. "Jack!" I cupped his face in my hands. "Please, stay with me. I'll get you help." I tried to pry the cell phone out of my pocket.

"The postcard," he whispered. "I shouldn't have sent it. They'll just find you, too. Then I'll have lost ... both my sisters."

I had only started to dial 9-1-1 when headlights illuminated the fog around us. The tuned-up engine of a car roared through the quiet night, and I looked up to see a silver Ford Mustang rocketing down Seaport Boulevard, heading for the bridge.

In a panic, I slipped out from under Jack and stood between him and the oncoming car. "Help!" I screamed, while frantically waving my arms over my head. I lit up my cell phone, praying that the driver would see the glow of the screen through the mist.

Instead, the driver accelerated. The Mustang reached the head of the bridge and I froze as the blinding twin headlights zeroed in on where I was standing.

No signs of braking.

No signs of veering.

The car was headed straight for us.

As time slowed down in that instant, I caught a glimpse of the driver inside, her smile gleaming with victory. And maybe it was a trick of the light playing over the windshield ...

... But I swear I saw two silvery horns spiraling out of her head.

It was the devil, come to collect.

Powerful arms shoved me from behind—Jack's. The hard push propelled me into the opposite lane where I hit the ground hard.

In the moments when I was tumbling to the pavement, I heard four things.

The final demonic crescendo of the Mustang's engine.

A fleshy thump.

The smash of something hitting the windshield.

A second, wetter thump.

25

North Palm Beach Library

By the time that I had righted myself, Jack lay in a mangled lump in the middle of the bridge, unmoving, while the Mustang zoomed off, disappearing into the entrance to Interstate 93.

Even as I screamed and ran to Jack's side, blood was already pooling in the street. I flipped Jack over, praying it would be just like the first time I caught him. He'd blink his dazzling green eyes up at me and everything would be okay.

Instead, those same eyes gazed lifelessly through me into the starless city sky and I knew that Jack was gone.

I tilted my head back and wailed into the night, a tortured, banshee scream, before I blacked out with my brother's broken body still cradled in my arms.

PERSONAL EFFECTS
ONE WEEK LATER

JACK WAS GONE, BUT THE FOG THAT HAD DESCENDED over the Seaport the night he died stalked me wherever I went.

For a whole week, I merely existed, a hollow vessel sailing through an endless mist with no captain and no destination. I loathed myself for not feeling during the times of numbness, but then prayed for the numbness when the harsh pain arthritically settled back into my bones. I stumbled through seven days of meetings with the police and arrangements with the funeral director and finally the funeral itself. My father howled loudest of anyone there, until the corrections officers escorting him had no choice but to drag him out of Saint George's and back to his cell at Cedar Junction.

Then there was Echo. My mother and I alternated shifts by her bedside, each of us taking the other's place when the grief overwhelmed the brave masks we wore to spare her from seeing us in agony. There had even been talk of whether we should conceal Jack's passing from her for the time being, for the sake of her health, but she was far more observant than the average third grader. We had to tell her.

Echo was the only thing that kept me going that interminable week. I feared that Jack's death would steal that last strand of vitality that my sister, my soldier, had clung to these last few months. So I watched over her every minute that I could, a stony gargoyle keeping sentry over the one life I treasured most.

27

The day after the funeral, while Mom watched Echo, I drove out to Cape Cod to visit Jack's favorite beach in Chatham. He always loved coming here in the fall, when the cool air and autumn storms had shooed the tourists and seasonal residents away until next summer. Jack had taught me to swim on this beach when I was five. At first I had refused to even set foot in the ocean, terrified of being carried out to sea by a swift rip current—ironic for a girl whose last name is "Tides." Jack, a patient and understanding old soul even when he was in first grade, had scooped up a handful of sand and slipped it into the back pocket of my shorts.

"What was that for?" I'd asked him.

He'd smiled at me. "If you take the beach with you wherever you go, you can never really drift away from it, can you?"

As I now stood at the water's edge, the dusk wind billowing my hoodie around me, I flung a message in a bottle out into the Atlantic and watched it slip soundlessly into the waves. It contained a short poem by Walt Whitman that I'd found framed on Jack's desk at home:

Keep your face always toward the sunshine
And shadows will fall behind you.

Before I left, as a tribute to Jack, I gathered a handful of the Cape Cod sand and stuffed it into the pocket of my jeans.

That lump of sand somehow gave me courage later that day as I walked into the police station in Government Center. An officer escorted me to a spare, forgettable room with cinderblock walls. I'd made an appointment for two o'clock, but it wasn't until an hour later that someone finally entered to greet me.

The detective couldn't have been older than forty. Between his thinning, close-cropped hair and general air of sternness, my first impression was that he must be ex-military. Instead of police blues, he sported a button-down shirt and tie, with freshly pressed slacks. He might have been a day trader if it weren't for the gun holstered by his suspenders.

He reached an enormous hand across the table and shook mine with a rock-crushing grip. "You must be Sabra. My name is Detective Louis Grimshaw."

I studied him warily. "You're in charge of my brother's case? I feel like I spoke to just about every other officer in the city last week—except for you."

"I took an active interest in the incident," he replied, settling into the chair. "Before we talk about anything else, I want to say how sorry I am for your loss."

The pleasantries of bereavement meant little to me. I'd heard nothing but how "sorry" people were for seven days now. What I really wanted were answers. "I don't want to waste your time, Detective, so I'll get right to it," I said. "I'm not here today to give a new statement. I'm here to address the final report that one of your officers released about …" My mind flashed back to the fog, the bridge, the Mustang. I swallowed hard. "… about what happened to Jack."

Detective Grimshaw flipped open the manila folder in front of him and thumbed through the papers until he found the summary in question. "I wrote that report myself, and I promise I was remarkably thorough with the information that I collected. Did you feel like something was missing?"

"How about the truth?"

He gazed over the top of the folder. "Care to elaborate, Ms. Tides?" In an instant, the compassion and patience he'd shown a minute ago evaporated.

I softened my tone. "The police log said that he was killed in a hit-and-run, most likely by a drunk driver who fled the scene of the accident when she realized what she'd done."

The detective blinked twice. "And?"

"And if you'd listened to any of what I told the investigators, you'd know that this wasn't an accident at all." The detective looked ready to interrupt me already, but I soldiered on. "Look at the evidence. When my brother called me, he was clearly being pursued by someone who wished him harm. In fact, he was running with a limp, which means that he must have escaped an attack when I got the call. Then there was the car itself." I counted another piece of evidence on my fingers. "You say it was a drunk driver? Then why did she speed up when she saw me? Why did she aim the car for us? The report claims that the Mustang lost control and veered into our lane, but *I was there*. The driver was in complete control the whole time."

"Ah, yes. The driver who you observed had"—Grimshaw glanced down at the file—"devil's horns?" The corner of his lips twitched. Was he trying to suppress a smile?

I refused to be bullied. The fog that had surrounded me all week had suddenly lifted. Every detail from that night reemerged. "What about the brake marks?"

"There were no brake marks," Grimshaw replied quickly.

I pounded my fist on the table. "*Exactly*. Try to put yourself in the brain of a drunk driver. You're three sheets to the wind, your reflexes are slow, and your vision is swimming. Even if you somehow didn't see us in the path of your car until it was too late, what would be the first thing you'd do after that body struck your windshield?" I waited, hoping that the detective would answer for me, but he remained silent. "You'd hit the brakes, Detective Grimshaw. You'd hit them hard. Even if you then decided to jet off onto I-93 northbound to save your own ass before the police responded, for a split second, your brain would succumb to pure reflexes—and reflex says your foot goes straight for the brake pedal. There. Were. No. Brake marks." I tapped each word with finality against the wooden tabletop.

Grimshaw made a steeple with his fingers. "So you're saying that the absence of brake marks is concrete proof that your brother's hit-and-run was intentional?" His voice was flat, patronizing. "While I admire your deductive reasoning skills, drawing a whole bunch of ill-founded conclusions based on the intoxicated ravings of your brother and some theory about brake marks isn't 'evidence,' as you called it. It's conjecture." I opened my mouth to interrupt, but this time, Grimshaw cut me off. "Furthermore, as for your brother's inebriation and the injury he sustained to his leg, those can all be explained. Another witness came forward."

I squinted at Grimshaw. "What other witness?" Had they been purposely withholding knowledge about my brother's whereabouts that night from me?

The detective seemed to be considering how much to divulge. "A bartender who was on duty at the Nightingale, a nightclub in the Seaport, on the evening of the *accident.*" He stressed the final word like he was trying to stick another dagger through my heart. "Apparently, your brother snuck into the Nightingale with a fake ID and went on quite the bender. Downed a few too many shots of bourbon, started throwing pint glasses at the bartender's head. Two bouncers had to drag him out of the place, and when he took a swing at one of them, they tossed him out into the street, where he busted his knee. As for his raving about being pursued ..." Grimshaw shrugged. "Probably paranoia that the bouncers were following him."

"What's the bartender's name?" I demanded.

"Why, so you can harass my witness? Fat chance."

"Because my brother was a saint and everyone knows it." I had raised my voice enough that a female officer walking by the room's solitary window stared in at me. She could come in and taser me for all I cared. "Tell me how a straight-A history dork goes from spending his nights researching obscure Revolutionary War texts to getting completely hammered, tearing apart a bar, and brawling with bouncers."

"Pull the wool off your eyes," Grimshaw barked. "The pressures of college, a deadbeat father doing ten-to-fifteen in max-security, a sister who's battling cancer, and a mother who's probably not around all that much? I've got no doubt in my mind that your brother, as angelic as you thought he was, finally hit his breaking point. People have snapped for less." He closed the file in front of him. "It's perfectly natural for someone in your position to look for meaning in a senseless tragedy. But the real tragedy is that sometimes there's no meaning to be found."

My ears burned hot. I couldn't stop shaking. "What was the bartender's name?" I asked again slowly.

Grimshaw ignored me. "Focus on your family, Sabra. Go spend some time with your little sister—Echo was it? And most importantly, leave justice up to us. We'll find the Mustang and its driver soon enough. I promise."

I opened my mouth. "I ..." My eyes rolled up behind my eyelids and I fainted backwards. Next thing I knew, my chair hit the floor and I spilled limply off the seat onto the hard tiles.

Grimshaw stooped by my side. "You okay, kid?"

I blinked dazedly around the room and rubbed the back of my head. "Yes, I—I think I'm just dehydrated."

The detective helped me to my feet and carefully lowered me into another chair. "I'll go get you a glass of water. Stay put." Then he hurried out of the room.

As soon as Grimshaw was gone, I dropped the fainting act, walked to the other side of the table, and opened my brother's file. It took minimal leafing to find the pink carbon copy of a witness report taken in the Seaport two days after Jack's death.

The name of the witness was Samuel Smithwick.

"Bingo," I whispered.

I shut the file, and without waiting for Grimshaw to return, I slipped stealthily out of the police station.

Boston University

Tempting as it was to head straight to the Nightingale to confront Samuel, I needed time to develop a plan first. I'd get nowhere by crashing through the doors in the middle of the afternoon, tearing up the place, and demanding answers.

I called the nightclub, pretending to be a regular who'd been doting on Samuel Smithwick from afar. Sam—or "Smitty" as the manager on the phone called him—must not have been much of a looker, because his boss seemed all too amused that he had an admirer. The manager assured me that if I stopped by after five o'clock, I'd catch the object of my affection running the evening shift.

With several hours to kill, I decided to take care of an unsavory task I'd been putting off since the funeral: visiting Jack's dorm room to claim the items he'd left behind.

The Boston University campus was the city-loving student's dream. It wasn't the typical sprawling, green-quad, Sesame Street existence of most American universities, but a decidedly urban stretch of buildings that dominated the western edge of Boston proper.

Smack dab in its center loomed the Warren Towers, three dormitories that rose eighteen stories out of Commonwealth Avenue and cast a tall shadow over the trolley cars below. Side by side, they almost looked as though the tines of a massive trident had been speared through the asphalt.

I played the grief card with the security officer at the front desk. I didn't even have to fake the tears in my eyes before he waved me past to go sift through the remnants of my brother's ill-fated freshman year. Jack's room was on the thirteenth floor, and the door was protected by a ten-digit keypad lock. This was a setback I had prepared for. On a small note card, I had jotted down a list of every crucial date in early U.S. history that I could find, prioritizing the historical events that Jack blathered on about most frequently. It took a handful of tries, but the door finally popped open after I entered the code 3-1-7-7-6. March 17, 1776 was Evacuation Day, when General Washington had fortified the city of Boston, forcing the British army to retreat north to Canada.

Jack's room was a standard double, and I could instantly tell which side had belonged to him.

The left side was neat and spare. The bed was made so tightly you could bounce a quarter off the sheets. Between the spartan walls—not a poster in sight—and the desk, which was empty save an old lobster trap that was used to store textbooks, it looked as though Jack's roommate had never fully moved in. However, I noticed that the toothbrush on the bureau looked freshly wet, so it was safe to say that the roommate had recently returned.

The right side of the room was chaos incarnate. A river of books flowed down off an already overcrowded bookshelf and onto the unmade bed. The makeshift library covered the mattress so completely that I could only see a few patches of my brother's faded bedspread, which was embroidered with lines from the Gettysburg Address.

He'd been sleeping under that comforter since the fourth grade.

I shook off the memory of Jack at age ten and focused on the mountain of library texts. They were mostly history and geography, the intellectual fuel that my brother had voraciously consumed for as long as I could remember. Jack had been insatiable when it came to stories of centuries past. As far as I knew, his obsession could be traced back to the day Dad told him that one of our ancestors had signed the Declaration of Independence.

That, like so many other things our pathologically lying father said, had turned out to be a total fabrication. A story that was meant to make Buck Tides feel like a hero for a few minutes, as though that would make up for all of his other shortcomings as a father figure.

As I perused the titles on the spines of the different books, I looked for a common thread between them. The keywords that jumped out at me spanned centuries and continents. Some of Jack's favorite historical periods were well-represented, from the Jefferson Purchase to the Underground Railroad. But then there were other obscure titles, like:

The Distance They Journeyed: The Slaves of Tanzania.
Mount Kilimanjaro: In the Shadows of a Giant.
Orchids from around the World.

After a minute of pawing through the books, I had a premonition that I wasn't alone. Sure enough, when I turned back to the door, a boy stood there watching me.

He must have come from a workout, given the sweats he was wearing and the gym bag slung over his shoulder. He wasn't particularly tall, but even his baggy gray hoodie couldn't conceal his powerful shoulders, which verged on being disproportionately broad for his build.

The boy broke the silence first. "You look just like him."

It was the first time since Jack died that someone had greeted me with something other than how sorry they were. It felt refreshing. "My little sister came out the spitting image of my mother, but both Jack and I were the unwilling recipients of our father's puffy cheeks." I sighed. "At least one of us won the genetic coin toss."

The boy dropped his duffel onto the neater of the two beds. "I'm adopted," he explained, "so while I can't tell you exactly whose features I got in the lottery, my eyelashes did come out suspiciously feminine." He ran his fingers along his jawline, indicating the three days' growth of beard. "That's why I use the stubble to balance it out."

"Haven't you been to the movies lately? The pretty-boy look is in." I was suddenly self-conscious of the fact that I'd broken into this boy's room, uninvited. At least he'd put two and two together that I was Jack's sister. "I'm Sabra, by the way."

"Atlas." He extended a big hand, which I took. Where the sleeve of his hooded sweatshirt bunched up closer to his elbow, I caught a flicker of a tattoo. Before I could read it, he retracted his arm and rolled the sleeve back down.

I didn't need Echo's Greek mythology text to recognize his name. Atlas had been the titan responsible for holding up the celestial heavens, lest they come crashing down to earth. "Atlas, huh?" I said. "Do you have a particularly large burden to bear?" He certainly had the shoulders to support a heavy load or two.

He smiled. "Atlas is my last name. I just go by it because my first name royally blows."

"Oh, give me a break. I have to share my name with a brand of hummus," I said flatly. "How bad could yours possibly be?"

"That," he replied, "is a secret that stays between me and my driver's license." He pantomimed zipping his mouth closed and tossing the key into the waste basket.

My attention drifted back toward the mound of books on Jack's bed. "How well did you know my brother, Atlas?"

He considered this. "I was probably his best friend here," he said, then added, "which is to say I hardly knew him at all."

I frowned. My brother was a bookworm, sure, but not the awkward, social outcast variety. Jack moved fluidly through his teenage years with more social ease than anyone I knew. The guy had an open invitation to any social circle he wanted in high

36

school. He ate lunch with the gamers, played pickup basketball with the jocks, and dated the homecoming queen for an entire year, before she cheated on him and broke his heart.

So to hear Atlas suggest that Jack was some kind of introvert at a school with thirty thousand students didn't compute. "You're telling me that Jack had no real friends here?"

Atlas must have seen how upset I was getting, because he held up his hands in conciliation. "Hey, maybe I'm wrong. I work a job as the concierge for a luxury condominium complex in the South End, sometimes during the graveyard shift, so our paths mostly crossed in the mornings when I was just getting home. But ..."

I was sick of people tiptoeing around my grief like it was thin ice. "Look. I've got a gut feeling the size of a bowling ball that my brother got into something deep before he died, something real bad, and I'm running out of leads to chase. So if you noticed anything suspicious, no matter how small, that might help me understand how a straight-laced kid at the top of his class with a full ride to seven colleges ended up on a bridge in Southie drunk, beaten half-to-death, and then ..." My voice broke and tears welled in my eyes. I fixed my pleading gaze on Atlas. "Please," I whispered. "Tell me everything and don't hold back."

Atlas nodded and sat down on his bed. "For starters, those books?" He pointed to the mountain of texts behind me. "Those subjects don't match any of the classes on the schedule he taped to his mirror. I figured at first that a bright guy like Jack might be doing a special research project for one of his courses—but I'm not sure he was even *going* to class. One of his professors left a voicemail on our dorm phone asking where Jack had been the last three seminars."

My arms prickled with goose bumps. College wasn't supposed to be like high school—here, they only checked in on you if they thought you'd been kidnapped or if the FBI issued a warrant for your arrest. "What else?"

"I wasn't the only occupant of this room pulling all-nighters. Your brother found himself some job at a shady nightclub in the Seaport. It had a bird in the name."

"The Nightingale?" I chimed in.

Atlas snapped his fingers. "That's the one. Jack was a barback there, I guess, washing dishes, putting clean pint glasses out front, tapping a new keg when one kicked. Guy like that, I figured if he wanted to work for peanuts, he'd get a job in the library or as a research assistant."

So Jack had actually *worked* at the Nightingale—the same bar where he'd allegedly been thrown out of for going on a drunken rampage. How the hell had that slipped through the cracks during Detective Grimshaw's allegedly thorough investigation?

Now I had twice as much reason to pay Smitty a visit.

I could tell that there was something else on Atlas's mind that he was withholding. His gaze had gone opaque, like he was reliving a memory and its significance was just settling in.

"Jack said something to you, didn't he?" I asked.

Atlas smoothed out a wrinkle in his sheets. "It was the night before he died. The last time I saw him alive, actually. I'd gotten a night off from work and was catching up on sleep. It must have been two, maybe three in the morning, when I woke up to some weird noises. Your brother was standing on his desk and fishing around in the ceiling."

I looked up. The ceiling was made up of a series of tiles that looked like they could be moved if necessary. I found myself standing up and walking over to Jack's desk.

"It was dark and I was still half-asleep," Atlas went on, "but I could see Jack come down clutching some sort of old-looking paper, sealed in a plastic laminate. Then he picked up his pea coat and made for the door, like he was about to leave."

With one sweep of my arm, I cleared the books off the desk and climbed onto it. It wobbled uncertainly beneath me.

Atlas jumped up to help steady it and continued his story as he held on. "I was lying there quiet as a rock, but your brother must have sensed me watching him, because he paused at the door. And he turned to speak over his shoulder."

Among the tiles over the desk, I spotted one that was turned slightly askew, as though it had recently been disturbed. As I balanced on the desk's built-in hutch, I pushed aside the misplaced tile and felt around in the rafter space above.

But my groping hands found only air. Whatever Jack had been stowing away, he must have never returned it in the twenty-four hours before he was killed.

Atlas helped me down, and I sat, deflated, on the edge of the desk. "What did my brother say?"

Atlas drew in a deep breath as he tried to recall the words. "He said, 'She's going to want to follow me. But you have to stop her. I can't lose them both.'" Atlas exhaled. "Then he was gone."

An arctic chill passed through my veins. *She's going to follow me.* I felt fairly confident that Jack was referring to me. But follow him where?

Whatever meaning was behind his ominous final words to Atlas, one thing was crystal clear:

Jack had *sensed* that something horrible was about to befall him.

Somehow, out of the gloom, I found the smallest of smiles for Atlas. "Thank you," I whispered.

"For what?" Atlas asked, confused.

"Because," I said, "for the first time in over a week, it feels like someone is actually telling me the truth."

I gave a final defeated look at the mountain range of books on Jack's bed. I couldn't exactly throw them all in the back of my pedicab, so I'd have to leave them here for now.

Atlas was studying me intently again. "You really believe there was something more to Jack's death, don't you?"

The answer resounded up from my core. "What happened on that bridge was no accident. It was an assassination."

Something sparked behind Atlas's eyes and he walked over to his almost barren desk. He found a marker, but after a quick search through his drawers turned up no paper, he rummaged around in his gym bag and withdrew a white t-shirt. Several flourished scribbles later and he handed the vandalized shirt to me.

I unfurled the rumpled white T and laughed—my first in over a week—when I saw the ten digits written on it. "You do realize that one of the perks of living in the twenty-first century is that we have magical phones where we can program numbers right in without having to deface innocent gym clothes."

"I strive for memorable first impressions." Atlas's face turned somber. "Look, I don't know what your brother was talking about the last time I saw him alive, and maybe it was just crazy babble. But for whatever reason, it sounded like he wanted me to stop you from going down whatever road got him into trouble. I think I owe it to him to see that promise through."

This unexpected blast of chivalry was endearing, but ultimately misplaced. "My brother, who was essentially a stranger to you, mumbled three cryptic sentences while you were half-asleep. You're in no way obligated to him or to me." Flustered, I avoided eye contact as I stuffed the ratty t-shirt into my knapsack. "I'm under a lot of stress, and given everything that's happened, I need to look after myself right now. Thanks for your help—seriously,." I headed for the door, anxious to get back out into the open air of Comm. Ave.

"I have a sister," Atlas said firmly

I stopped in the entryway.

"She's fourteen," he continued. "Next year, she starts high school. All I could think when I walked in and saw you going through your brother's things—when I see you standing here now—is that if something ever happened to me, I'd hope that someone would be there to watch over her. Even if it was just some crazy final message I left to a roommate I barely knew." He took a step forward, closing the distance between us. "So you never have to dial that number if you don't want. But if you even have the tiniest flicker of a thought that you need my help, no matter how big or how small it might be, don't you dare hesitate to call."

If I were a bridge, then his words would have severed every last one of my supports. I had to hold onto the doorknob tight to keep from caving in on myself. My father was in jail, my mother was attending to my sick sister, and my brother, my rock, was dead. How far had I fallen, how low and pathetic had I become, to cling to the promises of total strangers?

In my moment of vulnerability, I blurted out a morbid, off-topic question that had been nagging me since I'd walked into the dorm room. "Is it true that if your roommate dies, the school doesn't try to replace him with another student? That they leave his bed empty for the rest of the school year?" It was stupid, but I mostly needed to know that the world wouldn't entirely steamroll on as though my brother had never existed.

Atlas surprised me by smiling softly. "If they try to stick me with a new roommate, I'll fight them off tooth and nail," he said. "Some people just can't be replaced."

DEN OF SIN
THE SEAPORT

AS I SURVEYED THE THE STEADY STREAM OF PATRONS entering the Nightingale beneath its gaudy neon marquee, I had an overwhelming suspicion that I stood at a crossroads. It was an ominous sense that my life could take two wildly divergent paths from here on out, and to walk through the nightclub's metal-studded doors was to irrevocably commit myself to a journey from which I might not come back.

Down one path, I could willingly bow out now, take the train home, and try to pick up the pieces of my broken family, my tattered life. I wanted answers, but I didn't even really know what the *questions* were. Anything I learned now wouldn't bring my brother back from the dead.

But then, like I had so many times in the dark this past week, I saw the headlights of that Mustang speeding down the road toward me with murderous purpose. As those twin beams burned into my retinas, I felt the anger grow, and with that fury came certainty:

Somewhere out there lurked a sinister truth.

And I was going to chase it down.

I crossed the street and shouldered through the nightclub's heavy doors.

The entrance to the Nightingale opened into a long, dark foyer, indulgently decorated in crimson draperies and espresso wood. Ahead of me, an imposing, broad-shouldered bouncer guarded a curtain that led into the nightclub beyond, from which the melancholy song of a trumpet echoed out.

I tried to look nonchalant as I approached, even though my stomach felt like a soggy dish towel being tied into knots. When I reached the enormous man, I handed him my ID, a fake driver's license I'd acquired through one of Rufus's shady contacts that afternoon. It had cost me 150 dollars and a trip to a dodgy attic apartment in Andrew Square, where the windows were covered in tie-dye quilts and the air reeked of something herbal that definitely wasn't incense.

I tried to keep my hand steady as I passed the ID to the bouncer. The picture on it was my own, but the rest of the information had been fabricated. For tonight, I was twenty-three-year-old Sherry DuPont of Acorn Street.

The bouncer's gaze alternated between the license and my face. "When's your birthday?" he quizzed me. He crossed his arms over his barrel chest, his pectorals bulging out of his shirt.

I casually recited the date that I'd memorized on the ride over. "April fourteenth. Why, you going to bake me a cake?"

The bouncer's threatening scowl endured for a moment longer, before his face broke out into a broad grin. "Nah, always been more of a brownie man, myself." He drew aside the curtain.

As soon as I passed through to the other side, I felt like I'd been transported eighty years into the past.

The Nightingale was no dive bar—it was a gauche, cavernous space, more of a grand ballroom than a hole-in-the-wall. The crown jewel of the vaulted ceiling was a silver chandelier the size of a compact car. The room itself was shaped like a bowl, with tiers of leather booths terraced down toward the dance floor and stage, where a ten-piece brass band launched into an old Billie Holiday standard. The lighting was dim, bright enough that you could see the man or woman you were flirting with, but dark enough to mask all of his or her imperfections. With the workday over, the booths were filling up with cuddling couples and sharply dressed traders who'd wandered over from the Financial District.

It was like something straight out of an old gangster film, where men in zoot suits and fedoras smoked cigars, leering at "dames" in flapper dresses. Where uniformed soldiers danced the jitterbug with the fiancées they were leaving behind as they hopped on a boat to Normandy.

I reached the oak bar on the far side of the room and slid into a leather stool. The sole bartender was dressed in a tuxedo vest and a white collared shirt cuffed at the elbows. He sported an impressive handlebar mustache the same carrot color as his slicked back hair.

Although he wasn't wearing a name tag, I felt fairly certain that the quirky, mustached ginger standing in front of me was Smitty.

"What can I get you, stranger?" the bartender asked without looking up. He busied himself polishing one of the numerous vodka bottles that lined the long mirror behind the bar. I had tried vodka once at a friend's house party and found it to be perfectly dreadful. Why a bar would stock forty varieties of something that tasted like nail polish was beyond me.

Since I didn't drink, I panicked and blurted out something I remembered a character ordering in a movie I'd watched recently. "I'll have a whiskey, neat."

For the first time, Smitty looked at me, with a quizzical expression that told me I'd ordered something completely out of character. "You trying to grow some hair on your chest?"

"It's been a rough week," I replied.

"In that case, we better bust out the big guns." Smitty reached for a bottle of brown liquid on the top shelf. "My favorite eighteen-year scotch. First round's on the house. Just don't tell my boss." His eyes flicked up toward a series of tinted windows overlooking the orchestra pit, some sort of VIP room.

Smitty expertly poured a healthy dose into two tumblers, then held up one. Instinctively, I picked up the other, clinked glasses with his, and took a sip. It tasted horrible—smoky like a cigar, bitter like gasoline, and it burned the whole way down. Smitty was clearly observing me, so it was all I could do to hide my displeasure as the acrid liquid spiraled down my esophagus and ignited a small brushfire in my belly. "Good stuff," I said hoarsely as I set the tumbler down.

Smitty withdrew a few limes from beneath the counter and began slicing them into wedges with a paring knife. "So why the rough week?" he asked. "You get fired? You working a shit job where you *wish* they'd fire you?" When I didn't reply, he rattled off more suggestions. "Got your heart broken? Broke somebody else's heart? Your cat ran away? TV broke right before the Patriots game on Sunday?"

"Death in the family," I said finally.

Those four words derailed whatever banter Smitty was trying to drum up with me. His knife paused mid-stroke. "Shit, I'm sorry," he said. I scrutinized his face to see if there was any recognition at all, but found none. I didn't resemble Jack as much as Atlas had suggested—you had to be looking for it to see the same cherubic curve of our jaws and the swatch of Irish freckles beneath our eyes.

"You're sorry?" I echoed. "What are you sorry for?"

"It's just an expression," Smitty mumbled, noticeably unnerved. He glanced toward the end of the bar, looking for another customer he could serve. Unfortunately for him, the only patrons to be found were sitting in booths, watching the band. He wiped his brow and carved up another lime.

"You know," I said, my gaze sweeping over the Nightingale. "My brother would have hated a place like this. He loved *real*

45

history, not garish imitations of it." Smitty's face twitched and his knife strokes picked up pace. "Not to mention that my brother was a straight-edge dork who probably wouldn't drink a beer unless you convinced him that it had been brewed by George Washington himself." My hand slid the scotch glass aside as I leaned over the bar. "That's why it boggles my mind why some random bartender would fabricate a bullshit story for the police about how the night that Jack died, he got belligerently drunk here and tore up the place." I narrowed my eyes. "So I'll ask again: What exactly are you sorry for, *Smitty*?"

As I said the bartender's name, he brought his knife down too hard. The lime split in two with such force that both halves skittered away.

When Smitty lifted his gaze to meet mine, there was no warmth left in it. "You should leave," he said. His hand had tightened around the handle of the knife. Lime juice dripped off the tip of the blade—*drip, drip, drip.*

"You gonna stab me?" I asked. "I thought poison, beatings, and vehicular homicide were more your people's style."

"You got no idea what you're talking about, little girl." Smitty glanced up at the tinted windows over the stage again.

With one look of fear, he'd told me more than he'd probably intended. "Why are you so afraid of your boss? Did he pay you to lie? Was he involved in my brother's—?"

"Enough," Smitty rasped sharply. "I may not have recognized you, but someone here will before long. Then we're both toast." He relaxed his hand around the knife and began to skirt his way down the counter, away from me.

"This can go down one of two ways," I said, before Smitty could get out of earshot. "You can tell me everything—and I mean *everything*—that I want to know. About what my brother was doing here. About why somebody wanted him dead. About why you're covering it up. Or," I continued, "I make a scene.

Maybe I start flipping barstools. Maybe I go pound on the door to that sleazy VIP room and find out who you're so afraid of. But when I come face-to-face with whoever it is you're lying to protect, I'm going to tell him that I know everything, and that you sold him out faster than a two-brownie bake sale to save your own ass."

I had made no effort to keep my voice down, and Smitty looked so terrified that I thought he might take off running for the door, never to return. Part of me had initially wondered if he played a more active role in my brother's death. My gut said that the squirming mess of a man in front of me, who looked like he might soil himself, was no killer.

Smitty came back. His face had regained some element of composure, but his hand shook as he picked up his tumbler of scotch and pounded it in one gulp. Then he reached across the counter and did the same with mine, without even so much as a grimace. His eyes lingered closed, and when they reopened, his pupils looked dull and resigned. "Two a.m. Windward Bluffs Country Club in Rockport, eleventh green. I will feel only relief if you don't show. But if you're your brother's sister, you'll be there."

"Count on it," I said. Eight hours was a long time to wait when the curiosity was burning my insides like battery acid, but I knew that I'd learn nothing more from Smitty as long as he was under this roof. I stood up and headed for the exit.

I only made it two steps when I heard him say quietly, guiltily, "I always liked your brother."

I said nothing, but I thought to myself: *Somebody sure didn't.*

POSTCARDS FROM THE DEAD
CHILDREN'S HOSPITAL

MY TONGUE STILL TINGLED WITH THE BITTER TASTE of scotch when I stopped by the hospital to see Echo. Visiting hours would soon end for the night, but I knew the halls well enough at this point to sneak in if I ever needed to.

Echo was asleep when I arrived. Mom, too, appeared to be napping in the chair next to the bed, with her head resting in the crook of her elbow.

The gentle click of the door behind me was enough to wake my mother, who bristled, blinked rapidly, and turned to Echo in a motherly panic. But my sister remained fast asleep, her breath whistling reassuringly through the gap between her two front teeth.

Mom flashed me an ephemeral smile, more an unsure twitch of the lips than anything else. For the entire time that Echo had been sick, smiles in the Tides family always felt like a patch of thin ice. Either you treaded softly, or you'd plunge right through, only to watch the ice seal back up over you, trapping you in a dark, airless abyss.

Now the ice had thawed even more.

"What have you been up to?" Mom asked, a yawn muddling the end of her sentence.

Just sneaking into a seedy nightclub and interrogating the bartender who's lying to the police about the circumstances surrounding Jack's death. "Working," I said.

"Well, my shift starts in twenty, so you're right on time for the changing of the guard." Mom stood up—only to nearly collapse back into the chair. I caught her by the arm as she swayed precariously on one foot. "I'm fine, I'm fine," she mumbled, her eyes glazed. Only then did I notice that my mother was slurring her words.

I glanced down at her pocket book. The childproof cap of a bottle of anti-anxiety medication poked out between the zippers.

I considered telling her to call out from work, but in all honesty, I knew she needed the distraction. Everyone upstairs was well aware of her recent loss, and she had been relegated to desk duty for the foreseeable future. No one was going to fault her for dropping a few Xanax to get through the night. I planted a kiss on her cheek and said, "I'll hang out for a while and sneak out later." If I wanted to catch the last train out of Boston to meet Smitty, I would need to get to North Station by midnight.

"My daughter, the renegade," Mom said, though it sounded soulless. As the door closed behind her, I realized that our relationship over the last year boiled down to a few words here and there. It was as though we had boarded separate boats sailing in opposite directions, and we were always trying to hold a conversation as our ships passed each other in the night.

At the foot of the chair, a stack of mail came up to my knees. Mom must have finally gone home, a task that she'd avoided since the funeral by sleeping in the spare cot here in Echo's room.

The thought of reading one more bereavement card made me want to throw up. I picked up the hefty stack. So this was the weight of the people we touched: When you die, you leave an immeasurable, crushing burden on the shoulders of the few people closest to you. Everyone else sends Hallmark.

Among the mix of uniform, off-white sympathy cards and letter envelopes containing past-due reminders for utility bills Mom had neglected to pay, I spotted a single splash of color toward the bottom. Curious, I pried out the postcard and held it up to the light.

The picture on the front was of an old oil painting. On first impression, the ocean scene depicted a beautiful chaos of orange, copper, red, and muted blues. In the distance, in front of the setting sun, a magnificent ship sailed into the churning, frothing waters of an approaching storm. Its sails and masts glowed red, beneath the dark umbra of the squall that was bearing down on it.

It was only when my gaze gravitated to the foreground that I noticed the horrific scene that was unfolding: men, dying men. Their faces weren't visible—they were all in the process of drowning in the stormy sea—but their shackled hands reached out of the violent waves one last time. A partial leg was visible in the surf, bound in iron chains, while fish surrounded the limb, preparing for their next meal. Sea gulls descended on the water where it was tinged with the first brushes of crimson blood.

I shuddered at the macabre image and flipped the postcard over. According to the caption, the painting was called *Slave Ship* by an artist named J. M. W. Turner, and it currently resided at the Museum of Fine Arts in Boston, only a few blocks from here. But it was the short message scrawled on the postcard that took me by surprise.

It was addressed to me.

The name under the signature was someone I didn't know.

But the handwriting, without a doubt, belonged to my dearly departed brother.

And it was dated the night that he died.

Dear Sabra,

Greetings from your old summer camp bunkmate.
Hard to believe it was nine years ago that you rode with me to the
hospital when my appendix burst out on the trail.
Don't hit the books too hard senior year.
I miss you dearly …

Love,
Aedon Philomel

The postcard trembled in my hands. This might have been the last thing Jack had ever written, and it was even more nonsensical than our cryptic phone conversation right before the deadly hit-and-run on the bridge. It wasn't until my tears dropped onto the messy scrawl of the postcard, causing the ink to run, that I realized I was crying.

I miss you dearly, he'd written.

Had he known the end was so close?

While my second instinct was to experience an updraft of frustration—here I was trying to put the pieces of Jack's death together, and he had yet to leave me any straightforward answers—I remembered back to when I was in elementary school, before Echo was even born. Every year, on my birthday, Jack would hide my presents around the house, and write me rhyming clues on scraps of notepaper to guide me from one location to the next. Back then, my parents were struggling to make mortgage payments, so birthday gifts were never anything extravagant, but I didn't care. It was Jack's riddles and treasure hunt that I looked forward to, not the loot at the end.

Jack had done this every year, right up until my most recent birthday, which is one of the reasons I had instantly recognized his handwriting. As I got older, he'd expanded the area of the gift hunt to the entire neighborhood, and made the clues harder as well, since "I bet you five bucks / that the next clue's beneath some rubber ducks" didn't really pose the same intellectual challenge at age seventeen that it had at age seven.

The more I reread the postcard, the more I grew confident that it was another of his riddles.

I started with the basics. The postcard was in my brother's handwriting, but it was even sloppier and more illegible than usual, as though he had written the note in a hurry. The letters T and I were respectively crossed and dotted in haphazard places, a sign that my brother might have been writing in near darkness, possibly in hiding. That he'd signed the letter from a strange name could mean that he thought whoever was after him might be on the lookout for a message sent to his family. The idea of some goon at my childhood home, rifling through my mailbox, gave me the willies.

Then there was the message itself. On face value, it was nonsense. I'd never been to summer camp. I'd never ridden in an ambulance with any friend after her appendix burst. And I had no friends named Aedon.

I plucked a pen from the nightstand and began to underline the keywords in the note that jumped out. *Camp. Bunkmate. Nine years. Hospital. Appendix. Books.*

None of those words immediately meant anything to me, so I turned to the name. When I typed Aedon Philomel into the web browser on my phone, the search results informed me that Aedon and Philomel were actually two different women.

But not real ones. They were figures from Greek mythology.

In both myths, they had been transformed into nightingales.

I revisited the words I'd underlined in Jack's message, and watched them magically fall into order in my mind. *Book. Hospital bunk. Appendix.*

And nine years ago, back when I would have been eight years old ... just like Echo.

I turned to Echo's bed. The Greek mythology text that Jack was reading to her that fateful night was right there, lying half-tangled in her blankets by her elbow. She must have fallen asleep reading or looking at the pictures.

Careful not to wake my sister, I picked up the book and immediately flipped to the very end—the appendix. Nothing stood out to me as I fanned through the index pages. But when I came to where the red endpaper was glued to the back cover, I saw that Jack had lightly penciled a tiny sketch in the corner.

A bird that might have been a nightingale.

I fumbled through my clutch until I found the Swiss-army knife attachment on my keychain. I flicked out the blade and carefully carved the endpaper away from the back cover, like I was opening an envelope.

As I undid the bottom, a single piece of paper, ragged and yellowed with age, dropped out and landed at my feet.

I gingerly picked it up, my trembling fingers grasping the brittle document by the corner. There was writing on both sides, but by two different hands. On one side, someone had scrawled a letter on journal stationery, the cursive barely legible, the tiny words spilling out to the margins. On the reverse, a second person had copied a short, twelve-line poem with measured, precise pen strokes.

A poem that read suspiciously like another riddle.

The full gravity of what I was holding didn't sink in until I read the date scrawled below the letterhead at the very top of the journal entry.

February 13, 1865.

"Holy shit," I whispered.

Dearest Adelaide,

It has been four months now since the carnage I witnessed at Winchester, four months since I fled the Shenandoah Valley. Every night, the events of that ruinous month haunt my dreams. I can hardly close my eyes without seeing the spilled blood of my brethren painting the banks of the Cedar.

However, my fear for our future weighs on me far heavier than any wartime atrocities. I fear that I shall never get to send these letters, and that you will never know how hard I tried to return to Baton Rouge to take my rightful spot at your side. I fear that General Early himself will track me down and string me from the gallows, a deserter's death. More than anything, I fear that even if heaven consents to bring me home, you will not desire a coward for a husband.

Still, I must put aside these woes for now to tell you of the queerest thing that happened this evening, so peculiar, indeed, that I eagerly write this now by lantern light.

Six days had I spent in the forests outside Charleston, with no roof over my head and rarely a morsel to be eaten. The Carolina rains sought to best me. And so, needing refuge from the elements, I found a barn on the outskirts where I could nest a bed for myself amongst the cattle and hay.

I had hardly made myself at home in my new sanctuary when I discerned a glow from an empty stall. It was a radiant blue the likes that I had never in this world seen. Though the source of the light was in part shrouded under a burlap concealment, I instantly knew I was in the presence of something divine, and so I edged closer with cautious trepidation.

My approach came to an unexpected stop when I felt the edge of a blade pressed against my neck. Holding the knife was a dark man of impressive stature—a slave, I assumed, by the fresh lashings recently branded upon his bare flesh.

"Please, sir. I am a friend," I promised him, though I expected he may doubt my honesty given my pallor and the soiled gray of my uniform. I noted a particularly inflamed wound upon his chest, tinged with the earliest whispers of infection, and I added, "I am also a doctor."

After much wordless scrutiny, he relented, and answered my prayers when he sheathed his blade.

My curiosity overcame my relief, and so, as my new companion knelt in the hay beside the glowing artifact, of which he seemed quite familiar, I dared to ask, "What is that heavenly thing?"

His silence endured so long I deemed that he may be a mute. In time, however, he whispered, "Yakuti Serengeti." Then, remarkably, he spoke to me in English, his accent harsh and alien, but his words powerful and certain in a way I shall never forget. "It is the Serengeti Sapphire," he said. "And it is the only thing that can save my son."

And then he promptly collapsed.

On castle grounds
'Top drumlin's perch
Where griffins gaze
O'er shore and shoals

Where statues flank
Long halls of pine
The hill rolls down
To taste the sea

As roses watch
The fount' runs dry
The truth entombed
Exhumed at last.

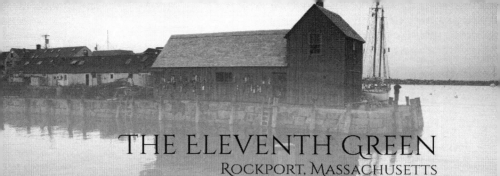

THE ELEVENTH GREEN
ROCKPORT, MASSACHUSETTS

BY THE TIME THE TRAIN CHUGGED SLOWLY INTO THE final station, it was after 1 a.m. and I was the only passenger remaining in my car. An attendant in a black cap strutted down the aisle and called out, "Rockport—end of the line."

I hoped he was only being literal.

As I stepped off the train onto the cement platform, I anxiously touched the pouch of my hooded sweatshirt to make sure the journal page was still there. I didn't know much about the preservation of artifacts, but I imagined that a few museum curators might faint at the thought of me stuffing a 150-year-old document into a hoodie. Still, my brother had gone to great lengths to conceal it from somebody, and I had no intentions of letting it out of my sight.

I left the railroad tracks in my dust, leaving the conductor to put the purple-striped train to bed for the night. I followed the main road on foot, toward the smell of the ocean. Surrounded on three sides by the sea, Rockport formed the eastern terminus of the Cape Ann peninsula, one of the earliest landing sites for English settlers traveling to the New World.

Today, the town was a strange relic of an old family fishing industry. Throughout the generations of fishermen, the Atlantic had reportedly claimed the lives of more than ten thousand of Cape Ann's husbands and sons. To this day, their names were inscribed in the nearby town hall of Gloucester.

It was amazing, I realized as I reflected on this historical trivia that had lain dormant in my brain, how much information I'd actually absorbed from Jack's frequent historical ravings.

The road curved through Bearskin Neck, the quaint but touristy stretch of town that overlooked a ship-dotted harbor. With its tiny, sea-weathered storefronts and colorful infestation of ships, the village was a popular destination for film crews in search of a rustic, coastal, all-American feel.

In the dead of night, it was so quiet that I could practically hear the buoys bobbing with the soft swell of the sea.

A short walk later, I arrived at the Windward Bluffs Country Club. The golf course's perimeter was protected only by a low metal fence, which was probably intended more to keep rogue balls from smashing car windows than it was to keep out late-night intruders. In the brush near the cart trail, I spotted a score card that somebody had discarded, and I used its map to navigate my way to the eleventh green.

As I hiked across the dark, empty fairway, my path lit only by a thin veil of moonlight filtering through the tall pines, I suddenly grew aware of how stupidly dangerous this trip to Rockport could be. I'd agreed to come to an empty golf course to meet a near stranger, who was at least tangentially involved in the death of my brother.

And I'd told absolutely no one where I was going.

It would be easy enough for Smitty and whoever else to ambush me, lash me to an anchor, and drop me into the middle of Sandy Bay. No one would ever hear from me again, until the ropes binding me one day rotted through and my fish-nibbled body washed ashore by the yacht club.

When I reached the eleventh green, I could see why Smitty had picked it as the spot for our clandestine rendezvous. It was the highest point in the whole course, situated at the top of a hill so you could see in all directions if somebody was coming.

For better or worse, the skittish bartender had yet to arrive, so I plopped down on the edge of a bunker. In the spirit of superstition, I pocketed a small handful of sand from the trap, just as Jack had taught me while he was teaching me to swim. Granted, this was a country club, not the beach, but there were dark currents at play now, and a little spiritual protection from my brother couldn't hurt.

While I waited, the automatic sprinklers clicked on, popping out of their hiding places around the green like steel gophers. Soon, a fine mist floated through the air, and even though it was probably too cold out to be getting wet, I found the dewy touch against my face refreshing.

After this past week, it was nice to feel something other than confusion, anger, or sorrow.

It felt like I'd been waiting forever when I heard the hum of a motor approaching. A golf cart rolled swiftly over the fairway, making its way up the hill. I stood and grabbed the sand rake from the bunker to use as a weapon if I needed.

Fortunately, Smitty had come alone. With a final dying *put-put-put*, the cart's motor idled into silence and Smitty rolled to a stop beside the green.

"Nice wheels," I said.

Smitty didn't smile. He stuffed his hands into his trousers—he was still wearing his uniform from the Nightingale. He looked so tense that his face might crack if the cape breeze hit him the wrong way. "Sorry to haul you all the way out here," he said. "This is where I grew up. I've been caddying at this golf course every summer since I was fourteen. I guess I wanted to be somewhere I felt safe."

"Safe from whom, Smitty?" I asked.

Smitty didn't answer at first. He floated a few steps across the green and ran a finger down the flag pole. Finally, without meeting my gaze, he said, "Horace Nox."

The name snapped a guitar string in my mind. *Horace Nox*. I didn't know him, per se, but most people who lived in Boston or even picked up a copy of the *Globe* had at least heard of him. He was an entrepreneur. He was also purportedly a "gangster," whatever that meant these days.

"Is that who killed my brother?" I asked, my voice dead.

Smitty looked sharply at me. "Did you come here just for the spoilers?" he snapped. "Or did you want the whole story?"

I swallowed the anger that had billowed up at the sound of Nox's name and nodded at Smitty. The *how* and the *why* were every bit as important as the *who*.

Smitty wandered over to the sand trap. I tossed the rake away and took a seat beside him. "How much do you know about Nox?" he asked me.

"Not much." Newspaper images and snippets of news footage surfaced in my memory. Nox was most notorious for wanting to open up a casino on the South Shore a few years back. The city council members shut him down before he could ever break ground. Officially, they claimed it was because he failed to produce viable evidence that he was one-eighth Algonquin Indian, as he had claimed, and that the influx of gamblers consuming copious amounts of alcohol posed a threat to the safety of their citizens.

Off the record, it was because of Nox's unsavory reputation.

Smitty scooped up a handful of sand. "A lot of what I'm about to tell you is stitched together from little stories I've heard in whispers here and there. Horace Nox is not the kind of guy who has a clean little bio you can read about on Wikipedia. He's a ghost who you don't touch and you don't talk about. The pieces of his story are like dinosaur bones in a desert—you dust them off one at a time, and at the end of the day, you hope you've got enough to glue them together and get a glimpse of the whole monster. Still," the bartender said solemnly as he opened his fingers and let the sand sift through, "I believe every word of what I'm about to tell you."

"Start at the beginning," I said. "Leave nothing out."

Smitty cleared his throat. "They say he grew up just outside Boston, down in Dorchester—your hometown, from what I gather. Don't know much about his parents, but Nox had an older brother named Wilbur, so if you ask me, his folks had no idea what side of the nineteenth century they were on. Even though Wilbur grew up perfectly healthy, Nox got the shit end of the gene pool and was born with some rare autoimmune disease that left him in constant pain, so bad that his hair turned permanently gray from the trauma by the time he finished elementary school. His muscles atrophied. Arthritis feasted on his joints. His kidneys started to fail. Nobody thought the kid would make it past his twelfth birthday."

I tightened my fingers around a tuft of grass at the edge of the sand trap, savoring the *snap* as each blade ripped free. "I usually root for sick children to pull through, but in his case ..."

"He probably wouldn't have, if it weren't for his big brother," Smitty continued. "See, Wilbur was a science geek, a bona fide prodigy, and he doted on Horace. He had his PhD in biochemistry by the time he turned twenty-one, but his true passion was botany."

"Botany? Like plants?"

"Sounds dumb when you put it that way, right? But many of the world's drugs, good and bad, come from plants and fungus—antibiotics, pharmaceuticals, narcotics—so it's not all that bizarre. In the end, because he loved Horace, Wilbur agreed to do whatever it took to find something that would alleviate his little brother's pain. The elder Nox experimented using plants from every continent, until he stumbled across a curious little organism from the Brazilian rainforest. Some sort of lichen that grows on the banks of the Amazon River. With

61

the right processes, Wilbur figured out how to distill it down into a serum that stabilized Horace's immune system, stimulated his muscle growth, and restored function to his failing organs. A chemical that finally quelled Nox's pain." Smitty paused, then added, "That's how they discovered Blyss."

The last word was one that I'd come to know well, especially since I started pedicabbing and seeing the "late-night" side of Boston. Blyss was fairly new to the drug world, but it was gaining popularity fast.

To illustrate his story, Smitty pulled a vial of the potion out of his pocket, rolling it between his thumb and pointer finger. In the darkness of the golf course, the Blyss phosphoresced softly, the murky contents undulating. At first glance, it was white and milky, like someone had bottled a cloud and it was trying to break out of the glass. Because you drank it instead of smoking it or injecting it, it was easy to consume in public without arousing suspicion. I had never tried it, but I knew plenty of people who had, including Rufus, who indulged whenever he had the cash. Out of curiosity, I had asked him once what it felt like.

"Cleanest high you'll ever get," Rufus had mused. "Suddenly, you feel this molten energy radiating out of everything around you, and your body soaks it up. Your senses of sight, sound, taste, and smell are heightened until you notice all the little details that you'd never given a damn about before —the scent of the perfume of the girl who walked past you, the screech of the train's brakes as it comes into Bowdoin. Meanwhile, it slows your reflexes and fries your sense of touch. Hell, I walked around Beacon Hill for three straight hours in bare feet, and it was like I was gliding over the cobblestones. And for a short while, I felt completely invincible ..."

It had scared me to hear Rufus like that, the tendrils of addiction in his voice, as though he were talking about a new lover he couldn't get enough of. But he wasn't alone. I'd seen some of my fares sharing sips from a flask in the back of my pedicab, giggling for no other reason than how the wind whistled past their ears. Kids from my high school parked in dark fields and lay in their truck beds, drinking Blyss until the stars swallowed them up.

I'd never known where the drug got its start.

Smitty fished a pack of cigarettes out of his trousers and tapped it against the edge of his palm until one came loose. "Mind if I smoke?" he asked.

I scooted away from him. "As long as you don't die from emphysema before you reach the end of the story."

When Smitty lifted the cigarette to his lips, I saw how bad the man was trembling. He dropped it twice into his lap before he managed to slip the end into his mouth and light it.

Smitty took a long drag, closed his eyes, and let a gray cloud billow out of him, like he was trying to exhale his fear. The tremor in his voice quieted as he picked up the tale again. "Within weeks of starting Horace on daily doses of Blyss, the symptoms of his disease began to retreat. His internal organs sprang back to life. His muscles grew strong. All that pain faded away. By the time Nox graduated from high school, he was in such peak health that he enlisted in the Marines and headed off to Iraq. While he was there, his convoy tripped an explosive device in the road, but Nox survived the ambush with just a few shrapnel wounds and a scratchy voice. Suddenly, the kid who once seemed doomed to wither away had transformed into a man of steel."

The few newspaper clippings I'd read had mentioned Nox's wartime exploits. They painted him as a war hero who'd fallen from grace once he'd returned to the mainland. "If he's some superman," I said, "then let's talk about his kryptonite."

Smitty's eyes lit up. "Now that involves a bit of irony. See, the problem for Horace is that in the early days, Wilbur hadn't quite perfected the recipe for Blyss. While the drug was taking away Nox's pain and kickstarting his immune system, it was also silently planting the seeds of a little something nasty that's been growing in him all these years."

"Nox … has cancer?" I asked.

Smitty shrugged. "Something like that. Something the doctors had never seen. Something they couldn't cure. Either way, the man is dying." He dropped his cigarette into the sand and toed it out in the dirt.

So the very plant that Nox had thought would be his guardian angel turned out to be the grim reaper in disguise. "Great bedtime story," I told Smitty. "But it's about time you get to the part where my brother ended up on the bad side of a dying, drug-dealing kingpin."

Something came over Smitty's face, and I could tell he was struggling with how to phrase what happened next. Was that shame in his expression?

He drew in a deep breath. "The night your brother died, I was working the bar, like the police report said. And your brother was at the Nightingale, too. Only he wasn't upstairs pounding shots."

Whatever excitement I'd felt before at the prospect of finally getting answers turned to ice.

Smitty's eyes were glassy. Tears pooled in the corners, ready to spill over. "Toward the end of my shift, we ran out of Newport Lager, so I went downstairs to change the keg. Partway down the steps, I heard Nox interrogating your brother. Had a couple of his goons with him, too."

"Was one of those goons," I asked slowly, "a chick with some interesting metal hardware on her head?" My mind chillingly flashed to the grin of the horned driver who'd run down my brother.

Smitty nodded. "That's Aries, his dealer up in Salem. Nox seems to favor her because she *enjoys* doing the unsavory stuff. Lets Nox keep his hands clean, relatively speaking."

My fingers balled into a fist so tight that I could feel the bones bend in protest.

"It sounded like your brother had taken something from Nox," Smitty said. "Some page from an old journal or something. And from the tone of Nox's voice, he would do anything to get it back."

I slipped a hand into my hoodie pocket and brushed my fingers across the fragile surface of the journal page. There was no doubt in my mind: The old document in my possession was the very thing that Nox had been grilling Jack for.

Something about it was so important to Nox that it cost Jack his life.

"So you're telling me that you just stood there while they interrogated my brother?" I pictured Jack limping across the bridge, the pained twist in his face every time he put weight on his bad leg. "While they beat and tortured him?"

"What was I supposed to do?" Smitty wailed, the sharp peak of his voice carrying down the quiet hill. "You think I should have run upstairs and called the cops? Nox has a fixer in the Boston Police Department—a dirty cop on his payroll who smoothes everything over."

It had only been twelve hours ago that I was in the precinct, going toe-to-toe with a detective who'd taken a sudden interest in my brother's case. Could Detective Grimshaw be Nox's inside man? "Dirty how?"

"Rumor has it that this detective put money on the wrong horses at Suffolk Downs and got in deep with a local Armenian bookie named Georg. Now the cop and Nox have an agreement: Nox keeps Georg from coming to collect, so long as the cop makes sure Nox's name stays out of the police ledgers. Who do you think falsified that report? Who do you think coerced *me* into signing it?"

All day, I'd figured Grimshaw was being unhelpful because he thought I was suffering from delusions. What if he was actually trying to sweep the murder under the rug for the drug dealer who was paying off his gambling debts?

"You have to believe me!" Smitty pleaded, sounding like he was trying to convince himself as much as he was me. "Nox's guys are roughnecks, but I had no idea they were going to kill him."

"What did you think, that they were going to throw him a birthday party?" I asked.

Smitty bowed his head. "Later that night, once I got home to my wife and my baby daughter, I woke up to a scraping sound. It was Aries, sharpening a knife at the foot of my bed. Sharpening them on the horns sprouting out of her skull." The fear had returned to his voice twofold. "Aries told me, very calmly, that they'd caught me on security camera, eavesdropping on the staircase. That a witness report would appear at the police station the next day with my name on it, and I better corroborate everything it said. Then she was gone."

"*Aries*," I repeated the name, letting it sit bitterly on my tongue. It tasted like bleach.

There were so many people who needed to pay for Jack's murder. Nox for ordering it. Whatever goons held my brother down in that basement. Detective Grimshaw for covering it up.

But Aries was the one behind the wheel of the Mustang.

For that, she was going to pay most dearly.

"That's all I know," Smitty said. "Do I feel shame for not trying harder to save your brother? Words cannot even describe. I liked the guy, a lot. Smart as a whip, and I learned more from his historical babble in two months than I learned in four years at Salem State. But I have a family to think about. I risked my life and theirs to share this information with you, because you at least deserve the truth."

Smitty rattled off a string of apologies and excuses, but I was lost in thought as I gazed out over the harbor at Thacher Island, its outline dark against the indigo sea. Its two lighthouses winked at me with each sweep of their lights. The last time I'd been to Rockport, I had tagged along with Jack for a research project he was doing. Standing on the pier next to a buoy-covered boathouse, he'd pointed animatedly at Thacher. During the Revolutionary War, the colonists had decided that the lighthouses were inadvertently helping guide the Redcoats to safe harbor, so a group of minutemen stormed the island and extinguished the twin lanterns.

So much knowledge trapped in Jack's head, so much verve for life, and he hadn't lived to see his nineteenth birthday.

"What are you going to do?" Smitty was asking when I snapped out of my reverie. "As long as he has his inside man, going to the police is a death sentence. And if you try to cross Nox, he will filet you like a cod and stew you in his chowder."

I didn't dare tell Smitty that I had the journal page Nox was looking for. Smitty had helped me so far, but only under duress. He would clearly do anything to survive, or at least to protect his family, and if Nox turned his interrogation techniques on this fragile bartender, he would crow like a rooster.

I let my fingers close resolutely around the edge of the riddle. "I'm going to find what Nox is looking for," I said.

"And then what?" Smitty asked.

My eyes narrowed with cold fury. "Retribution."

HOME INVASION
DORCHESTER, MASSACHUSETTS

WHEN I OPENED MY EYES THE FOLLOWING DAY, IT took several moments of confusion to figure out why I wasn't in my own bed.

I'd fallen asleep in Jack's old bedroom.

It was the blue flannel sheets I recognized first, followed by the smell of Jack's citrusy cologne, which still lingered on the unwashed pillowcases. Jack hadn't been home since he'd left for college, but the "old-man scent" that he generously spritzed himself with had always clung stubbornly to fabrics like moss to a stone.

Without looking at the alarm clock, I knew that I'd slept right through the morning and into the afternoon. Jack's room faced west, and I'd woken up because the low October sun had been streaming onto my face, through the window over Jack's bed. Even now my cheek felt warm to the touch.

I leaned out the window, gazing out over the endless clusters of triple-decker houses that made up Dorchester's Savin Hill neighborhood. The Boston skyline looked like a miniature on the horizon. My hometown was one of the last bastions of true diversity in the city. Irish, black, Vietnamese, Cape Verdean—you could find a little bit of each coexisting on every street in Dorchester. Sure, we had our problems like any other city, but at the end of the day, we all shared one common thread: Everyone here was just trying to get by.

Now, however, I had far greater concerns than breaking into the middle class.

At dawn, I'd taken the earliest train home from Rockport, after waiting two hours, curled up on a bench at the commuter rail station, digesting everything Smitty had told me. *Treat the story like the riddles Jack used to leave you*, I told myself. *Start simple, and let the answers reveal themselves to you as you go.*

But for every conclusion I reached, two more questions took its place.

My first conclusion: It was no coincidence that Jack ended up working at the Nightingale. Twenty-four hours ago, I might have convinced myself that the allure of extra pocket cash had drawn Jack to a job at a seedy nightclub. But it was a little too much to swallow, given Jack's obsession with American history, that he'd arrived at the Nightingale with no ulterior motives, when the bar's owner happened to be in possession of a priceless journal page from the 1800s.

So Jack had planted himself in Nox's organization in the least suspicious position possible. Some place where Nox might not even notice he existed, washing dishes and the floors. He'd bided his time and listened to the whispers around him.

And then he'd stolen the journal page from Nox.

Then there was the artifact itself. Jack's interest in it made sense, but what significance could it have to Nox? I didn't want to stereotype, but I couldn't imagine that an ex-commando drug kingpin could be interested in it strictly for its historical value. Maybe it was old enough that it was worth a fortune. However, Nox owned a nightclub and reigned over the Blyss drug ring. He had enough money that he didn't need to sell some journal page at the Antiques Roadshow.

So if Nox wasn't interested in it for the sake of history or monetary gain, then why had he killed my brother for stealing it?

This question still haunted me as I wandered over to Jack's cluttered mahogany desk. I rubbed the residual sleep from my eyes and idly flipped over my brother's antique hourglass.

Something happened as I watched the white sand slowly filter through the timepiece. My mind went still for the first time since I could remember, as I listened to the gentle hiss of the grains collecting in the lower glass orb.

"*Time*," I whispered.

Nox had power and money. But if he was truly dying, then what he didn't have was time. Neither power nor money could buy that back. And Nox had already proven in the past that he was willing to go to extraordinary lengths to stay alive.

Jack, on the other hand, hadn't been dying himself, but his youngest sister was on the losing end of a battle with cancer. Just as Nox would do anything to survive, Jack would have done anything to give Echo her childhood back.

Then there was the runaway slave from the journal, who was convinced that the "Serengeti Sapphire"—some sort of mystical gem?—would save his son.

My next thought was so crazy that I almost stopped myself from thinking it, but the idea bubbled up anyway.

What if Jack and Nox were both after something that could restore health to the ill?

What if they were both after the Serengeti Sapphire?

The idea was preposterous, yet it filled me with such hope that the concept began planting roots in my brain as soon as I thought it. I felt those roots slithering deep into the soil of my consciousness, and the more they grew, the more I felt like I'd stumbled upon something that finally made sense.

When I'd first examined the books that Jack had hoarded in his dorm room, I struggled to identify any common themes among them, but now a few titles jumped out in my memory: *The Lazarus Myths. Alchemy and the Quest for the Philosopher's Stone.*

La Fontaine de Jouvence—French for "the Fountain of Youth." All legends concerned with prolonging human life beyond natural means. Regeneration. Resurrection.

Immortality.

Beyond the telltale book titles, Jack's actions in his final hours had completely contradicted themselves. He'd instructed his roommate, who I didn't even know, to prevent me from following his quest. Then, mere hours before he died, he'd secretly left me with the very object that had gotten him killed, and sent me a cryptic postcard to guide me to it.

Maybe he'd been torn between the prospect of saving one sister and the possibility of endangering the other.

Of course, my theory about my brother searching for some sapphire with healing properties could be completely off-base. Even if he had been, even if both Jack and Nox believed in it, it didn't mean it was real.

However, one thing my brother and I shared in common was this: If there was even a fraction of a chance that something could cure Echo, we'd follow that lead to the ends of the earth.

Despite all these revelations, one question still fiercely bothered me. Jack had concealed the journal page within that Greek mythology book, yet he'd dropped it off in Echo's hospital room, instead of leaving it at our house in Dorchester. Why?

That's when I noticed little details I'd missed before. Jack's tightly packed bookshelves were all arranged alphabetically by author, exactly the way he liked it. However, the thin layer of dust on the shelves, which had accumulated since Jack went to college, had recently been disturbed. Then there was my brother's chair, which was tucked neatly into his desk, flush against the wood. The thing was, one of Jack's favorite historical figures was General George Patton. Patton's statue at West Point, where he'd attended college, faced the library, because it had been said that Patton never felt like he'd done enough reading. Jack had found this so novel that he always left his desk chair facing his own library, away from his desk.

One of Nox's people had been here recently, searching for the journal page.

Here. In my house.

I instantly felt violated at the thought of one of the men responsible for Jack's death pawing through his things, through all of our things, while we weren't home.

I pulled the journal page out of my pocket. I traced my finger along the jagged edge where the paper had been ripped from the binding of the actual journal. If Nox was after this page as though it belonged to him …

Then maybe Nox was in possession of the rest of the journal as well.

In the past twenty-four hours, I had done my fair share of stupid reckless things. I'd badgered a dirty detective. I'd snuck into a nightclub to interrogate a bartender. I'd agreed to meet a complete stranger who had ties to my brother's killers in the dead of night on an empty golf course.

The plan formulating as I watched the sand in the hourglass trickle down put all of those to shame.

My brother had stolen one page from the journal.

I was going to steal the rest.

I sat down at Jack's desk and powered on his old desktop computer. When the dusty relic finally opened a web browser, I ran a search for "Horace Nox" and began reading through public records until I found what I was looking for:

His home address.

I smiled and ran my fingernail down the orb of the hourglass. "You break into my house," I said, "I break into yours …"

———

Apparently, the Blyss trade was more lucrative in New England than I initially realized.

Because Nox lived in one of the most colossal mansions I'd ever seen.

Not a mansion, I corrected myself as I studied the house from the obscurity of the trees across the street. *This is a fortress.*

Between the high brick-and-mortar wall that ran the perimeter of the grounds, the wrought-iron gates monogrammed "HDN," and a single lookout tower reaching up into the sky, Nox's residence looked like it had been built to withstand a siege. Hell, throw in a drawbridge and a moat with a few crocodiles and it would be downright medieval.

Once again, I'd boarded one of the commuter rail's many tentacles to escape the city, this time to the town of Cohasset, southeast of Boston. The idea of a gangster living in plain sight here of all places was especially amusing, since Cohasset had a reputation for being one of the most cookie-cutter hamlets in Massachusetts. Nestled on a quiet stretch of coastline, the town was named for a Native American word meaning "rocky shore," but the lifestyle here was anything but rocky. With its quaint little town green, complete with a duck pond and a cutesy white church, it was a far cry from the neighborhood in Dorchester where I was born and raised.

In short, it was not the place where you'd expect a high school student to be breaking into the mansion of a murderer.

Yet here I was, lying at the edge of the trees within viewing distance of Nox's estate. I hoped that the brown hoodie that I was wearing might camouflage me with the bed of leaves to anyone driving by.

I lurked there for an hour before the gates parted. A silver Cadillac with tinted windows rolled out onto the main drag, and I flattened myself to the ground, pressing my face into the dew-covered leaves. The rumble of the engine grew louder, and for a paranoid second, I felt certain that Nox would spot me. That I'd hear the screech of the car's brakes, then feel the cold barrel of a gun against the back of my head.

I exhaled with relief as the Cadillac zipped by me.

Instinct took over in the seconds that followed. As I lifted my head and peeled a wet leaf off my cheek, I noticed that the front gates to Nox Manor were lingering open. There were plenty of things I should have considered then. Was his fortress equipped with surveillance cameras? Did he have private security or attack dogs waiting on the other side?

Rather than weighing any of these questions seriously, I staggered to my feet and ran.

It took several strides to shake the stiffness from my knees, after all that time lying on the roadside, but I channeled my inner Olympic sprinter and barreled toward the gates. They had already begun to swing mechanically closed, and in a matter of seconds, I would be back to square one.

I wasn't about to let that happen. With one last dash of speed, I angled my body through the remaining gap, my arms brushing the metal gate on each side as I threaded the needle.

I landed hard on the gravel entryway right as the doors clanged shut behind me.

I rose to my feet, brushing off the gravel pebbles embedded in my scraped knees. Now that I was inside the compound, I could see that I hadn't been far off calling the mansion a "fortress." Its walls were constructed of massive stone blocks and the narrow windows were latticed with steel, which meant that the "smash the glass" method of breaking and entering was a no-go. The metal-plated front doors looked like they could withstand an all-day assault from a battering ram.

The landscaping was no less intimidating. A collection of thorny botanical sculptures leered over me as I made my way around the house. A horse's head, a castle tower, a shapeless body with a crown—the topiaries were all giant chess pieces. It was a fitting garden for someone who probably viewed life as a game, a man willing to watch all of the pieces fall around him, so long as the king still stood victorious in the end. Had Nox seen my brother as just another pawn to be sacrificed?

By the time I reached the backyard, I was close to giving up. How easy had I thought this was going to be? I wasn't a jewel thief. I had no tools with which to successfully break into a house. The windows were reinforced and if I even attempted to scale the stone walls, I'd probably slip and kill myself.

I stopped at the end of the yard, where the Kentucky blue grass ended abruptly at a cliff's edge overlooking the rocky shore below. I was staring off over the restless sea, feeling like a total failure, when a light breeze coursed through the yard. It carried with it the odor of something pungent, something stronger than the salty aroma of the sea.

I followed the smell back across the lawn, until I found the culprit, still smoking in the grass: the butt of a cigar. My father had always loved smoking these with my godfather after work, one of his many filthy habits, so I recognized the scent. My initial thought was that Nox must have lit up in his backyard before he headed out.

But then I noticed the balcony protruding from the manor's second floor. I'd been so fixated on the ground level that I'd ignored it on my first pass. I could picture Nox wandering out of his study, puffing a lit cigar beneath his teeth like he had the whole world wrapped around his finger.

When I gazed up at the glass balcony doors leading into the house, I noticed another encouraging detail: one of them had been left ajar.

A smile crossed my lips. "You careless bastard," I whispered. Building a castle meant jack shit if you couldn't remember to close your patio doors.

I took off at a run toward the wall, as though I were about to crash right through it. At the last second, I found a toehold in the mortar between the rocks. I kicked off with all my might, extending my arms up.

Before gravity could catch up with me, my fingers wrapped around the balcony's edge, so that I dangled over the grass below. It took upper-body strength I didn't know I had—I was a cyclist, not a gymnast—but I eventually pulled myself up and climbed over the railing.

When I slipped through the open patio doors, I half-expected an alarm to go off, for several Dobermans to come racing across the floor, lunging for my jugular with gnashing, spittle-slick teeth. But there was only the creak of the floorboards under the oriental carpet.

The parlor was nothing I wouldn't have expected from a wealthy, self-indulgent man. The mahogany room boasted a billiard table with the silhouette of a nightingale on the green felt top. His wet bar was stocked with more bourbon than a Tennessee distillery and unmarked bottles filled with milky Blyss.

Other than testifying to Nox's history of substance abuse, the parlor contained nothing of note, so I headed for the exit, moving deeper into his mansion.

What lay beyond those doors was far more interesting.

Horace Nox had an indoor jungle.

I found myself at a railing, staring down on a central courtyard overgrown with trees. As far as I could tell, every room in the square-shaped estate opened into this massive greenhouse. Whereas the parlor had been air-conditioned, the climate out here was sticky and hot like an equatorial rainforest. Sunlight shone through the massive glass steeple over the courtyard, and the light took on a green tint as it filtered down through the canopy.

Even more bizarre, the courtyard was surrounded by mesh netting, as though there was something inside the jungle that Nox wanted to keep out of the rest of his house.

Yet I could see nothing dangerous lurking in the foliage, nor could I hear anything but the babble of running water somewhere in the underbrush.

As I traveled along the corridor, I discovered that each room in the house was labeled with a gold plaque. The sign over the parlor doors read "Knavery." The room next door, "Insomnia," turned out to be a small movie theater with only one seat, dead-center, so apparently Nox wasn't fond of date nights. A popcorn cart sat in the corner, and the projector whirred idly, casting a flickering glow onto the red curtains.

I nearly vomited when I stepped into "Game," a walk-in freezer populated with the carcasses of exotic animals dangling from steel hooks. Kangaroo, caribou, ostrich, lion—the hunks of frozen meat were only identifiable thanks to the morgue tags attached to them.

Things only got stranger through the door marked "Triumph."

The space beyond was initially cloaked in darkness, but seconds later several gas torches bloomed on the walls, revealing a spiral staircase cut into stone. Basked in firelight, I descended one story, then another, and a third. By the time the staircase spat me out into a dark chamber, I estimated that I must be forty feet underground.

More torches flickered to life, illuminating the limestone walls and the vaulted ceiling. The Triumph room had a decidedly tomb-like quality to it, only instead of a sarcophagus, there was a wooden desk at its center, directly under a solitary skylight. The desk was covered with an enormous map of New England and faced a glass screen embedded in the stone walls.

But the screen wasn't a television, I realized as I approached. The portal in the wall was a glass case with six pages pinned inside.

Aged, yellowed pages.

Pages that looked like they belonged to the same journal as the one in my pocket.

Each of the six documents featured a twelve-line poem, and I felt certain that if I flipped them over, I'd find additional journal entries from Dr. Cumberland Warwick. From my pocket, I withdrew the riddle Jack had left me, which I'd protectively coated in a plastic sleeve, and I pressed it to the glass. Just as I remembered, it had the number seven inscribed in the corner.

After snapping hi-res pictures of the new riddles using my phone, I revisited the map on the desk. Nox had placed a number of pins within a hundred miles of Boston. The pin numbered "1" was located right in the heart of the city, next to a picture of an old library—the Boston Athenaeum, according to the short description attached. A string connected the first marker to a second one outside city limits, which depicted an old grist mill with a spinning water wheel. One by one, I traced the journey along the string to different landmarks throughout New England.

#3: Provincetown Harbor on the tip of Cape Cod, where the Mayflower first moored on its journey to the New World.

#4: The U.S.S. Constitution, a massive forty-gun frigate that was one of the first-ever ships in the U.S. Naval fleet.

#5: The Portland Head Light, the oldest lighthouse in Maine, which George Washington had commissioned in 1791.

#6: The House of the Seven Gables, long associated with the city of Salem's sordid history of witchcraft-related persecutions.

#7: Block Island, the site of an infamous colonial massacre of Pequot Indians. This particular flag had a big red X through it, along with a photograph of an empty treasure chest.

The final picture was of the Museum of Fine Arts, which had the #8 and a big question mark next to it.

As the dots connected in my head, I dropped down heavily into the desk's leather chair.

Nox had six pages from the old journal. If I were interpreting the map correctly, each one had been discovered in a different historical landmark around New England. They formed some sort of circuitous path that Nox had been following, page by page.

That is, until my brother had beaten him to the seventh. The map on Nox's desk suggested the possible location of the eighth page as the MFA, the same museum from which Jack had mailed me that cryptic postcard the night of his murder. Maybe Nox or his men had followed Jack there, hoping he'd uncover the eighth riddle for him. However, that page was missing from Nox's collection, which meant that it must still be at large.

With a quaking hand, I withdrew the journal page once more. The riddle had sounded like gibberish at first, but I now knew exactly what was encoded within its twelve lines:

The location of the next page.

This whole thing was one big goddamn scavenger hunt.

Tiny warning alarms rang in my head, reminding me that it was probably time to hightail it out of Nox's compound. I sprinted out of the chamber and up the stairs.

On my way out of the mansion, curiosity seized me as I passed the courtyard. It didn't take a psychoanalyst to recognize that each of the peculiarly labeled rooms in the house had something to say about Nox's twisted psyche. To truly understand the man who killed my brother, nothing would be more revealing than finding out what he'd constructed in the very heart of his fortress.

I passed through a gap in the mesh and out into the indoor jungle. The humidity in the greenhouse pressed down on me like a sodden blanket. The trees were tall, brushing up against the glass overhead, and I wondered how the roots weren't tearing the mansion's foundation apart—although the thought of the house caving in on Nox brought a smile to my lips.

The path snaked through the trees, alongside a small manmade brook. When I looked closely, I saw that the water was propelled downstream by a series of motors. Like everything else in the mansion, Nox had paid a meticulous attention to detail when he designed this courtyard. But to what end? To have a quiet indoor forest where he could come to reflect? Why would a man who prided himself on a raucous nightclub create an oasis like this? And more pressingly: What was with all the nets?

These questions were interrupted by a door crashing open somewhere in the complex, followed by a male voice, coarse and deep as the bottom of a ravine, saying:

"Take him to the birdcage."

CARRION
COHASSET, MASSACHUSETTS

PANIC EXPLODED IN ME. MY FIRST INSTINCT WAS TO run back the way I came, but in the echoing vastness of the courtyard, I couldn't be sure which direction the voice was originating from.

In a move of pure desperation, I sought refuge in the thickest bush I could find and drew my hood over my head for camouflage. Then I waited, while silently praying, *Please choose any room but this one.*

They entered the courtyard through the same hallway I had. I remained still, hoping that the brook would conceal any rustling I made. As the sound of footsteps approached, I could also hear the whimpering of some kind of animal.

No, not an animal. They were the muffled cries of a human being who'd been gagged.

Through the thick undergrowth, I saw a giant of a man— he had to be pushing seven feet tall and nearly half as wide. Although he walked with a discernible limp, the brute effortlessly carried a much smaller man draped over one of his mammoth shoulders. His captive was bound at the ankles and wrists and shrieked in short bursts of terror through the duct tape over his mouth. I recognized the hostage's sweat-matted red hair.

Smitty.

The bartender still wore the formal vest and suit pants of his Nightingale uniform, but his face had been beaten into a checkerboard of black and blue, blotting out his freckles.

I had little time to fear for Smitty's life, because the next three people who entered brought my blood to a full boil.

Detective Grimshaw wore a long black trench coat with his police badge pinned to the lapel.

The spiky-haired she-devil behind him didn't have a face that I would know, but the metal ram's horns spiraling out of her head had haunted my dreams every night since Jack's death. She had a croquet mallet strapped to her back, and her eyes were visibly bloodshot from whatever drugs she'd been using.

Last but not least, an imposing man in a three-piece suit strode confidently onto the brick path. Horace Nox's irises were so piercingly blue that they should belong to a movie star, not a killer. He kept his prematurely silver hair long and unencumbered now that he'd left the military for a life of drugs and terror, and he sported a necklace with a slender shard of blood-tinged shrapnel.

The gangster who'd ordered Jack's execution, the succubus who'd carried it out, and the detective who'd covered it up, all in one room, a short ten yards away from me.

What I wouldn't give to have a gun right now.

The giant unshouldered Smitty and forced him down onto his knees. As he squirmed, Aries sauntered forward, twirling her croquet mallet. She held up the handle end, which had been whittled down to a sharp point. "You try to run," she said, "and I'll make you sit on this." Immediately, the bartender stopped fidgeting, but he whimpered as Aries sawed through the string binding his wrists and ankles. A cry burst out of him as she ripped the duct tape off his mouth, tearing away half of his mustache in the process.

I ducked lower in the bushes as Nox squatted in front of his kneeling captive. Even from my leafy vantage point, I could see that the drug baron was a lot like his nightclub: a paper-thin layer of class lacquered over a cheap, warped skeleton.

Nox put a finger to his lips. "Shh. There's no need to fret, Smitty. I just have three easy questions to ask you, and if you answer them all honestly, then I'll have Drumm drive you right back to the Nightingale. I'll even throw in a bottle of that Macallan you love so much to compensate you for this traumatic ordeal. What do you say?"

Smitty swallowed hard. "I'm a Magic Eight-Ball, boss. Give me a light shake and I'll tell you whatever you like."

Nox clapped his hands together. "Wonderful. Question one: When you were growing up, did you ever want to be an astronomer?"

The bizarre inquiry visibly caught Smitty off-guard. "No, boss," he stammered. "I wasn't very good at science and the only telescope I used was to spy into the room of the girl next door."

Nox smiled but didn't laugh. "You mangy dog. Question two: How is your golf game these days?"

"Golf game?" A wetness spread through the seat of Smitty's trousers. "Terrible, boss. Hard to be any good on the fairways when one of your legs is shorter than the other."

"Which brings us to question three," Nox mused. "Why would someone who doesn't like stargazing and is no good with a three-iron *possibly* want to visit a golf course in the dead of night?"

So they'd kidnapped Smitty because of me. I had bullied him into meeting up with me at the country club. Nox's men had followed him. Now the bartender was at the mercy of killers.

If I didn't get the hell out of here, I would be, too.

"Boss," Smitty pleaded. "It was nothing shady, I promise. The country club has me on call for maintenance, and I got a message that the sprinkler system was backed up. You know rich guys and golf—one piece of dry grass on a perfectly manicured fairway and it's the end of the world." He attempted a laugh. It sounded like the shrill giggle of a man who was already dead.

Nox straightened up and slapped a palm against his own forehead. "Smitty, I am *so* sorry. Wow, do I feel embarrassed." He pointed to the punk with the horns. "See, Aries tailed you last night to Rockport and I made this crazy assumption that you were up to no good. You know how I can leap to paranoid conclusions sometimes. I've been in this business for a few years now, but I can honestly say this is the first time I've ever wrongfully kidnapped someone for performing sprinkler maintenance. Is there any chance we can put this whole misunderstanding behind us?" He extended his hand to Smitty.

Smitty eyed the gangster warily but shook hands with him. "We all make mistakes," he said, his voice still trembling. "You don't even have to give me a raise."

Nox shrugged and released the bartender's hand. "How about an early bonus then?" His eyed flicked to the burly mutant who'd dragged Smitty into the greenhouse. "Drumm?"

Drumm picked up a vat of something that had been hidden in a nearby thicket. He held the tank over Smitty, who looked up right as ten gallons of viscous, dark red liquid poured down over his head.

Smitty screamed, and I clamped my hand over my mouth, assuming that the mysterious chemical was acid. But after several seconds, it was clear that Smitty wasn't burning alive. He clawed the substance away from his face and retched. "What *is* this?" he burbled.

"Horse blood," Nox said matter-of-factly, as though he'd said "Pepsi" instead.

Even Detective Grimshaw gagged. Aries twitched with anticipation. Something awful was about to happen.

The trees came alive then. Throughout the canopy, several enormous birds that had been concealed in the foliage bristled on their perches. One of the creatures landed on a branch over my hiding place, and as soon as I saw it, I couldn't believe I'd missed it before. It was a vulture of incredible size, with a white hood and a rubbery red projection above its beak. Its black wings spanned twice my height. Its beady eyes ignored me and fixed on the man who was now covered in blood.

"Here's the problem," Nox said. "Sprinkler maintenance doesn't explain the redhead who you rendezvoused with at the golf course last night. Or why that same girl showed up in our surveillance tapes from earlier in the day, talking with you at the bar. Or why she matches the description of the overly inquisitive bitch who peppered Grimshaw with all sorts of questions. yesterday. So tell me, Smitty ..." All at once, Nox's cool façade dissolved and his voice rose into an apoplectic scream. "Why were you talking with the sister of the meddling loser that *I just put in the fucking ground?*"

"I was ... I was only trying ... to see how much ... she knew!" Smitty wailed, his sentence punctuated by sobs. "I figured if she trusted me ... I could find out whether you needed ... to have her taken care of."

Nox lifted his eyes to the trees. "Those birds watching you right now are Andean Condors. Some of the largest birds in the world. They feed mostly on the carcasses of dead animals. And this"—Nox took what looked like a fire extinguisher from Aries—"is a tank full of *ethyl mercaptan*, which is, quite literally, the stench of death. A few sprays from this, and those hungry condors will mistake you for carrion. See, that's all liars like you are to me: rotting, stinking corpses."

Nox angled the tank's nozzle at Smitty, ready to turn him into condor chow. The bartender raised his hands. "Wait, Horace! Wait! There's something you need to know! Wait!"

To my surprise, Nox set the canister down. The path must have been uneven, because it toppled over and rolled slowly, slowly ...

And when it was done rolling, the tank stopped right in front of my leafy hiding spot.

Nox put one hand to his ear and leaned toward Smitty, waiting for the bartender to elaborate.

"She knows how her brother died." Smitty swallowed hard. "And she knows about the journal."

Nox stiffened at the word "journal," as though an electric current had passed through his body. "Well," he said. "That is all *very* good information for me to know." A pause. "However, my pets are still famished."

While Smitty pleaded for his life, Nox started toward the tank. I knew that if the drug lord got close enough to pick it up, he would see me.

Then Jack's killers would murder me, too.

But more than that, I pictured Echo wasting away in that hospital bed, waiting for a miracle treatment that would never come.

So I did the only thing that made sense to me in that moment: I decided to draw first blood.

I sprang out of the bushes and Nox froze mid-step. That extra second was all I needed. I scooped up the tank, leveled the nozzle at the bastard's face, and pulled the trigger.

The spray hit him in his steely eyes and he bellowed in pain. The chemical smelled foul, like rotting eggs and onions, and I didn't relent until the acrid fog enveloped us both. Nox swung his arms blindly, hoping to connect with me, but I ducked under them. Detective Grimshaw and Drumm both rushed at me, so I sent two bursts of the chemical into each of their faces, blinding them as well.

Something hard and unforgiving pressed into my throat. Aries had snuck up behind me and was choking me with the shaft of her croquet mallet. "You *look* like your brother," she rasped. "But do you whimper like him, too?"

The scent of the ethyl mercaptan must have finally reached the condors, because they descended through the mist in a cacophony of hisses and fluttering wings. One bird swooped toward my face, its wingspan spread the full ten feet. I grabbed Aries's mallet and spun the two of us 180 degrees, forcing her into the path of the condor. She shrieked as it latched onto her spiral horns and tackled her to the ground. I wheezed a hoarse, relieved breath as the pressure came off my windpipe.

Through the flash of wings and mayhem, I saw Drumm come at me again, but Smitty wrapped his arms around the titan's legs, impeding his progress. The distraction gave me enough time to scoop up the empty canister, wind up, and strike Drumm hard in the face. His nose collapsed on impact, blood pouring out onto his shirt, and he dropped face-first to the ground.

I fought off a condor, then seized Smitty by his bloody hand, pulling him toward the exit to the greenhouse. Nearby, Aries had wrestled one bird to the ground only to have a second land on her back. Cowardly Detective Grimshaw crawled into the bushes while two more condors raked at his flesh.

Nox, however, had swatted away the bird attacking him and drew a gun from his waistband. His eyes blinked rapidly, bleary from the chemicals, but I saw a smile tickle his lips when he saw us. He raised the gun.

With a deep, raspy squawk, the largest condor of all dropped down from its perch. Its talons sank into Nox's shoulders and the gunshot went wide, blowing a hole in the tree trunk next to my head. The bird dragged Nox back into the manmade river with a satisfying splash, allowing Smitty and me to escape the greenhouse with our lives.

We weren't out of the woods yet. I led him out the nearest exit I could find, and we spilled out into the backyard. This was the part that was *really* going to take courage.

Because I knew the condors inside the greenhouse wouldn't hold the four gangsters for long. If we went for the main road on foot, Nox and his men would chase us down in cars.

They would never expect us to escape via the ocean.

As I sprinted across the lawn toward the cliff, Smitty realized exactly what I intended. "Are you nuts?" he said, out of breath.

"Do you want to see your wife and kid again?" I asked.

Even through the crimson sheen of blood covering his face, I saw the grim determination that came over him. He ran faster. If we were going to clear the rocks at the base of the cliff and have any chance of survival, we would need to leap as far out to sea as we could.

We were almost to the cliff when I heard the gunshot. Smitty's body snapped forward. I almost slowed down to help him, but as he rolled across the grass, I saw the gaping wound the bullet had drilled into the back of his skull. He was gone.

I raced the last few yards to the cliff's edge, and with no hesitation, I hurled myself into the air. The jump was awkward and my body rotated mid-leap, enough that my last image before I plummeted to the water was of Nox standing in his backyard with a gun trained on me.

Then gravity dragged me downward in a death spiral toward the rocky shallows below.

MEANWHILE, BACK AT NOX MANOR

As soon as the Tides girl disappeared over the cliff, Horace Nox relaxed his finger on the trigger, then finally let the gun fall to his side altogether. By the time he reached the edge, Sabra had already been carried a football field away by the south-roving current, her head bobbing in and out of the surf. Nox was a pretty good marksman, but he had only intended to maim her—you couldn't milk a dead cow, after all—and at this distance, there was no guarantee he wouldn't accidentally pop her melon. The last thing he needed was a corpse washing up in one of his neighbor's backyards.

One by one, Aries, Drumm, and Grimshaw emerged from the mansion, all nursing various flesh wounds from the buzzard attack. Drumm swayed on his feet, still dazed, with his mangled nose resembling a flattened beet.

Despite the tic-tac-toe board of claw marks on her face, Aries still buzzed with excitement thanks to the fresh dose of Blyss flowing through her veins. "Want me to fire up the boat?" she asked. "I have a harpoon I'd like to introduce that bitch to."

Nox shook his head. Sabra Tides had come crawling around the Nightingale and then broke into his mansion. Her brother must have bequeathed her with some information about the riddle he'd found. With any luck, he'd left her the page itself.

So why not step back and let her find the eighth riddle for him?

He addressed Drumm first. "I want you to stake out the MFA. We know her brother had a lead on the next riddle somewhere in the museum, so maybe she'll pick up the trail there, too." To Aries, he said, "I want you to case her house tonight. Get something with her stink on it so Pearce's hounds can pick up her trail. If she's smart enough not to show her face by morning, put eyes on the hospital. Sooner or later, she's going to drop by to visit that diseased little brat." Aries gleefully gave her boss a mock salute before galloping off across the lawn.

Nox turned to Detective Grimshaw last. "I want red flags on her credit cards. The moment she even buys a bag of peanuts at a gas station, you call me immediately. Get a warrant to put tabs on her cell phone, too, if you can." He leaned close to the detective, then pointed at the steaming remains of Smitty. "And take out my garbage before it starts to stink."

With his troops dispatched, Nox sat down on the cliff's edge and lit a cigar. Behind him, the detective grunted as he dragged Smitty's corpse toward the landscaping shed. A minute later, the wood chipper sputtered to life.

Nox tuned out the drone of the machine and listened to the water lapping at the rocks below. He took a puff of his cigar then exhaled a smoke ring in the direction where Sabra had disappeared. "The thing about throwing a snail out to sea," he said to no one at all, "is that sooner or later, the tide will carry it right back to you."

THE DOLLHOUSE
COHASSET, MASSACHUSETTS

I HAD NEVER FALLEN THIRTY FEET BEFORE, BUT THE descent was over before I had time to wonder how badly it was going to hurt. I hit the surface of the water so hard and with such poor form that I thought for sure I'd landed on the rocks, my body smashing into little chunks of watermelon while my consciousness lingered just long enough to process its final few seconds of life.

But then, remarkably, I was underwater. The frigid embrace of the Atlantic momentarily deadened everything but my sense of touch. As soon as I'd gathered my wits, I resurfaced with a panicked breath and swam with the current. It wouldn't be long before Nox reached the cliff's edge, and the bullets in his gun definitely moved quicker than I could breaststroke.

I couldn't be sure how long I was in the water or how far I drifted. Whenever my arms grew too tired to carry me any farther, I would flip onto my back and float. All the while, I fought to keep a safe distance from the mainland, in case Nox's men were scouring the area.

Eventually I spotted the protective mouth of a harbor and the thin yellow smile of a beach. With no strength left in my limbs, I ultimately let the tide carry my exhausted, battered body the remaining journey to shore.

The first thing I did when I reached land was check my hoodie pocket. Once I was certain that the journal page had miraculously stayed with me, still dry in its laminate, I collapsed.

Frigid and feeling very much alone, I lay with my face pressed into the wet sand of Bassing Beach.

I am dead, I thought.

I might have escaped Nox's lair, but I had only postponed the inevitable. He knew who I was. I'd witnessed Smitty's murder firsthand and had information connecting Nox to the homicide of my brother. Sure, he had Detective Grimshaw on the payroll to sweep this under the rug, but I was still a loose end that Nox would want snipped.

With Jack dead and my father in jail, I had no one to turn to for help. If I brought Mom into this, I'd be endangering both her and Echo. From what little I knew of Nox, the man did his research, which meant he'd probably post his men at both my house and Children's Hospital to wait for me.

When I racked my brain, I realized there *was* one person who I could call that Nox wouldn't be on the lookout for.

I took the cell phone out of my soggy pocket. In my line of work, I often found myself in sudden downpours, pedaling my cab through torrential rain. For this reason, I'd opted for a waterproof phone case. When I'd purchased it last year, I never thought it would one day come in handy when making an aquatic escape from a murderous drug lord.

I only had to scroll to the "A" section before I saw the name and number that I'd recently copied off a dirty gym shirt.

Atlas picked up on the second ring. "You know," he said, "they say you're supposed to wait three full days after getting a guy's number before you call. So you don't seem too eager."

How he'd guessed it was me, I didn't know, but I decided the best time-saver would be to lay my situation on him as matter-of-factly as possible. "I just nearly died. I'm stuck in Cohasset without a car. There are bad men on their way to my house as we speak to finish the job, and given what I'm into, even the police can't help me." I added, "How's *that* for eager?"

There was a short pause, then his voice returned, grave and assertive. "Give me an address and twenty minutes."

In the end I waited the better part of an hour for Atlas to arrive—even his willingness to play knight in shining armor was no match for the traffic that plagued I-93, which even Moses couldn't part. I climbed into the passenger's seat of Atlas's rusty Chevy Silverado. I could feel the alarm in his eyes as he studied me—my soaked clothes, my shivering, hypothermic body, the crimson splash of Smitty's blood on my hoodie. Meanwhile, I could only stare blankly through the windshield. Dark clouds had rolled over the harbor and a warning volley of raindrops speckled the glass.

"Look," I said when it became clear that he wasn't going to drive anywhere without an explanation. "I didn't want to play the damsel-in-distress card. I don't want to drag you into this. All I need right now is a ride downtown and a place to crash for the night."

Atlas responded by cranking up the truck's heat and angling the vents in my direction. As the cocoon of warmth lapped at my damp skin, I felt it thaw the resilient, tough-as-nails front I'd put up for the last week. All at once, my face was wet with tears and I couldn't even remember starting to cry.

Atlas squeezed my knee. His voice was quiet, but it was the confidence with which he spoke that I found most calming. "Here's what's going to happen. I'm going to drive you some place safe. You're going to take a long shower until the hot water tank runs dry. And *then* we're going to talk this out."

I simply nodded with my face buried in my hands.

The truck ride back to Boston was silent except for the rhythmic *squeak-squeak* of the windshield wipers, until Atlas pulled off the highway five exits earlier than I'd expected, taking us into Boston's South End. "Where are you taking me?" I demanded. "I thought we were going back to the university."

Atlas shook his head. "The dorm room has been ... compromised. When I got back from class this morning, all of Jack's stuff was gone. That mountain of books, his clothes, even his goddamn toothbrush—everything vanished." He glanced sideways at me. "Even if that weren't the case, I'm pretty sure that taking a girl in a bloody sweatshirt onto a campus where thirty thousand undergraduates are walking to dinner would be an excellent way to draw unwanted attention."

I drew in deep breaths, squashing my paranoid thoughts. *Not everyone is trying to kill you*, I reminded myself. "Where to then?"

"I'm taking you to the Dollhouse," he replied, with no further explanation. His voice fluttered with amusement.

The South End was an interesting place. It bordered some of the rougher boroughs in Boston and used to have a similar reputation itself. It featured heavily into the tales my father told Jack and me about his mischievous youth. Of course, whenever my mother overheard Buck reciting any of those stories, she would rip him a new one, which simply made us want to hear them more.

Over the last two decades, the South End had transformed into the posh cultural epicenter of Boston—in came the haves and out went the have-nots. Young professionals and families scrambled to move into its iconic brownstones and property values tripled. Seemingly overnight, developers gutted decrepit buildings and filled the renovated spaces with art galleries and upscale French bistros. Some of the best tips I made driving my pedicab were from passengers dining in the South End.

Atlas took a hard right toward an old factory that had been converted into loft-style apartments. The setting sun illuminated the luxury building's massive windows in an electric shade of orange. The road dipped, and the metal gates of the subterranean garage magically parted to let us through.

Once we'd parked, he made me turn my bloodstained hoodie inside out before he would let me out of the truck. He herded me through the lobby, which was so decadent that it featured an indoor waterfall and a grand player piano that performed a Gershwin tune on its own. If the ghosts of the destitute factory workers who had slaved away here a century earlier could see the space now, they'd die a second time.

I pointed to the empty mahogany desk in front of the elevators. "Think the doorman is taking a nap somewhere?"

"Nah, he probably abandoned his post to rescue some stranded teenage girl." Now I remembered him telling me during our very first meeting that he worked as a concierge.

Atlas took me up to the eighth floor, to a condo labeled *8D*. After he fumbled with an obnoxiously full key ring, he found the one he was looking for. "Welcome to the Dollhouse," he said as he cast open the door and flipped the light switch inside.

The condo was gorgeous, from its cherry hardwood floors to the stainless steel appliances in the kitchen. Massive French windows lined the back wall, providing an astonishing view of downtown Boston. The John Hancock Tower, Boston's tallest building, dominated the skyline, a sleek column of reflective blue glass that looked transparent to the sky beyond it.

I wandered into the room and steadied my exhausted body against one of the leather sofas. "This whole day has been like a movie. It started out *The Godfather* and apparently now I'm Julia Roberts in *Pretty Woman*."

Atlas laughed. "It's not a real condo, just a model staged to look like people actually live here. Whenever new tenants come to consider buying a unit in the building, the realtors show them this one. That's why we call it the Dollhouse: It's where adults come to play house in their imagination."

"I can't stay here," I protested.

"You can and you will," Atlas replied. "Unless you'd rather let Witness Protection hide you away in some Podunk swamp hut. Besides"—He gestured to the glass—"it's criminal that a view like this only gets two visitors a month. Now go take a shower, try to relax, and I'll be back as soon as I close out my shift."

I had neither the strength nor the will to put up a fight. After I'd locked the deadbolt behind Atlas, I stripped out of my soggy clothes and filed into the elegant shower. I cranked the dial until it was scalding, then sat down heavily on the tiles, with my bare back pressed against the opaque glass door. I let the steam swallow me up.

When I emerged thirty minutes later, the wet clothes I'd balled up outside the bathroom were gone, replaced with a red Boston University sweatshirt and a pair of plaid men's pajama pants, folded on top of a fresh towel.

Swaddled in my new wardrobe, I wandered down the hall and found a pizza and a two-liter of Coke waiting for me on the kitchen counter. In the living room, Atlas stood in front of a crackling fire, and if I wasn't mistaken, it was my hoodie and jeans that were currently being consumed by the flames.

Atlas had changed, too, trading his doorman's suit for jeans and a flannel shirt that hugged his broad shoulders like a sock might fit a bowling ball. "I know you're a far cry from XL, but those clothes were the best I could do on short notice," he said.

"Right now I'd wear a garbage bag as long as it was dry."

He poked at my smoldering clothes with a fire iron. "There are plenty beneath the sink if black non-biodegradable plastic is more your style."

I set a course for the pizza box. My stomach had been in knots since I witnessed Smitty's murder, but my appetite caught up with me now that I was temporarily safe. I shoveled the better part of an entire slice into my mouth before I remembered to mumble, "Thanks for dinner. And for saving my ass."

"I think it's about time that you explain why exactly your ass required saving. I have a sneaking suspicion ..." He paused mid-sentence, set the fire poker aside, and picked up something off the mantle: an old piece of paper encased in plastic. "... that it has something to do with this."

It was the journal page, which to my great relief he had salvaged from my pocket before he cremated my hoodie. I was such a zombie that the riddle hadn't even crossed my mind when I saw my sweatshirt in flames.

Part of me wanted to resist sharing anything with this boy I barely knew. Jack was *my* brother. Echo was *my* sister. This should be my quest to bear alone.

But Atlas had a right to know just how dangerous it was for him to be harboring me, even talking with me. The last man I'd discussed the journal page with was currently missing the back of his skull and a heartbeat.

So as soon as we'd settled into the sofa, I told Atlas everything. He listened pensively, without interruption, as the firelight danced in his unblinking eyes. And when it was over, I felt something unexpected: relief.

I had committed myself to following the path of these riddles. Even if there was only an infinitesimal chance that what lay at the end could save Echo. Even if the Serengeti Sapphire turned out to be a hoax. Even if there was a high probability that Nox would catch and kill me before I was through.

My relief was because now, if I died, at least one person in the world would know what *really* happened to me.

Atlas didn't respond at first. He leaned back and stared into the fire, his arms draped over the back of the sofa. Then he said, "Well, I've got good news and bad news, Sabra."

"Is this the beginning of a bad joke?" I asked him. Two young men were dead, I was on the mob's hit list, my sister's life hung in the balance—yet I couldn't tell whether Atlas was taking me seriously.

"The bad news," he went on, unfazed, "is that you're going to have to cut and color your hair."

I glared at him. "Are you getting high off the odor of burning hoodie?"

"Don't get me wrong—the ruby-red vixen look goes well with your dimples, but that's exactly what that son of a bitch will be looking for." He pulled a box from a pharmacy bag he'd hidden beneath the coffee table and tossed it to me. It was black hair dye. "They'll never see a brunette with a pixie cut coming, though."

I couldn't decide whether Atlas was an idiot or a genius. "Strangely practical, which I can't argue with. Although it does make me wonder whether you've done this whole harboring-a-fugitive thing before. So what's the good news?"

"The good news is that I'm going to help you find the Serengeti Sapphire, whether you like it or not."

"What makes you think I need your help?" I asked. "What makes you think I'll still be here in the morning when you come to check on me?" *However grateful I am for all you've done*, I conceded silently.

"Because I can tell that you'd do anything to save Echo, and you know that you have a better shot at seeing this thing through if you have someone to watch your back—especially someone as well-versed in American history as your brother."

"Wait." I held up a hand.

Atlas failed to suppress a smile. "Did you think it was by a random dormitory lottery that I got paired with Jack?"

This changed everything. For every historical fact I'd absorbed from my brother's nerdy ramblings over the years, there were a thousand more I didn't know. And this quest, this path of journal pages, reeked of history. It was Jack's bottomless knowledge on the subject that had probably let him get the drop on Nox, before Nox ultimately got the drop on him.

"So you're telling me"—I tapped the journal page on the table—"That you might be able to solve that riddle?"

"No," Atlas replied. "I'm telling you that I already did."

WHERE GRIFFINS GAZE
THE SOUTH END

"YOU ALREADY FIGURED IT OUT?" I ECHOED incredulously. "You're telling me that in the thirty minutes I was in that bathroom, you obtained spare clothes for me, ordered a pizza, bought hair dye, lit a fire—and you *still* found time to solve a century-old riddle, which as far as I can tell is total gibberish?"

"I'm sure hieroglyphics looked like a game of Pictionary the first time an explorer wandered into the pyramids, but only because he didn't speak the language. Here, watch this."

From his backpack, Atlas produced a pen and a notepad. While I looked on, he copied the text of the poem onto the paper. He only glanced at the journal page once, which led me to wonder whether my new friend had some sort of photographic memory.

ON CASTLE GROUNDS
'TOP DRUMLIN'S PERCH
WHERE GRIFFINS GAZE
O'ER SHORE AND SHOALS

WHERE STATUES FLANK
LONG HALLS OF PINE
THE HILL ROLLS DOWN
TO TASTE THE SEA

AS ROSES WATCH
THE FOUNT' RUNS DRY
THE TRUTH ENTOMBED
EXHUMED AT LAST.

Atlas then combed through the riddle, underlining keywords like *castle*, *griffin*, and *entombed*, just as I had done with Jack's postcard. "It's easy to see why your brother followed the riddle to the Museum of Fine Arts. It does resemble a castle—stone masonry, a central courtyard—and the objects mentioned throughout the three stanzas sound like the kind of things that would only coexist in a museum. The MFA is full of statues, and *entombed* could refer to the Egyptology room, which houses a collection of mummies and sarcophagi."

I read between the lines. "But you think he was wrong." It was hard to imagine Jack being incorrect at anything, especially history. He was the kind of kid who even aced tests he never studied for.

Atlas squinted into the fire. "I don't know what was going through Jack's head. Maybe he had a few places in mind and that's the one where he got caught. Or maybe he knew the bloodhounds were on his trail, and he was trying to steer them down the wrong path. It's impossible to say."

I pictured Nox sending his men to futilely sweep through the MFA, looking for a page they'd never find. It was almost enough to make me smile. "So where is this poetic compass actually pointing us?"

"North." He grinned. "But that's all you're getting for now."

I stood up angrily. "This isn't a game, Atlas. If you know where the next page is, then this conversation only ends with you drawing me a map with a big red X on it. The last person who helped me just had his brain matter sprayed over a backyard in Cohasset, so from now on, I'm on my own."

That last sentence sparked something fierce and dark in Atlas. He rolled up his flannel shirt sleeve and turned his left palm upward, exposing his wrist. He was showing me a tattoo below his elbow, the one I'd noticed when I first met him.

It was the name *Selene* written across a crescent moon. The tattoo artist had done something interesting to the final *e* in the name: The edges of the letter erupted into a flock of sparrows, taking flight until they disappeared around Atlas's arm.

This was one riddle that I *could* solve.

I thought back to meeting Atlas, when he mentioned his sister. The distant look in his eyes as he talked about her going to high school, something I now realized was only a tragic hypothetical. "What happened to her?" I asked softly.

Atlas bit the inside of his lip. "Two summers ago, for her thirteenth birthday, Selene decided to have a little camping trip in the woods behind our house. Couple of friends, couple of cute boys. My parents were away on business, and she lied to me that she was sleeping over at a friend's house." Atlas paused. "I guess one of the guys at the campfire had a brother who was a dealer, so he'd stolen a bottle of Blyss from his private stash. Thought it would liven up the party."

Now I remembered how Atlas had remained remarkably still throughout my entire story—except for an almost imperceptible flinch when I mentioned Nox's connection to the Blyss trade.

"My sister was the birthday girl, so she took the first shot. Selene's heart stopped within seconds. Her friends freaked out when she collapsed beside the fire. They were so afraid they'd get in trouble that they just ..." The words *left her there* evaporated off Atlas's tongue. "One of the girls was so hysterical by the time she got home that her mother grilled her until she came clean. The police found Selene soon after. The coroner confirmed later, after the autopsy, that the Blyss had been dosed with poison. Apparently it's not uncommon for dealers to sabotage their competition by slipping what they call 'bad apples' into their product."

Everything that I wanted to say sounded like a cliché—"I'm so sorry," or "It wasn't your fault"—all the things I'd loathed hearing after Jack died. I said nothing.

"So while I'm sure it was desperation that made your brother tell me to look after you, and while I know that if a psychologist were here right now, he'd tell me I'm displacing my guilt for Selene's death onto someone else's little sister, believe me when I say that *I don't give a shit*. Because when you find out that your little sister died cold and alone in the woods not far from the recliner where you fell asleep watching *Jeopardy*, you earn the right to be irrationally protective of people you hardly know." He rolled his sleeve back down, covering the tattoo.

I put a hand on his elbow. It was in my nature to resist help from others. When your father was a crook and your mother was a workaholic, fending for yourself became second nature. But I sensed now that we both needed each other: I needed Atlas to help me find the next journal page, and Atlas needed this quest as catharsis for the death of his sister.

"Okay," I said.

Atlas bristled. He probably hadn't expected me to cave so easily. "Okay?"

"But if you join me," I continued, "it isn't me that you're signing onto protect. It's *my* little sister. Survival doesn't mean anything to me if Echo doesn't come through this, too. So help me, stand by my side—but you can never ask me to give up."

He regarded me for an intense moment, perhaps trying to compute the possibility that in order for Echo to live, he might have to watch me die trying to save her. Eventually, he squeezed my hand. "Rest up," he said. "History field trip starts tomorrow."

———

I slept restlessly, my dreams haunted by the flap of buzzards' wings. Their red eyes peered through the cloud of death and their talons tore into a lifeless, faceless body that could have been Smitty's.

Or it could have been my own.

I felt something flutter onto my bed sheets and lashed out, aiming to break the bird's neck before it pecked out my eyes.

Instead, I discovered that the creature responsible for the "fluttering" was a lacy peach-colored dress. Even stranger, Atlas was leaning in my bedroom doorway wearing a tuxedo. He twirled a bowtie rakishly around his fingers.

I pulled the sheets up around my neck. "Should I ask whether you want your martini shaken or stirred?" I asked, my voice still groggy with sleep.

"It's too early to start drinking, Moneypenny," Atlas said in a British accent. "I have no clue whether that dress is your size. I had to 'borrow' what was available in the basement. Some of the wealthier residents here have us dry-clean things, then never remember to collect them."

I rubbed my eyes. "Let me guess. The clues in the riddle are sending us to a high school prom."

Atlas chuckled mischievously. "That guess was less ridiculous than you think. Get dressed. Party starts in one hour." He vanished out the door.

I had slept well into the morning, so by the time I pulled myself together, it was nearly noon. The dress fit loose in the chest and tight in the hips, a catalog of all my self-consciousness, but it sure beat a soggy, bloodstained hoodie.

Atlas offered no clues about our destination as we drove north, but when we arrived in the town of Ipswich, I caught faint whiffs of the ocean air through the truck's open windows. Eventually, Atlas turned onto a long drive past a sign that welcomed us to "The Crane Estate at Castle Hill."

Reading the word "castle" gave me a tingle of excitement. I pulled out the riddle and traced my fingers over the first sentence. "*On castle grounds ...*" I read aloud.

Atlas grinned without taking his eyes off the road.

A security guard emerged from a small hut to meet us. His eyes took in Atlas's tuxedo and my dress without a touch of surprise. "Here for the Ramapo wedding?" he asked.

"About time those crazy kids got hitched!" Atlas replied. The guard laughed and gestured toward the parking lot ahead.

I waited until we'd exited the truck and were strolling up a hillside path to berate Atlas. "Please don't tell me that we're crashing some stranger's wedding."

He mouthed the word "oops" at me.

The winding path eventually spat us out in front of the most breathtaking house I'd ever seen. I whistled through my teeth. "Not exactly a castle," I said, "but it will do."

The Crane Estate was an enormous masterpiece of red bricks and picturesque windows, elegant chimneys, and a high cupola in the middle that glowed softly against the overcast sky. It looked like the kind of palace that belonged in the English countryside, where the royal family would spend summer playing polo and drinking tea out on the lawn. A place where the BBC would film a television drama about how the elite and their servants lived at the turn of the century.

It did not resemble something that belonged on a random hill in the Boston suburbs.

Hordes of wedding guests were milling about in the house's circular drive. Atlas tightened his bowtie. "I figured we could use the wedding to our advantage. We look like we belong here. But if Nox's horned sidekick shows up, she's going to stick out like a wolf in a sheep's pen."

I nodded, admiring my companion. I held up the riddle. "So we have a sort-of castle, which takes care of the first line, and it's at the top of a big hill, which explains *drumlin's perch* in the second. That leaves ten more lines you need to sell me on."

"Challenge accepted." Atlas looped his arm through mine.

The backyard, as it turned out, was even more impressive than the front. In fact, to even call it a yard felt like a disservice. From the back steps of the mansion, a vibrantly green lawn extended for a quarter mile toward the ocean. It cut a perfectly straight line fifty yards wide through a forest of pine, spruce, and cedar trees. The grass undulated in magnificent hills, up and down, up and down, all the way to a cliff overlooking the sea.

"What do you think?" Atlas asked.

I put my hands on my hips and absorbed the magnificent view. "I would have killed to have all this open space when I was a kid. Our 'yard' in Dorchester was a patch of cracked asphalt barely big enough for us to play catch." I gazed back at the mansion behind me. "What the hell *is* this place?"

"I won't bore you with historical context." Atlas paused. "Scratch that, I can't help myself. The quick version: A hundred years ago, a super-rich guy named Crane bought all this land and built a mansion for himself and his wife. It was a beautiful Italian-style villa like you might find in Tuscany. His wife absolutely hated it. Crane promised her that if she didn't warm up to it after ten years, he'd build her a completely new home. Exactly ten years later, she said 'Yep, this place still blows,' so he constructed the sixty-room estate you see now."

"Right," I said, "because only a savage would live in a fifty-nine-room house."

"You know what they say: 'Happy wife, happy life.'" Atlas tapped the riddle in my hands. "Let's see if we can make sense of the rest of this. First, I need you to close your eyes."

I reluctantly indulged him and Atlas took my arm and led me across the lawn. We stopped after twenty paces. "Okay, you can open them," he said.

When I did, I found myself face-to-face with the piercing eyes of a golden-brown creature.

"No way," I whispered.

The statue had the beak and talons of an eagle but a lion's ears to match its feline body. It had been sculpted with a tongue darting out of its open beak and squatted half-risen on its haunches as though about to take flight. A second identical statue perched on the opposite side of the mansion's terrace.

"*Where griffins gaze,*" Atlas read from the riddle, pointing to the two mythical creatures. Then he turned me around. "*O'er shore and shoals.* At the base of the cliff is Crane Beach, and on a good day they say you can see all the way to the Isle of Shoals, off the coast of Maine."

I followed Atlas out onto the lawn next. To either side of the green, white classical statues of people dressed in ancient garb stood on pedestals. Behind them, the evergreen trees towered a hundred feet. "*Where statues flank / long halls of pine,*" I quoted from the text. My gaze returned to the wavy green lawn that descended toward the beach. "*The hills roll down / to taste the sea.*" While this was all promising, that still only accounted for the poem's first eight lines. "What about the final stanza, though? I don't see any roses or fountains."

Atlas frowned pensively at the riddle. "Damn. Well, I guess I was completely wrong. We can head back to the truck now." A smile broke across his face. "Unless …"

With a gleeful shriek that caused a cluster of wedding attendees to glance our way, Atlas took off toward the edge of the house in a horse-like gallop. I sighed and raced after him, although it was a struggle to keep pace in the oversized flats that Atlas had scrounged up to go with my dress.

The pursuit took me down a tree-lined path toward a garden that resembled the ruins of an ancient city, lost in the jungle. Massive stone columns topped with elegant mermaid

107

statues guarded its entrance, and I nearly lost my footing rushing down the steps. I expected Atlas to stop there, but he simply yelled, "the Italian garden!" before rushing excitedly across the grass. The rectangular lawn was enclosed by stone walls on all sides. Atlas paused in the exit on the opposite end and waited for me to catch up.

As in shape as I was, I was breathless by the time I reached Atlas's side. He grabbed my hand and tugged me down another short path. A second garden awaited us, a circular terrace surrounded by more stone columns.

In the middle of the small green was a stone fountain that had long run dry. Its centerpiece was a bowl-shaped urn, where the water might have once pooled for bathing birds.

Atlas lowered his voice reverently. "The Cranes commissioned several famous landscapers to craft these beautiful gardens. This"—Atlas spread his arms wide—"is called the Rose Garden. It used to contain six hundred varieties of the flower."

I kicked the sandals off my blistered feet. The moment my toes hit the grass, it felt like someone passed an electric wand over my body. I strode slowly but purposefully over to the old fountain. Stepped over the lip and down into the stone basin.

"*As roses watch*," I whispered, "*the fount' runs dry.*"

Atlas entered the fountain with me and cast a glance toward the entrance to make sure we were alone. "Just to be clear, what we're about to do is vandalism and the defacement of a historical landmark of immeasurable value."

My eyes glistened as I looked earnestly at Atlas. "The only thing of immeasurable value, as far as I'm concerned, is my sister's life."

I squatted down and wrapped my arms around the edge of the fountain's stone centerpiece, bear-hugging it. Atlas tried to nudge his way in to help, but I scolded him away.

I channeled all the love I had for my broken family—all the things I'd never get to say to Jack, all the things I'd say to Echo if it wouldn't break her—and I lifted. The heavy urn looked like it was solidly attached, but some makeshift plaster crumbled away when I really put my legs into it.

Ten seconds later, with my face red as a Maraschino and every muscle in my body nearly torn or trembling, I toppled the urn onto its side.

Atlas caught me under my armpits before I could go down with it. Once he made sure I was steady, we both turned to the piece of paper that had until seconds ago been covered by the urn.

It was heavily coated in stone and plaster dust, so I dropped to my knees, put my face close, and blew with all the air left in my lungs. The dust flew off the yellowed page, revealing the familiar cursive scrawl of a man from another century.

"The truth entombed," I said, *"Exhumed at last."*

Together, the two of us sat on a grassy step and read the journal page—the riddle on one side and the next installment of Cumberland Warwick's story on the other. And when we were done, I let out a long, trembling breath. "The Serengeti Sapphire isn't a gem at all," I said.

"It's a flower."

Dearest Adelaide,

Morning has come, and the giant survives.

All night, his brow burned feverish, his sleep fitful, as he fought the infection that festered within. And all night, I tended to him, soaking a cloth in the cool rainwater to dispel his fever, cleaning his wounds as best I could. All the while, I found spare moments by lantern light to write my letter to you, my beloved. The Serengeti Sapphire, the object of my new companion's fixed concern, never strayed far from my thoughts, nor my awestruck gaze. I shall try to sketch the Sapphire in the margins, though my humble artistry can do it no justice.

A stranger flower I had never seen. Its cerulean petals gleamed in such a way that, even in the dark, they truly earned the name of the gemstone for which they were named.

When the giant finally came to with a parched gasp, he wasted no time in doting on the flower and would not relax until he was certain that not a petal was out of sorts. "It is safe," I assured him. "And so are you. Now tell me about your son."

I cannot fault him for being wary of a white stranger, but in time, he let flow a story that spanned an ocean. For reasons that will become clear, I will summarize his tale with brutal precision.

Malaika and his wife had been farmers in their native Africa, harvesting tea leaves in the fertile valley within the shadow of a massive mountain. They often traded with the Arab and British merchants, thus his proficiency in the English tongue. They had one son, Jaro, who had been born with the most beautiful eyes, golden and flecked with stardust, but the boy had been plagued by an unshakable sickness since infancy. The symptoms Malaika described matched a chronic illness that, from my years as a traveling physician, I knew was endemic to the male slave population on the Louisianian plantations.

As the illness progressed, desperation drove Malaika up the mountain in search of a local legend: a rare blue orchid that could irreversibly cure even the most corrosive malady. After three days of climbing, he found it, a singular blue flower nestled in the snowy crater atop the formidable summit.

His triumphant return quickly turned to tragedy. Slavers had come during his absence, taking both his wife and his sickly son.

So Malaika followed the slavers' trail through the Dark Continent and back to America, stowing aboard a ship that came in through the West Indies and then South Carolina. In Charleston, he narrowly escaped a lynching on his flight from the city, and the mob had imparted on him numerous wounds before he found shelter in this barn.

Adelaide, I hope you can forgive me for the words I said next, as they will undoubtedly forestall my return to you, and have irrevocably intertwined my destiny with that of a man whose people I once fought to keep in servitude. In truth, when I looked at Malaika, cold, beaten, yet determined, I saw only a father whose love for his son knew no manacles. So I leaned toward him and said, "My name is Cumberland Warwick. And I'm going to help you find your boy."

A CLASH OF TWO DREADNOUGHTS
ONE FERRIC, ONE ICE,
A VICTOR GLOATS COLDLY
O'ER THE COLOSSUS'S GRAVE.

A THOUSAND SOULS SWALLOWED
DOWN THE DARK, FRIGID MAW,
WHILE A LIBRARY SINKS
WITH ITS SCHOLAR IN TOW.

BUT HE'LL STUDY ETERNAL
IN WHAT LOOKS JUST LIKE HOME,
WHILE DREAMING OF BLACK SPOTS,
ISLANDS, AND GOLD.

SONG OF ORPHEUS
THE SOUTH END

I STOOD IN FRONT OF THE BATHROOM MIRROR WITH a lock of my red hair curled around one finger and a pair of scissors in the other hand. Despite everything that had happened in the last two weeks, I felt a shameful wave of vanity at the thought of lopping off my hair.

But this was a transformation as necessary to Echo's survival as it was to my own. Nox by himself would be bad enough, but with a detective on his payroll, the kingpin had at his disposal all the same resources as the police department. Security camera footage. Credit card statements. If I made even one misstep, Nox would sniff me out like a bloodhound. And then he would put me down.

Knowing all this, I had instructed Atlas to take a random detour through the suburb of Burlington on the drive home, where I stopped at a branch of my bank. While he stood sentry outside the ATM, I withdrew as much money as I could from my account, feeling the beady eye of the closed-circuit camera watching me the whole time. No doubt, the use of my debit card was already sending a ping to Detective Grimshaw. If anything, I hoped it would distract him and Nox's men with a search on the completely wrong side of the city.

After that, we stopped at a thrift store so that I could replenish my supply of clothes with something other than Atlas's baggy hand-me-downs: black jeans, black t-shirts, a mound of underwear and socks, and a black hooded sweatshirt that caught my eye on the way to checkout. It had the outline of a large bird stitched into the back.

Atlas eyed the dark, rumpled lump of clothes in my basket. "You have a vendetta against color?" He noticed the design on the back of the hoodie. "Sweet bird, though."

I took the sweatshirt off the hanger and tugged it over my head. It fit perfectly. "I'm going to take everything from Nox," I explained. "Why not start with the symbol he built his empire around."

Now, back in the Dollhouse, I made swift, decisive cuts, while the mound of hair in the sink slowly pile up. The instant I finished, I dropped the shears and set to work massaging the dye into my hair. I let it sit for the full hour before rinsing it out.

When I finally toweled my hair dry and gazed back into the mirror, I couldn't help but gasp at the transformation. I now sported a haphazard pixie cut, black as a well of ink.

And I kind of liked it.

Before Atlas had left for his evening seminar at BU, he made me promise to stay put, vowing in return to bring me dim sum from the best restaurant Chinatown had to offer.

This was a promise that I had no intention of honoring. I had two loose ends in the Fenway area, so I made the half-mile walk to the Broadway subway station. As I waited on the platform, I experienced a rare flicker of nostalgia for a man I almost never thought about these days: my father.

Jack Tides Sr. had spent his whole life living in the same eight-block radius of the Dorchester neighborhood where he was born. Thanks to the stag tattoo on his neck, inspired by the logo of his favorite whiskey, his unsavory friends had nicknamed him Buck. His father had been a subway car driver for the MBTA, an alcoholic, and an all-around bastard, and Dad hated him so intensely that he grew up to be exactly like him. Even though my father held a steady job behind the throttle of a Red

Line car, a job that should have been enough to make ends meet for his wife and three kids, he never lost that chip on his shoulder that he wanted—no, *deserved*—more than his lot in life. "I'm so sick of breakin' even," he would mutter at dinner, huddling over his TV table and stabbing furiously at mom's casserole with his fork. "Is it too much to ask to get ahead in life for once?"

A series of failed get-rich-quick schemes forced our family further into debt, which was when Dad abandoned the law altogether. Unfortunately, Buck Tides was an incompetent thief. Ten minutes into a botched robbery at a chemical warehouse, my father found himself writhing face-down on the concrete floor with a bullet lodged in his thigh and a SWAT officer kneeling on his spine.

In the end, his two associates—including my degenerate godfather—took plea bargains from the DA and squealed on him, which bought Buck fifteen years. When the bailiffs led him out of the courtroom, he'd yelled to my mother, "I was just trying to provide for you! That's all I ever wanted!" I had only been ten at the time, but even then, I knew he was full of shit.

Still, as much as my father was a nonperson in my life, I thought of him every time I heard the screech of the subway car's brakes as it slowed into the station. When I was a kid, I'd stand out on the platform, watching the train crest the hill. It looked like a long steel caterpillar with a red stripe. Back then, I imagined that my father was behind the wheel of *every* subway car, looking dapper in his blue vest.

I climbed into the trolley and pushed my father out of my mind. After all, he was wearing a different uniform these days.

I had arranged to rendezvous with Rufus at a riverside glade in the Longwood area, and was waiting there when the gangly man-child biked up beside me. He leaped off the pedicab with about as much grace as an orangutan dismounting a racehorse, stumbling forward several steps and letting his riderless cab collide with a tree. "Sabra Tides," Rufus said, and noting my hair added, "Now available in black."

"I figured I'd get a haircut for the both of us." I ruffled the disheveled nest on his head. "Let this grow any longer and the National Park Service is going to declare it a wildlife sanctuary."

Rufus responded unexpectedly by wrapping me in a tight hug. "Sorry about your brother, lass," he said into my ear. "Good kid like that deserved at least a century."

I swallowed hard and refused to squeeze him back. I'd crack if I did. "You would have liked him."

Rufus gazed around the wooded clearing, which was empty save a few twilight joggers. "So after two weeks without you on the pedicab circuit, you ask for a clandestine meeting. What's up, chica? Please tell me there's mischief afoot."

A cool wind swept through the trees and I tightened my hoodie's drawstrings. "The abridged version: I need to get into the hospital to see Echo, but there are possibly some bad people outside. I need the help of someone trustworthy and knowledgeable about Boston's shadier residents. And who meets those criteria more perfectly than the only part-time private detective in my contact list?"

Rufus's left eye twitched. "Sweet buttered biscuits, Sabra. First you ask me for a fake ID. Now this. Exactly how deep are you in?"

"Ever watch one of those documentaries about the ocean's trenches, where no sunlight penetrates and the pressure is so intense that it can crumple submarines? A little deeper than that."

At first I thought that Rufus would say no to helping me. He exhaled a long breath. "Well, the Sabra I know wouldn't let anything stand in the way of a visit with her sister. So if I can't stop you, then I guess I better help you. Give me the unabridged version as we walk."

On our journey to the hospital, we made a quick detour by Fenway Park, where Yawkey Way was a red and blue sea of tourists lining up for tonight's game. At his direction, I bought us Red Sox shirts and caps from a vendor cart for camouflage. Then we swung by Children's Hospital, where we camped out on a bench across the street from the entrance. At first, I saw no trace of any armed mercenaries waiting to intercept me.

I was starting to feel foolish about dragging Rufus along when he said, "I count two of them: police officer by the ambulance and the guy making balloon animals."

I scanned the milieu of people around the long circular drive until I found the two men he was talking about. "How can you tell?" The cop looked just like every officer you could find patrolling the streets of Boston, stern-faced behind a pair of shades, and if there was a reasonable place for a balloon artist to be, it was a hospital full of children.

"The truth is in the details." Rufus nodded to the cop first. "His shirt is a different shade of blue than the BPD wears, his radio is clipped in the wrong spot, and his shoes aren't regulation."

"Wow," I said. "Spoken like someone who's had a few brushes with the law. What about the wannabe clown?"

"He sucks at making balloon animals," Rufus replied, a little offended. "What is that even supposed to be, a walrus? If that doesn't convince you, he's been fiddling with the same balloon since we got here, without offering it to any of the kids who've walked by."

I'd always seen Rufus as a man lacking ambition, so I'd never taken his P.I. business seriously. Now I was impressed. "You must have been killer at *Where's Waldo?* as a kid."

"You haven't seen anything yet." Rufus flagged down a kid in baggy jeans and a Metallica t-shirt who was strutting by. "Hey, chief, wanna make an easy five bucks?" With the boy's attention, Rufus pulled a noise popper from his pocket, the kind you could buy at a party store. He pressed it into the kid's hand with the promised cash. "Cross the street and pull this as you walk by the entrance."

The boy looked at Rufus like he was nuts and shrugged. "Your dime, dude."

"Why do you even have one of those on you?" I asked Rufus, as I watched the boy make his way toward the hospital.

"You never know when you'll need a distraction." He put two fingers to his eyes, then pointed to the balloon artist. "Keep your gaze on the clown."

Ten seconds later, a loud pop of the noisemaker echoed across the street. The balloon artist instantly dropped the animal in his hands and reached for his right hip, exposing a concealed holster and a firearm. His hand relaxed once he realized that it wasn't a gunshot, but in that one reflexive motion, he'd given himself away.

"A balloon artist who's packing?" Rufus said. "I think not."

There was a moment, too, when the cop and the artist locked eyes to acknowledge each other, before they went back to looking busy.

"So how do we—?"

Rufus waved off my question. "Leave it to me." He pulled out his phone and rapidly dialed a number. After someone on the other end picked up, Rufus began to ramble in a panicked voice. "Hello, Boston Police? I'm trying to leave Children's Hospital with my six-year-old daughter, but this creep making balloon animals just offered her a pot brownie. He's about six-foot-two, two hundred pounds, and—" Abruptly, Rufus held the phone away from his face and screamed, "You get that flask away from her, you sick bastard!" Then he hung up.

"You are one twisted genius," I said in genuine awe.

Rufus tapped his watch. "I give them about two minutes response time."

In reality, it only took ninety seconds for a police cruiser to whip around the long drive. Two cops—real ones—spilled out of the doors and cornered the balloon artist. The mercenary had only started to protest when they slammed him face-first down onto the bench. After patting him down, one of the officers found the concealed pistol, which is when the shit *really* hit the fan. The balloon artist bucked free, but only made it three steps down the sidewalk when the second cop zapped the nape of his neck with a taser. His body convulsed on the ground while they kneeled down to cuff him.

Meanwhile, I saw the fake cop slink away into the shadows, then break into a fast stride away from the hospital.

I clapped Rufus on the back. "That's my cue. Just let me know what your going rate is and I can reimburse you."

Rufus waved me off with his hat. "You're on the friends and family plan. Besides, it was cheaper and more entertaining than a movie. Be careful, kid. I'd suggest using an auxiliary exit when you exfiltrate, in case they send replacement dirtbags." In true Rufus fashion, my companion reached into the pocket of his cargo shorts, pulled out a partially consumed hotdog, and ate the rest as he watched the mercenary get stuffed into the back of the squad car.

I was grateful to find Echo alone in her hospital room, without my mother—I would deal with her next. My sister was sleeping fitfully, her brow slick with sweat, her blanket cast to the floor. Ordinarily, I made a rule not to wake her, but tonight this visit needed to be as efficient as possible.

Even though for the time being it would be my last.

I placed a hand on Echo's cheek. "Hey, little nugget."

Echo blinked lethargically. Her eyes widened as they gravitated to my hair. "What did you *do*, Sabra?" she asked shrilly.

I put a finger to my lips. "Weirdest thing happened on my way here. First, some landscaper thought I was a bush, so he used hedge trimmers on my hair. Then it started raining dark chocolate, and I couldn't find any shampoo that would rinse it out."

Echo giggled. "Maybe you can shampoo with whip cream."

I squinted at her. "I don't exactly know where you're going with this—but I like it."

My sister's happy expression swerved into nausea. I reached for the bedpan but Echo shook her head. She swallowed and wiped the tears from her eyes with the back of her hand. "I'm fine," she protested.

"You're not a good liar like your older sister." I set down the bedpan. "Seriously, you'd make, like, the worst poker player ever."

This time Echo didn't laugh. "You *are* a liar. You promised you were going to visit last night. I waited up for you."

There were few feelings worse than disappointing Echo. "Sorry, kiddo." I tried not to picture yesterday's grisly events. "I had to work."

"Mom says your job is stupid," Echo said. "Mom says that a smart girl like you shouldn't waste her nights dragging tourists around like a . . . like a horse pulling a stagecoach."

The invisible knife in my gut twisted. If Calista Tides wanted to criticize my life choices, she should do it to my face, rather than venting to a sick eight-year-old.

I warehoused that anger for now so that I could focus on the task at hand: explaining to my sister why I might not see her for a while. While my initial instinct had been to tell Echo what

I was really up to—that I was on the trail of something that might save her life—false hope and unfulfilled promises could be as deadly to a young psyche as cancer was to the body. What if the Serengeti Sapphire wasn't real? What if I never found it? What if I got killed and Echo realized with despair one day that her sister was never coming back to save her?

"I have to tell you something," I said. "Something difficult to hear. I have to go away for a little while. Could be a few days, could be a few weeks. But I promise that when I get back, I'm coming straight here. I'll walk barefoot through a blizzard if I have to."

With a dispirited sigh, Echo pressed her face into the pillow. "Why is everyone in this family always leaving?" she asked, her voice muffled through cotton and feathers.

I grimaced. I rolled Echo back over so she'd have to look at me. "The truth is," I said, "that Jack was looking for something before ... before he passed. Something that could be very important to our family."

Echo perked up. "Treasure?" she asked hopefully.

I laughed. Knowing her, she was probably picturing a pirate's chest overflowing with gold doubloons and gem-encrusted chalices. "Something like that. But I won't know exactly what that treasure is until I follow the clues he left behind. Now, if you want to help me find the treasure, you have to do one thing for me."

Echo lingered on my every word with bated breath. "Anything," she whispered.

I glanced toward the door. "You can't tell a soul about what I told you tonight. Not your doctors. Not the police. Not even Mom." Echo narrowed her eyes. "I know this is hard to understand, but when she gets frantic, thinking I've gone missing, you need to let her think that."

And this was the critical conclusion that I'd reached earlier, as I stared pensively into a crackling fire at the Dollhouse.

121

Tomorrow was Monday. While my mother had spent too much time at the hospital to notice that I hadn't slept in my bed since Friday night, my high school would eventually call her to report my unexplained absence. She would then call me, only to discover that my cell phone had been disconnected. The night before, I had tossed it into the Mystic River so that Detective Grimshaw couldn't use his resources to triangulate my location.

Later, she'd get the message I dropped in the hospital mailbox, saying that I couldn't take it anymore, that I'd run away.

In order to keep my family safe, I needed my mother to think I'd gone off the grid. I needed her to call the police, because eventually that information would make its way to Detective Grimshaw. If her distress seemed sincere and unrehearsed, they'd hopefully rule out the possibility that she knew anything about my quest to track down the Sapphire.

So while it broke my heart to think of Mom frantic with worry, and so soon after Jack's death, it needed to be done.

Echo frowned at me. "You want me to lie to Mom. Didn't you just call me a horrible liar?"

I gazed into her keenly intelligent eyes, marveling, unsure whether to cry or laugh. Most days, Echo seemed so much younger than eight. Spending more time in the hospital than at school around kids her age had seemingly stunted her ability to grow up. But there were other times, like now, when I realized how damn smart and cunning my sister was—and how brilliant she'd grow up to be, if only the disease that had swept through her body like a typhoon would leave her the fuck alone.

"I hate asking you to lie," I said. "Most of the time, lies only hurt people. But every once in a while, you need to hide the truth to protect the people you love."

This last part went over Echo's head, but I could see her fading fast again anyway. She nestled sleepily back into her blankets. "Tell me another story before you go?" she asked.

Even knowing full well that Nox could have men roaming the hospital, no goon was going to stop me from reading my sister to sleep for what might be the final time. I picked up the book of Greek myths from the nightstand and flipped through, until I saw an illustration with a harp on it. A story about music seemed benign enough to read to an eight-year-old.

I got partway through the tale of Orpheus and Eurydice before I realized that it was just as dark and depressing as the other myths, but it didn't matter. Echo was softly snoring by the time I reached page two. Still, desperate to buy more time with her, I read the story aloud until the very end. Orpheus tried to lead his beloved Eurydice out of the underworld, playing his harp so that she would follow his song—but he prematurely gazed back at her, breaking his pact with Hades and casting Eurydice's spirit permanently into the land of the dead.

I set the book down. I leaned over Echo, pushed aside her hair, and pressed my lips to her ashen cheek. Even in sleep, her smile twitched.

"Promise me something," I whispered into her ear. "Promise me that you'll hang on."

Then I turned and strode toward the door. Much like Orpheus, I broke my own heart when I made the mistake of looking back as I left.

OVERDOSE
MUSEUM OF FINE ARTS

AS I STOOD IN FRONT OF THE MUSEUM, I COULD SEE why my brother had followed the seventh riddle here. Bathed in spotlights, the MFA's imposing castle-like façade gleamed bright against the night sky. Four pillars towered like golems over the entrance, draped with crimson banners fit for a royal court.

A bronze statue stood in the center of the lawn, a Native American in a headdress, riding a horse with his hands spread wide and his face upturned to the heavens as he searched for answers. I remembered Jack calling it *The Appeal to the Great Spirit* when he dragged me here.

I paused in front of the statue. "Did the Great Spirit answer your prayers yet?" I asked. When it didn't respond, I flicked my eyes skyward. "Mine neither."

I camouflaged myself in the midst of a pod of tourists entering the museum, in case Nox had posted men here. Inside, as I climbed the grand staircase up to the golden-hued rotunda, I couldn't tear my eyes from the mural over the archway. The painting depicted a helmet-clad Athena, goddess of wisdom, sheltering three mortals under her shield. Behind her, Death lurked with his scythe wound up to unleash a killing blow should Athena remove her protection. I shuddered. From now on, wisdom would be my only haven from death, too.

My destination was the Art of Europe wing. I'd memorized the museum's floor plan prior to my arrival, so I could make a beeline for the painting on Jack's postcard. One moment lingered too long in hostile territory could spell the end of me.

My first impression of the gallery was that the nineteenth century must have been a bleak time for Europe. All the paintings conveyed dark themes. Warriors hunting lions. Moses raining hail and fire down on the city of Thebes.

And there, front and center, was the one I'd been searching for. In person, *The Slave Ship* was far more impressive than on a postcard. As soon as I set eyes on it, the hairs on the nape of my neck rose. I sat down on the wooden bench in front of it and pulled out the battered postcard with a trembling hand.

Jack was meticulous to a fault—even in his haste, he would have purposely chosen *this* postcard. I also knew that when it came to historical landmarks in New England, my brother was a sponge. So while I could accept that Jack, being human, had made a rare error in following the clues to the MFA, there was no way he believed *The Slave Ship* was the answer to the seventh riddle. It made zero sense given the poem's final stanza. There were no gardens in the painting, no fountains or roses.

He must have realized that Nox's men were onto him, and visited this room to throw their scent off the real trail. I could picture him in this gallery, putting on a performance as he stared in fake vexation at this painting, while sitting in *this* seat.

"This seat," I repeated aloud.

If Jack sent me that postcard, it meant that for some reason he wanted me to come here, to look at what he was looking at.

To sit where he had been sitting.

I ran my fingers along the bottom of the bench. To my disgust, I immediately encountered a mountain range of old gum pressed into the wood. But when I reached back far enough, my fingertips grazed the corner of a piece of card stock.

Bingo.

It was a business card that had been adhered to the bench with a wad of gum. The embossed name read "Charlotte Shepherd, PhD—senior lecturer in history at Boston University." Just as Jack had done in the Greek mythology book, he'd pencilled a little nightingale in the corner, his signature so I'd know it was from him.

The fact that he was carrying this historian's card could only mean that they'd met before he died. By leaving it for me, he was indicating that I should make her acquaintance as well. After all, Jack knew I wasn't a history buff like him, which dramatically diminished my chances of finding the Sapphire on my own. He had no way of knowing that I'd team up with his brilliant roommate. Maybe he'd hoped the postcard would put me on the trail of the eighth page, while giving me a resource to turn to if the seventh riddle stumped me.

I was so entranced by my discovery that I didn't register the heavy, limping footsteps until it was too late. The hulking form stopped directly behind my bench, and it took all of my willpower not to turn around. I slowly stuffed the business card into my pocket.

A tense minute later, an enormous man with the build of an NFL linebacker shuffled past the bench, edging closer to *The Slave Ship*. As soon as I saw him in profile, with bandages crisscrossing his broken nose like crime scene tape, I recognized him as Drumm—the one that I'd drilled in the face with a metal tank during my escape yesterday. He had one hand tucked into his sweatshirt; in his other, he held three steel stress balls. He rolled them around his palm and between his salami-sized fingers. They clinked unnervingly every time they collided with each other.

As tempting as it was for me to see what Drumm did next, I knew that it would only take him one good look at my face and I'd be finished. I casually stood up and walked toward the gallery's exit. Still, as I crossed the marble floor, every step echoed like the thunderous gait of a T-Rex.

At the threshold of the next gallery, I chanced a quick look over my shoulder.

Big mistake.

Drumm had been studying *The Slave Ship*, but the motion of my turning head was enough to rouse his attention. In just the two seconds that I looked back, his eyes darted to my face and focused. Even with my new hair color, I could see his eyebrows draw taut with recognition.

Shit. I tried to maintain a casual pace, hoping Drumm might second-guess himself. No dice. I heard his limping footsteps resume in double time. The shark smelled blood in the water and he wasn't about to let an injury get in his way.

I kept my face forward and walked as fast as my stride would allow. What would Drumm do if he caught me? Had Nox ordered my capture, alive, so they could force me to divulge the latest riddle? Or would he simply erase me from the equation and try to find the page on his own? The museum was a public place, but with closing time approaching, the halls were emptying out fast. With four floors and a hundred rooms, there were plenty of quiet corners for Drumm to finish the job and leave me to bleed out in the shadows ...

The image of a "withering body" gave me a crazy idea. My memories of the MFA from field trips were mostly a blur of art and mild boredom, but there was one room that had made a big impression on me.

I waited until I reached the entrance to the glass stairwell, then broke into a run. I descended the stairs two at a time, and still I could hear the lumbering trail of Drumm keeping pace behind me. At the bottom, I darted across the central atrium that connected the various wings, setting a course for "The Art of the Ancient World."

127

The Egyptology exhibit was exactly as I remembered it. A giant glass case contained an old mummy and the various layers of the sarcophagus that once entombed it. Animal-headed canopic jars lined the walls, each containing the bodily organs of long-dead pharaohs. But the object I sought wasn't behind glass at all: the outer stone shell of a sarcophagus, etched with reliefs. A lid was suspended eight inches above it, casting shadows over the coffin's interior. I recalled staring into its dark recesses during my last visit, overcome by panic at the thought of being buried alive inside of it—not afraid like a normal person at the prospect of suffocation, but because more than anything I was terrified by the idea of true dead silence.

Now, with the Egyptology room momentarily to myself and Drumm's footsteps fast approaching down the corridor, I willingly thrust my body through the gap between the lid and the sarcophagus and dropped into its dark embrace.

The hardest part was not making a noise when I landed on my elbow. I listened as Drumm's steps slowed outside. *Come on,* I urged him. *Go check the next room like a good dog.*

He grumbled a curse and I heard the electronic chirp of a walkie-talkie. "Canary sighting in the building," he said. "Be ready with the hounds out on Huntington in case she tries to run for the Green Line."

After a few tense moments, the clinking of Drumm's metal balls drifted away as he moved his search into the Greek and Roman exhibits. I peered out over the lip of the sarcophagus.

I'd barely raised my head when a piercing scream resounded through the Egyptology room. In another stroke of bad luck, a five-year-old boy and his mother had entered right in time to see me rising up out of the coffin.

I was playing the world's deadliest game of hide-and-seek and a kindergartener had totally blown my cover.

I propelled myself out of the sarcophagus and barreled past the family, dodging the swing of the mother's pocketbook. I abandoned all attempts at stealth and fled through the atrium in a full-out sprint. A security officer shouted after me. Since Drumm had instructed his dog handler to patrol Huntington Avenue, I set a course for the rear exit, which emptied out into the tangled marshlands of the Fens.

I stumbled down the museum's steps and crossed the desolate street. The Fens lay silent, and as I darted over the footbridge and into the park, I acknowledged the gamble I'd made. Sure, there were no hounds to sniff me out back here, but there would be no witnesses either if anything happened to me. As beautiful as the Fens were during the daytime, they were a favorite ambush point for muggers, so most people avoided it after sundown.

The trees fanned out and the park opened up into the war memorial. When I glimpsed the well-lit neighborhoods beyond the Fens, a thrill ran through me. Maybe I'd escaped Nox's clutches once again.

I heard a strange whooshing sound behind me. If I didn't know any better, it sounded like someone was twirling an object around their head over and over again and—

Something snagged around my ankles, tethering them together. Before I could extend my hands to break my fall, I landed chin-first in the grass. The half-frozen ground raked my face. My body skidded to a halt in front of the sixteenth-century Japanese temple bell that belonged to the Fenway War Memorial.

The old bell was a symbol of peace and I was about to be slaughtered in front of it.

My ankles were bound tight by several lengths of wire, anchored with the three metal balls Drumm had been rolling around in his hands. Not stress balls at all, but bolas, a projectile snare used by hunters to bring down their prey.

I fumbled in my pocket for my Swiss-army knife keychain, but time had run out. With uncanny strength, Drumm hoisted me to my feet. He clamped my body to his with one bear-like arm, pinning my elbows at my sides. With his other hand, he pressed the unforgiving metal tip of something to my neck.

A syringe.

"Listen carefully," Drumm whispered into my ear. "You get one shot to tell me where the journal page is. Not two, not three—*one shot*. If you even begin to say, 'I don't know,' I inject this concentrated dose of Blyss straight into your jugular. I promise it will feel *real* good, right up until your heart stops sixty seconds later."

I closed my eyes. I pictured seeing Drumm in the buzzard's cage yesterday and at the museum tonight. I listened in my mind to the rhythm of his limp, the shortened, tentative step every time one of his sneakers hit the floor. *Clip-clop. Clip-clop. Clip-clop.* One of his legs was injured, but which one? I thought harder, envisioning the moment I'd gazed back at him as he followed me through the atrium.

Left-right. Left-right. Left-right.

I was pulled so tight against Drumm that I could actually feel the slight bulge of the bandage wrapped around his left leg.

Drumm sighed. "No one will be surprised when they find your body tomorrow. Just another junkie who didn't know her limits, taking after her big brother—"

I drove my thumb into his bandage. With a sickening twist, I felt the stitches cinching the wound together snap.

Drumm howled and slackened his grip on me, dropping the syringe in the process. Without him to hold me upright, I flopped to the grass. I instinctively snatched the syringe out of the dirt. Then I thrust the needlepoint up into my captor's good thigh and depressed the plunger, expelling its lethal contents.

Whereas Drumm had been thrashing about in pain before, he stopped completely in his tracks. He stared dumbfounded at the syringe protruding from his flesh. This bought me enough time to whip out my knife and saw through the bolas around my ankles with a few heavy strokes.

Drumm snapped back into action, lifting his boot to stomp down on my chest, but I rolled away. His eyes quickly clouded over as the concentrated Blyss flowed through his body.

I defensively rose to my feet in front of the war memorial's venerable oak tree. Drumm lunged for me. His meaty fist drew back, ready to crush my skull in a single blow. The Blyss hadn't sapped his strength yet.

It had, however, dulled his reflexes. I easily saw the punch coming and dodged left. Instead of intercepting my face, his powerful cross connected with the tree trunk. A loud crack resounded on impact, and I couldn't be sure whether it was the bones shattering in his hand or the oak tree splitting down the middle.

The Blyss must have overloaded Drumm's nerve endings by then, because he didn't even cry out. He held his mangled hand up to his face in awed bewilderment, studying his fingers, now twisted in unnatural directions. Two of his knuckle bones protruded from the skin.

I watched the fight drain out of him. In fact, in his drug-induced haze, he seemed to forget that I was standing a few feet away with a knife gripped in my hand. He took a few uneasy steps before he collapsed against the bell, the back of his skull clanging against the bronze as he slipped into a sitting position against the stone base.

Even as tears streamed from his eyes, Drumm unexpectedly began to laugh, a high-pitched giggle as though he'd heard the funniest joke. "He sent me to collect a brother and a sister," he said between gasps, "and you both stuck me with a syringe. Like a couple of fucking doctors."

The laughter stopped abruptly as the high from the Blyss passed. His expression sobered and his chest rapidly huffed in and out with shallow, hyperventilating breaths. Soon, his chest stopped moving at all. In a final moment of lucidity, he looked me straight in the eyes and whispered, "I hate this job."

Then his head lolled to the side. The gaze from his dead eyes landed on the crack he'd made in the oak tree.

As I stared at the mercenary's corpse, my whole body trembled. My survival instincts screamed *run, run, you have to run*, but I stood frozen, trying to process that the soulless vessel in front of me had been a breathing, thinking human being just a minute ago. Trying to process that I had been the one who'd snatched the life from him.

I wanted to feel some wave of victory, the thrill of vengeance. This man had played a role in the murders of both Smitty and my brother. Given a few more seconds, he would have killed me, too. I could still feel the tender spot on my neck where he'd pressed the needle.

So why, I asked myself as I touched my cheeks and my fingers came back wet, was I crying?

For the first time, I truly grasped the long and ugly road ahead of me. This wasn't just a race to find the Sapphire, it was a game of last man standing. My family would be in grave danger so long as Grimshaw and Aries and Nox still breathed.

Before this would all be over, the three of them would have to go. Did I have it in me to see this through to the end?

I gathered my wits enough to wipe down the syringe's handle to remove any fingerprints. I slipped the needle into Drumm's hand, which even in death, had closed into a fist.

In the direction of the museum, I heard the barking of dogs. I sprinted across the park, heading toward the light.

Horace Nox stood inside an eight-foot-tall glass cylinder, completely naked except for the electrodes on his chest and neck to monitor his vital signs. Encased within the human-sized test tube, he watched transfixed as the opaque, silvery liquid bubbled up out of the metal grate beneath his feet. The fluid lapped at his toes, rising around his ankles, then began its ascent up his shins. In less than sixty seconds, he would be totally immersed in the cold slime.

Someone tapped on the glass. The man on the other side looked like a distorted reflection of Nox, taller and awkwardly shaped, as though the crime lord was gazing into a funhouse mirror. He had a pronounced hunch in his upper back that was visible beneath his lab coat, and the left side of his face twitched uncontrollably. With great difficulty, Wilbur Nox stuttered out the same seven words that he'd repeated to Horace so many times since they were kids:

"I'm g-going to f-fix you, little br-brother."

But Horace knew that the chemical soup creeping past his knees was no cure. It was just a temporary patch to get his rotting body through another month. The liquid was fully oxygenated and breathable, an experimental treatment that had originally been developed for the lungs of cystic fibrosis patients. "At f-first," Wilbur had warned him, "it will feel like you're dr-drowning."

Once the serum had filled his airway and lungs, it would deliver its medical payload, a series of plant-based drugs that Wilbur had genetically engineered to suppress the symptoms of Horace's terminal condition. A fungal spore to reduce pulmonary inflammation. Cedar resin to restore elasticity to his alveoli. A mutation of rhubarb that would slow but not entirely inhibit the growth of the strange tumors that had networked through his torso.

Nox shivered as the liquid climbed over his buttocks and genitals and up his abdomen. When it reached his neck, he drew in a deep breath and pressed his palm to the glass to brace himself. On the other side, Wilbur placed his hand reassuringly over his brother's. The serum soon covered Nox's face, and the laboratory outside the tube disappeared through the murk.

When Nox could hold his breath no longer, he opened his mouth and inhaled.

The first minute truly did feel like drowning. Nox thrashed wildly, pounding his fists on the cylinder wall, screaming muffled pleas for Wilbur to open the watertight doors.

But then, miraculously, Nox felt a calm settle over him. The liquid coated the air sacs in his lungs, nourishing his oxygen-starved bloodstream. He could breathe again, just not the way he was accustomed to. It was uncomfortable, but his panic subsided and he let himself float, suspended in the watery abyss.

An indeterminate time later, a loud *clack* echoed up from below his feet. The fluid rapidly drained out of the tube and the cylinder doors parted. Nox collapsed out onto the lab floor.

On his hands and knees, he vomited what felt like a gallon of liquid onto the white tile. Toward the end, as he hacked the final remnants from his airway, he could see where the serum had been tinged dark red, stained with the bloodied mucus it had cleaned from his lungs. This would allow him to breathe easier for a time, until the mutation filled his insides with more detritus. Then it would once again feel like he was breathing through gravel.

Wilbur rubbed his brother's back with a spindly hand. "I'm s-sorry," he stammered. "I w-wish I could g-give you more than b-borrowed time."

Nox actually found himself smiling. "Every day of my life has been borrowed time. But soon, I'll steal eternity."

A half hour later, Nox wandered into a room in his mansion labeled "Chrysalis." Its whitewashed walls contained only two objects: a sledge hammer and the gnarled remains of a secondhand wheelchair, the metal prison that had confined Nox for much of his childhood. Once a week, he came here to take a crack at it with the hammer, to the point that it was hardly recognizable as a wheelchair anymore.

Nox picked up the shaft of the sledgehammer but hesitated. He felt so refreshed from his treatment that maybe he didn't need to take a swing today.

The phone in his pocket vibrated with an incoming voicemail. At first all he could hear was the barking of hounds, before Pearce finally said in his croaky Southern twang, "Drumm's dead. Girl's gone." The line went dead after that. Pearce wasn't much of a talker.

Nox let the cell phone clatter to the floor. With a scream that reverberated out of the room and across the indoor jungle, he hoisted the sledge hammer over his head and drove it down onto the warped wheelchair with all his might—splitting it right down the middle.

SMALL COMFORTS
THE SOUTH END

BACK AT THE DOLLHOUSE, I KNEW THAT SOMETHING was wrong the moment I stepped out of the elevator. The condo's door had been left ajar, a sliver of red-tinged light glowing through the crack. I could hear the rustling movements of somebody inside, as well as the clatter of something glass. My hand flew to the knife on my keychain and I held it out in front of me. Had Nox discovered my whereabouts? The eighth journal page was still in there and I would protect it at all costs.

As I edged closer, though, I could hear something else: a familiar song from my childhood, one of my mother's holiday favorites. I'd recognize the dulcet tones of Andy Williams singing "Sleigh Ride" anywhere.

I folded up my knife and pushed open the door.

The inside of the condo had transformed in the few hours I'd been gone. Evergreen garlands decorated the ceiling trim, intertwined with strings of red lights. An enormous mound of gingerbread cookies dominated the kitchen counter, and the sweet aroma of another batch in the oven permeated the air.

Most perplexing of all was the Christmas tree by the windows, so tall that the halo on the angel topper grazed the lofted ceiling. Atlas balanced precariously on a step ladder, hanging a series of Norman Rockwell ornaments. When he spotted me, he froze. "I can explain," he said.

I leaned against the doorway. "What is there to explain? You celebrate Halloween a little differently than the other kids at school,

136

and that's okay. I mean, I typically carve pumpkins and decide whether I'm going to be a cat or a sexy ninja this year, but if you want to go crazy with tinsel and holly, who am I to judge?"

Atlas glared at me. "Are you done?"

I flicked the mistletoe hanging over the door. "Oh, now I see what's really going on here. I'm into it, but we need to lay a few ground rules. First, you can call me Mrs. Clause, but only if you decorate the bed like a sleigh. Second, as soon as reindeer get involved, I am *out*. Number three—"

Atlas jumped down off the ladder. "Careful: The fortuneteller at my tenth birthday party told me I'd marry a sarcastic girl one day." He frowned. "She also told me I'd grow up to be a dolphin trainer."

I wandered over to the cookies, and after poking one to make sure it wasn't made of wax, I popped it into my mouth. "You should have been a baker instead. But seriously, why does the condo look like the Polar Express just threw up on it?"

"Boss's orders." Atlas stood back and admired his tree. "They're having trouble selling a few condos downstairs, so they decided that with the holidays coming up, we should dress up the model unit to feel more welcoming and festive."

"Uh-huh," I mumbled through another mouthful of cookie. "And when a realtor brings a family through here and they find me sleeping in the master bedroom?"

Atlas shrugged. "I'll just tell them I went overboard when they said I should make the model unit feel 'lived in.'" He slapped my hand away as I reached for a third cookie. "Easy on the props, Cookie Monster. These need to last through October. How was your visit to the hospital?"

My hand unconsciously drifted to the sore spot on my neck. I pictured my harrowing escape through the museum and the gardens, then Drumm's dead eyes at the War Memorial. "Dull," I replied. If I wanted to preserve my freedom to come and go from the condo without Atlas trying to play bodyguard, lying was my only choice.

Atlas's jaw drew tight. He'd obviously been worrying about me. "I can't tell you not to visit your sick sister. But next time I wish you'd let me escort you, rather than making me come home to find nothing but a scribbled note."

"*Escort* me?" I echoed. "Back that horse up, Don Quixote. You're not my bodyguard; you are my history textbook."

The moment I said it, I knew I'd gone too far. Atlas wouldn't meet my gaze. He took a potholder out of the drawer and dropped it onto the counter. "Take the next batch of cookies out of the oven when the timer goes off," he said quietly. "Your history textbook will be in the second bedroom trying to solve your next riddle for you." He marched over the carpet and peeled it back, the hiding spot where we'd agreed to store the loose journal page.

I knelt beside him and laid my hand gently over his. "I'm sorry. I just had to say goodbye to Echo for the foreseeable future, so I'm wound a little tight. I shouldn't have unloaded on you like that."

"How'd she take it?" Atlas didn't move to retrieve his hand from under mine.

"As well as any sick kid would after her older sister said she had to go off the grid." I bit my lip to stop it from trembling. "The thing is, Atlas: Echo needs you. I need you. I inherited all of my father's street smarts, but absorbed very little of Jack's book smarts, so I could stare at this riddle for days and get nowhere. But with you, Echo actually has a shot."

Atlas squinted. "Just to be clear, you're saying that I'm the brains and you're the brawn? Because that wouldn't be at all emasculating." Still, the idea didn't seem to offend him.

"The point is," I continued, "that I need to minimize the opportunities Nox and his people have to see us together. Right now, he has no idea where I am and who I'm working with. But if he identifies you, he will figure out where you work. He will find this condo. He will corner the two of us. And then it will be that bastard who's being healed by the Sapphire, while Echo …" I trailed off. A tear fell from my face onto the riddle's laminate coating.

Atlas wiped the wet trail from my cheek. Then he asked me something that made no sense. "*Home Alone* or *Elf?*"

When I stared blankly at him, Atlas hopped over the couch. He returned from the coffee table clutching an armful of DVDs and dropped them onto the carpet. They were all holiday-themed movies.

Atlas touched the one titled *Christmas Vacation*. "This is one of my favorites, but it doesn't feel like a Chevy Chase kind of night. *Scrooged* is a little too dark, *Mixed Nuts* is a little too wacky, and *It's a Wonderful Life* is way too sappy. So I figured if we wanted the right balance of funny and hopeful, our best bets are Will Ferrell running around Manhattan in an elf suit or Joe Pesci getting hit in the face with a can of paint."

"You want to watch a movie?" I asked. "Right now?" My eyes drifted to the journal page.

"Trust me, I'm going to solve it," Atlas promised. "But I've been working on that riddle all day, searching keywords, poring through library texts, and racking my brain as I put up all these decorations. I know it so well that I can recite it to you backwards. Whenever I hit a problem like this I can't solve, the most helpful thing I can do is to empty my mind and come back fresh. Something tells me that you could use a few hours of non-thinking yourself."

He was right. Even if I wanted to search tirelessly for the Sapphire, exhausting ourselves would only be counterproductive.

So I pointed to a DVD in the pile. "This one."

Atlas actually looked impressed. "*White Christmas*—a classic."

I shrugged. "Between Bing Crosby's sultry eyes and Danny Kaye's dance moves, how could a girl choose anything else?"

"You have good taste in men," Atlas said.

I barked out a laugh. "My mother might disagree."

Next thing I knew, we were curled up on opposite ends of the couch, watching a movie I'd probably seen fifty times as a child, while the heat from the fireplace warmed the room. On screen, Bing Crosby sang in his smoky baritone to his troops, who were huddled up in the war-scarred shell of an old city.

For the first time, I truly understood this part of the film. Even when your world was falling to rubble around you, it was human nature to grasp for small, familiar comforts.

Yet oddly I was more familiar with this movie than with the boy who I was watching it with. I blurted out, "Who *are* you, Atlas?"

He smiled patiently. "Don't you think one riddle is enough for the night?"

I shook my head. "If you're going to continue to harbor me as a fugitive, I need to get to know you three-dimensionally. At the moment you're just sort of a paper doll."

"You want, like, Atlas trivia?" he asked through a yawn. "Like how I enjoy the smell of lawnmower exhaust, or that I was afraid of the moon until I was five years old, or how I find the sensation of plucking out a stray hair to be strangely pleasant? I can keep going but it only gets weirder from here."

I planted my hands on my hips. "Take this seriously."

Atlas drummed his fingers on the armrest and his eyes lit up. "Well, if I'm some sort of enigmatic onion to you, I know just the game to start peeling away the layers."

He rummaged through the coffee table drawer until he found a deck of what looked like playing cards. With a flourish of his hands, he rapidly shuffled the deck, then held them out for me to pick one.

When I flipped my chosen card over, there was no suit or number. "Who was your first kiss?" I read aloud. "Omit no details." It was then I realized that the cards were a series of icebreaker questions.

"Ooh, a juicy one." Atlas folded his hands under his chin and waited for me to launch into a story. "Do tell."

I didn't take the bait. "I'm not sure that a drinking game intended for a sorority mixer was what I had in mind. This is like the Milton Bradley version of 'getting-to-know-you.'"

"Call me crazy," Atlas said, "but I think you can learn a lot about a person based on whose tongue they first invited into their mouth."

In his defense, I found this to be an ironclad argument. "His name was Chad Barnes."

"He was your first kiss, *too*?" Atlas mock-pouted. "And he told me I was special."

I brandished the card. "I am on the precipice of paper-cutting your jugular right now." Atlas held up his hands in surrender. "In the seventh grade," I continued, "I was best friends with his sister, Melissa. Chad was in eighth grade and one of those junior high heartthrobs who develops earlier than everyone else, so we all had his name doodled in our notebooks with hearts around it. Melissa had a sleepover for her thirteenth birthday. Later that night, we were all passed out on her living room floor. I woke up when I heard the floor creaking. The TV was still on, muted, so I could see Chad tiptoeing his way through the labyrinth of sleeping bags."

Atlas couldn't contain himself. "I figured you were going to tell me some cute story about a kiss beneath the bleachers at the football game. This sounds straight-up creepy."

"Well, to a thirteen-year-old, it seemed romantic. Chad knelt next to me and put a finger to his lips. Then he asked, 'Do you like me?' I nodded and suddenly we were kissing. He tasted like

141

Cheetos and Mountain Dew and I nearly asphyxiated on his tongue, but I was an idiot with a crush, so it didn't seem disgusting then. My heart was beating so fast by the time he left that I couldn't fall back asleep." I paused. "Which turned out to be a good thing, because I was still awake an hour later when I heard his voice whisper, 'Do you like me?'—only this time it was to Tanya Lanigan on the other side of the room."

Atlas cringed and clasped his hands over his chest. "The preteen heartbreak is almost palpable."

I grinned slyly. "Well, that player double-timed the wrong girl. A few days later, I came back to school with a duffle bag full of 'gentlemen's magazines' from the secret stash my Dad kept behind the paint cans in the garage. I broke into Chad's locker and rigged a stack so they'd fall out the next time he opened the door. He got suspended for two days—then for another week when they found the ones I stuffed in his desk. His parents sent him to Jesus camp that summer."

"And so Sabra Tides's life of retribution got a precocious start," Atlas said.

I flipped the playing card onto Atlas's lap. "Your turn, Casanova. Let me guess: It was on a field trip to Gettysburg, and your studious knowledge of Confederate military strategy got her all hot and bothered."

"Actually, it was in a blueberry patch."

I held up a hand to stop him. "Before you go any further, is this story going to permanently ruin one of my favorite types of pancakes?"

"It's disappointingly less racy than you think," he said. "Every summer, my family used to vacation on Chebeague Island, off the coast of Maine. I was good friends with one of our neighbors, Sophia, who lived in the cottage next door with her lobsterman father. She taught me how to clam for razors and steamers on the beach, and how to run across the sandbar

142

to the little island when it was low tide. When we were fourteen, we both got jobs at the golf course." Atlas stared distantly into the fireplace. "For my final night on the island that summer, she stole a bottle of champagne from the country club's bar. We sat in this one blueberry patch that was 'our spot,' taking turns drinking from the bottle. And when the champagne was gone, and the drunken giggling had faded, the moment sort of clicked, and we both went in for the kiss at the same time."

I waited for Atlas to say more, but he offered nothing else. "Wow," I said. "If you're going to be a historian, you really have to learn to tell a better story, because that one royally sucked. Where was the passion? Where was the *ending*? Is Sophia back on the island, even now, pining for the day when you'll return and put a ring on it?"

Atlas shook his head. "When I returned the next summer, there was a new family living in Sophia's cottage. It was a bad year for lobstering, so she and her father moved north to Bar Harbor. The year after that, my dad lost his job, and we sold the cottage." I still looked disappointed. He let out an exasperated sigh. "Sometimes romance ends in a whimper instead of a bang. But that doesn't mean it didn't shape the trajectory of your life, even in a little way."

"I'm not sure I'm comfortable giving that much credit to all the frogs I've kissed," I replied. "If that's the case, I should be more discriminating about who 'shapes my trajectory.'"

"Did you know that kissing in wedding ceremonies started in ancient Rome?" Atlas asked. "A lot of people were illiterate and couldn't read a contract, so the kiss became a way to legally seal the marriage."

The way Atlas popped out random historical facts like a gumball machine reminded me so much of Jack. I realized with a pang of sadness that given more time, the two of them could have become fast friends. "For what it's worth," I said, "I'm glad they stuck Jack with you as a roommate. The guy had offers to every Ivy League school from Harvard to Stanford, but it was as though fate conspired to send him to BU, so he could meet someone the same rare species of nerd that he was."

Atlas squinted at me funny, his expression indecipherable. "Say that again," he said slowly.

"Say what again? Don't tell me you're offended because I called you a nerd."

"Not offended." His voice swelled with excitement. "*Inspired.*"

Atlas hurdled over the couch and peeled back the carpet, revealing the eighth riddle. After a few moments of scrutiny, he opened his mouth and I watched clarity wash over his face, like a combination lock in his mind had clicked to the final number. "You clever son of a bitch," he whispered.

"You figured it out?" I asked hopefully.

"The first part at least." Atlas hurried over to the floor in front of the fireplace. I knelt beside him and we read through the riddle as the firelight played over the page.

A CLASH OF TWO DREADNOUGHTS
ONE FERRIC, ONE ICE,
A VICTOR GLOATS COLDLY
O'ER THE COLOSSUS'S GRAVE.

A THOUSAND SOULS SWALLOWED
DOWN THE DARK, FRIGID MAW.
A LIBRARY SINKS
WITH ITS SCHOLAR IN TOW.

BUT HE'LL STUDY ETERNAL
IN WHAT LOOKS JUST LIKE HOME,
WHILE DREAMING OF BLACK SPOTS,
ISLANDS, AND GOLD.

"At first," Atlas explained spiritedly, "I thought this riddle was referring to a myth or folktale about a battle between two monsters, one made of iron—*ferric*—and one made of ice. But after an hour or two, I realized that maybe I wasn't taking this literally enough. A dreadnought is another name for a battleship. Tell me: How much do you know about the sinking of the *RMS Titanic*?"

"Um, I saw the movie a few times, but all I remember is that it was a huge ocean liner that sank in the Atlantic. And that Leonardo DiCaprio is super adorable with bangs."

Atlas rolled his eyes. "A little over a century ago, in April of 1912, the *Titanic* set sail from Liverpool, England, and picked up passengers in France and Ireland on route to America. But in the dead of night, somewhere far off the coast of Newfoundland, the ship struck an iceberg, which tore into its watertight compartments and sunk the boat in a matter of hours." He jabbed his finger at the page. "These opening lines —*A clash of two dreadnoughts / One ferric, one ice*—refer to the ship and the iceberg. The accident caused fifteen hundred people to freeze or drown in the cold ocean waters, hence the lines *A thousand souls swallowed / Down the dark, frigid maw*. The problem? If we're to believe the map you found at Nox's mansion, all of the journal pages so far have been hidden in New England, in places with historical relevance to Boston. But the destination of the *Titanic*'s maiden voyage was New York City."

"Maybe there's a museum or a memorial somewhere around here," I suggested.

"That was my thought, too. Unfortunately, the only in-state museum I could find is way out in Western Massachusetts, and when I searched through the registry of artifacts, not a single object made sense of the rest of the poem."

"What about this part?" I underscored the seventh and eighth lines with my fingertip. *A library sinks / With its scholar in tow.* "If the *Titanic* was so luxurious, it must have had a library, and probably a librarian, too."

"*Two* libraries, in fact. One for the first class, one for the second class, and none for the lower class." Atlas beamed. "But it wasn't until you mentioned Harvard a few minutes ago that I realized the riddle is referring to a different library altogether."

He whipped out his cell phone, furiously typing something into the web browser. After a few strokes on the keypad, the condo's television flickered and the synced image from his phone replaced Rosemary Clooney on the screen.

I wandered closer to read the article that Atlas had pulled up. It featured a black-and-white portrait of a handsome young man with piercing eyes and his hair parted immaculately down the center. He might have looked overly serious in his dapper suit had it not been for the ghost of a smile on his lips. I read the caption aloud: "Harry Elkins Widener."

According to the article, Harry had been a graduate of Harvard College best known for his impressive collection of books. Shortly after his twenty-seventh birthday, the bibliophile and his parents had traveled to France to collect a rare text.

For the return voyage, Harry had unfortunately purchased a ticket aboard the doomed *Titanic*. While he and his father had perished in the frigid Atlantic, his mother survived and donated two million dollars to Harvard to construct a library in his name.

I felt an excited chill as my eyes landed on the article's final picture. It showed a beautiful study, complete with a fireplace, a large antique desk, and tall bookcases recessed into oak walls. This, I knew instantly, was the place we'd find the ninth journal page. "Oh my God," I whispered. "There's a memorial in the middle of the library that's a replica of Widener's study?"

Atlas laughed darkly, before reciting in a singsong voice, "*But he'll study eternal / In what looks just like home.*"

THE BLACK SPOT
HARVARD SQUARE

I'D ALWAYS HAD MIXED FEELINGS ABOUT CAMBRIDGE, the sprawling city on the opposite bank of the Charles River. It was an eclectic blend of high-tech and old-fashioned, wealthy and impoverished, enlightened and uneducated—one great big patchwork quilt of a town. Hell, it was even divided into "squares." Kendall Square, to the far east, was Boston's answer to Silicon Valley, a hub of cutting-edge computer science and engineering that siphoned the brightest recruits from nearby MIT. Only a few blocks from Kendall's modern expanse of steel and glass lay Central Square, a squat line of vegan restaurants and bars that fed on the wallets of grad students. No matter the time of day, Massachusetts Avenue teemed with throngs of belligerent locals.

Then there was Harvard Square, the beating heart of Cambridge, where all these worlds collided. It was my favorite part of town. At least once a week, I biked across the river to pig out at a Sicilian pizza place tucked away in an alley.

As Atlas and I stepped off the railcar and into the subway station, a musician with dreadlocks and a colorful hat strummed out a funky tune on his electric guitar. Beside him, his drummer smiled toothlessly at passersby while his drumsticks *rat-a-tat-tatted* over the tile floor. It was a shining example of why I loved Harvard Square so much:

It was weird. Truly, deeply weird.

We passed a peddler who was selling both jewelry and extension cords off a hemp rug, and Atlas whispered, "I call this place the Twilight Zone of Boston."

Aboveground, the two of us were swallowed by a deluge of tourists that had just spilled out of a bus. A horn blared as a taxi nearly mowed down a camera-wielding man who had wandered into traffic. I wondered what the life expectancy of tourists was around here.

We shouldered our way through the milling crowd and under the wrought-iron gates to Harvard University. We hadn't traveled a dozen paces onto campus before Atlas stopped to admire a red brick building with a sextet of chimney stacks. "This," he said excitedly, "is Massachusetts Hall. During the Siege of Boston in 1775, an entire garrison of colonial troops stayed here while the British—"

I snapped my fingers in front of his face. "Focus. There's plenty of history waiting for us at the library."

His focus only lasted another sixty seconds. As we crossed Harvard Yard, a sweeping quad with towering oaks, Atlas pointed to a bronze statue of a clergyman in colonial garb— John Harvard himself. A gaggle of tourists had formed a line and were rubbing the statue's left foot, one by one. While the last two centuries had weathered the rest of the monument a dark, dull brown, the toe of his right boot gleamed, polished to its original bronze thanks to whatever weird daily tradition I was observing. "What the hell are they doing?" I asked.

Atlas released a girlish giggle and leaned closer so that only I could hear him. "Each day, the tour guides tell the visitors that rubbing John Harvard's left foot will bring them good luck. And each night, the students piss on it."

We both doubled over with laughter when the next tourist in line stood on his tiptoes to kiss the boot.

A short walk later we arrived at Widener Library. Unlike Jack, I had never been the bookish type, but as I gazed up at the towering columns, I thought that this was the kind of place I could curl up with an issue of *Vogue* for a few hours.

Which was for the best, since according to our plan, I'd be spending the better part of the evening inside.

Atlas suddenly looked nervous. "I'm really starting to rethink letting you do this alone," he said.

I sighed. Even after I'd explained all the logical reasons why I needed to fly solo tonight, I knew he'd play the macho card at the last minute. "If I get caught by myself, at least you'll be free to try again. But if they catch us both trespassing, there will be no one to finish this quest for Echo. Besides, even if we were to escape together, Detective Grimshaw will have access to the security footage, and if he identifies you then the Dollhouse is compromised." I'd been hesitant to even let him ride the subway with me—there were cameras everywhere, these days—but I'd made that concession to get him off my back.

Atlas slouched in defeat. "But we don't even have a student ID for you to get into the library. We don't know *where* in the memorial room the journal page is hidden, either. You're going to need my help—"

"—Which I'll be able to get instantly by texting the History Dork Hotline, because you'll be staring anxiously at your phone the entire time you're working your concierge shift."

I spied a girl coming down the library stairs carrying a stack of books up to her chin. Laced in her fingers, dangling in front of her, was the lanyard attached to her student ID.

I backed away from Atlas. "Just remember, you may be the book smarts of this operation ..." I tapped my temple. "... But I'm the street smarts."

Then I turned and intentionally crashed into the student.

The girl's book tower toppled, scattering over the steps. "I am *so* sorry," she apologized timidly, as though it were her fault.

I bent down to help her wrangle the books. "Please, I'm the klutz." I spotted her ID sticking out from beneath a copy of Camus's *The Stranger*. While she was distracted, I deftly palmed the badge. Then I placed the last book on the towering pile the girl had once again collected in her arms. "On your next visit to the library," I suggested, "consider bringing a wheel barrow."

The bookworm smiled and waddled off. As I jogged up the library steps, I triumphantly repeated "Street smarts!" over my shoulder to Atlas. I slipped between the pillars and swiped the stolen ID to gain access through the metal turnstiles. I was in.

The Harry Elkins Widener Memorial Room was at the top of the first flight of stairs, beneath a dazzling chandelier. Because it was in such a high-profile location, searching it during the daytime was out of the question. For now, I stood in front of the stanchions that corded off the room from visitors and reacquainted myself with its layout, while mentally cataloging all the places where the ninth riddle could be hiding.

Tall bookcases lined the walls, crammed end to end with dusty texts. Widener's handsome portrait hung over the ornate fireplace and a red Persian carpet spanned most of the floor. I'd pegged the desk as the riddle's most likely location. I made a note to check its drawers for false bottoms.

The room's crown jewel was the display case containing a copy of the Gutenberg Bible, the first book ever printed using movable type. Only twenty-one copies in the world had survived since the fifteenth century. I would look in that case only as a last resort. I wasn't superstitious by any means, but tampering with a priceless religious text was asking for bad juju.

After I had absorbed as much as I could, I ventured deeper into the library to find an isolated study carol, where I'd carry out the most agonizing component of my plan: waiting.

When I had explained the next phase to Atlas, he had replied, "So your master plan essentially boils down to how well you can play hide-and-seek?"

He was absolutely right.

When the P.A. system crackled on at last and a librarian announced closing time, I slipped into the women's bathroom. I walled myself in one of the stalls until I heard the door swing open. I tucked my feet up onto the toilet seat.

"All clear in here?" the security guard asked. Without waiting for a response, he disappeared off to finish his rounds.

It was close to eleven when I cautiously emerged from the restroom, listening for any signs of movement—late-night librarians, security patrols, cleaning crews. But there was only a deep and pervasive silence.

On my way up to the Memorial Room, I worried I'd trip hidden motion detectors, setting off blaring alarms and flashing red lights, but the university probably didn't expect anyone to "Trojan Horse" their way into some place as boring as the library.

The memorial had gone dark except for its dim auxiliary lighting, so I unclipped an LED flashlight from my belt as I stepped over the stanchion. A vase containing flowers glinted under the light. I had read in my research that they'd put a fresh bouquet on the desk every week for the last hundred years, a stipulation made by Harry Widener's mother.

In comparing the last two riddles, I had deciphered a pattern: each poem was structured to move from general to specific, like a funnel. With the most recent riddle, the opening lines introduced the idea of the *Titanic*'s victims, then narrowed the location down to Widener Library, then the Memorial Room— which meant that the final stanza should tell me exactly *where* in the memorial to look. I had memorized the last few lines so if I got caught, they wouldn't find the journal page on me:

While Dreaming of Black Spots, Islands, and Gold.

As my light passed over the walls and the library shelves, I struggled to find anything that made sense of those lines. Not the carpet, not the moldings, not the portrait over the fireplace.

The words "black spots" haunted me as I rifled through the desk, an old memory clawing to get out. I closed my eyes and zeroed in on the image that was drifting just out of reach.

Then it all clicked.

The memory that surfaced was of a movie I'd watched in grade school years ago. One of pirates, adventure, distant islands, and golden treasure. A story about a one-legged cook aboard a ship who organized a mutiny. A story that began with an aging pirate receiving a death sentence—a black spot.

Treasure Island.

I ran a search on my phone to confirm this theory. The results were promising: According to the top article, one of Widener's favorite authors was Robert Louis Stevenson, and his private collection contained several first editions of Stevenson's works.

I jogged over to the bookshelves and meticulously scanned the titles. My search paid off when my flashlight illuminated a sage-green text with *Treasure Island* on its spine.

My gloved hands trembled as I opened the glass case and withdrew the novel. Despite being 130 years old, it remained in good condition, though I feared that the old book might flake apart, its binding withering to ash under my touch.

My care of the book became more frantic as I failed to find any sign of the ninth riddle. I fanned through every page in case it was wedged between them. I ran my fingers over the endpaper to see if it might be hidden beneath. Nothing.

I cursed, tempted to throw the book across the room in my frustration. I was about to reshelve it when I glimpsed something inside the front cover. It was an antique book plate. I was sure that plenty of the library's volumes bore Widener's name—

Only this one was embossed with golden vines.

This one had a splotch of black ink in the corner.

And where the signature should have been, this one contained a four-line poem, written in the same jagged scrawl as the other riddles.

I held my flashlight closer to the page.

THE CINDERS STOP SMOLDERING
THE FLAMES NOW EFFETE
BUT HIS GAZE WATCHES, VIGILANT,
WHILE HIS GILDED HEART BEATS

I rubbed the bridge of my nose. A riddle within a riddle?

You can figure this out, I coached myself. *You don't need Atlas's help on everything.* I traced my finger through the stanzas and isolated the keywords.

Cinders.

Flames.

Gaze.

Gilded.

Something else caught my attention. At the end of the word *heart*, the cursive trail extending from the letter "t" was looping and misshapen, as though the pen had trailed on too long. When I squinted at the page, I realized it wasn't accidental at all. That squiggle was actually the letter "h."

The word was *hearth*.

My head snapped to the left. There was the fireplace, cold and unused—its cinders no longer smoldering, its flames long since dead. There was the portrait of Harry Widener gazing vigilantly.

And sandwiched between the portrait above and the fireplace below was a golden inlay in the wood.

A gilded hearth.

I knelt in front of the fireplace. My hands groped around the gold ornament for any sign of weakness, but it was firmly attached to the wall. However, when I slipped my arm inside the flue, I discovered a loose brick directly behind it.

I dug blindly, raking at the loose mortar with my nails, until at last the stone popped free into my hand. On its exposed side, it was a normal brick, its craggy surface stained with soot. But when I flipped it over, I found that someone had carved out the middle and placed a rolled up page inside.

The ninth riddle.

I tucked the journal page into my pocket, brick and all, and drew my hood tight around my face. Then I walked briskly down the main staircase, inhaled a deep breath, and unlocked the library's front doors.

The alarms sounded instantly. Outside, a group of freshman girls standing on the quad turned in surprise. When they saw me barreling down the stone steps with all but my eyes concealed, they shrieked and ran in the opposite direction.

The university police had a better response time then I'd anticipated. I turned the corner just as a public safety van came barreling across the quad.

But they wouldn't find me. By the time I heard the car doors slamming and the chatter from the officers as they hurdled up the stairs, I was already disappearing through a side gate. I cast off my hood as I stepped out onto Mass Ave. so I wouldn't look suspicious, before making my way back to the subway station.

I didn't breathe a sigh of relief until the train car jerked forward, heading away from the platform and back downtown, toward the safety of the Dollhouse. The car was empty except for a blind man with a seeing-eye dog, who'd boarded right before the doors hissed closed. Still, I resisted the urge to take out the riddle and read it. I kept one hand delicately draped over the bulge the brick formed in my pocket.

With the car in motion, I finally remembered to text Atlas. *Chill the champagne*, I wrote, just enough to put his anxiety to rest.

Only a few passengers boarded over the next few stops, and I tried my best to avoid eye contact. Before long, I developed this strange, unshakable feeling that somebody was watching me. I felt this way sometimes late at night, walking alone through Dorchester after a pedicab shift. Usually, in those cases, it turned out to be nothing. But tonight ...

I subtly glanced from passenger to passenger, profiling anyone who might be a threat. An elderly man with two bags of groceries in his walker. Three college girls wearing thigh-length cocktail dresses beneath their pea coats, gabbing about some party. A boy who couldn't have been older than middle school, his earbuds cranking out music so loud that I could recognize the tune. He seemed far more interested in ogling the female undergrads than checking me out.

That left only the blind man across the aisle. He was middle-aged, with a receding hairline that had gone gray at the temples. He had one hand wrapped tightly around his dog's harness and the other tucked into the pocket of his leather jacket. At first glance, I had believed he was gazing unseeingly up at the ceiling, but behind the dark tint of his aviator sunglasses, it was impossible to know for sure.

Hadn't Drumm, before he died, called an accomplice on his radio—someone with hounds? Was it possible that same man had picked up my trail, and was biding his time to steal the riddle I'd just uncovered?

Maybe it was paranoia. I had just broken into one of the most famous libraries in the world, so I had a right to be on edge.

To put my fears to rest, I took out my phone and opened the camera app. With no warning, I clicked the shutter button.

The flash went off. The hound whined in discomfort. And in that sudden burst of light, even with the aviators covering his eyes, I could see the corner of the man's eyes crinkle as he winced.

Blind, my ass.

My stomach somersaulted. I tried not to look at him, pretending that the camera flash had been a harmless accident. The train slowed down as it rolled into Park Street Station. I waited for the doors to part and then, seeing that the man had made no move to get up, I darted out onto the platform.

I didn't turn around at first. Instead, I approached a street meat vendor and ordered a sausage. Ordinarily, I'd never buy anything cooked in a dirty subway station, but a wild, desperate idea was brewing in my brain.

As I traded a five-spot for the sausage, I casually glanced behind me. Sure enough, the man and his dog were idly skulking nearby. He was pretending to ask for directions, but the Rhodesian ridgeback stared fixedly at me. It dipped its nose to the ground then sniffed the air, clinging to my scent trail.

I set a fast clip for the opposite end of the platform. While I walked, I tore off a piece of the charcoal-grilled meat and dropped it. As I suspected, the dog handler had resumed his slow pursuit. He'd cast off his sunglasses and his eyes homed in on me. The dog stopped to eat the piece of sausage I'd tossed, but its handler cursed and urged it forward.

Fifteen yards down the platform, I dropped another piece. This time I heard the dog yelp in pain when the man jerked on the leash, robbing it of its snack.

A robotic voice announced over the loudspeaker, "Attention passengers: The next train to Ashmont is now approaching."

Ahead, the sounds of the incoming train echoed out of the tunnel. My path would soon be obstructed by a wall. For better or worse, that would be where I made my last stand.

When I reached the dead end, I spun around to face my pursuer. The dog handler quickened his pace, sensing victory.

"Don't take another step," I warned him. My voice sounded feeble and terrified and barely carried over the clatter of wheels on steel tracks.

The dog handler responded by pulling a black object from his pocket—a gun. Its silencer glinted under the approaching headlights from the train.

I had never wanted to see my crazy plan through. But given another few seconds, I had no doubt that this degenerate would put a bullet between my eyes and steal the journal page from my corpse.

What I was about to do wasn't solely for my own survival. It was for Echo.

This time, I steeled my voice as I said, "You should really learn to treat that dog better."

Then I threw the rest of the sausage over the tracks.

The hound, underfed and ravenous, instantly leaped after the airborne meat. It was a sinewy, muscular dog, and its pounce safely landed it on the opposite platform, out of harm's way.

The same couldn't be said for the dog handler. To keep the hound on task, he'd wrapped his hand so firmly around the leash that when the hound hurdled the tracks, it pulled the man right along with him. My pursuer lost his balance on the edge of the platform and toppled over the safety strip, falling onto the steel rails.

Only a fleeting, doomed moan escaped his mouth before the incoming subway car plowed right over him.

Even though I knew it was coming, I wasn't fully prepared for the ugly cacophony of steel trampling flesh and bone. I hunched over and vomited onto the concrete.

Screams erupted farther up the tracks, as the train pushed whatever remained of the mercenary past the smattering of late-night passengers. Their hysterical shrieks could be heard even over the subway car's screeching brakes.

When there was nothing left in my stomach for me to throw up, I wiped the spittle from my mouth and whispered, "Why? Why couldn't you have just left me alone?"

Another noise interrupted my stupefied horror. It was the whimper of the Rhodesian ridgeback on the opposite platform, searching for its master. I could hear it shuffling around, its harness jingling as it dragged behind the dog. When the hound realized that it was truly alone, it let out a forlorn, bloodcurdling howl.

Somehow that sound was so much worse than anything else.

I exited the station as quickly as possible, keeping my hood up and my head low so the cameras wouldn't catch my face. As much as the man deserved it, as much as I'd do it all over again in the same situation, one thought haunted the long, cold walk back to the safe house:

I had just killed another man, and this time, I didn't even know his name.

Dearest Adelaide,

My resourceful companion overcame many obstacles to find himself on our shores. Yet there remained at large one vital clove of information, the absence of which threatened to render his struggle futile: the location of his son. The slaves in the region's cotton fields number in the thousands, so I nearly wrote off our journey as impossible before it had even begun.

However, Malaika had obtained one indispensable lead. The slave ship that his child had been forced onto bore a crest on its sails of a winged lion and fleur-de-lis. This heraldry belonged to the Gold Coast Company of Charleston, the offices of which were tucked away in the Cannonborough district, not far—much to my alarm—from the Citadel military academy.

So it was that Malaika and I returned to the city where the first shots of this cursed war rung righteously. For the purposes of camouflage, we assumed the roles of slaver and slave, costuming ourselves in vesture we purloined from a clothesline outside city limits. On our journey through the Charleston streets, Malaika kept his head bowed and concealed the Sapphire hidden beneath his tattered cloak.

Upon our arrival, we were greeted by the Gold Coast proprietor, a man by the name of Lourde with snow-white muttonchops. I introduced myself as a proxy for a wealthy plantation owner from Goose Creek, who had sent me to acquire new labor for his tobacco fields.

The promise of money makes fast friends, and so we retired to his study to conduct business, while Malaika remained outside.

The slaver's office was richly furnished, the spoils of a sordid trade, but my keen eye glossed over all these extravagancies in favor of his library of leather-bound manifests. "I see your bookkeeping knows no bounds of meticulousness," I said.

He grinned. "Organization is, after all, the foundation of success."

"I wonder then," I told him, "if your records are so thorough that you would be able to ascertain the specifics of a particular transaction for me: a boy of twelve years from Africa's eastern coast, sold in the summer of '64."

Lourde's good will transformed to suspicion. "Forgive me, sir, but the only transaction of my concern at present is the exchange of your gold for four of my finest brutes."

"I have in mind a more lucrative deal." I brandished the pistol I'd pilfered earlier from the citadel. "Your life for one name."

Lourde blanched at the sight of my pistol, but recovered quickly. "I have made a career of working with some truly squalid men. And I don't believe you have a killer's constitution."

"Perhaps not," I agreed. "But when my companion finishes with you, you shall wish I weren't such a pacifist." Malaika, who had silently scaled up to the second-story window, emerged from the shadows behind Lourde and clamped his impressive hands down on the proprietor's shoulders. So stricken was he with terror, and so hard did Malaika squeeze, that I quite thought his head my burst like a tomato.

"Malaika and I respectfully invite you to assist us in our endeavor." I smiled at the proprietor. "And we thank you in advance for your utmost cooperation."

In the valley of a river swift,
Four set down roots to make a home,
But when thirst insatiably cursed the land,
The great flood swept in to drown them all.

Four ghosts now stand at water's edge,
But one mourns loudest to the east,
A lonely siren calling you
To her long-since-vacant watering hole.

So tread carefully, friend, off the cornerstone
Ten paces to starboard, and thrice that to bow,
Then two down to willingly bury yourself
In the land of the dead, abandoned.

FLOODS AND SPARKS
THE SOUTH END

THE BEREFT CRY OF THAT DOG PUNCTUATED MY FITFUL sleep and the succession of nightmares that plagued it. In the worst and final dream, I found myself lying paralyzed on a pair of train tracks. With my cheek pressed against the steel rail, I couldn't look away from the dismembered corpse of the dog handler lying at my side. Soon, the noise of the approaching train grew from a susurrus into a deafening roar. My body refused to move, no matter how much I struggled. With the engine's headlights growing brighter and only seconds to go before impact, the dog handler's decapitated head rolled to the side and gazed into my soul. "There is a darkness in your heart, Sabra Tides," he croaked.

I awoke with a start to a net being dragged over my body. I defensively rolled onto my back, expecting the worst, that Horace Nox had infiltrated the Dollhouse.

But when my bleary eyes focused, I saw that it was Atlas, his face softly lit by the muted television as he tucked a blanket over me. I must have unintentionally passed out on the living room sofa while I was studying the journal page.

I had avoided the concierge desk on my way upstairs, because I knew Atlas would pepper me with questions. I was nowhere near ready to relive the gruesome confrontation in the subway.

"Oh, look," I muttered drowsily. "My overprotective roommate is home, right on time." I waved an imaginary flag. "Hooray."

Atlas held up the ninth journal page. "You must have been studying hard, since I found this stuck to your cheek."

"I hope none of the ink smudged off on my face."

Atlas's mouth opened like he was about to ask a question, but a news report on the television caught his eye. I recognized the images of the subway station that I'd narrowly escaped hours ago. According to the closed captions, a man had been crushed to death by an oncoming train after his dog had dragged him onto the tracks.

Whereas I should be relieved that the police weren't looking for a fugitive murderess, I felt a wave of nausea as the news report sucked me right back to that platform.

Atlas pointed to the TV. "Please tell me that doesn't have anything to do with ..." His sentence trailed off as I began to cry.

"He had a gun," I whispered.

I expected a lecture from Atlas, maybe an I-told-you-so for pursuing the ninth riddle without him. He surprised me by reaching out and affectionately drawing me to him. I let it happen, pressing my tear-stained cheek against his shoulder.

Atlas rubbed my back. "You know, Thomas Jefferson once wrote, 'The tree of liberty must be refreshed from time to time with the blood of patriots and tyrants.' These people who are after the Serengeti Sapphire—after you—will not hesitate to erase you from the equation. If that guy infringed on your right to live, then he deserved what he got." He grabbed the clicker and turned off the television.

I closed my eyes and listened to Atlas's heartbeat, willing my own to slow down in tandem with his. "Tell me a story," I said, desperate for a distraction. "Even a nerdy historical one."

"Why tell you a story when I can show you one." From his back pocket, Atlas produced a felt-covered jewelry box.

163

I feigned a smile. "Two days, and not only did you ask me to move in with you, but now you're trying to put a ring on it?"

"A different kind of ring." He popped open the box, revealing a tiny silver bell not much bigger than a marble, hanging on the end of a simple chain. The year 1792 was etched into the metal. "Paul Revere cast this bell," Atlas explained.

"*The* Paul Revere?" I blinked in surprise. "The same one who rode through the countryside warning the American colonists that the British were coming?"

Atlas nodded. "He was a silversmith by trade before he was a patriot. Once the Revolutionary War was over, he opened a foundry to cast bells for churches and shipyards. Some of them are still in service two centuries later. While he was skilled at forging large bells, some weighing thousands of pounds, he never quite mastered casting them on the smaller scale."

To test this theory, I rattled the bell. Instead of the high-pitched peel that I expected to hear, the clapper inside made only a dull clack. "It's broken?"

"Well, I couldn't exactly give a bell that rings properly to a girl who needs to stealthily break into historical landmarks. May I?" As Atlas slipped the chain around my neck and fastened it in the back, I could tell he was avoiding eye contact. "More than anything, I think it's a good reminder that even the tasks we expect to be easiest come with unexpected complications."

"You were an unexpected complication," I said. "Unexpected, but not unwelcome."

Atlas's hand lingered on the tiny bell as it found a home in the hollow of my neck.

Before the tension between us could reach critical mass, I averted my gaze and tapped the newest riddle. "So—any idea where our enigmatic friend is pointing to this time?"

"Yeah," he said without even looking at it. "Straight to bed. I know that you're never supposed to say this to a woman, but with all due respect: You look like hell."

"But Pop, I'm not even tired," I said, though a yawn betrayed me. As exhausted as I was, I couldn't stomach the thought of being alone right now, awake or in slumber. I sat upright, folding the blanket over my lap. "Come on, let's burn the midnight oil and solve this tricky bastard."

Atlas looked equally drained, but that nerdy, fiery spark rekindled in his eyes. I couldn't help but smile at how easily my companion was manipulated at the promise of reliving history. *Sucker.*

"Before I passed out, I think I had a lead." I pointed to the words *great flood* in the first stanza. "Now, I'm not exactly a practicing Christian, but I did learn a few things before I dropped out of Sunday parochial classes. One of those stories was about Noah's Ark."

Atlas made an intrigued humming noise. "A reference to the flood narrative in Genesis." He snapped his fingers. "So all we have to do now is find the wreckage of the Ark. Don't worry, I bet Noah crash-landed it in Boston."

I slugged him on the arm. "Not the real ark, doofus—just something related to it. It could be a monument, a painting, maybe even a piece of wood that's allegedly from the hull?"

"Not a bad start," Atlas said. "There's just one problem." On his phone, he pulled up the Museum of Fine Arts web page.

When he searched for "ark" the system retrieved more than fifty items in the museum's collections. Lithographs, oil paintings, wood engravings. And that was just *one* museum in *one* city.

"We're talking about one of the most popularly depicted episodes from the Bible. Its image appears in everything from picture books to the Sistine Chapel."

My spirit deflated. "Well, I figured out the first line. You get to narrow down our choices with the other eleven."

He patted my knee. "The king of nerds accepts your challenge. But first, we need some riddle-solving ambience."

And so it was that we curled up on the couch together, sipping hot cocoa and sharing a wool blanket. *The Nightmare Before Christmas* played in the background while we pored over the yellowed journal page. I had every intention of staying up until we solved the riddle, but bathed in the warmth of both the fireplace and Atlas's body next to me, I lost the fight to keep my eyes open. One minute, Jack Skellington was saving Halloweentown on the television, and the next I'd fallen into my first dreamless sleep in weeks.

When I awoke, I was in motion, suspended over the floor. Atlas cradled me in his arms, carrying me to the bedroom. Through the darkness, I glimpsed his square jaw in profile as he lowered me carefully into my bed. I closed my eyes again, feigning sleep, while he drew the covers up to my neck. A few seconds later, I heard his footsteps recede across the hardwood toward the door.

Without my permission, three words escaped my mouth, half-whispered into my pillow. "Stay with me ..." Then another. "Please?"

His silhouette lingered in the doorway. A longing that I hadn't anticipated coursed through my body in the seconds that followed. It was agonizing.

Maybe he hadn't heard me. Maybe he had. But then the door creaked closed, and Atlas was gone.

I emerged from my bedroom the next morning to find a stack of banana pancakes on the kitchen counter, powdered with sugar and a square of butter melting on top. Beside them,

166

Atlas had left me a laptop, with a note that read, "Tarzan go to library. Jane stay here, use glowy-book thing."

"Dork," I muttered, though I was swallowed by the memory of the previous night, drifting in and out of sleep nearly until dawn, hoping he'd reappear in my doorway.

What followed was an hour of fruitless searches on the web, combining language from the riddle with keywords like "Boston" and "Massachusetts." When none of those results panned out, I scrolled endlessly through the artwork on various museum pages, searching for details that mirrored anything encoded in the riddle.

By the time the Dollhouse's grandfather clock tolled noon, I was ready to hurl the laptop against the wall and piss on its useless electronic remains.

In my frustration, I stuffed my hands into my hoodie and yelped as something paper-cut my finger. It was the business card Jack had left for me at the museum, now stamped with my bloody fingerprint.

With no other leads to follow, I typed the name on the card into the search engine. Professor Charlotte Shepherd had an impressive résumé. Eight published works on the Revolutionary and Civil Wars, speeches delivered at White House events, collaborations on PBS documentaries. She had led the kind of industrious career as a historian that Jack would have achieved one day, if he'd been given the chance to survive past eighteen.

If Professor Shepherd had been some sort of mentor to him in his final months, she might have information crucial to his quest. And if he'd left this business card for me, he must have trusted her enough not to betray his sister.

Under the website's "Events" page, I discovered something even more promising: Professor Shepherd was hosting a public launch party for her latest book in Charlestown today.

One hour from now.

On a new sticky note, I left Atlas a short message and adhered it to the laptop screen:

Jane gone to smart woman lecture;
Tarzan can give Jane his own lecture later.

STORMING THE HILL
CHARLESTOWN, MASSACHUSETTS

CHARLOTTE SHEPHERD HAD DECIDED TO HOST HER launch party in the shadow of the Bunker Hill Monument, a 220-foot-tall granite obelisk that perched over the community of Charlestown. The towering pillar commemorated one of the first major battles during the Revolutionary War, and it immediately summoned one of my earliest memories of Jack's inexhaustible dorkiness.

Ten years ago, we had gone on a tour of the historical Freedom Trail with our dad, during one of Buck's rare attempts to do something fatherly with his children. Throughout the course of the tour, eight-year-old Jack had corrected our guide —an underemployed actor dressed as Benjamin Franklin—no fewer than seventeen times. Our father, already at his boiling point because of the summer heat and the length of time that had passed since his last beer, threatened to cut our tour short if Jack opened his mouth again. Still, as we stood on the edge of the hilltop green, craning our heads to look at the monument, Jack couldn't help himself.

"Imagine that you're a member of the colonial militia," the guide said, "outnumbered and staring down your musket as a wave of redcoats storms up Bunker Hill."

Jack had cleared his throat. "Sir—I mean, Mr. Franklin— this is Breed's Hill." He pointed north. "Bunker Hill is actually over there." An awkward silence followed, which Jack misinterpreted as an invitation to continue. "See, the British initially intended to capture Bunker Hill, but the colonial forces decided Breed's would have a better field position for them to make a stand, so the names of both the battle and the monument are really kind of a misnomer that—"

Our father had seized Jack by the ear before he could finish and dragged the two of us to Old Sully's pub. We sat silent as ghosts in the corner, sharing a basket of chicken fingers while Buck ordered a shot of Jameson and two tallboys in order to cool down.

Some days, I truly hated my father for insinuating himself into otherwise smile-worthy memories of my brother.

Today a chilly October breeze had descended on the exposed hill. I shivered in my hoodie until I reached the edge of the party and entered an unexpected bubble of warmth, courtesy of several portable space heaters hidden beneath the cocktail tables. So that was why the guests all looked so comfortable.

I snagged a flute of hot cider off a passing waiter's tray and scanned the audience. The launch party had drawn an eclectic mix of older history buffs and college students, so at least I didn't look totally out of place.

Somewhere closer to the monument, a fork clinked against a glass and the crowd fell silent. A stout African American woman stepped onto a box so that she could be seen over the crowd. Charlotte Shepherd was probably in her forties and clearly eccentric. Between her bomber jacket, flight cap, and goggles, she looked like Amelia Earhart—and it was a week too early for Halloween.

"Friends and fellow Bostonians," she began warmly in a Southern accent, her cheeks puffing out like a blowfish when she talked. "Thank you so much for joining me on this joyous day as I give birth"—She held up a copy of her latest book —"to a one-pound, eleven-inch, four-hundred-page bundle of

170

joy. He may not be a human child, but like a real infant, he has certainly kept me up late into the night for the several years."

What a cheeseball. I stared judgmentally at the college guy laughing like an idiot next to me. Maybe Professor Shepherd's students got extra credit for pretending she was funny.

"Breathe in the world around you." She wafted the air in front of her nose, then exhaled dramatically. "This city is so rich with history that you can taste it. But there are countless hidden gems in Boston's rich four-hundred-year legacy that go overlooked every day."

A projector whirred on, casting an image onto the granite monument. It depicted a stone bust of a half-woman, half-lion wearing the headdress of an Egyptian pharaoh. "Is this sphinx from the pyramids of Giza, nestled in the desert sands?" The image zoomed out to reveal green gardens and tombstones around the creature's elongated body. "Or is it a Civil War memorial a few miles away in Mount Auburn Cemetery?

"What about this?" The image on screen morphed into a picture of a busy city intersection. "Today it looks like your average street corner in Chinatown. But two hundred and fifty years ago it was the site of the Liberty Tree, a beautiful elm where brave colonial protestors first rallied against the Stamp Act and incited a revolution. A few years later, when the British laid siege to Boston, they cut the tree down and incinerated it to enrage the patriots."

Professor Shepherd flew through slide after slide. The thirteenth pew in King's Church, where death-row prisoners in the 1700s would say their final prayers before they marched to the gallows. An illustration of the Green Dragon Tavern, where the Sons of Liberty met to scheme against the redcoats.

"These tales only scratch the surface of what I chronicle in my new book, *Liberty's Roots.*" She lifted her glass. "I hope you'll join me in a toast to the centuries of history beneath our very feet, waiting to be excavated. A toast to our city."

Everyone raised their drinks. I did as well, although I rolled my eyes at the presumptuousness of someone with a drawl referring to Boston as "our city."

Over the next half an hour, I lurked at the party's fringes as guest after guest converged on Professor Shepherd, the old and young alike kissing her ass and lavishing her with questions about her research. Something about her rubbed me the wrong way, but if Jack had believed her to be an ally, I wanted to give her the benefit of the doubt, too.

Once the queue of adoring fans had abated, I approached the professor before I could second-guess myself. "Professor Shepherd? My name is … Autumn," I said, using my middle name at the last minute. "It is such an honor to meet you."

She shook my hand and grinned so broadly that I was surprised her makeup didn't crack. "A lovely name." She closed her eyes and quoted theatrically, "'Though she chide as loud as thunder / when the clouds in Autumn crack.' *Taming of the Shrew* by William Shakespeare."

"I'll add it to my Netflix queue. Look, I don't want to take too much of your time on your big day, so I'll cut to the chase. I'm here because I think my brother wanted us to meet."

The professor hummed thoughtfully. "Oh really? Is he a budding historian?"

"He was," I said shortly.

The corner of her eye twitched. Her perma-smile drooped like someone had dumped a wheelbarrow of rocks on top of it.

"I think he might have been a student of yours. Jack Tides?"

Again, that same tick of the eye. "In my sophomore seminar on the American Revolution, I have ninety-seven students—and that's just one of three courses I teach." She shook her head. "I'm afraid getting to know all of them on a

172

first-name basis is simply impossible for an aging, unreliable memory like mine. Excuse me." And just like that, she brusquely sidestepped me, walked to the makeshift bar, and greeted a fan clutching an armful of her books.

I studied her from a distance, taking in her forced smile. Like Smitty, Charlotte Shepherd had probably been intimidated into silence, but I still swelled with anger at her cowardice. A boy was dead, a student who had probably looked up to her, and she was content to let his memory disperse like smoke in the wind, when information she had could help me avenge his death?

Well, if Smitty had proved anything, it was that even the most frightened rabbits on Nox's payroll could be coerced into honesty.

I downed my glass of cider and strode purposefully through the milling guests. Professor Shepherd was mid-conversation with two students, gesticulating wildly. She didn't even notice me until I was upon her.

I leaned in so that we were nearly cheek-to-cheek and whispered into her ear, "You're a liar."

Meanwhile, my fingers stealthily closed around the keychain I'd spotted inside her jacket pocket. Without her noticing, I palmed the keys and exited the party.

It took me fifteen minutes of wandering through Charlestown, periodically clicking the unlock button on her keychain, before I heard the telltale *chirp-chirp* in front of me. It was a blue BMW parked on a side street. Its vanity plate read "L1BRTY." With a grim smile, I placed her keys on the pavement beneath the driver-side door. Then I tucked myself away in her backseat, hiding beneath a winter pea coat.

It wasn't long before I heard someone shuffling around outside, followed by a relieved sigh and the jingling of keys. The door opened and the leather seat crinkled. As Professor

Shepherd buckled herself in, I pressed a tube of lipstick into the back of her neck.

She squealed in fear and instinctively reached for her phone.

I pressed the lipstick harder into the bumpy flesh over her spine. "Don't even think about dialing nine-one-one."

Her terrified eyes tracked over to the rearview mirror. "You?" she stammered. "What do you want from me?"

"My brother thought it was so important for us to meet that he risked his life to ensure that we did. I want to know why. Lie to me, and the next owner of this car will need to get it reupholstered."

The professor exhaled. Her body visibly sagged under the weight of a memory. "Your brother came to my office two weeks ago. He was stumped on a project he was working on and wanted my historical expertise."

"He asked you to help him solve a riddle," I said. "To help him find the Serengeti Sapphire."

She cocked her head, looking surprised that I knew this much. "Yes. I told him that going after the Sapphire was a fool's errand, but he was obnoxiously persistent. I agreed to assist him merely as an academic exercise. He would only show me the first eight lines of the riddle, so I interpreted as best I could and suggested he try the Museum of Fine Arts."

I smirked despite myself. Atlas's ego would have a field day if he knew he'd solved a riddle in five minutes that had stumped a Pulitzer-winning historian.

Professor Shepherd's hands tightened around the leather steering wheel. "A few days later, the day that I found out your brother died, I came home late from a lecture at Tufts. When I walked into my kitchen, I knew something was out of place. There was a black object hanging on my fridge. It ..." Her voice broke. "It was my cat, Wally. Someone had dipped him in tar, covered him in feathers, and strung him up by the tail."

The image made me want to vomit. I knew from conversations with Jack that tarring and feathering was a form of torture popular during the Revolutionary War.

"Next thing I knew, someone wrapped a hand around my mouth. She forced me to stare at my poor dead Wally and rasped into my ear, 'This is what happens when you interfere with history.' Then she made me sit down and write out the riddle Jack had shown me as best as I could remember."

"By chance was this cretin high as a satellite and sporting a pair of metal horns?" I asked.

The professor nodded. "I could only remember a few phrases, and the bitch did kill my cat, so I fabricated some lines, enough to keep her walking around in circles in the museum for a few days. When it was all written out, I figured I was a goner, but she said I would stay alive as long as I was useful to her boss. That I'd be a 'historical consultant.' And if I went to the police or tried to flee the city, she would—how did she put it? —*personally flay me and pin my hide to the State House steps.*"

The professor was lucky she'd believed Aries. Detective Grimshaw had ears everywhere.

Something she'd said earlier had been troubling me. "Why did you say that searching for the Sapphire is a fool's errand?"

"Oh, come on," she muttered. "The Sapphire is a hoax—an elaborate and impressive one to be sure, but a ruse nonetheless."

While I was committed to this quest, I knew very little about the journal's origins. "Convince me," I challenged her.

"For starters, the riddles were added over a century after the journal was originally written."

"What?" Anyone could see that the riddles and the journal entries had been written by two different hands. Was it possible that the authors had existed a lifetime apart?

"The journal itself originally came into the possession of the Boston Athenaeum library in the early 1900s," the professor continued. "Historians authenticated the existence of Cumberland Warwick, but only the most superstitious zealots believed the story to be anything but a folktale. A Confederate deserter helping an African tea farmer transport a magical plant to heal his enslaved son's sickle cell anemia—seriously? Still, it was kept on display beneath a glass case in the Athenaeum for many decades, until one night in the 1970s, when a thief broke into the library and stole it."

So that theft couldn't have been Nox, unless he'd been a really enterprising fetus.

"The Athenaeum assumed it would never see the manuscript again, that it had been pawned on the black market. One morning, a curator came to work and discovered something peculiar: the first page of the journal, torn from its bindings and stowed back in the glass case as though it had never left. Even stranger, someone had scribbled a poem on the reverse side, which had previously been blank."

My soul sank into despair. If this was all true, then the riddles could be nothing more than forgeries, the graffiti of some historically inclined trickster. Part of me had truly believed that the quest had been left by Cumberland Warwick himself, or at least someone close to him who might have kept the Sapphire alive all these years.

The rest of the story seemed pretty obvious to me. At some point, Nox had stolen that first riddle from the Athenaeum and started following the clues. My brother had caught wind of this and hijacked the quest. We know how that journey ended.

I'd been so lost in my distress that I didn't notice Professor Shepherd turn around. She closed her hand gently around the tube of lipstick in my hand. I expected anger from her, but her expression had softened. "Who's dying?"

So Jack had omitted that part when he enlisted her help. "My sister. She's not doing so well. Cancer in her lymph nodes."

176

"I'm sorry to hear that," Charlotte said, and despite all her showboating and panache, I believed her. "Here's the best advice I can give you: Go spend time with your sister. Make every day count. Don't waste it chasing after white whales."

Her words cut deep because they echoed the excruciating questions that had been haunting me. What if I *was* wasting time I could be sharing with Echo? What if this quest was total bullshit, a dead end that was stealing memories I could be creating with my sister? What if Echo blamed me for running out on her and she took a turn for the worse while I was away? What if her last impression of me was that I had abandoned her during her time of need?

But it would be even worse to turn back empty-handed now.

And as long as Nox, Grimshaw, and Aries were still alive, they would stop at nothing to "contain" me, which meant that I would be putting Echo and Mom in grave danger every time I set foot in that hospital.

"Can I trust you?" I asked quietly.

In response, Charlotte folded down the car's sun visor. There were a series of photographs there, all of the professor with the same woman. In the last picture, the woman lay in a hospital bed, her face gaunter, her hair shorn, her smile duller, with Charlotte's lips pressed to her forehead. A prayer card accompanied the final picture, along with a string of rosary beads.

Charlotte touched her fingers to a faded picture, back when the two women couldn't have been much older than me. "I've lived a mostly selfish existence. But when you lose someone that your world revolved around, you realize we're all in this together."

I pulled out my phone and showed her a screenshot of the latest riddle's first eight lines. It was a risk to show her even this much, but with Echo's health on the decline, time was a luxury I didn't have.

Professor Shepherd's eyes darted across the screen, absorbing each line. When she reached the end of the second stanza, a smile played over her lips.

"Dana," she said. "Dana, Massachusetts."

An entire town was a dispiritingly large target, but hopefully Atlas could decode the final four lines into something more specific. "You're absolutely sure this time? You didn't exactly ace the first riddle."

"Far more certain than I was before. Besides"—She tapped my hand— "this time I know what's at stake."

After thanking her for the lead and apologizing for pretending to hold her at gunpoint, I stood on the curb, watching her BMW speed away. I couldn't blame her for wanting to put as much distance between us as possible. I dialed Atlas and he picked up on the first ring, immediately launching into a frustrated rant about all the dead ends he'd reached at the library.

I cut him off. "What do you know about Dana, Massachusetts?"

There was a long silence on the other end. I could practically hear the cogs click as they turned in his head. "Holy shit," he whispered. "Put on a coat. I'll pick you up at the condo in ten."

I winced, glancing at the street sign above me. "Actually …"

Fifteen minutes later, Atlas's pickup careened around the corner and screeched to a halt next to me. As I climbed into the passenger seat, he nodded toward the Bunker Hill Monument. "Do I want to know?"

I shook my head. I reached for the GPS on his dashboard and started to type the letters "D-A-N-A."

Atlas chuckled and pulled the truck away from the curb, heading back toward the interstate. "Don't bother. You won't find it in there."

Sure enough, the GPS returned with zero results. Even though I knew he was absolutely dying to tell me, I asked, "And why, oh wise King Nerd, does the magical black dashboard box not know the route to Dana?"

His eyes flashed with excitement. "Because Dana doesn't exist!"

Meanwhile, in the North End

Charlotte Shepherd navigated the tightly packed tables of the restaurant *Ombra*. Around her, couples flirted and clumsily mispronounced the Italian dishes on the menu, to the disdain of their black-tied waiters. They were all having a great old time, unaware that the woman solemnly walking past them was about to do a truly deplorable thing.

When the professor parted a curtain and stepped out onto *Ombra*'s private outdoor grotto, she found herself alone with the one man she'd hoped she would never see again. Horace Nox sat at a wrought-iron table, a small feast laid out before him. Two gaslit torches cast a bubble of heat onto the patio, warding off the autumn chill, but Charlotte felt no warmth as she took the seat across from him.

Horace didn't look up as her chair's metal feet grated over the bricks. He twirled the fork in his hand and speared a slab of salami off the antipasti plate. She watched, disgusted, as he chewed, his teeth stained magenta from the half-empty bottle of wine on the table.

Eventually, he picked up a bright red lobster off a plate and dangled it in front of her. "You look famished, Charlotte. How about some surf and turf?" He brandished the crustacean's red claws, a child playing with his food.

The professor wrinkled her nose and leaned away. "I'm allergic, so I think I'll pass."

"A shellfish allergy, in a city built on the blood and sweat of fishermen?" He wagged a finger. "Now *that* should be a crime."

Charlotte was sick of Nox's cat-and-mouse conversations. It was time to cut the bullshit. "I want some guarantees," she demanded. "You tell your minions to stay away from my daughter's dorm, especially that psycho with the horns. I don't ever want them within a square mile of her again."

He finally made eye contact. "Done. If your information pans out of course."

So she told him every detail from Sabra's visit, including the destination that the poor girl was probably headed at this very moment. And when Charlotte was done, she could only think: *God forgive me.*

Nox regarded her coolly as he poured two glasses of red wine. When he slid one of them across the table, she didn't lift a finger to touch it. She wasn't going to break bread with this monster.

The crime lord shook his head. "You call yourself a historian, yet you reject the opportunity to taste history when it's put right in front of you?" He held up the scuffed bottle. "This Syrah comes from a vineyard in Tunisia that's over two thousand years old. That means it's older than *Jesus*, for Christ's sake—literally! The Phoenicians planted grapes outside Carthage, on the banks of the Bagradas. When the Romans destroyed the city during the Punic Wars, the vineyard miraculously survived and flourished as the wind scattered Carthage's ashes over the river valley. So to ingest this wine is to taste the ruin of an entire empire."

Nox picked up a piece of focaccia and swabbed it in a saucer of green liquid, drawing lazy circles while the porous bread soaked it in. "Then there's this olive oil. It's squeezed from the olives of one of the oldest trees in the world, an *Olea europaea* that has refused to die, even as civilizations rose and fell around it."

"If I wanted a history lesson," Charlotte said, "I would read one of my own books." Still, parched from the stress of condemning a young girl to die, she absently picked up her glass and took a long gulp, as though she were chugging a beer instead of a priceless wine that sold for a thousand dollars an ounce.

"The point is," Nox went on, "that if you want to live to be three thousand years old, you have to be able to thrive in the midst of destruction, to stonily watch the world crumble around you. That's why, in another three millennia, that vineyard will still be producing wine, and that olive tree will still be making oil, and I'll still be sitting on a gilded throne."

Charlotte had started sweating profusely under the gas lamps. "You've got the narrative all twisted around. Those plants have lived as long as they have because *they're fucking plants*. They don't make enemies and they don't start wars." She swallowed hard and tugged at the neck of her cardigan to let in more air. "You want to sit at the top of the world, Horace? If there's one lesson you should take a way from seven thousand years of human history, it's that every throne is a death sentence. And the bigger the throne, the bigger the ..." The professor cleared her throat once, twice. "The bigger the ..." The word 'fall' never left her lips because her throat had completely closed up.

Horace's taut face didn't even twitch as she futilely gasped for air. "You look feverish," he said. "Maybe it's the gas lamps. Or maybe I swabbed the inside of your wine glass with oyster juice before you sat down."

Charlotte's eyes bulged. She desperately fumbled for the clasp of her pants pocket, where she kept an epinephrine pen in case of emergencies.

In a flash, Nox was out of his seat and kneeling next to her. His hands fastened down on hers, clamping them to her thighs.

She wriggled to free herself. The EpiPen, her ticket to oxygen, was so tantalizingly close.

Nox brought his sallow face up to hers, until the enlarged pores on his nose looked deep as wishing wells. If she'd been able to breathe, she could have smelled the sickness on him. "My men will never go near your daughter again," he promised. "But unfortunately, neither will you."

The professor's eyes rolled back into her head. After a minute of convulsions, after her brain starved for air that would never come, neurons screaming and dying, her body finally went still and her head drooped. When Nox released her hands, her arms unfolded limply to either side of her.

Nox straightened his tie. On his way back through the restaurant, he found his waiter, Armando. "Some vagrant crashed my dinner, but I'm not one to turn away a hungry soul. You should have seen her eyes light up when she tried the oysters!" Nox slipped a crisp twenty into the waiter's breast pocket. "Check on her again in fifteen minutes, and if she wants anything else, put it on my tab."

"Absolutely, sir." Armando bowed with a chipper smile.

When Nox reached the street, his livery driver rolled the Cadillac up to the curb. As soon as he was in the privacy of the backseat, Nox speed-dialed Louis Grimshaw. "Good evening, detective," he said. "I'm going to need you to drop whatever you're doing and visit an imaginary town."

GHOST TOWN
PETERSHAM, MASSACHUSETTS

IT BEGAN TO SNOW ON OUR DRIVE WEST, A GIFT FROM New England's notoriously temperamental weather. With the flurries whirling around Atlas's truck, I felt strangely safe for once. Even back at the Dollhouse, I experienced a low, steady hum of anxiety, that instinct that if I stayed still for one second too long, Nox would batter down the doors and slaughter us both.

But for now, as the world rushed by our sixty-mile-an-hour snow globe, it felt like maybe, just maybe, this quest had the possibility of coming to a safe and happy conclusion.

Atlas gave me a crash course on the history of Dana as he drove. His statement about the town being imaginary had been slightly misleading. While it was true that Dana no longer existed, eighty years ago it had been very real.

In the decades following the Civil War, the population of Massachusetts boomed, increasing the demand for drinking water. Fearing an inevitable shortage, the state had conceived an extraordinary plan: They would divert the Swift River into a nearby valley to create a manmade reservoir vastly bigger than New England had ever seen.

To do it, they would have to flood four towns.

The townships of Prescott, Enfield, Greenwich, and Dana were all condemned to be swallowed by the river in April of 1938. People evacuated the houses their families had inhabited for generations. Graveyards were disinterred, the bodies reburied

183

elsewhere. Churches, schoolhouses, hotels, roads, and railroad tracks—over the seven years it took for the Quabbin Reservoir to fill the valley, all of these were drowned beneath more than four hundred *billion* gallons of water.

In my seventeen years as a Boston resident, I'd never wondered where the water that I used every day to drink, brush my teeth, and shower originated.

Atlas's history lesson raised one alarming question. "If Dana is at the bottom of the reservoir, then what are we going to do? Scuba dive to find the next riddle?"

"I rented a submersible," Atlas replied. When he got no laugh from me, he sighed. "Part of the town highlands are still above water, on a peninsula that juts out into the reservoir. The foundations of the buildings are all that remain of Dana, but if we're interpreting the riddle correctly, I'm banking on there being a little something more than history buried within the town limits."

Eventually, Atlas pulled the truck off the highway onto a woodsy backroad. Modern-day Petersham, Massachusetts, had absorbed Dana's remnants. It was practically a ghost town itself, though a beautiful one. The houses on the "main road" were few and far between, separated by long stretches of woods. Having grown up in Dorchester, where the streets were so densely packed that you could reach out your window and touch your neighbor's house, it was hard to believe that a place like this existed only an hour away. Ten minutes driving through this town and I could already feel time itself slowing down.

Atlas launched into yet another impromptu history lesson when we passed the town green. Shortly after the Revolutionary War, in the 1780s, a rebel band of subsistence farmers had struck out against the state, taking up arms to protest the oppressive tax and debt collection that threatened their way of life. After a failed attempt to seize the local armory, Shay's

Rebellion set up camp in Petersham, only to be ambushed and defeated by the militia.

"It's funny," I said after he finished the story. "It's been two hundred and fifty years, and the have-nots are still protesting against the haves."

Atlas grunted in agreement. "The only difference is that now we do it with strongly worded Facebook posts instead of muskets and cannon fire."

Atlas pulled over onto a dirt road and parked the car. A series of metal rods obstructed the path ahead to automobile traffic, so our journey would have to continue on foot.

After raiding the bed of his pickup, Atlas found what he was looking for: two shovels, one of which he tossed to me.

I caught the wooden handle and gazed skeptically at Atlas. "So you just happen to keep a collection of shovels in your truck? Is this the part where I ask where the bodies are buried?"

Atlas sheepishly scratched the back of his head. "I compete in sandcastle-building competitions every summer. Not the coolest of hobbies, but it's something I did with my sister when she was younger. It seemed wrong to stop after she was gone."

Every time I thought Atlas couldn't get more interesting, I learned something new and weird about him. And I knew all too well what it was like to hold onto someone's ghost. "I mean this in the most complimentary way possible," I said, "but you are one big labyrinth of a human being."

He considered this. "I think if you boil me down to what drives me—to what I truly want—you'll find I'm not so complicated at all."

"And what *do* you want, Atlas?"

He evasively rifled around in his truck until he found an electric lantern. As the bulb flickered and cast an orange orb of light out into the snowy darkness, I saw uncertainty in his eyes. "Right now?" he answered. "To dig."

185

We walked in near silence for about a mile. The light powder accumulating on the trail dampened the sound of our footfalls. The maples lining the path had spouts hammered into them, where local farmers had tapped for syrup. At one point, I knelt and scooped a handful of loose topsoil, stuffing it into my back pocket for good luck. When Atlas raised an eyebrow, I explained, "A ritual my brother taught me. For safe passage."

The forest eventually gave way to a clearing. The entrance was marked with a disquieting, weather-faded stone that read, "*Site of Dana Common, 1801–1938. To all those who sacrificed their homes and way of life.*" It was like seeing a grave marker for an entire town.

A gunshot sounded deep in the woods and I instinctively jumped toward Atlas, trying to flatten him to the ground. He caught me in his broad arms, and to my surprise, he smiled. "Probably just some local hunters. But it's adorable to know that you would have taken a bullet for me."

"Or maybe I intended to use you as a human shield." Again, I felt that unwelcome urge to let him hold me longer than necessary. I slipped out of his grasp, embarrassed.

Not much remained of the village once known as Dana, just a creepy series of cellar holes overgrown with weeds. Atlas paused beside a deteriorating foundation that was larger than the others. "When we were under the assumption that the riddle involved Noah's Ark, I figured *watering hole* referred to where the animals would go to drink. In actuality, it meant where *humans* go to drink." He spread his arms and gazed around at imaginary walls. "This used to be the Eagle Hotel, which in its early days served as the village tavern."

"Do you think this bar was owned by a murderous, immortality-seeking mobster, too?" I asked.

"I think you just described most entrepreneurs." Atlas took

out the ninth riddle and held it under the lantern's glow. "Now, this part—*ten paces to starboard and thrice that to bow*—sounded like it was describing the dimensions of a ship. But since we're clearly on land, *starboard* and *bow* could indicate directions on a compass rose, east and north, respectively. And the *paces* mean literal strides that we're supposed to take."

"Isn't it a little imprecise to count steps?" I challenged him. "You, me, and the crazy riddler probably all have different lengths to our strides."

Atlas's face got that look like he was boiling over with excitement at the prospect of schooling me. "It's incredibly precise. The Roman *passus*, or two steps, is equivalent to exactly one-point-four-eight meters. With some simple arithmetic and the handy digital tape measure app on my phone ..."

We began at the defunct hotel's northeastern corner, where the cornerstone was laid according to Freemasonry, and the starting point according to the riddle's final stanza: *So tread carefully, friend, off the cornerstone.* From there, we walked due east, crossing the grassless path that had once been Main Street. Fifty feet later, the red light on Atlas's phone blinked green, and we rotated ninety degrees to face north. This time we traveled for nearly half a football field, crossing into a broad clearing that was delineated with stone fence posts.

We were in Dana's old graveyard, the one where the bodies and headstones had all been dug up and moved before the flood.

Only something else was buried here now.

Deep into the field, the digital tape measure pinged again. I dropped to my knees and swept aside the thin layer of snow, revealing a stone half-buried in the earth. It was charcoal gray, with white veins of quartz spiderwebbed across the surface.

"That's soapstone," Atlas said. "They used to mine it in quarries not too far from here."

Curious, I carefully worked the tip of my shovel under the stone's edge. With a little leverage, the small boulder popped free and flipped onto its back like a helpless turtle.

Its underside had been polished near smooth, except for five letters carved into the surface.

Chini.

Atlas ran a search on his phone for the word. "It's Swahili. And it means *down.*"

Neither of us needed to be told twice. It was hard work—the soil beneath the top layer was dense and I had to use the heel of my boot to drive the shovel head downward. Atlas and I fell into a natural rhythm of *spear, scoop, toss, repeat.* The hole beneath us deepened and widened, as the mound of excavated earth grew taller beside us.

Six feet down, the tip of my shovel struck something hard, disengaging me from auto-pilot. Eager to excavate the object but knowing that my shovel could damage it, I scraped away the remaining earth with my bare hands. I exposed more of the same soapstone we'd seen before, this time on an item roughly the size and shape of a bowling pin.

It was a bottle.

Once I'd climbed out of the hole with our prize, I let some snow melt in my hand and scrubbed away the bottle's coating of dirt. An image had been delicately etched into the soapstone, the leaves and petals of an orchid.

The top was plugged with a stopper, which it took Atlas's muscular forearms to finally uncork. I cast the lantern light down the bottleneck until we saw what we were looking for: an old paper, the same color and texture of the other journal pages, rolled into a tight scroll.

Joy can be a powerful intoxicant. And in that moment, as Atlas and I both laughed excitedly, overwhelmed with relief, our chests still heaving hard from the exhaustion of all that digging,

Atlas took one curious look at me in the lantern glow. Then he rushed forward, cupped my face in his hands, and kissed me.

I was so caught off-guard that I nearly fell into the gaping hole we'd dug. Atlas pulled away as suddenly as he'd swooped in, his jaw hung open in shock. He looked as surprised as I was about the kiss and more than a little guilty. "I …" he started. "I'm sorry. That was wrong. You're my dead roommate's little sister and I'm here to protect you, not to …" He trailed off, lost for words.

When I finally regained control of my tongue, I said, "It's depraved and you should be ashamed of yourself." I dropped the bottle into the snow and walked determinedly toward him. "Do it again."

This time, there was no holding back. Any restraint had been dynamited away and our lips met in a kiss far deeper than the chasm we'd just scored into the earth, all of the *want* and *need,* and not a whisper of the *shouldn't.* It was wild and lusty, lips in perpetual motion, hearts thundering, hands roving, teeth occasionally bumping.

It was me who finally put a hand to his chest and pushed him away just enough for me to get air. My fingers lingered on my raw lips, feeling the ghost of Atlas's touch everywhere. We began to laugh again, our foreheads touching as we gripped each other, as though one of us might blow away in the cold wind. When I could bear the separation no longer, I grabbed a fistful of his shirt and yanked him down on top of me. Together, we collapsed against the mound of dirt we'd created.

We'd just hit the ground when our embrace was interrupted by the crack of a gunshot.

This one, unlike those I'd heard before, was not intended for a deer.

It was meant for the two of us.

PREDATOR, PREY
DANA, MASSACHUSETTS

THE EARTHEN MOUND BESIDE US EXPLODED, SENDING a cloud of dirt spraying into our faces.

As time slowed down, a number of things happened. Atlas and I tangled with each other, our instincts both to shelter the other's body with our own. His brute strength won out and he shoved me roughly forward, urging me to my feet and toward the line of trees ten yards away. Through the haze of earth, snow, and darkness, I saw the outline of a harsh-faced man briskly marching across the old cemetery toward us. It was Detective Grimshaw, and he was loading another shell into his break-action shotgun.

I slipped through Atlas's grasp, running back toward danger to retrieve the bottle. My hand had barely wrapped around its soapstone neck when Atlas seized me by the waist and propelled me away from Grimshaw.

We both raced across the cemetery, only a few paces apart, and hit the edge of the forest as the second shotgun blast went off. The slug detonated the tree trunk three feet to my left, so close that a barrage of splinters pelted my cheek.

As we penetrated deeper into the forest, riding a surge of fear and adrenaline, I came to several concerning conclusions. First, losing Grimshaw in the woods was a hopeless endeavor. The snow was proving to be our greatest enemy, preserving a perfect record of our footsteps through the trees. While pedicabbing had sculpted my legs into peak physical shape, Atlas was bulkier and lacked my endurance. He was already starting to lag behind my pace—five feet, ten feet, then fifteen.

The trees spaced out in front of us and we abruptly hit the rocky shore of the Quabbin Reservoir. We cut a course along the waterline, but our new tact left us even more exposed to the hunter who was still in pursuit.

Ahead of us, a gnarled oak tree stood resolute on the banks of the Quabbin, clinging to its foliage late into autumn. Seized by a desperate idea, I slowed down to fall into rhythm beside Atlas. "If you want us both to live, you need to follow my next instructions exactly," I said breathlessly. "I need you to keep running and don't look back, no matter what I do." Atlas opened his mouth to protest, but I cut him off. "Trust me. Remember who's got the street smarts."

Before he could argue, I dropped behind him, following his footsteps precisely through the snow so we would only leave a singular trail. As our path drew closer to the gnarled oak, I cast the soapstone bottle into the snow, took a deep breath, and leapt for one of the tree's low-lying branches.

Success. I steadied myself against the trunk and rapidly ascended its spiraling limbs. My bicycle-toe boots, while less than ideal for running, helped me to find traction on the slippery bark.

Atlas must have had to fight all of his protective instincts not to turn around, but when I peered out through the foliage, I saw him racing up the shoreline as I'd instructed him.

I didn't stop until I'd reached a perch twenty feet up, and not a moment too soon. Detective Grimshaw plunged out of the forest onto the reservoir banks, hot on the trail of our footprints. He spotted the bottle containing the riddle where I'd abandoned it and paused beneath my tree, taking the bait.

Meanwhile, up the shore, Atlas was losing steam. In his exhaustion, his foot snagged on a stone, sending him tumbling over the beach.

Grimshaw sensed an imminent victory. He raised his shotgun and glared down the sights. I could practically feel his finger settling on the trigger as he drew a bead on Atlas, who was frantically clambering to his feet.

So I pounced out of the tree, setting myself on a fast downward trajectory toward Grimshaw.

The rustle of the leaves gave me away and the detective snapped the shotgun barrel skyward, ready to fire. But gravity was my ally and I hit him like a cannonball before he could get a shot off. Pain exploded in me as we collided. Somewhere in the tangle of bodies, the top of his head rammed into my chest, and one of my ankles twisted torturously beneath me as I landed. I crumpled to the rocky shore.

Grimshaw got it even worse, though. The sheer velocity of my impact knocked the weapon from his hands and cast him backward into the shallows of the Quabbin.

I lifted my head from the snowy ground and saw the detective, dazed as he was, scrambling on his hands and knees toward where his shotgun had landed on the water's edge.

I spotted the soapstone bottle in the snow between the detective and me. Knowing that Grimshaw would never miss at this close proximity, I sprung forward and scooped up the bottle. The detective let out a victory cry as his fumbling fingers found the shotgun's stock and yanked it toward him.

He whipped the barrel around to face me, right as I cocked the bottle back and took a major-league swing at his head.

Crack. The impact of the bottle against his jaw was so loud that at first I thought the shotgun had gone off. It resonated through my fingers and up my arms. The light behind the detective's eyes burst like a broken tungsten filament.

With that, he collapsed cheek-down into the shallows, his dislocated jaw hanging open idiotically. Three bloody, broken teeth bobbed to the surface of the water next to his face.

Lumbering footsteps snapped me from my stupor, a winded Atlas returning to the scene of the crime.

Not really sure what else to say, I held up the bottle. I'd hit Grimshaw with it so hard that the bottom had snapped clean off. The tenth riddle poked out of the base. "I, uh, opened it."

Still panting hard, Atlas wrapped his arms around me and I squeezed him right back. This was my fourth brush with death in as many days, yet there was something infinitely more terrifying when someone you cared for was in the crosshairs.

Atlas nodded to the body in the water. "Before we even take a crack at that riddle, we should probably figure out what to do with our dead assassin friend." He flinched when Grimshaw's back rose upward in a sudden convulsing breath. "Make that half-dead assassin friend."

"Half-dead cop, actually," I corrected him. Atlas's face blanched. "He's on Nox's payroll. Grimshaw covered up my brother's murder in exchange for Nox paying off his gambling debts to some Armenian bookie. Must have been a rough week at the blackjack table if he was willing to hunt us down in cold blood for the riddle."

I stepped into the shallows and pressed my boot to Grimshaw's spine. As I applied pressure, a wheezy breath escaped his mouth. All it would take was a slight turn of the detective's head and he'd drown in three inches of water without ever waking up.

"Sabra," Atlas said softly. "I stand behind you no matter how you want to handle this. That coward tried to shoot us in the back, and I have no doubt the world would be a better place without him. But if his body turns up somewhere, we could be one DNA sample away from having both Nox *and* the entire Boston Police Department after us."

He was right, of course. This forest was one big playground of forensics evidence. Grimshaw also didn't magically teleport to the reservoir, which meant we probably had a car to get rid of, too. One that could have a tracking device installed in it.

On the other hand, we couldn't leave him to wake up with a broken jaw and let him seek vengeance. We had no idea how he'd traced us here, and worst of all, he'd seen me with Atlas. It was only a matter of time before the Dollhouse was compromised.

What we needed was somebody to clean up our mess for us.

When I saw the answer, I whipped out my cell phone and dialed Rufus.

Atlas narrowed his eyes. "What's with the light bulb hanging over your head, Thomas Edison? Who are you calling?"

"The maid," I replied.

After three rings, Rufus picked up. Our connection crackled as wind whipped past the receiver on his end—he must have been on his pedicab downtown—so I was grateful when his singsong voice came on the line. "You've reached the Flintstones Taxi Service, how can I yabba-dabba help you?"

"It's Sabra. Look, I'm sort of in a bind yet again. I need to obtain a private number that's going to be next to impossible to come by, and I need it fast. Think you can do me another solid?"

He scoffed. "A single, measly phone number? Piece of crème brûlée. One sec while I take care of something first." On the other end, I heard Rufus slam on the bike's brakes and curtly say to his passengers, *"Get out, losers."* His fares started to protest about not being at their destination yet. *"Yeah, well this taxi just ran out of gas. And you're wearing Yankees jerseys in the wrong town."* He came back on the line. "Okay, babycakes, lay that name on me."

I gave it to him, knowing full well he wasn't going to like it.

194

He didn't. "Jesus, Sabra. I was really hoping you just wanted the number of some guy you met at the mall. But this dude is straight-up bad news."

"Believe it or not, he won't be the most dangerous bastard I've dealt with this week. In fact, I don't think he'll even crack the top five. Text me that number as soon as you get it." I hung up before he could try to talk me out of it.

I returned my attention to the other time-sensitive issue: Grimshaw. After flipping him over and searching his pockets, amidst a collection of faded stubs from the Suffolk Downs racetrack, I found two particularly useful items: his car keys and a small bottle of chloroform. He must have been prepared to capture us with more "peaceful" measures, but decided to save himself the trouble of taking hostages when he'd seen that we'd unearthed the tenth riddle.

Grimshaw was already starting to moan and stir. I uncorked the chloroform, soaked the edge of his coat with it, and held the wool over his mouth until the chemical fumes stilled his body.

Atlas and I positioned ourselves on either side of him and hoisted his body out of the water, with me holding his ankles and Atlas carrying him under the armpits. Together, we began the arduous journey of hauling the detective through the woods.

Fortunately for us, Grimshaw had circumvented the front gates and driven his unmarked Crown Vic down the pedestrian path, which meant we didn't have to carry him another mile back to the main road. I made a quick stroke on his key fob, popping open the trunk, and we unceremoniously dumped the bastard on top of his spare tire. "Let me do the honors," I said, then slammed the trunk door hard.

My phone vibrated. Rufus had come through with the number, which he appended with a final warning: *Stay safe, little dingo.*

I clicked *Send*, even though I knew I could be making a game-ending mistake. I'd assaulted a cop and crammed his body into a state-issued police vehicle, and now I was about to entrust this information with a total stranger. A disreputable stranger no less. In my panic, I contemplated hanging up.

Georg Tankian, the Armenian racketeer from Watertown, picked up before I could chicken out. "This better be important," he said in his thick accent, without introduction. "You're interrupting ninth inning in game seven, and Red Sox are down by two points. It is real nail-biter."

I swallowed hard and tried to restore the confident edge to my voice. "The gift I'm about to offer you is better than a World Series ring," I said.

I heard the crunch of leather as Georg leaned forward in his seat. "Who is this? Girl Scout? This is private number."

No turning back now. "This is the Girl Scout who has a detective named Louis Grimshaw stuffed in the trunk of a car." I let this sink in. "I've heard he's been a bit of a pain in your ass?"

Georg made an ambivalent noise. "He has not simply been pain in ass—he is full-blown hemorrhoid. However, his master pays his dues now, so let that North Shore trash keep betting on lame horses. Goodbye, crazy girl stranger."

"Wait!" I barked. I had to think fast. What did Georg want that I could offer him? I had researched him after his name came up during my clandestine golf course meeting with Smitty. Georg owned the Mad Raven nightclub, one of the Nightingale's chief competitors. Nox had won the bidding war for the last slice of waterfront real estate in the Seaport, leaving Georg to build in a less desirable location.

Which meant that Georg and Nox were rivals.

I smiled darkly. Atlas, who was leaning against Grimshaw's car, furrowed his snow-covered brow as if to say *Oh, God, what could you possibly be doing now?*

"What if I told you," I said, "that his master wouldn't be around to pay his dues in seventy-two hours—which would leave the Nightingale ownerless. Do I have your attention now?"

A pregnant pause. "Hypothetically."

In my research on Georg, I'd learned that he had three daughters, the youngest of whom was Echo's age. As illegitimate as Georg Tankian's enterprises in Boston might be, he was still a father. For me to persuade him to help me, I was going to have to play to his more sensitive side.

"Here's the story, as concise as I can tell it," I said. "My eight-year-old sister has cancer. If Horace Nox gets his way, she could die in the very near future." On the other end, Georg grumbled a string of what must have been Armenian curses, which if translated into English would have probably made even my father say a Hail Mary. "I'm going to take Nox out of the game to make sure that doesn't happen. But for me to have the freedom to do that, this cop car—along with the detective in its trunk, who very recently tried to murder me—needs to disappear." I walked him through a rough plan that I'd concocted on the spot, one that would allow Grimshaw to survive, but make him wish he hadn't. His credibility would be destroyed and his ability to retaliate would be neutralized.

Georg took an unnerving amount of time to respond, perhaps while he tried to intuit whether I was another cop trying to entrap him. I knew I'd checkmated him when he muted the Red Sox game in the background. "And, again hypothetically, where would this troublesome vehicle be located?"

I told him.

"The last time I saw Horace," Georg said slowly, "I invited him out to brunch at my finest restaurant. I figure, we both have respectable business to run in same town, so why not be civil and bury hatchet. Do you know what that Irish punk called me? Gypsy. *Gypsy!* That's not right country. Not even right side of *Black Sea*." He sighed. "Well, crazy girl stranger, I am no criminal. That said, sometimes when people forget keys in ignition, cars get stolen. This world we live in is—how you say?—*bananas*. Have lovely evening."

While Georg had, outright, admitted to nothing, he had surreptitiously given me the green light. "Go Sox," I added.

As I hung up, a pounding came from the Crown Vic's trunk. Grimshaw's muffled screaming followed, but the words came out of his broken jaw as warbling, unintelligible mush, like his mouth was stuffed with cotton balls.

"Someone sounds happy," Atlas said.

I inserted the key into the ignition, then wiped down everything I'd touched. "If you think he's excited now, just wait until Georg sends an Armenian chauffeur to pick him up."

Atlas was clearly ready to book it out of the area, but I crouched at the bumper of the Crown Vic. Grimshaw continued to holler inside the trunk until I pounded on it to shut him up. "Never forget," I said sharply to the keyhole, "that I showed you mercy when I could have drowned you like the rat you are. And if you ever do anything to jeopardize my sister's health again, I will make what your bookie is about to do to you feel like a ride on Splash Mountain."

Immediately, Grimshaw's screams resumed, more pleading this time, all vowels and no consonants, beseeching me to spare him from the wrath of Georg Tankian.

As we walked down the lightless path back to the truck, with the wind stirring the snow around us, Atlas said, "You are one scary-ass chick, Sabra Tides."

My hand slipped into his and squeezed until I felt like the lifeline of his palm had been tattooed into my skin. "That's what he gets for interrupting the best kiss of my life."

Dearest Adelaide,

I write from a bed of ashes. It can only be by divine intervention that I have survived to share my tale, to watch dusk fall upon a city in cinders. Yet if God indeed had a hand in today's events, I must believe that He is a cruel purveyor of circumstance, doling out miracle and tragedy in equal measure.

For three days, Malaika and I journeyed tirelessly from Charleston to Columbia. There we would find Magnolia Black, the plantation to which the craven Gold Coast proprietor had sold young Jaro. We traveled fifty miles a day, until our soles grew rife with blisters. We clung to the riverbanks, from the Cooper to the Congaree, using the waters as our guide. At night, Malaika slept with one arm always around the Sapphire. All the while, I prayed that neither illness nor the barbarous cotton fields had prematurely snatched Jaro from this earth.

On the third day, we emerged from the cypresses to the most disconcerting of visions: Columbia was in flames. Smoke cloaked the sky in curtains. Heavy winds fanned the fire through the heart of the city. By whom it was set, whether by retreating Confederates or Union sabotage, remained unclear, but the magnitude of its rampant destruction was incontestable.

The chaos intensified as we navigated the city streets. Everywhere, citizens and soldiers alike had erupted in riotous frenzy. Looters smashed windows. Men staggered through the streets, bottles in hand, drunk from tavern raids. The State House burned while a mob darted into the flames to steal from its wealth of luxuries. It was this pandemonium that should have portended the grievous calamity to follow.

Upon our arrival at Magnolia Black, fire raged ungovernably through the plantation. On the manse's burning porch, the field supervisor brandished his whip to ward off a cluster of liberated slaves. In time, he was overrun by the men he had long subjugated. I could only watch in macabre stupefaction as they strung him up from the rafters with his own scourge.

We skirted the scene of the lynching and set a course for the slave quarters, which were in dire straits. The shanty was immersed in an all-devouring inferno, transforming the space beneath the cheap tin roof into an oven and fanning us with an unbearable heat. Malaika bellowed Jaro's name. His calls were met with no reply through the smoky penumbra.

Before I could caution him otherwise, my companion thrust the Serengeti Sapphire into my hands and plunged into the conflagration. For an interminable time, I waited at the shanty's threshold, praying for Malaika to emerge from the hut. I even contemplated joining him in the furnace, though I'm loathe to admit that my cowardice bested me.

Deep in the structure's flickering recesses, I saw a magnificent silhouette materialize through the smoke. It was Malaika, and cradled in his arms was a miracle. Long legs. Spindly arms.

A boy.

My triumphant glee proved ephemeral. A soul-rending crack resounded from the rafters. I screamed for my companion to watch out, but pitiless destiny had other plans. Malaika had only time to cast a forlorn look upward before the roof's flaming timbers caved in, burying father and son, dragging them away into the dark frontier that we all fear to one day explore.

200

The first stop for enemies from afar,
The last for enemies from within,
Five brazen stone-faced soldiers
To keep their city sound and safe.

A widow mourns a lonely walk,
Her grave mistake, her husband's ruin,
And roams the beach eternally
Grieving in black amongst the gray.

Her gallows long since rendered tinder,
The promise of life springs anew
Where the five petals converge
On the cinquefoil in bloom.

BURNING GAUNTLET
THE SOUTH END

IN THE INITIAL HOUR AFTER WE ARRIVED HOME AT the Dollhouse, Atlas and I made a valiant attempt to interpret the tenth riddle. Unfortunately, with our spiked adrenaline levels bottoming out, we surrendered to our stifled yawns and bleary eyes. I led Atlas by the hand to my bed. The cuffs of our jeans were still wet from our trip to the reservoir, but we climbed under the quilt without changing just the same.

The yearning I felt for him had only intensified, but with a good night's rest—and the solution to the latest riddle—of far greater urgency, I took a raincheck on seeing where our snowy union in the woods would lead us. I contented myself to take pleasure in Atlas's muscular body spooning my own. He imparted one last kiss to the nape of my neck before he fell asleep. My last sensation before I closed my eyes was the steady pulse of his warm breath whispering through my hair.

I couldn't have been out for long when a noise in the condo woke me. Dazed, I had trouble immediately placing the strange sound, so I closed my eyes again, listening closely.

There it was: a rattling, like the patter of rain against a window, repeating in two-second bursts.

I slipped out from under Atlas's thick arm. He was a heavy sleeper and didn't even stir as I walked out into the living room.

My cell phone, the throwaway that no one outside of Atlas and the two people I'd called tonight should possibly know the number to, was ringing on the glass coffee table. My gut squirmed uneasily as I crossed the room. I hadn't set up a voicemail, so the phone continued to slowly skitter across the table with each ring, the screen lighting up with a number I didn't recognize.

Maybe it was Rufus calling from a hardline. Maybe Georg wanted to update me on the fate of Detective Grimshaw. The illogical part of me feared that it was my mother calling to break bad news about Echo. There was no possible way for her to have this number, but my paranoid imagination misfired just the same.

When I picked up, I didn't say anything at first. I held the receiver up to my ear and listened for the caller to chime in.

While I'd heard the husky female voice on the other end only once before, it was one I'd never forget, just as I'd never forget the haunting sentence Aries spoke next.

"Do you want to hear the sound your brother made when he died?"

Her voice was immediately followed by a recording.

The rumble of a car engine.

The stick shift moving up a gear.

The engine's aggressive crescendo as the car accelerated.

Thump.

Crack.

Tumble-tumble.

Then a cold, low chuckle.

My heart rate skyrocketed. My eyes watered. In spite of all my strength these past few days, a pathetic sob escaped my lips, a high-pitched hiccup as that miserable, homicidal junkie forced me to relive the worst moment of my life.

"I figured I'd record it as a trophy," Aries said casually. "I made it my ringtone, so I could wake up to it every morning. Really start the day off on a positive note, you know?"

I was quaking so much that the phone slipped out of my clammy hand. When I picked it up, I held the microphone close

203

to my mouth. "The only trophy is going to be your bloodstained horns nailed over my mantle, you bitch."

Aries yawned. "Let's not resort to petty violence, *gatita*. Look, I have a race to get to, so I'm going to keep my proposition brief. Our little game of citywide hide-and-seek was fun in the beginning, but I'm getting *so* bored, and there's a bonus payday in it for me if I get these silly riddles back for Horace. So this is how it's going to go down: There's a gazebo on the far corner of Castle Island. You're going to surrender the latest riddle to me there at sunrise. If you don't, then I'm going to pay a visit to Children's Hospital."

A polar vortex swept through my body. "And do what?" I snapped. "Go on, say it. Give me another reason to make you suffer."

"How about a demonstration?" Aries asked. "Grimshaw traced your new phone to the South End, but with the signal playing pinball off the sides of all those buildings, we couldn't triangulate an exact location. Still, look out the nearest window."

I crept carefully over to the large floor-to-ceiling panes and parted the curtains an inch.

An SUV three doors down lit up, the car alarm wailing into the night, the headlights flashing an SOS pulse.

Then a more intense light emanated from the vehicle's back seat and it exploded.

The whole neighborhood shook. The glass windows of the surrounding buildings shattered, and the blast punched a hole in the brick wall of the art gallery behind it, large enough for elephants to comfortably march through. Debris rained down on the nearby cars, before they were swallowed by the smoke billowing down the street. Screams echoed from the condo units above and below me, as people ran to their windows to see the smoldering inferno of the SUV's remains.

Aries applauded herself. "Sounds like I was pretty close! That's what Echo can look forward to if her big sister doesn't bring me what I want. 6 a.m. Castle Island. No phone calls to the cops or hospital." Then she hung up.

The bedroom door burst open. The blast had woken Atlas, who grabbed me by the shoulders. "You okay?" he asked, frantic.

I nodded dumbly.

"I need to go out there and see if anyone needs help. Stay here." He wrapped me in a brief hug and sprinted out of the Dollhouse.

As I emerged from my shock, I found myself dialing Rufus's number once more. "It's your favorite troublemaker," I said when he picked up. "I need to know where someone is going to be—tonight." While I didn't know Aries's real name, her alias and the metal hardware on her head shouldn't make her hard to track down.

Rufus clucked his tongue thoughtfully after I'd dictated everything I knew about Aries. "I know a guy," he mused. "Dealt Blyss for a few years, until the feds caught a whiff of him, so he quit the game before he got burned. Mostly keeps to himself these days, living in some shithole up in Everett, but with a little financial incentive, his lips might loosen enough to say a thing or two about your charming, antlered acquaintance."

"Whatever you need," I promised him.

With Rufus on the job, I jacked Atlas's car keys from the kitchen counter. I traced the outline of a truck on the fridge's dry-erase board, with a note that said, "Last time. I promise."

Then I was in the parking garage, starting the engine to Atlas's Silverado, and roaring out of the back entrance to avoid the carnage left by the car bomb.

I hadn't been on the road long when, bless his heart, Rufus emailed me a full dossier of information. Aries's full name. Her drug territories on the North Shore. A rough map of the illegal street race she competed in every Tuesday at 3 a.m. without fail.

The race she would be competing in tonight.

You're the most industrious stoner I know, I texted Rufus back, before shutting the phone off altogether, so Aries couldn't trace my drive north and Atlas wouldn't try to stop me.

I sped toward Salem, Massachusetts, the heart of the infamous witch trials over three hundred years ago, which sent nineteen women to the gallows for allegations of sorcery.

Tonight, a different kind of witch was going to hang.

WITCHING HOUR
SALEM, MASSACHUSETTS

DEPENDING ON WHOM YOU ASKED, OCTOBER WAS either the best or the worst month to visit Salem.

Eleven months out of the year, it was a typical middle-class suburb, known for its restaurants and ocean views. Before my dad's mounting debt forced him to sell his boat, a used Catalina that he couldn't afford in the first place, he kept it moored here. Some of my only good memories of Buck Tides were of that summer when I was nine. Every Tuesday, we'd set sail out of Hawthorne Cove, with my father smiling at the wheel, and Jack, Mom, and me sprawled out in the back of the little fishing boat. My mother was pregnant with Echo then and always kept her hands gently folded over the swell of her belly. She seemed to infinitely glow that summer, like their marriage had entered a renaissance, though that glow would dim every time my father reached into the cooler for another Busch Light. Or when my godfather, Dec, would come along for the ride and drunkenly piss off the side of the boat.

Two months later, Buck Tides went to prison.

That was the Salem that I remember. However, for the entire month of October, the town annually embraced its paranormal legacy and transformed into a touristy magnet of haunted houses, graveyard tours, and Wiccan boutiques. Like the eighth biblical plague, hordes of teenagers would descend on Salem in the weeks leading up to Halloween, costumed and invincible, shrieking as they incited mischief in the streets.

When I pulled into town, the nightly bedlam was beginning to die down. The haunted houses had all closed for the evening, but I passed a trio of teens in bloodied steampunk costumes, who were inexplicably lighting a handkerchief on fire. A guide in Puritan-era wardrobe held a lantern aloft while he led a gaggle of tourists to Proctor's Ledge, the site of the seventeenth-century witch executions.

My destination was on the northeast tip of town, a waterfront park known as Salem Willows, named after the iconic trees that lined the property. I parked by a dilapidated arcade and popped my hood as I entered the grounds. It was a look that would scream "sketchy" anywhere else, but in Salem, I was just another delinquent who was up to no good.

Beyond the gates, I could hear a distant ruckus. I followed the sound across the park to the wharf and paused to watch from the shadows of a silent carousel, its plastic horses in suspended animation on their metal rods.

A large gang of punks had gathered around two flaming trash cans. Between the thirty of them, they had enough piercings and metal hardware to give any MRI technician an anxiety attack. *What the hell is this?* I wondered. *The fucking Thunderdome?*

Bottles of milky, glowing Blyss made their rounds, and even from my vantage point, I could feel the palpable electricity circulating with it. It was like being at a pet shop: If you rattled one cage, *all* the animals would start yowling.

The tension thickened when a tall skeleton of a man stepped forward. He must have been three heads taller than anyone else, yet probably weighed less than I did, with emaciated arms that dangled nearly to his knees. His ripped jeans were so tight that they looked like they'd been painted onto his pipe-cleaner legs.

Half of the crowd cheered as he mounted one of the motorcycles parked between the flaming trash cans, and it was only then that I realized the punks were divided into two camps. They were all so uniform in their alternativeness.

The opposite side exploded in their own cheers as a spiky-haired girl stepped out to meet the tall man's challenge. Her face had been painted as a Mexican sugar skull—chalk white, with a spider web across her forehead, violet flowers encircling her eyes, a black nose, and a lipless, toothy grin. Leather clung to her curves and she had a wooden croquet mallet strapped to her back.

The gangly man jammed a black helmet down onto his tiny head and climbed onto his bike, revving the engine twice in challenge.

The skull-faced girl rolled her eyes and made an obscene jerking motion with her hand, to the laughter of her gang members. She, too, straddled her motorcycle. Instead of a helmet, she unholstered two steel ram's horns from her belt. She screwed the prostheses in place one at a time, first the left, then the right, until they were firmly attached to the metal bolts protruding from her scalp.

My fingernails dug into plastic saddle of the carousel horse I was hiding behind. *Aries.*

Her real name, I had learned according to Rufus's source, was Dominika Calderón, a drug dealer who'd emigrated from Venezuela. Little was known about her prior to a few years ago, but she'd apparently made an impressively cutthroat ascent through Nox's organization, slowly commandeering his respect by sabotaging the markets for Blyss's competitors. Marijuana greenhouses burned. Meth labs exploded. Heroin supplies laced. Ecstasy, oxy, and Molly swapped for deadly pills. She had poisoned every well she could to ensure that addicts and recreational drug users alike would, in their fear, turn to the one drug that was consistent, tamper-free, and bountiful. It was basic supply and demand. Apparently, she would have made a brilliant economist in another life.

Somewhere along the way, Dominika had adopted an alias from the zodiac and started sporting demonic headgear to match it. Apparently her ruthlessness trumped her young age in Nox's eyes, because he'd quickly promoted her to oversee all Blyss distribution in the northeast. All that responsibility, and she still found time after her "day job" for illegal street-racing.

I was reminded of another interesting fact from Rufus's intel as Aries rolled up her sleeve and injected a syringe into her track-marked arm: Aries was a thrill junkie. As if racing her bike around public streets wasn't dangerous enough, she took a hit of Blyss mixed with a mild hallucinogen, intravenously for quicker results, and let the drug transform the streets around her. All of that, without wearing a helmet.

Well, if she had a death wish, it was about to be granted.

One goon stepped up to the starting line, holding bundles in each hand. When he dropped the first into the burning trash barrel, the flames turned yellow. Both competitors revved their engines. The "official" opened his right hand this time, and as soon as the second package hit the fire, green flames spewed out.

Both bikes shot forward. They whipped past my hiding spot, already jostling for the lead as they rattled down the narrow path. The last I saw of Aries was her popping a wheelie over the curb and speeding through the parking lot.

With the race underway and Aries now positively identified as a participant, I had probably no more than twenty minutes to get to the waypoint I'd chosen to make my last stand.

Then it would only be a matter of looking for the horns.

I hid on the grassy shoulder of Derby Street, the course's waterfront home stretch, which ran parallel to Salem Sound. Behind me, moored at the end of a long wharf, was the

Friendship, one of Salem's many tourist attractions. The enormous three-masted clipper ship loomed silently over the bay, its rigging occasionally groaning in the night breeze.

With a pair of binoculars, I gazed down the straightaway, which was devoid of traffic this time of night. It wasn't long before I heard the distant, excited hum of two motorcycles, growing louder on their approach. The tall man rounded the bend in the road first, his head low to the handlebars as he clung to his narrow lead.

Then I saw the telltale glint of metal horns. Aries was a hundred feet behind her competitor and her Yamaha jerked forward hard as she tried to close the distance. I wouldn't put it past her to jam her croquet mallet into his spokes if it meant the difference between winning or losing.

I readied my bundle at the roadside, a booby trap hastily constructed from materials I'd bought at a twenty-four-hour department store. The grandmotherly cashier had given me a strange look when, well after midnight, I'd dropped a long runner carpet and a box of nails onto the checkout belt. "Late-night home improvement," I'd explained.

Now it would all come down to timing. I lowered my body deeper into the weeds as the gangly punk flew by me at seventy miles an hour.

I popped out of the grass, pushed my palms against the rolled-up carpet, and shoved it toward the street. The twelve-foot rug unfurled across the road, and as it opened, the rows of nails that I'd hammered into it pointed skyward, snapping into place like hidden fangs.

The homemade spike strip had barely finished unspooling when Aries's bike sizzled over it. *Pop-pop.* The nails shredded the front tire, then the back. Her momentum was so great that as the bike's rims grated harshly against the asphalt, I feared that Aries might simply slow down and pull over, unfazed.

But then the front rim caught a dip in the road and bucked sideways. Aries flew over the handlebars headfirst, while the motorcycle clattered across Derby Street. Pieces of the plastic shell snapped off in chunks until the riderless bike slammed into a light pole.

Meanwhile, Aries hit the pavement and continued to slide across it. Sparks blossomed from the tips of her horns as they traced two blackened lines across the asphalt, before her body finally came to rest by the roadside.

I yanked the trap out of the street and threw it into the grass. Then I walked determinedly toward Aries.

I'd hoped the crash itself would put an end to her, but cockroach that she was, she was already peeling herself off the pavement. Her hands were bloodied and raw and the road rash had burned away her leather suit in patches. The tips of her horns glowed a fierce red, with smoke trails faintly rising from them.

I'm not sure what the cocktail of designer hallucinogens in her system made her see as I marched toward her, but as her hazy eyes struggled to focus, she groaned, "What *are* you?"

I drew back my hood to let her get a good look at the face of the girl she should never have crossed. "*I'm the nightingale*," I rasped.

I was nearly upon her when one of her bloodstained hands opened and she blew a handful of powder into my face.

The particles stung my eyes, momentarily blinding me, and I inhaled sharply before I could think better. The pixie dust unpleasantly coated the inside of my nose and mouth and I gagged on its pungent, chemical taste.

While I coughed out the wretched substance, Aries popped up to her feet in one feline movement and took off running down the wharf. The murderess was fast despite her road-chafed knees.

I wiped my eyes clear and pursued her, but I took my time since the jetty was a dead end. She would have no choice but to either turn and face me or dive into the frigid waters of Salem Sound. Unlike the mercy I'd shown Grimshaw, I would happily hold her punk head underwater until her legs stopped kicking.

Aries had other plans. She cut a hard right where the clipper ship was docked. The *Friendship*'s boarding ramp had been withdrawn for the night, but Aries planted her feet on the wharf's edge and leaped over the water with her gazelle-like legs. Her hands found the edge of the main deck, and after a few seconds of frantic writhing, she hauled herself aboard.

An unpleasant sensation swept through my brain as I reached the *Friendship*. The world around me distorted and the colors grew brighter. With my vision in a constant state of flux, I nearly misjudged my leap onto the boat. Pain exploded in my knees as they struck the pine hull, and it was only by a miracle that my hands found the deck's edge. My boots scrabbled blindly until I found a notch in the wood, which gave me enough leverage to drag my body up over the railing.

I assumed a defensive stance as soon as I could rally to my feet, but Aries was nowhere to be seen. The pixie-dust drug had me in its grip, assaulting me with a fresh wave of vertigo. The floorboards of the deck undulated beneath me, making every footstep I took uncertain. Even the masts twisted back and forth, like sky-bound serpents rising out of their coils.

Something fist-sized nailed me directly between my shoulder blades—Aries's croquet mallet hammering my spine. I staggered forward and caught the mast before I went down. Footsteps thudded across the deck behind me, and I whipped around to see the mallet on a collision course for my head.

I ducked just in time and Aries's major league swing connected with the mast instead, leaving a dent in the wood and

213

shattering the mallet. The impact rattled her, and I seized the opportunity to punch the demoness right in the throat.

She clutched her windpipe, inhaling ragged breaths. I came at her again, ready to bash her horns into her drug-addled brain.

Aries grabbed a cannonball from a supply rack and side-armed it at me. The round shot slammed into my ribs, doubling me over. The world around me burst into a kaleidoscope of color.

I heard Aries laugh as she took another unexpected path of retreat: up the rope ladders that ascended the mainmast. As she clambered up the rigging, she hoarsely sang, *"The itsy-bitsy spider crawled up the waterspout ..."*

The *Friendship*'s mast must have been over a hundred feet tall. As I ascended after Aries, the ropes squirmed beneath my fingers, snakes ready to sink their fangs into my flesh. I kept my focus on the trail of her bloody handprints and tried not to look down at the deck of the ship that was growing smaller.

At the top of the ladder, Aries pulled herself up onto the yardbar, the long piece of lumber that supported the topsail. She shimmied out to the edge, holding onto a rigging line to steady herself. "Come on up," she taunted me. "The view's to die for."

When I neared the yardbar, I climbed onto the beam's opposite end, putting myself out of reach from Aries so she couldn't kick me in the head on my way up. We now stood with only a handful of steps and the mainmast between us. My adrenaline was finally overpowering the drug, but the beam was narrow. If the line in my hand snapped, I'd fall for sure.

Aries's Cheshire grin broadened as she drew a knife from her waistband and flicked out the blade. "Perfect," she cooed. "You'll make an even bigger splat than your brother."

She crossed the beam slowly, knifepoint extended. She'd be on me in seconds.

My free hand slipped into the back pocket of my jeans. I felt the sand from Salem Sound that I'd tucked away earlier for

214

good luck. Aries was three steps from me now, making quick jabs to try to spook me off the edge. The next slice would find my flesh.

I closed my fingers into a fist and withdrew the sand from my pocket. My eyes smoldered as I met Aries's bestial, gloating gaze for the last time. Then I asked her, "Do you want to hear the sound you made when you died?"

I flung the sand into Aries's eyes right as she lunged. Instinctively, she let go of both the knife and her handhold to wipe them, tottering precariously on the yardbar. I grabbed the rigging above me with both hands, swung toward her, and kicked her in the chest with my boots as hard as I could.

Aries flew back off the beam and began the long drop to the deck below. Her rapid descent was interrupted three-quarters of the way down when one of her looping horns snagged on a line between the masts.

Even sixty feet up, I could hear the harsh *crack* when the sudden stop separated her skull from her spine.

My feet fumbled to find a perch again, and I didn't breathe a sigh of relief until I'd lowered myself back to the ladder. I squeezed it for dear life. Beneath me, Aries's body listed slowly from side to side on her makeshift gallows, her arms slack and her head bent at an unnatural angle on her broken neck.

I marveled at the remains of the sand that still coated my fingertips. When I was five, my brother had stuffed a handful of the Cape Cod beach into my pockets. Little had he known then that, twelve years later, his advice would save my life and avenge his own murder.

THE LADY IN BLACK
THE SOUTH END

IT WAS DAWN BY THE TIME I RETURNED TO THE SOUTH
End. I knew I was going to have to face the protective wrath of
Atlas the moment I opened the Dollhouse door.

As luck would have it, I didn't even have to wait that long.
After I'd rolled the truck into the condo's underground garage,
my headlights illuminated Atlas, swaddled in a bathrobe and
wearing an expression that hopscotched between fury and
relief. He had set up a beach chair in the spot where his
Silverado should have been, and I had no doubt he'd been
staking out the garage for hours, stewing miserably.

To be fair, I had stolen his truck with no explanation, right
after a car bomb left a crater outside our safe house.

After I'd parked and he stood there fuming, waiting for my
explanation, I tried to muster an apologetic façade, knowing full
well that I couldn't pull off the "puppy dog" look with any
shred of sincerity. "Would you believe," I asked, "that I was
taking the Silverado out for a car wash?"

Atlas crossed his arms tightly enough to pulverize a
cinderblock. "You," he replied, "are a panic attack personified.
If you keep this up, I'll be on blood pressure medication before
I turn nineteen."

There was no way I was going to evade explaining myself
this time, so we climbed into the bed of the truck and I told
him everything, from Aries's phone call to her lynching aboard
the *Friendship*. The ice melted off Atlas throughout the story, fury

giving way to understanding, tinged with disapproval. In the end, his primary concern came down to whether or not I could be connected to the death of Aries.

"I don't know," I answered. "With any luck, they'll run a toxicology test and her blood will light up like Times Square. Hopefully they'll see a girl who was so strung out on uppers and hallucinogens that she crashed her bike, tried to use a clipper ship as her own personal jungle gym, and accidentally belly-flopped off the topsail. Even if they suspected foul play, they'd have to sort through the fingerprints of thousands of tourists on the ship to find any of mine."

Atlas withdrew the tenth journal page from his pocket, and I felt immediately grateful for the change in subject. "I had a few hours to kill while I was waiting here to make sure you were alive, so I dug into the latest riddle."

"Any headway?" I asked.

"To be honest, I feel like I'm chasing my own tail again." He flattened the page against the rubber lining of the truck bed, and we studied it under the glow of the jaundiced garage light. One by one he pointed to words that he'd highlighted on the document's protective sleeve:

THE FIRST STOP FOR ENEMIES FROM AFAR,
THE LAST FOR ENEMIES FROM WITHIN,
FIVE BRAZEN STONE-FACED SOLDIERS
TO KEEP THEIR CITY SOUND AND SAFE.

A WIDOW MOURNS A LONELY WALK,
HER GRAVE MISTAKE, HER HUSBAND'S RUIN,
AND ROAMS THE BEACH ETERNALLY
GRIEVING IN BLACK AMONGST THE GRAY.

HER GALLOWS LONG SINCE RENDERED TINDER, THE PROMISE OF LIFE SPRINGS ANEW WHERE THE FIVE PETALS CONVERGE ON THE CINQUEFOIL IN BLOOM.

"To put it academically: There's a lot of weird shit going on," Atlas said. "Note how the number five comes up repeatedly. A *cinquefoil* is a five-petaled flower, so maybe we're looking for a garden. But it also refers to the pentagram, a star within a pentagon, a symbol commonly associated with witchcraft."

"Pentagon" made something in my memory twitch, but I couldn't summon it to the surface. "Witchcraft isn't a bad starting point. After all, I did just come from Salem, the witchcraft capital of the country. And there is that reference to the gallows."

"My thoughts initially as well." He tapped twice on the opening lines. "But what do protecting the city and *stone-faced soldiers* have to do with the witch trials? And what about this mourning widow—*her grave mistake, her husband's ruin*? I cross-referenced that second stanza with the full list of the accused witches who were executed by hanging. A few of them were widowed, but none of the stories mentioned anything about them being responsible for the death of their husbands, so I have no idea what to make of this lady in black."

The words *lady in black* again caused an ancient memory to stir. I could visualize the widow drifting eerily down the beach, her black robes billowing around her, only her toes touching the sand as they dragged two spectral lines through the surf. Where had I seen this image before?

Still, the memory frustratingly drifted away from me, like the lady in black herself.

My eyes landed on the fourth line. "Wait—why are these two words reversed?"

"Reversed?" Atlas leaned closer to the poem.

"It says *to keep the city sound and safe*. But the expression is typically *safe and sound*. Unless ..."

Unless the poem was trying to put emphasis on *sound*. My brain ran with this idea. *Sound* had a handful of meanings: it could mean in good condition or healthy. It could mean noise.

It could also mean the stretch of water that separated the mainland from an island.

And just like that, everything lined up in my mind, a slot machine coming up all sevens.

Island. Pentagon. Lady in black.

I don't know if it was because I was exhausted, or because I was euphoric at solving the riddle, or maybe because of the utter ridiculousness of where the memory came from, but I started to laugh hysterically, until my eyes watered and my ribs hurt where the cannonball had struck me earlier. "You've got to be kidding me," I said.

Atlas was looking at me like I had smallpox, so I tried to regain composure. "You had the wrong supernatural creature all along," I explained. "We're not looking for a witch. We're looking for a ghost."

His mouth formed an *O* of surprise. "Did you just solve the riddle?"

"Actually, you're never going to believe this." I wiped the tears from my eyes. "But my deadbeat father solved it for us."

MEANWHILE, AT NOX MANOR

Sunrise came and went, and Horace Nox was still waiting in his study for the phone to ring. Sunrise, Aries had promised him. At sunrise, the latest journal page would be his, the Tides bitch would be buzzard bait, and he would be one step closer to killing the infernal malady that was gnawing at his cells.

One step closer to resurrection.

But the sun had breached the horizon and began its autumnal ascent across the sky. While he restlessly waited for Aries's confirmation, he turned on the television, only to see a familiar face in the news.

A wild-eyed Louis Grimshaw was being led across a lawn in handcuffs by a horde of police officers. In the background, a handful of women in various states of undress were also being shepherded out of a dilapidated house. Grimshaw looked like he'd been pumped so full of drugs that he couldn't remember his own name. "Corruption in the BPD," the caption read. "Drug and prostitution bust leads to the arrest of a twenty-year veteran of the force."

When the buzzer announced that someone had arrived at the front gates, Nox hurried past the buzzard cage and through the mansion. "About damn time," he muttered as he arrived at the imposing front doors.

But the person on the other side wasn't Aries. It was one of her underlings, a North Shore drug dealer with a mohawk. Between the piercings in his ears, nose, and eyebrows, he had more rings than Saturn.

Once Nox had allowed him inside, the dealer reached into his bag with trembling hands and pulled out a scuffed metal object. His whole body quaked with fear—nobody liked to be the bearer of bad news to Horace Nox—but he gingerly held the item out for his boss to take.

It was a single, steel ram's horn, the forward tip worn down to a nub and the base coated in dried blood.

Nox stared at the horn, without ever really focusing. Finally, he reached into the holster tucked into his suit pants. "I know this is going to seem really cliché," he said almost apologetically.

Then he drew the gun and fired two rounds into the messenger's head.

Before the boy's corpse even hit the ground, Nox's phone was ringing in his pocket. He expected even more bad news when he answered, but as it turned out, his luck was about to change.

"One of your hunches panned out," said the man on the other end, his final remaining contact in the police, now that Grimshaw had been decommissioned. "Tides's roommate came up clean at first, until I looked into his employment history. Turns out he works at the Haven Halls Condominiums. It's in the South End, same neighborhood where we got the ping from that disposable phone."

Nox couldn't help it—he started to laugh. *I found your new nest, little bird.*

"It gets better," the dirty cop went on. "I just ran his credit cards and Atlas made an interesting purchase this morning: He rented a boat out of Marblehead."

And now, Nox thought, *I'm going to clip your wings. And saw off your beak. And pluck you clean until you beg me to throw you in the skillet.*

As soon as he'd hung up the phone, he stepped over the body and the pool of crimson that was slowing spreading over his tiles. In the blood and brain splatter on his wall, he dipped his finger and slowly doodled two words:

Gone fishin'.

PRISONERS OF THE SEA
THE BOSTON HARBOR ISLANDS

WHILE THE DUSK SUN LANGUISHED ON THE HORIZON, our pontoon boat skimmed over the gentle waves of Boston Harbor. Atlas stood at the helm, navigating the obstacle course of buoys and danger markers. The harbor's tallest lighthouse, which sat on a chunk of rock known as "The Graves," pulsed rhythmically as we motored by. Meanwhile, I let the wind race through my hair and gazed south toward our destination: a series of islands that loomed like coal silhouettes against the darkening sky.

If the Boston Harbor Islands were a cross-section of the city's history, you'd see the Four Horsemen of the Apocalypse: Famine, Conquest, War, and Death. Today, the thirty-four islands scattered throughout the harbor mostly played home to family-friendly recreation and gull watching. Every weekend from April until September, throngs of visitors squeezed onto boats out of Long Wharf and descended on the archipelago with picnic baskets and quilts. Slathered in sunscreen, they'd bask in the ocean air and eat hot dogs from concession stands, while wondering how such a pastoral oasis could coexist so close to Boston's skyline.

Most of these tourists remained oblivious to the uglier rubble of history beneath their feet. Take Spectacle Island, for instance. It got its name because its two hills made it look like a misshapen pair of eyeglasses. Visitors loved to climb its drumlins, which were terraced with shrubs and flowers and offered a beautiful view of the city.

What these hikers often failed to realize was that they were standing on what used to be mountains of century-old garbage, toxins, and disease.

Prior to its cleanup, Spectacle was home to a garbage incinerator for many years. Eventually, the city of Boston began to dump trash on the island, until the mid-twentieth century, when the heaps became so immense that the rubbish swallowed a bulldozer whole. To deal with this issue, the city proposed an innovative solution: From the highway tunnel they had trenched through Boston, they would take five thousand barges dirt and dump it on the remaining garbage. They landscaped the whole island into a park, added a visiting center and a marina for incoming ships, and *voila!* Instant nature preserve.

The island's colorful history didn't stop there. Spectacle had also been home to a grease reclamation plant that processed garbage fluid to make soap; a facility that rendered horse carcasses into glue and brushes; a series of hotels, which were shut down for gambling and prostitution; and a smallpox quarantine station, through which the disease eventually killed much of the Native American population that had fished the island's coast for centuries.

Atlas eased off the throttle as we floated deeper into the domicile of these stone giants. To our starboard side, a pyramid striped black and white rose out of the water to prevent sailors from running aground on Nixes Mate, a tiny island with a macabre history. In 1726, the buccaneer William Fly had been captured after a mutiny aboard the *Elizabeth*, which he and his fellow mutineers renamed the *Fame's Revenge*. Fly was sent to the gallows in Boston, and he was such a badass that he'd chastised his executioner for improperly tying his noose—then made the proper hangman's knot himself. Fly's remains had been displayed on the rocks of Nixes Mate as a public warning to all would-be pirates.

Atlas was watching me intently. "Nostalgic smile, thousand-yard gaze—something reminded you of Jack, didn't it?"

"I can't even sail past a rock at high tide without hearing the echoes of some yarn he once told me," I said. "All those times that I begged him not to give me another unsolicited history lecture, and now I'd trade a year off my life just to hear him recite one more stupid fact."

Atlas cut the engine as we arrived at our final destination: George's Island. I hopped off the boat first, catching the tow line from Atlas and lashing it to the pier.

While the other islands in the harbor were steeped with colorful histories and folklore, *this* was the one that seemed to have an answer for every line in the tenth riddle.

THE FIRST STOP FOR ENEMIES FROM AFAR,

George's Island was home to Fort Warren, a 150-year-old military fortification that had guarded Boston Harbor from marine attacks during the Civil War, the Spanish-American War, and World Wars I and II.

THE LAST FOR ENEMIES FROM WITHIN,

During the Civil War, the island had served as an offshore prison camp for captured Confederates, including several generals and the vice president of the Confederacy.

FIVE BRAZEN STONE-FACED SOLDIERS
TO KEEP THEIR CITY SOUND AND SAFE.

Fort Warren had been constructed in the shape of a pentagon for defensive reasons. Its five massive walls were the first line of protection against enemy artillery fire.

A WIDOW MOURNS A LONELY WALK, HER GRAVE MISTAKE, HER HUSBAND'S RUIN,

This was the part where I regrettably had to give my father credit. Buck Tides wasn't what you'd call a learned man, but as a fourth-generation Boston resident, he'd inherited a wealth of "unofficial history," including ghost stories that he liked to scare Jack and me with when we were little.

One his favorites was "The Lady in Black."

According to the folktale, the wife of a Confederate prisoner conspired to liberate her husband and infiltrated the island, dressed as a man. During her botched attempt at a jailbreak, her pistol misfired, accidentally killing her husband.

AND ROAMS THE BEACH ETERNALLY GRIEVING IN BLACK AMONGST THE GRAY.

The widow was sentenced to death for treason, and for her execution, she wore the only female clothing they could find on the island: a black dress, instead of the gray of the Confederate uniform. Her spirit purportedly still haunted the shores of George's Island, and many who spent the twilight hours here reported hearing her wailing on the beach, lamenting her *grave mistake*.

Atlas and I gathered the required materials we'd brought with us, and I took inventory to make sure we weren't leaving anything behind: two shovels, a laser pointer, a hundred-yard spool of twine, and one athletic field marker, the rolling machine that sports teams used to paint lines on the turf.

225

"Ready to play ball?" Atlas asked me.

I hoisted the shovel onto my shoulder. "Batter up."

I'd underestimated how eerie the island would be at night. The buildings sat in complete darkness, including the explosives warehouse that had, hilariously, been transformed into a visitor center. A cannon pointed ominously at the empty Adirondack chairs lining the beach. You could easily imagine the wraith of a dead widow gliding between them.

We journeyed down the dark tunnel that led into the heart of Fort Warren, the sweeping parade grounds where soldiers had once trained and prisoners had stretched their stiff legs after long nights in confinement. The five stone walls rose around us. Although it was dead quiet, I could almost hear the bombastic crack of artillery fire echo through history, the morning bugle call coaxing tired soldiers from the barracks into the cold embrace of dawn.

In the middle of the vast green, Atlas stopped, drew in a deep breath, and tilted his head to the starry sky. "I used to play vintage baseball games here every summer," he said. "It was a history nerd's dream—dressing in nineteenth-century uniforms, playing without gloves like *real* men. The pitcher's mound would have been somewhere around here."

I dumped my equipment on the ground. "You'd make one hell of a personal ad, you know that? 'Sandcastle-building vintage baseball player seeks history-loving woman who enjoys a seductive frolic in the blueberry patch.'"

"Well, I don't know what the future holds for my love life," he said as he handed me the end of our twine spool, "but you've set the bar unreasonably high for first dates. How am I supposed to go back to 'dinner and a movie' after this?"

Our plan to conquer the third stanza of the riddle involved as much geometry as it did history. The final lines had told us to look where the five petals of the cinquefoil converged, which

Atlas and I agreed must be the fort's geometrical center. To calculate this location more precisely, we'd devised a plan:

We were going to draw a big-ass star.

Over the course of the next hour, we repeatedly stretched the rope from one corner of the fort to another. As soon as it was taut, we'd flash the laser pointers at each other to indicate that we were in place. Then we'd roll the athletic line marker along the length of twine, using it like a gigantic ruler to guide the white aerosol paint. When we were done, the five lines formed a star so enormous that even the passengers of a jetliner would be able to see it from cruising altitude.

The convergence of the five lines left a smaller pentagon in their center. We repeated the process inside it, painting a smaller star, and then again within that one, until our kaleidoscope of lines left us with an innermost pentagon six feet across. This marked the center of the courtyard.

In unison, Atlas and I both scooped up our shovels and clinked the heads together like champagne glasses. *"The promise of life springs anew,"* I quoted the riddle.

The digging was easier this time, since the moist harbor ground wasn't frozen like the soil in Dana. Still, it wasn't until we had excavated enough dirt for the hole to rise over my head that my shovel struck something. If the hollow metallic *bong* that resonated on impact gave any indication, it was enormous.

We vigorously uncovered the iron shell, which was several feet in diameter and perfectly round. When the top half of the sphere was fully exposed, Atlas gave a low whistle.

"You know what this is?" I asked him.

He cleared his throat. "It, uh, appears to be a submarine mine."

"A mine?" I screeched. "Of the explosive variety?" I took a step back toward the edge of our deep hole. I entertained a horrific vision of the shell detonating, of feeling a short-lived

227

burst of unfathomable, fiery pain before my consciousness was squelched out and my liquefied flesh painted the parade grounds.

Atlas seemed less concerned. He knelt down and began to scrape the remaining dirt off the casing, using water from his canteen to loosen it up. "Something tells me that this one isn't stuffed with dynamite, unless the person who designed this riddle quest was a psychotic nihilist. Mines like this were manually detonated by a long series of electrical wires. If it was touch-activated, it *probably* would have blown up when you harpooned it with your shovel."

I waited tensely while Atlas pulled a knife from his pocket. He found a metal cap that covered an entry point into the mine and scored the dirt away from the seam. "At one point, during World War II, there were more than five hundred of these buoyed beneath the surface of Boston Harbor, fifty tons of dynamite ready to shred any German U-boats. Kind of makes you wonder if they forgot one, and it's still floating out in the water somewhere …"

With the cap loosened, Atlas grasped it by the metal ring on top. "Last chance to get out of the hole before I pull the pin on this ginormous grenade."

"And let you be the sole martyr? Fat chance." I steeled myself for the worst as the muscles in Atlas's forearm tensed. With his eyes scrunched shut, he gave the cap a hard yank.

Pop. The plug came free and the torpedo expelled a plume of musty air, a long sigh decades in the making. Relieved that we hadn't been incinerated, I dove for the mine and slipped my arm down into the sphere. It took some grasping around the inside, but eventually my hand found something thin and papery plastered to the interior wall. I carefully pried it from the adhesive holding it in place. "Either we just opened the world's biggest fortune cookie"—I pulled the eleventh journal page through the opening—"or we found the next riddle."

Tempted as we were to start reading, we agreed to make ourselves scarce. Getting caught by harbor patrol on an island that we vandalized, with the paint still drying on what looked like the symbol from an occult ritual, would put a definite kink in our plans.

Our excited smiles lasted only until we emerged from the other end of the tunnel. Because when we reached the beach, that's when we heard the boat.

Atlas and I lunged for cover behind the ornamental cannon as the motor approached. At first, we could only make out the ship's outline through the all-consuming darkness. A spotlight bloomed on the bow and swiveled around until it landed on our little Sun Cruiser.

"The Coast Guard?" I whispered to Atlas. I squinted to make out the name painted on the hull.

Someone on the ship lobbed a green baseball-sized object through the air. It landed in the bed of our Sun Cruiser.

Atlas understood what he was seeing before I did. He flattened me to the sand.

The grenade exploded, rending our boat into fiery scraps of wood and scorched fiberglass. The heat wave hit my face from across the beach and debris clattered down around us.

It was all I could do not to cry out as our ticket off this island burned in the shallows.

The spotlight swiveled again, this time pinning down our location behind the cannon. We raced back toward the tunnel, into the fort, eliciting a chorus of shouts from our pursuers. I glanced back as four mercenaries in tactical gear leaped onto the dock.

Leading the charge, his long gunmetal hair bathed in the orange light from our burning boat, was Horace Nox.

Back inside the fort walls, Atlas held tight to my hand as we fled across the starlit parade grounds. He directed us toward the

229

far corner, where we plunged through an archway and into the dark bowels of the fortress.

It was nearly impossible to see inside so we clung to the walls, running our fingers over the damp stone to guide us. With each passing cell, I felt hope slip away. Even if we found another exit, we were still stranded on this island. What were we going to do without a boat? Swim a mile to the nearest shore? Risk destroying the new riddle in the process?

Any specter of hope for our survival vanished when we reached a dead end. We had entered a dank, empty cell, with no furniture to hide behind and only a single window, latticed with metal bars. A wheezy sob escaped my lips as I violently jerked at the grill, trying to rip it free from the stone. The island was a dead zone for cellular service, so we couldn't call the police, and it was too late to turn back to the other rooms. I could hear the footsteps of Nox and his men descending on us down the hallway.

Atlas, who had barricaded the door shut using the only chair in the room, spun me around and cupped my face in his hands. "Listen to me—Sabra, listen to me!" he whispered harshly, until I stopped crying. "What if I told you that there *is* a way to get us off this island alive? What if I told you that in twenty-four hours, you'll know the location of the final riddle? Would you trust me?"

I nodded vigorously. I couldn't form the words to agree with him.

"Then no matter what happens next, you *cannot* stop what I'm about to do," he said. "First, I need the journal page."

Atlas produced a lighter from his pocket. His fingers were shaking, so it took a few tries for him to ignite it, but once he did, he snatched the new riddle from me. In the flickering glow, his eyes rapidly scanned the page.

After he'd read it once, he brought the flame to the corner.

"What are you—?" I started to cry out.

He silenced me with a finger to his lips and mouthed the words 'Have faith.' The edge of the paper crackled and blackened. The burn was apparently too slow for Atlas—he dropped the riddle to the ground and snapped the lighter's shell over it. The butane from the fuel chamber drizzled onto the page. Fire spread rapidly over the surface, hungrily following the trail of lighter fluid. I watched helplessly as the flames consumed Cumberland Warwick's cursive. In less than a minute, the riddle, the only chance I had to end the blight that had stolen my sister's childhood from her, was gone.

Atlas wasn't watching the page burn, nor was he watching the door, where any minute now Nox and his men would burst through. Instead, he closed his eyes. The lumps of his pupils danced behind his eyelids. His lips formed a string of words, to the point that he appeared to be chanting to himself.

Someone on the other side of the door kicked it hard. On the second kick, the old wood began to buckle. With the third, the chair flew out from under the knob and clattered to the floor, and a fourth sprung the door open altogether.

The squad of mercenaries fanned out into the room, shining their flashlights on our faces and hollering at us to hold our hands over our heads.

The last person to enter the room was Horace Nox.

The drug baron held a pistol in one hand and a flashlight in the other. He opened his mouth to say something, but then his gaze fell on the riddle's burning remains. His eyes widened as the fire devoured the last surviving word.

"No!" he howled, then again, "No, no, no!" He threw himself to his knees and attempted to slap out the remaining fire, but he was too late. The riddle was nothing but embers now.

Driven mad with rage, he pointed the pistol at my head. I drew in my last breath. "I'm sorry, Echo ..." I whispered.

But right before Nox could pull the trigger, Atlas's eyes sprung open and he screamed, "I have an eidetic memory!"

While I had no idea what that meant, his words clearly meant something to Nox. The gangster kept his gun trained on my face, but his finger relaxed on the trigger. "Explain," he ordered.

Atlas swallowed hard and stepped in front of me to interrupt Nox's line of fire. "It's not a perfect photographic memory," he went on, "but I can picture the words on the page, and using some mnemonic devices, I'll be able to tell you exactly what the riddle said—word for word."

Nox seized Atlas by his short hair. He pressed the barrel of his pistol to the soft fleshy spot under Atlas's jaw. "Then get on your knees and write those words in the dirt, and for your troubles, I will mercifully let your maggoty existence extend an extra sixty seconds."

"No," Atlas replied. Nox drilled the gun harder into his neck. Still, Atlas held his ground. "You'll get the eleventh riddle —and the Serengeti Sapphire—but only on my terms."

Nox took a step back and impatiently massaged the bridge of his nose. "Please, *please* tell me that you're not about to bore me with some ultimatum to spare your life."

"Not my life." Atlas tilted his head in my direction. "Just hers."

Nox sauntered around Atlas and up to me. I tried not to flinch as he ran the pistol's barrel down the side of my face in a perverse caress. I'd killed the woman who'd murdered my brother, I'd destroyed the man who'd covered it up, yet here was the human stain who was behind all of my family's recent suffering, close enough that I had to share oxygen molecules with him—and I could do nothing.

"I'm excellent at reading character," Nox said. He jerked his thumb back at Atlas. "Your man, there, is a petunia who hasn't an ounce of violence in him. But you ...” He released a shuddering breath, odorous with the cabbage-like smell of death, thanks to the illness rotting his insides. “I can taste the violence in you. Drumm, Pearce, Aries—their deaths were all your doing, weren’t they?”

“*Oops*,” I replied.

“Hey, douchebag,” Atlas snapped. “Do you want your magical plant or not?”

Nox turned back to Atlas. “Okay, cupcake. What are your terms of surrender?”

“This is how it’s going to go down,” Atlas said firmly. “You’re going to hold me for one day, some place away from Boston, off the grid, so I know that you’re personally not anywhere *near* Sabra. Over the course of those twenty-four hours, she is going to get a head start fleeing as far away from the city as she possibly can.” I started to protest, but Atlas spoke louder to cut me off. “After that time has elapsed, she’s going to call me so I know that she’s found haven somewhere beyond your reach. Once I hear her voice, *then* I will dictate to you the contents of the riddle and even help you solve it. But if I don’t hear from her, then you might as well make your own funeral arrangements, because the contents of the riddle will die with me.”

Nox mulled over Atlas’s proposition. “So you’ll *willingly* help me find the Sapphire, even though that means condemning youngest Tides runt to death.”

Atlas turned his gaze on me. His eyes were so stony that even *I* was convinced by what he said next. “To be brutally honest, I think you’re all a bunch of pathetic daydreamers who are chasing an antidote that doesn’t exist. So, yes, I will lead you down the rabbit hole, if only to watch you writhe with desperation when you realize you’ve wasted your final days chasing a white whale.”

It dawned on me exactly what Atlas was orchestrating. After everything he'd gone through with his own sister, after everything *we'd* gone through over the last few days, he would never betray Echo and lead Nox to our miracle cure. *What if I told you that in twenty-four hours, you'll know the location of the final riddle?* he'd said to me before our capture. *Would you trust me?*

Atlas was going to solve the riddle in his own head.

When I called tomorrow, he would tell me where to find the next journal page and hope that I could race there before Nox did.

And as soon as he did that, he was a dead man.

Nox, who'd been studying Atlas for any trace of bullshit, must have realized that he had no other option but to cooperate. Atlas was, after all, the only 'copy' of the remaining riddle. If he died, so did the final link to the Sapphire.

So Nox unclipped a satellite phone from the belt of his black jeans, dialed a number, and held it to his ear. "Hello, dear brother," he sang. "Get the Greenhouse ready for a visitor." He smiled at Atlas. "I have a new petunia for your garden."

Several minutes later, Atlas and I were ushered aboard Nox's boat, which had been sadistically named *The Last Hope*. The two of us were isolated on separate ends of the ship.

The captain slowed the vessel off the coast of Hull, at which point I was manhandled by two mercenaries, who held me by my arms as Nox approached. He reached out and traced a finger down the silver chain around my neck, until his fingertip came to rest on Paul Revere's silver bell. He tightened a fist around the trinket, and with a rough yank, he ripped the necklace off me. Tiny silver links scattered over the deck as the chain snapped, and I could feel blood bead on the nape of my neck.

"Before I toss you back out to sea," Nox said, "I can't help but ask: What is it with your family and stealing from me? What sort of strange compulsion makes all of you so unable to keep your hands off my shit?" He searched my eyes for an answer. "After three Tides in nine years, I have to believe that you suffer from some genetically predisposed death wish."

"*Three* Tides?" I repeated. "What the hell are you talking about?"

Nox's eyes lit up. "Wait—you really don't know, do you?" He laughed from his belly. "Oh, this is fresh. Whose warehouse do you think your old man was trying to roll over when the pigs busted him? Who do you think he was trying to rip off?"

I shook my head. "That's ... not possible. The man who owned the warehouse testified against my dad." It had been almost a decade since the trial, and I'd been a kid then, sure, but I would have remembered if Horace Nox had been involved.

"You think I'm cotton-headed enough to put my own name on the deed to a warehouse full of drugs? That guy who testified against your father was only my marionette." Nox pantomimed a puppet with his hand. "Of course, Buck was too dumb to realize he'd been duped. And he had no idea he was setting the Tides bloodline on a collision course for extinction."

I was still struggling to process this twist when Nox jabbed a finger down at the water. "Let's reunite the Tides with the surf, shall we boys?"

The two mercenaries hefted me over their heads with strong arms and tossed me overboard. I landed in a yellow lifeboat that they'd lowered into the water. One of them dropped a single paddle on top of me.

Once I had peeled myself off the raft's plastic lining, Nox threw something else before I drifted away. It was a five-dollar bill wrapped around a rock. "Buy Echo a cheeseburger," he shouted. "I hear she's got a voracious appetite these days."

I roared and threw the stone right back at him, aiming for his face. It pathetically missed and struck the side of the ship.

The rock gouged a hole in the word *Hope* before the harbor waters swallowed it up.

I didn't cry until my raft washed ashore on the banks of Hull. I collapsed in the sand. I had come so far—*so far*—only to have the penultimate riddle stripped from me, along with the one person who had been my bedrock during these backbreaking last few days. We'd repeatedly overcome insurmountable odds to complete the trials of the Sapphire quest, and it had all been for nothing. Atlas would likely die in Nox's confines, my own days were numbered, and Echo would never get her miracle cure.

As I wept on the beach, the cold surf lapping at my legs, I pictured the last moment I'd seen Atlas aboard the ship—potentially the last time I would ever see him alive. He hadn't said anything to me. He'd simply rolled up the sleeve of his sweatshirt and pressed two fingers to the tattoo of his sister's name.

That simple gesture gave me the strength to pick myself up off the beach. Despite the severe setbacks I'd been dealt, all of that dissolved, leaving behind only the simplicity of what I wanted, and what I would have to do to get it.

I wanted Echo to live. I needed the riddle to save her. Which meant that I had twenty-four hours to do whatever it took to find and free Atlas.

I pulled out my phone, which thankfully had service now that I was back on the mainland. I didn't even bother with a greeting when Rufus picked up. "I need two addresses this time," I said. The first, I explained, was the location of Nox's "greenhouse," where I assumed he grew Blyss's main ingredient. And as for the second ...

"Who the hell is Declan Kelly?" Rufus asked.

I speared the paddle from the life raft into the sand. "He's my godfather."

BACKWOODS RETRIBUTION
MOHAWK TRAIL FOREST

THE LAST TIME I'D SEEN DECLAN KELLY WAS ALMOST ten years ago, shortly before he took the stand to testify against my dad. But even in my memories of my godfather from before that unforgivable betrayal, the man was a real piece of shit.

Dec was an unofficial uncle to Jack and me when we were growing up, since my father was an only child and Mom's siblings lived back on Cyprus. Even now, I couldn't hear Dec's name without catching a whiff of his offensive breath, which smelled like a beer-soaked ashtray. As far as I knew, he only owned sleeveless t-shirts, none of them large enough to restrain the kidney-bean bulge of his stomach. His visits to the Tides household usually spiraled out of control shortly after he and my father retreated to our dilapidated porch with a deck of cards and a case of Harp.

Despite his short fuse and his countless deficits as a family man, my father mostly treated my mother with respect. But he slipped down to a spiteful place whenever Dec was around. He would make petty verbal jabs at Mom, picking at the scabs of old disagreements. All the while, I could hear my godfather sniggering through the porch's screen door, egging him on.

So while I didn't hate Dec for landing my father in Cedar Junction—Buck Tides had dug his own grave—I *did* hate Dec because he was an asshole.

That's why, in my time of crisis, I couldn't believe that I was driving two hours west to my godfather's trailer in the middle of the Mohawk Trail Forest. Dec was a gun collector, and I wasn't about to crash Nox's drug fields unarmed. Not that I actually knew how to fire a weapon, but I'd feel a hell of a lot safer with one to at least theatrically wave around.

Route 2 narrowed from three lanes to two lanes, then to one, until it ceased to be a highway altogether. The backroads took me through a covered bridge, the kind you only see in movies, and into a dense wood of towering oaks. When I finally parked Atlas's truck next to a mailbox plastered with a collage of Hooters stickers, it didn't take a GPS to confirm that I'd arrived at Dec's place.

The long dirt driveway spat me out in front of a trailer so dented and weathered that it looked like a giant had discarded an enormous beer can in the woods. It had been built on the banks of a brook that snaked through the trees, and reclined at an angle where the mossy earth was slowly repossessing it. Truth be told, I had some good rustic memories of summer days here—sipping root beer, trying to catch bullfrogs in the stream —but I didn't remember it ever being in such a sorry state.

I had no intention of meeting face-to-face with Dec. Hopefully, he was somewhere off-property sniping squirrels out of the trees, a favorite pastime of his. I peered through the dingy windows, looking for any signs of movement, but found none. His Harley was absent from the gravel drive.

To my relief, the old shipping container was still there. The long steel crate was the one place Jack and I had been banned from playing near. Considering the amount of rusty tools and scrap metal littering the riverside that we *had* been allowed to scamper around, it was obvious that there was something pretty damn dangerous inside the box.

The container's door was sealed shut with a flimsy lock. I scavenged around the yard until I found a lug wrench. Several hard swings later and the mangled lock dropped to the ground.

The inside of the shipping container was like a carnival of vices and contraband. I tripped over a crate of whiskey bottles as I entered. Buzzing UV lamps lined the walls, shining fake sunlight on a garden of plants that I felt reasonably certain weren't ferns. And in the back ...

"Bingo."

Dec kept all of his firearms on display in a glass cabinet: handguns, semiautomatics, a recurve bow with a bouquet of arrows. I decided to go small—homicidal drug lord or not, I had no intention of prancing around Nox's compound with an assault rifle. I had just settled on a revolver when someone behind me said in a butter-thick Boston accent, "Lay it down on the floor and turn around, real slow."

I did as I was told, exaggerating my movements. When I turned to face Dec, I was shocked to see a man who only loosely resembled the godfather from my childhood memories.

For starters, he was in a wheelchair now.

He had a sawed-off shotgun resting on the tartan quilt covering his lap. His finger hovered over the trigger.

"Hello, Uncle," I said.

His thin lips fell open as my face clicked in his memory with the eight-year-old girl he used to know. He let the shotgun clatter to the floor beside his wheelchair. "Jesus, Mary, and Bono," he whispered and groped for the crucifix tucked into the collar of his army surplus T.

"Isn't there a commandment against using U2's name in vain?" I asked.

As the shock of seeing me for the first time in a decade wore off, Dec folded his arms over his chest. "I might as well have shot you, because if your mother finds out you paid Uncle Dec a visit, she'll flay the both of us alive. So what the hell are you doing here?"

I toed at the Ruger on the floor. "I needed a gun."

"Clearly." He narrowed his eyes in suspicion. "Oh, I see what this is. I snitch on your Pop and a decade later you're here to collect your pound of flesh."

"Don't flatter yourself," I said evenly. "As far as I'm concerned, Buck can rot away in his orange jumpsuit, and you can keep living out your Duck Dynasty fantasies here in West Purgatory. I have a sister who needs me, and far worse people to worry about than two townie pricks who should have known they were too old to play cops and robbers." I bent down and picked up the revolver. "So with all due respect, roll back into your hobbit hole and stay out of my way."

To my surprise, Dec looked concerned. I would have preferred him angry. "Last time you visited me here," he said, "you were half as tall, splashing in the stream, and pretending to be a goose. I don't want to see that girl's face in an obituary, so for your own good, I won't hesitate to call the sheriff, if that's what it takes to keep you from heading down a dark road. But if you explain what brought you here to the last resort, maybe I'll change my mind." He pointed to the gun in my hand. "And even show you how to take the safety off."

There was nothing like being pitied by a paraplegic, reclusive ex-con to be reminded of what dire straits I'd come to. As much as I didn't want to spend another second with Dec on what would probably be my last day on earth, fifteen minutes was a small price to stay out of a holding cell. I tucked the revolver in the waistband of my jeans. "Got any coffee?"

We sat on the patio that overlooked the brook, which Dec called "his redneck Jacuzzi." He lit a joint and winked. "For my glaucoma—doctor's orders."

Between sips of coffee, I recounted an abridged version of the last two weeks. His hand tightened around the spokes of his wheelchair when I informed him of Jack's death. After I'd caught up to Atlas's capture, I finished with, "So that's why you're going to let me walk out of here without making a fuss. And if you try to stop me, I have no qualms about locking you in that shipping container."

Dec stared off into the forest, across the river, where a lone black bear was slowly ambling through the trees. Finally, he flicked the stub of his joint into the brook. "There's something you should see. Wait here." He popped a wheelie, spun 180 degrees, and glided down the rotting plank he used as a ramp.

After a minute of tinkering around inside of the shipping container, Dec returned to his spot beside me on the patio. He held a small object, metallic silver and about the size of an acorn. For some reason, it had been shrink-wrapped in plastic.

"What is that, a gumball?" I asked.

Dec slipped gardening gloves onto his hands. After gingerly unwrapping the weird marble, he cocked his arm back and threw it into the brook.

Then it exploded.

A geyser of water and pulverized stone jetted into the air. The severed head of an unlucky trout landed on the patio next to me, its body mutilated and cauterized below the gills. Its mouth opened and closed several times before its nervous system acknowledged that it was dead.

I rocketed out of my chair. "What the hell was that, Dec?"

"That," my godfather explained, "was what Horace Nox used to do *this*." He cast aside the afghan that covered the lower half of his body.

Both of his legs had been amputated above the knees.

If you'd asked me five minutes earlier if I thought it was possible to feel any sympathy for Dec, I would have called you crazy. "How?" I realized I was asking the wrong question. "Why?"

Dec drew the afghan back over the stubs of his legs. "Gangsters don't take kindly to people who take their things— especially their drugs."

241

So the story at my father's trial about his three-man crew trying to steal precious metals had been bullshit. "You're telling me," I said, "that you guys were trying to steal *Blyss*?"

"An early version of it, back when it first hit the scene in Boston." With some struggle, Dec bent over and picked up the singed fish head. "A rival dealer paid us to steal some cases, find out what this new high was all about. Nox was two steps ahead of us. The warehouse was stripped clean by the time we got there, and the cops weren't far behind." He launched the trout's corpse across the stream.

I was still trying to digest this, so Dec went on. "Fun fact about the Blyss production process: They have to manufacture it in a perfectly dry environment, then mix it with water later. You see, when they extract the drug from the plant, they're left with this unstable byproduct, a chemical they call 'Hydrobane' that reacts violently with water. I'm no chemistry major, but from what I've read, the reaction produces hydrogen gas and heat, which when you mix them together—" He mimed an expanding mushroom cloud with his hands and mouthed *boom*. "Instant Hindenburg. Nox apparently doesn't like it to go to waste, so he uses it on his enemies. For instance, say a man gets arrested for breaking into his warehouse. Say he beats his rap by ratting on a friend, but Nox doesn't like that he walked away scot-free. Say he decides to take his Harley out for a Saturday morning ride in the rain, with no clue that, during the night, Nox's men strapped a nugget of Hydrobane to the bottom of his bike. Say he hits a puddle at the end of his driveway." Dec left me to imagine the carnage. "I wasted years of my life plotting my revenge against the man. I even acquired several bricks of that stuff so I could watch him crawl on the ground after I took his own legs from him. But eventually I realized I'd rather live in the shadows than die in the cavalry charge."

Across the stream, the bear was pawing at the trout carcass. "Is this your way of trying to scare me into backing down?" I asked him.

"Damn right it is," Dec snapped. "You're off your nut if you think I'm going to give you my blessing to waltz onto his compound." There were tears in his eyes now. "I betrayed your daddy once. I'm not going to send his little girl to her death."

My phone chimed, a new disposable in case Nox was tracking the other. The email was from Rufus. He had come through with an elaborate dossier of information about Nox's greenhouse, the compound in Vermont where he grew and processed Blyss. Delivery routes, timetables, a crudely sketched map. I had no idea what channels Rufus had pursued to track down this information, but I owed my P.I. friend more than a positive Yelp review if I got out of this alive.

I turned back to Dec. While he would never be my favorite person in the world—or even break the top thousand—now more than ever, I could use someone who thought like a criminal. "This isn't about vengeance, anymore, Dec. It's about Echo's life. You can't change my mind." I held up the digital map of Nox's compound for him to see. "But you can help make sure I have the tools I need to come out alive. To send me in unprepared would be the *real* betrayal."

Dec folded his hands in his lap. He watched as the black bear rejected the dynamited trout and loped off into the forest. "What do you need?"

"Let's start with a way in," I replied, "and we'll see how hypothetically alive I still am after that."

SLASH AND BURN
NORTHEAST HIGHLANDS, VERMONT

DEEP IN A HARDWOOD FOREST ON THE BANKS OF Lake Willoughby, I waited in ambush by the roadside. To conquer Nox's stronghold, the insane plot I'd concocted with Dec's assistance would start with an old trick and end with a few new ones. According to my intel, it would all begin in sixty seconds, with the arrival of a maple syrup delivery truck.

Inside his trailer, Dec returned from the refrigerator with a bottle of syrup.

"It's a little late for pancakes, don't you think?" I asked.

He ripped the green label off the bottle and flattened it on the table. It depicted the silhouette of two mountains, overlaid with the gold-lettered brand name "Glacier Notch Farms" in the valley between them.

"This boutique maple farm," Dec explained, "is the front for the largest drug manufacturing operation in all of New England."

I squinted incredulously at him. "Are you trying to tell me that Horace Nox is Aunt Jemimah?" Now that I looked closer, I could see a dark bird flying away in the logo's corner.

"A savvy opportunist is what he is," Dec said. "When Nox and his brother first brought the Blyss lichen back from the Amazon, they had trouble getting it to survive outside of its rainforest habitat. They discovered that the lichen took a shine to the bark of sugar maple trees. A syrup company provided a convenient front for their operation."

I wandered over to the crude map of Nox's compound I'd copied onto the wall of the trailer. "So: How do I break into IHOP?"

Dec wheeled over and traced a finger around the perimeter. "There are two mountains to either side, a twelve-foot wall topped with razor-wire, and armed patrols circling the border. Unless you're an Olympic pole vaulter, you might be shit outta luck." He sounded hopeful, like a wall and a few guards would scare me into quitting.

Beside the map, I looked through the delivery schedule that Rufus had sent me. True to his military background, Nox ran all of his operations on a strict timetable. "What if I drive right through the main gates?"

Through my binoculars, I saw the green truck with the Glacier Notch Farms emblem round the bend. As soon as it neared my position, I rolled my makeshift spike strip across the road.

The nails shredded the truck's tires. Under the weight of its heavy cargo, it dropped onto four rims and rolled a ways before the driver pulled over. Good—I needed this truck intact.

With a gun in hand, I ran down the shoulder of the road. On the other side of the truck, the driver-side door opened and a woman swore as she examined the damage to her wheels.

She didn't hear me over the idling engine until I'd pressed the barrel of the revolver into the base of her skull. "On your knees, hands behind your head," I ordered. "I have no intention of pulling this trigger, but my finger gets real twitchy when fools try to surprise me."

The woman followed my instructions. She wore a green Glacier Notch uniform and quaked uncontrollably, but when I glimpsed her face in profile, I could see that something important was missing: surprise. When you drove around a truckload of drugs for a living, the possibility of being hijacked must always be in the back of your mind. "I have no cash," she said. "And even a few hundred cases of syrup won't buy you much crack. You can still walk away from this—I haven't seen your face."

I walked in front of her to let her see that I had no intention of going anywhere. "I'm not a junkie and I don't want your cargo. All I want is a ride back to the Notch."

"What are you, sixteen, seventeen?" She shook her head. "You're barely older than my daughter. Do your own mother a favor and leave now."

I sized up the driver. Presumably not everyone who worked for Nox was a bloodthirsty, merciless troll like Aries had been. Some were driven by greed, like Grimshaw and Drumm. Others, like Smitty, were prisoners to fear, but could be persuaded to help you if you pushed the right buttons. My gut was telling me that this driver fell into the latter category.

I'd have to appeal to her maternal instincts. "Your boss is one hour away from causing my eight-year-old sister to die. While that might sound crazy to you, you're clearly a smart woman. You know you're not working for the humanitarian-of-the-year. And if you're a mother, I'm sure you're probably just doing this to support your family. So ask yourself: If we were talking about your daughter, how far would you go to keep her safe from a tumor like Horace Nox?" I glanced down the road to make sure there were no cars coming. "I'm going to give you a simple choice. We climb in the truck, you drive us back through the compound gates, and all you have to do from that point on is say *nothing* and go back to living your life. But if you disobey me, then you are consciously putting an end to my sister's life, and your daughter will grow up motherless."

The woman nodded frantically. "There's a tarp in the passenger seat. You'll have to hide in the back of the cab until we're through the security checkpoint."

She climbed behind the wheel and I slipped beneath the tarp in the back. I tapped the gun against her seat to remind her not to mess with me. She made a sharp U-turn and headed north.

246

Fifteen minutes later, the truck came to a stop. We'd arrived at the gates to Nox's compound.

Through the open door, I heard the click of boot heels on the asphalt. A guard addressed the driver sounding less than pleased. "What are you doing back here?" he snapped. "You should be halfway to Conway by now."

I held my breath, expecting the driver to scream that there was an armed stowaway in the backseat. Bless her heart, she kept her voice calm. "There was broken glass from a car accident all over Lake Road. It shredded my tires to shit."

The guard grunted. "I can see that, Almeida."

"What did you expect me to do, call Triple A? Give me thirty in the garage and I'll slap on a new set."

I heard the loud groan of the compound's reinforced gates swinging open. "Better make it fifteen," the guard said. "Rumor has it the boss made a surprise visit today ..."

The truck rolled forward through the open gates. I was in.

I peeled the tarp off me. "Thank you," I said.

She kept her eyes forward on the dirt path. "You can thank me by tucking and rolling out of the truck exactly when I tell you. There's a camera blindspot on the passenger side up ahead. If you miss your window and they catch you on film, you might as well shoot us both."

I readied my hand on the door handle, and when she gave a brusque "Now!" I jumped out of the vehicle. I sprinted down the steep embankment beside the path, tripping on the gravel partway down and tumbling the remaining distance.

I landed in what I can only describe as an alien landscape.

A vast field of sugar maple trees arranged in tidy rows stretched as far as the eye could see. To observers during the day, the compound might appear to be an ordinary maple farm, but as the sun plunged beneath the horizon, the tree trunks had started to glow in the dark. According to Dec, the Blyss lichen absorbed sunlight, then phosphoresced throughout the night.

I heard the crunch of footsteps over dried leaves—a guard with a submachine gun doing rounds. I took shelter behind a maple, pressing my back into the spongy lichen-covered trunk and praying that its soft opalescence wouldn't cast my shadow.

The footsteps came and went, but I wasn't in the clear yet. The maple fields were teeming with armed mercenaries in black commando getups. They patrolled for unwelcome guests like me, while keeping a vigilant eye on the field workers who toiled late into the night, harvesting the lichen.

The glow-in-the-dark maples were hardly the weirdest feature of Glacier Notch Farms. That distinction went to the monstrous sequoia in the center of the compound, a tree thirty feet in diameter and four times as tall. Horace's crazy botanist brother, Wilbur, had genetically engineered the behemoth himself. A staircase wrapped around the trunk, spiraling upward like the threads on a screw, until it arrived at a glass globe at the top. Nox used the lookout as a bird's-eye view of the property that had made him a multimillionaire.

"I'd bet my life that you'll find Atlas there," Dec said. *"If the information in your boy's head is as important as you say it is, then Nox will want to keep him close to the chest—and in a place where he can see you coming. Which still leaves one difficult question."*

I touched the circular perimeter of the maple fields. *"How do I get from here"*—*I traced my finger to the center of the circle, where we'd marked the greenhouse—* *"to here, without taking a bullet?"*

"Or forty," *Dec added unhelpfully.*

I frowned at the map. Given the ambient light from the tree trunks, I might as well throw on a reflective vest with a neon target if my plan was to play hide-and-seek with the guards.

I recalled something from Rufus's dossier that hadn't seemed important on first read. Over the last year, the maple field had strained to meet the growing demand of Blyss. To increase production, Nox had invested in a new chemical to accelerate the growth of his product.

"Fertilizer ..." I whispered.

I used a marker to draw a big red X through Nox's circular compound, with the two lines intersecting at the massive treehouse in the center. "Four quadrants," I said, tapping each wedge of the pie, "north, east, south, and west. Each needs to be fertilized and watered once an hour. Since the fertilizer is toxic, the harvesters and sentinels are constantly moving clockwise around the compound to keep away from the sprinkler system—which means that for a few minutes every hour, one quadrant will be completely empty."

Dec looked unimpressed. "Uh, yeah, because it's being saturated in poison. What, are you going to wear a raincoat?"

I did a rough calculation of the circle's radius—it was close to a quarter mile from the perimeter to the treehouse. "A warning system supposedly gives a minute's notice for anyone who hasn't already cleared out. That will offer me a brief window to get from point A to point B."

Dec whistled. "How fast is your four-hundred-meter dash?"

As I lurked at the edge of the field, I heard the cog-like *clank-clank-clank* of machinery in the ground around me. Down the columns of maples, black sprinkler heads rose out of the dirt in synchrony. Red lights pulsed in warning, and the robotic voice of a woman made an announcement through speakers hidden among the trees:

"Sixty seconds until fertilization commences in West Quadrant."

I took off down the line of glowing trees. My legs pumped vigorously, toes digging into the soil, heels never touching the ground. For this to work, I was going to need to give it all the horsepower I had. If I was a second too slow, then I would die, and so in turn would Atlas and Echo, like precariously placed dominoes.

Partway through my mad dash across the field, I snatched one of the items from my bag and dropped it in my wake.

249

"*Thirty seconds until fertilization commences,*" the disconcertingly calm voice announced again. The greenhouse still seemed so far away.

By the time the voice started to count down from ten, I could see the open plaza that buffered the maple field from the towering sequoia. I spotted a potential sanctuary: a shadowed recess beneath the spiraling staircase, where the steps might shelter me from the fertilizer. With every bit of juice left in my veins, I rocketed forward and dove into that cubby, right as hundreds of sprinklers all hissed on in unison.

A fine green mist shrouded the western quadrant of the field. Some of the green water splattered the pavement in front of me. I covered my mouth with my sleeve and tucked my knapsack protectively behind my back.

Then I held my breath and watched the field in anticipation.

Dec still wasn't sold. "Even if you make like the Flash and beat the sprinklers, who's to say the greenhouse won't be swarming with guards?"

"Then I guess I'll have to empty the hive." And I had just the insane trick in mind to do it. "That chemical you threw into the river—Hydrobane, was it?—how much of that do you have?"

When it dawned on him what I was asking, Dec made the shape of the crucifix over his heart and muttered a prayer in Gaelic. "You've got to be kidding me, Sabra. You want to go running through sprinklers carrying a substance that explodes on contact with water?"

"Yep."

After some coaxing, Dec reluctantly led me out to the shipping container. He opened a cooler, revealing four lumps of the silvery Hydrobane laid in a row, each the size and shape of a brick and wrapped in plastic. If Dec's demonstration had used only a marble's worth, I could only imagine how much devastation an entire loaf could dole out.

"Each is coated in a resin made out of mineral oil. Even the humidity in the air can be enough to set off a reaction, so the coating keeps the moisture out. But once the resin washes off ..."

"Then I guess I better make sure tonight's forecast doesn't call for rain," I said.

Dec shut the lid of the cooler. "The hell do you need these for anyway?"

"Nox likes order. I'm going to introduce a little chaos."

Seconds later, an explosion rocked the compound. A blossom of fire rose up out of the green mist. The blast was so powerful that it ripped apart the tree trunks surrounding it, sending chunks of scorched, still-glowing bark to rain down over the orchard. The fertilizer being dispersed into the air must have been combustible, because right before my eyes, the flames spread through the network of tree canopies. In time, the sprinklers all turned into makeshift flamethrowers.

Shouts echoed from the field. Footsteps clattered down the stairs right over my head as Nox's security team fanned out across the compound, skirting around the edge of the war zone of toxins and fire. One of them screamed into his walkie-talkie as he ran. "Turn the sprinkler systems to water only!" he barked. "Do it now!"

I waited an extra minute until the last of them had exited the tower. Then I emerged from my hiding space and began the winding ascent around the outside of the sequoia. As I climbed, I was treated with a bird's-eye view of the compound. The devastating blast had left a crater fit for a meteorite. Even with the fertilizer shut off, the flames continued to spread in a ring that grew wider by the minute.

As I neared the greenhouse at the top, I pulled the gun from my waistband. For the last flight of steps, I edged cautiously around the trunk, keeping my back pressed to the bark. Then I stepped up onto the main platform.

The greenhouse was surrounded on all sides by a wraparound balcony, and the windows offered a 360-degree aerial perspective of the compound. Under less deadly circumstances, I might have taken the time to enjoy the panoramic view of Jay Peak and the highlands to the north.

The interior of the greenhouse contained rows of strange, exotic plants growing in boxes—an orchid with golden petals; cacti with dagger-sharp spines; a crimson briar patch with thorns that appeared to ooze blood. And in the middle of this freakish garden, a far stranger scene was unfolding.

Only two occupants remained in the greenhouse. Atlas had been bound by his hands and legs to a wheelchair. His head lolled from side to side, his vacant gaze passing right over me.

The other man had his back turned. He was freakishly tall even with the pronounced hunch in his back, and deathly thin as well, a gaunt wendigo of a man. He was tending to a pink-spotted vine with a pair of pruning shears, chattering insanely to himself. When I caught his face in profile, I knew exactly who he was.

The resemblance between Wilbur Nox and his younger brother was uncanny. Wilbur had the same cobalt eyes, the same harsh cheekbones. But whatever insanity possessed the elder Nox had left him emaciated, with the heavy eye bags of a chronic insomniac.

As I edged across the room, I noticed a tray full of syringes in front of Atlas. Their transparent tubes contained liquids of all colors and consistencies. They were crudely labeled with the penmanship of a madman: *Shivers. Fever. Sleep. Revive. Agony.*

Even more terrifying, three of the vials—*Truth, Nightmare,* and *Pain*—had nearly been used up. The Nox brothers had been using Wilbur's potions on Atlas to try to torture the riddle out of him.

My hand paused over the syringe labeled *Agony.* I was tempted to give Wilbur a taste of his own medicine, but getting Atlas out of here quietly was more important than vengeance. The last thing I needed was this psycho screaming in pain.

I picked up the *Sleep* syringe and padded quietly up behind Wilbur. The closer I got, the more I could make out his quiet ramblings. "That's right, my darling *Cucurbita tormentus*. You will be the one to make the little birdy squawk, where *Ferocactus verum* failed. Torment is the road to truth, I always say ..."

I wrapped my hand over Wilbur's mouth and rammed the needle into his back. He thrashed and gave a muffled scream into my hand, but I proved stronger than him. I expelled the contents of the syringe, and his frantic screeching and panicked movements calmed to nothing. His body crumpled. He was snoring by the time he hit the tile floor.

With the mad scientist incapacitated, I knelt by Atlas's wheelchair. His lips were so chapped from dehydration that they were bleeding. In his drug-induced haze, it was going to be difficult to get him off the compound, which wasn't exactly wheelchair accessible.

I lightly tapped him on the side of the face a few times. "Stay with me, Atlas. Do you know where you are?"

He burbled something incoherent, then whispered one name: "Selene ..."

Whatever freakish nightmare the drugs had conjured in his mind, it involved his dead sister.

Desperate, I grabbed the *Revive* syringe off the tray. While I didn't want to subject him to more of Wilbur's potions, I needed to wake him up so he could defend himself. I jammed the needle into his thigh and slowly depressed the plunger.

Atlas's eyes snapped open and he looked wildly around the room. I withdrew the needle and cupped his face. Where my thumb touched his neck, his pulse palpitated. "You're safe now," I said. "I'm getting you out of here."

I madly scanned the room for something to cut his restraints, until I saw the tiny pruning shears that Wilbur had been using. While I sawed through the ropes on one of his wrists, Atlas started to focus. "Sabra, I figured out where the final riddle is," he whispered with excitement. His voice was raspy and dry. "At least the general area, but it's a start."

"That's great," I reassured him. "You can tell me all about it once we get you the hell out of this tree." The shears finally snapped the first restraint.

With his newly freed hand, Atlas grabbed my wrist. "No, now. In case I don't make it out." I started to tell him that wasn't going to happen, but he plowed on. "Elderfield Hollow. It's a defunct agricultural college on an island just off the coast of Maine. The school has been closed for nearly half a century, but I'm positive the trail leads there."

I beamed at him, only admiration and awe in my heart. "Twenty-four hours of torture, drugs, and hallucinations, and you still managed to break the code?" My eyes filled with tears thinking about all that this boy, who was practically a stranger, had been through to save my sister—and to save me, too. "Clichés be damned, but I don't know what I would have done without you over the last week."

Atlas started to smile back at me, but his grin liquefied. His gaze had focused over my shoulder. The hairs on the nape of my neck bristled.

I spun around to find Horace Nox standing at the top of the stairs with a gun leveled at my head. "Didn't you see the sign?" he asked. "*No girls allowed in the treehouse.*"

TIMBER
GLACIER NOTCH FARMS

MY HAND FLEW TO THE BUTT OF THE REVOLVER TUCKED into my jeans, but Nox wagged a warning finger at me. "I don't think so. Take it out real slowly, lay it on the ground, and kick it toward me."

As I set my gun down, I contemplated trying to get a shot off, but I wasn't exactly a sharpshooter. Nox looked ready to pull the trigger if I so much as flinched. I felt all hope fade away as it skittered across the floor and stopped next to his shiny black shoes. I shrugged the knapsack off my back and tossed it to the floor as well.

With his gun still trained on me, Nox crossed the room to where his brother lay and felt his neck for a pulse. On cue, Wilbur let loose a phlegmy snore. "He seems charming," I said. "I can see where he gets his good looks and model physique."

Nox straightened up. "They should really change the Tides family name to 'Weeds.' But in a lot of ways, you've made this easier for me by coming here. In fact, you didn't even have to go the trouble of torching my field. I would have happily waved you right through the front gates. Because while this asshole"— He waved the gun at Atlas—"has done a bang-up job resisting torture, now I get to use you as leverage against him and him as leverage against you. A symbiosis of pain."

"What if you and I find the final riddle together?" I hated pleading with the man responsible for my brother's murder, but I was low on options. "If you let Atlas go, I swear I'll—"

255

Nox pulled the trigger and fired a shot so close to my head that my eardrum sang after the bullet whistled past. A window shattered behind me.

"No more ultimatums," he said. "This is how it's going to work: You're going to walk over to that tray full of delightful potions. You're going to pick up the syringe labeled *Agony*. And you're going to inject it into your heart. If you don't, I'm going to start putting bullets in your boyfriend, nonlethal shots first, into the most painful joints in his body. I'll start with his ankles and work my way up to the kneecaps, then his pelvis. Maybe even his manhood, since I'm in such a generous mood."

"I get the picture," I snapped.

"As for you, Mr. Atlas, I have a distinct feeling that while you proved adept at withstanding a lot of pain, you won't have the stomach to watch it inflicted on your girlfriend. And if you thought Wilbur's *Pain* potion was bad, he tells me that *Agony* is that multiplied by a hundred. We couldn't even use it on you because the pain from it is so unbearable that it can actually stop a person's heart. Her agony won't end until you tell me the answer to the last riddle."

Atlas was using his free hand to tug at his remaining restraints. "I don't know the answer, asshole," he said. "It's kind of tough to focus when instead of getting me the research materials I asked for, you give me torture and sleep deprivation."

Nox checked his watch. "You're full of shit and you're both wasting my time."

Through the loudspeaker in the corner of the greenhouse, the monotone female voice returned. "*Sixty seconds until fertilization commences in North Quadrant.*"

I glanced down at my knapsack. In dropping it, one of the remaining bricks of Hydrobane had partially slipped out. I could see it glinting silver under the top flap.

256

An idea congealed in my mind, but first I needed to figure out which direction was north. The plume of fire was rising to the west, which meant that if I turned ninety degrees clockwise ...

"Come on!" Nox ordered. "Pick up the syringe. Unless you want me to start playing Operation with your boyfriend." He took aim with the pistol at Atlas's lower extremities.

I held up my hands. "Okay, okay. I'm going." As I walked toward the tray with the needles, I stealthily snagged the brick of Hydrobane with my toe. With each shuffling step, I pushed it forward, never looking down so Nox wouldn't suspect. When I stepped behind a garden box, which briefly obscured my feet from him, I gave the brick a hard nudge. The *"Thirty seconds"* announcement covered the whisper of the brick gliding over the tiles. Like a hockey puck, it slid across the glossy greenhouse floor, heading toward the north-facing balcony. It tumbled off the edge toward the field below.

At the tray of syringes, I picked up the vial of *Agony*. A few beads of the golden poison spilled out of the needlepoint. "Sabra, don't," Atlas begged me. His faced had caved in with helpless torment. We both knew that as soon as he cracked and gave up the location of the final journal page, we were dead.

I pointed the needle toward my heart. "Before I do this, answer me just one question, Horace." Without giving him the opportunity to refuse, I asked anyway. "Why the Nightingale? You could have named your bar anything you wanted. But you chose to name it after a symbol of female revenge."

"Symbol of female revenge?" Nox snorted. "I've read every single myth and legend about resurrection and rebirth in existence, and let me tell you, the nightingale is the most brilliant practical joke in all of mythology. Women exacting vengeance, then getting transformed into nightingales, to forever sing some beautiful fucking song—female empowerment bullshit, blah,

blah, blah. But here's the punchline that you clearly missed: The Greeks had it all wrong, because in nature, it's only the *male* nightingale that sings." Over the loudspeaker, the announcer began the ten-second countdown. "Don't you see, you moron? The female nightingale has no voice." Nox clapped the butt of his gun on the edge of a garden box to underscore each of his final words. "The female. Nightingale. Doesn't. Sing."

I stared defiantly into Nox's eyes. "This one does."

In the northern quadrant below, the sprinklers hissed on, rinsing the resin off the brick of Hydrobane.

The explosion bucked the greenhouse hard, sending Nox and me to the ground. Under the force of the blast, the north-facing windows all shattered.

Something I hadn't expected happened next: The enormous tree began to list to one side. The blast must have been destructive enough to gouge a chunk out of the base. The floor beneath us tilted ten degrees, twenty degrees, then thirty. I grabbed hold of one of the garden boxes as the incline grew more pronounced. My knapsack, which contained the rest of the Hydrobane, landed next to me, and I prayed that there was nothing wet uphill. Meanwhile, Atlas's wheelchair started to roll forward. He latched onto the nearest flower box and braced himself.

The Nox brothers weren't so fortunate. Wilbur's unconscious body tumbled across the floor and right off the edge of the platform. Nox slipped helplessly over the tile, too, and for a second it looked like he might share his brother's grisly fate. At the last minute, as he approached the edge, he wrapped a hand around the railing and dangled there.

The tree's decline came to a jerking halt as what remained below of the damaged trunk held fast. My revolver, which had been lodged against one of the garden boxes uphill, skittered loose and raced past me before I could make a grab for it—

And landed right in the outstretched hand of Horace Nox. With his legs dangling over the void and his other hand still gripping the railing, he steadied his elbow on the tile and swiveled the gun in my direction, grinning with dark resolve.

I let go of my perch. My body slid fast over the tile floor on a collision course for Nox. Right as he zeroed in on me, I drilled my boot into his other hand, crushing his finger bones between my heel and the railing.

Nox screamed, and with his fingers too mangled to hold on, he fell. While I hugged the railing for dear life, I watched Horace Nox plummet into the canopy of burning trees eighty feet below. The inferno swallowed him whole. "How's that for agony?" I whispered.

Atlas cleared his throat. Upslope, he was dangling by one hand from a garden box, his forearm muscle bulging out of his skin under the weight of the wheelchair. "Glad we dropped a house on the wicked witch and all," he said in a strained voice, "but would you mind terribly cutting me out of this chair?"

I scaled back up the slope and pulled Atlas up to a safer perch, where I finished sawing through his restraints with a piece of broken glass. He was in rough shape—his body was stiff from being confined to the chair for the last twenty-four hours and he broke into a heavy sweat as the drugs made another cycle through his bloodstream. I wrapped his arm over my shoulder for support, scooped up my knapsack, and together we clambered over to the top of the staircase.

It was slow work climbing down. With the tree tilted nearly forty-five degrees, one unbalanced step could pitch us over the edge of the rickety bannister. As we journeyed downward, we were treated to an outstanding view of the fire that was spreading through the maples.

Our descent came to a halt at the site of the second explosion, where the staircase ended in a scorched, jagged lip.

The Hydrobane blast had decimated the bottom of the tree, leaving a chasm where the last flight of stairs used to be. Twenty feet below, the blackened crater still burned in patches.

The titanic tree groaned ominously. "I'd ask if you were okay to jump," I said, "but I don't think we have a choice."

Atlas smiled weakly. "Cannonball," he whispered, and we took a big step off the edge of the staircase.

A quick fall later, we hit the top lip of the crater. I braced myself for the impact and transferred my momentum into a roll down the shallow slope. I heard Atlas cry out as his ankle twisted beneath him. Before we'd even stopped tumbling, the mangled tree trunk looming over us gave another colossal groan. I picked Atlas up off the bed of charcoal and helped him limp across the crater. As we hobbled up the slope, the enormous tree cracked in half. I could feel the shadow of it coming down to hammer us into the earth.

With not a moment to spare, I gave Atlas a rough push from behind to force him up the final few feet and over the lip of the crater. A magnificent wind rushed around me as the trunk came so close to crushing us that I could almost feel the bark scrape down my backside. The ground quaked as the broken sequoia, reduced to a log of epic proportions, crashed to the earth, snapping an entire row of maples as if they were toothpicks. With any luck, the trunk had flattened Nox's corpse in the process.

We plowed through the burning maple fields toward the garage. Even with a sprained ankle and drugs pumping through his veins, Atlas soldiered on, one grimace-inducing step after another. The compound's security detail was too preoccupied with the fire to notice us limping through the chaos.

Our luck only lasted so long. We arrived at the garage right as a mercenary emerged from the door. He froze, noting our non-official attire. His hand strayed instinctively toward his holster.

"Excuse me, sir," Atlas said, then launched out of my grip with explosive speed. He drilled his meaty knuckles into the guard's temple in the most devastating punch I'd ever seen. The mercenary's head clanged against the garage's aluminum siding on his way to the ground, where he lay still.

Inside the garage, we ducked low and weaved through the armada of syrup delivery trucks. One of them idled, its diesel engine chugging away. The keys dangled from the ignition, abandoned by its driver at the sound of the explosions.

I helped Atlas into the passenger seat and climbed behind the wheel. As I reached for the stick shift, I realized that despite having my driver's license, I had never driven anything larger than Atlas's Silverado. Now, I was about to drive a box truck on a mad escape from a burning maple field.

"Just pretend it's a really big pedicab," Atlas suggested.

I taxied out of the garage, retracing the route the driver I'd taken hostage had followed. When I reached the main gates, they had been sealed closed. Fortunately, I had planned for this.

"Okay," Dec said, "so you've got your entrance, your distraction, and eventually, your man. But that doesn't mean shit if you can't get out." He stretched out of his wheelchair to poke the front gates on the map. "The moment you start burning the place down, those doors are going to snap shut to keep the feds out and trap you inside. And they're not some crappy chainlink fence you can drive through either—we're talking slabs of reinforced steel. You could drive a Mac truck into those at sixty miles per hour and you'd probably bounce right off."

Dec was, annoyingly, right. And without a ladder to scale the walls that circled the compound and bolt-cutters to hack through the razor wire on top, we might as well dig a hole to China to get out.

A squiggle on the map's southeastern edge caught my eye. According to our materials, it was a natural spring that Nox used as the primary reservoir for his sprinkler system.

I raised an eyebrow at Dec. "What if I made my own door?"

261

We sped past the sealed guard gate and down the access road. When the outline of the spring became visible beyond a nearby row of maples, I asked Atlas, "How strong is your arm?"

"I was an all-star pitcher on my baseball team. Of course, that was Little League …"

With one hand still on the wheel, I withdrew a brick of Hydrobane from my bag and handed it to Atlas. "Then pretend it's the final inning of the Little League World Series." I pointed to the approaching spring. "Hit the edge of that pond as close to the wall as you can."

Looking perplexed, Atlas pulled himself out the window and sat on the sill. He waited so long that I thought he might chicken out. If he threw it when we were too close to the spring, we'd be incinerated in the process.

He cocked back his arm, and with a cry of exertion, he finally let it rip. Through the windshield, I watched the brick soar through the air and tumble twice along the gravel road.

Then it plunged into the shallows of the spring.

I reached across the front seat and jerked Atlas back into the truck as the Hydrobane detonated. Half of the natural spring instantly turned into steam. The blast ripped through the wall as though it were made of papier-mâché.

I floored the accelerator so we'd have enough momentum to navigate the obstacle course ahead. The truck splashed down into the crater's soggy valley, popped up over the opposite lip, and barreled through a mound of rocky debris. As soon as we'd passed through the hole in the wall, I took a hard right to avoid the forest ahead.

A victory cry burst out of me when we reached the main road and the truck's wheels rumbled onto asphalt. "*Now* are you ready to admit that I've got street smarts?" I asked.

Atlas didn't respond. He had slouched down in his seat and was gaping around the truck's cab in unrestrained terror. From the sheen of sweat that had repopulated his brow, I knew that the mixture of drugs still loitering in his bloodstream had made an uninvited resurgence.

I snapped my fingers to get his attention. "Stay with me, Atlas. It's just an aftershock from those drugs. Keep looking at my face and everything will be okay."

Instead, his gaze had focused out the windshield on the road ahead, zeroing in on some imaginary horror. "Oh God," he whispered. "Oh God, oh God, oh God ..."

It was imperative that I get him to a hospital—he needed detox and an IV of fluids, fast. If the dehydration didn't kill him, the shock of these living nightmares might. "Tell me what you're seeing," I instructed him. "Maybe I can help you."

"I'm at the campfire for her birthday." His voice quivered. "She takes a sip of the Blyss, and I scream out for her to stop, but she can't hear me. Her eyes roll back and she starts to seize, so her friends all scatter, leaving her to die alone. I can do nothing, I can do absolutely ..." He petered off as his breathing escalated into full-blown hyperventilation.

I typed "hospital" into the truck's GPS, and chose the nearest one, in Saint Johnsbury. "It's only a nightmare, it's not real." But of course, Selene's death *had* been real, whether he'd been there or not, so I tried a different approach: distraction. "Tell me something I don't know about you. I've saved your life twice now, so I think I deserve to finally know your first name."

Atlas had covered his eyes with his hands, but he'd apparently heard me. "Gordon," he said. "Gordon Atlas. I was real chubby as a kid, so they used to call me El Gordo. It was traumatic."

I couldn't help but laugh. "Well you turned out okay in the looks department. Tell me something else. How about the riddle? You said it was at some old college in Maine?"

The color was starting to return to his face, though his eyes remained glazed over. "Elderfield Hollow, on a small island not

263

far off the coast. The college closed its doors fifty years ago—small schools throughout New England have come and gone like that for years." He swallowed hard. "The line *hallowed halls* told me it must be about a university, and there was something about a *snaw*, a popular ship among pirates. As far as I know, Elderfield Hollow is the only island with both a college and a history of piracy."

I glanced in the rearview mirror to make sure Nox's security force hadn't followed us. With their master dead and the drug fields reduced to ash, we were the least of their concerns now. "Was the riddle more specific about where to look, or are we going to have to dig up an entire island?"

Atlas forced himself to take deep breaths. "That part was unclear. The riddle mentioned the Garden of Hesperides. It's a Greek myth, an orchard that Hera owned on the edge of the world, with golden apple trees that could grant immortality."

My heart swelled with hope. "Plants with the power to give life? Sounds familiar." I fumbled around in the center console until I found a canteen of water. There wasn't much left, but it was better than nothing. "Drink this."

Atlas greedily poured the contents of the bottle over his chapped lips and down his throat, drinking so fast that he choked. When he was done sputtering, he continued. "According to myth, the divine hero Hercules was tasked with twelve labors—twelve feats of heroism—to earn the forgiveness of the gods. The eleventh labor required him to steal an apple from the orchard, which was guarded by a giant serpent." He shook his head. "That's honestly all I remember, but once I sit down with some research books, I swear—"

"You're going to sit down with a doctor first," I told him. "*Then* we will find this mythical garden of yours."

Thirty minutes later, I pulled up outside the hospital in Saint Johnsbury. The syrup truck earned more than a few bewildered looks as I helped Atlas down to the curb and through the emergency room's sliding doors.

The attendant took one look at the boy draped over my shoulders and paged for help. Two nurses assisted him into a wheelchair. "Not one of these again," he mumbled.

"Someone drugged his beer at a party," I lied. "I told him not to leave it unattended." This was the most plausible story I could come up with. The last thing we needed right now was an inquisition by the state police, the FBI, and the DEA.

The attending nurse looked skeptical, but in the end, she admitted him and firmly instructed me to stay put in the waiting room. Under the pretense of leaning in to plant a goodbye kiss on Atlas's forehead, I slipped my extra cell phone into his pocket.

As they rolled him away, Atlas hoarsely called out, "Promise me you won't go looking for the magical garden without me!" If they hadn't thought he was totally tripping before, they would now.

"I won't!" I yelled after him.

It was the second lie I'd told since we arrived at the hospital.

I walked back through the sliding doors and out to the truck. Atlas would be safe in hospital care for now. I couldn't bear the thought of waiting any longer when the Serengeti Sapphire was nearly within my grasp. And if the police came by the hospital and found a stolen delivery truck with a link to an incinerated drug compound up north, I'd end up locked up before I had a chance to complete the quest.

So I sent a telepathic apology to Atlas, plugged the coordinates to Elderfield Hollow into the truck's GPS, and began the four-hour drive to the Maine coast. With Horace Nox dead, there would be nothing to stop me from finding the Sapphire, nothing to hold me back from reuniting with Echo. By sunrise, I would have my life back.

———

Survival was all about timing. In most circumstances, the difference between life and certain death came down to a single choice you made in a tenth of a second, a weakness that you exploited, an opportunity that you seized.

Horace Nox knew all about timing. It was how he'd survived an ambush that had killed half his battalion twenty years ago. It was how he had risen to the throne atop his Boston empire.

So as he plummeted eight stories from the greenhouse, he rotated his body and let himself fall. Right as he plunged into the burning canopy of a maple tree, he reached out for one of its fiery limbs and seized it with his non-broken hand.

Nox had made a career of agony, but even this hurt. Under his incredible downward velocity and the weight of his body, his fingers snapped as he'd grabbed the burning branch. His shoulder ripped free of its socket. However, he slowed himself enough that when his body hit the ground below, it wasn't a meteoric impact.

Nox lay in the soil, stunned and taking inventory of his numerous injuries. Several broken ribs. Right shoulder dislocated. Minor burns covering his face and arms. Most of his fingers mangled. All the while, the canopy overhead seemed to burn in slow motion, dumping embers around him like a genocide of fireflies.

A heavy crack snapped Nox out of his stupor, and through the canopy he saw something else: the massive sequoia falling down to squash him. Adrenaline kicked in and he scampered through the trees. He could feel his twisted, bruised, and broken body resist his every movement. In the end, he escaped by a margin of a few feet. Any slower and the monstrous redwood would have crushed him at the ankles.

"Wilbur ..." he whispered, gazing at the fallen tree. His brother was undoubtedly dead somewhere under the log.

But above all, Horace Nox loved himself, so there was something far more important to do than mourning his brother: finding the Tides bitch and her boyfriend. While the girl could die a torturous death for all he cared, the boy was his last tether to the slave journal. If he died, so did the location of the Serengeti Sapphire.

After he'd rammed his arm into a nearby tree, popping his shoulder back into the socket, Nox limped through the burning field toward the crumpled knot of steel and shattered glass that used to be the greenhouse. He would tear the I-beams apart with his bare, broken hands if that's what it took to find the boy. And then he would squeeze him like a wet rag until the truth came out.

Nox wasted no time in assembling a team of his best mercenaries to comb through the wreckage for survivors. They had only begun to sift through the greenhouse debris when a third and final explosion rocked the compound.

Ten minutes later, he stood in front of the gaping, jagged hole in his perimeter wall. The underground spring was slowly replenishing the evaporated reservoir, filling in the tire tracks that the two little bastards had left during their escape.

The chief of his security force jogged up to his side. "Your suspicions were correct—they took one of the delivery trucks. How do you want us to proceed, sir?"

Nox pulled out his mobile phone. The screen was shattered, a spider web of misfiring pixels, but the processor inside had survived the fall. And as he pulled up the GPS locators that allowed him to see where all of his trucks were at any given time, he saw one blip heading east.

"Sir?" the mercenary repeated. "Do you want us to pursue the stolen truck?" He couldn't take his eyes off Nox's gnarled fingers, which were struggling to operate his phone. "Do you ... require medical attention?"

Nox took a vial of Blyss from his pocket and chugged it in one gulp. Over the next few minutes, it would slowly deaden him to the pain racking his body.

"Turn the fertilizer back on," Nox ordered the security chief. "In all quadrants. I want this field and all the product incinerated before the authorities get here. I'll handle our missing inventory." He pointed to the pistol strapped to the guard's hip. "Oh, and give me your sidearm."

The security chief handed over his weapon and Nox gingerly closed his fractured hand around its grip. The great thing about guns was that it didn't matter if you had nine broken fingers.

You only needed one to pull a trigger.

FROM THE JOURNAL OF DR. CUMBERLAND WARWICK
Columbia, South Carolina | February 17, 1865

In the moments following the slave quarters' implosion, I stood paralyzed with a despair incomparable even to the bloodiest nights of my military career. Staring at the mountain of fiery rubble that had collapsed on Malaika and his son, my beating heart petrified into cold, inanimate stone.

But when all seemed lost, over the fire's steady crackle, I heard a sound that filled me with optimism: a single cough. Then another. Forgetting my fear of fire, I set the Serengeti Sapphire aside and plunged into the wreckage. The smoldering wood and tin burned away the flesh on my fingers. Even now, it is with great pain that I hold the pen to write this letter. But hope trumps any agony, so I dug until my flesh puckered.

When the digging was done, I unearthed a bittersweet miracle.

Malaika had, to my great sorrow, perished in the collapse. His head hung askew where the largest rafter had broken his neck. I had little time to mourn because another weak cough escaped from below him. When I mustered the strength to roll my companion's tremendous form aside, I discovered the source of the signs of life: young Jaro. As his last dying act, his father had used his own mighty back, strong from a lifetime of tea leaf harvests, to shelter Jaro from the falling debris.

I scooped up the semiconscious boy in my arms and carried him away from the fiery ruins, so he would not wake to the sight of his father. Beneath the shelter of a weeping willow, I lay him among the roots. His face was streaked with soot and sweat. Smoke inhalation had aggravated his illness, rendering every breath ragged and uncertain. Any doubts that the boy sprawled before me was Malaika's son were whisked away when his gold-flecked eyes blinked open.

Upon seeing me, Jaro shrank back. I cannot fault him—he had probably seen no kindness from our people since the day of his kidnapping. I chose my next words carefully. "Jaro, I was sent by your father. Sent to bring you this." Spectacle speaks more convincingly than words, so I unsheathed the mystical Sapphire from its burlap sack.

As the orchid's azure glow lit Jaro's face, his eyes transformed from fear to wonder. "Yakuti ..." he whispered. His father, before cruel providence tore his son away, must have shared with him the legend of the flower, because Jaro excitedly plucked one of its radiant petals. Hope swelled in me as he pressed the blue curiosity to his tongue.

I was watching him chew when someone struck me savagely over the head. Consciousness forsook me. Hours later, my skull still throbs as fierce as my scorched fingers. When I regained my faculties, I was alone beneath the willow. The boy and the flower were gone. Through my bleary eyes, beyond the fiery mirage of the mansion, I observed a wagon speeding away down the long drive, away from Magnolia Black. I swear, from within the shadowed canopy of the carriage, I saw two eyes, filled with stardust and a thirst for life, gazing right back.

I fear I shall never know Jaro's fate, whether he escaped north, whether illness took him, or whether the Sapphire turned out to be the miracle Malaika zealously believed it to be.

To my dying day, however, I will think of that boy, and I will wonder.

IN A KINGDOM OF WAVES, THESE HALLOWED HALLS
TAUGHT WISE AND HARDY MEN TO TILL
AND OFT BEFRIENDED MUTINY,
A SAFE HARBOR FOR THE SCOURGE AND SNAW.

PART THE TIDES TO CROSS THE BRIDGE
AND ASCEND UP THROUGH THE STONE,
THEN NAVIGATE THE SERPENT'S TAIL
TO THE GARDEN OF HESPERIDES.

THE FINAL LABOUR AWAITS YOU THERE,
A HERCULEAN TASK OF FAITH:
TO FIND THE APPLE OF ETERNAL LIFE
YOU MUST FIRST KNOCK ON HADES'S DOOR.

THE HOLLOW
COAST OF MAINE

THE ISLAND OF ELDERFIELD HOLLOW LOOKED LIKE THE
Atlantic had tried to reclaim it many times, but failed.

It sat a quarter mile off a lonely section of coast and rose
dramatically out of the harbor. On all sides, erosion had carved
sheer cliff faces into the craggy gray rock. Black walnut trees
grew right up to the edges, arrogantly standing up to the
elements that had done their best to break the island.

I stood on the shoreline across from Elderfield Hollow,
leaning against the stolen delivery truck and waiting for my
ticket across the harbor. In the half hour since my arrival, not a
single car had come around the sharp bend in the road. I'd been
treated to the most stunning, interrupted symphony of the
waves gently lapping against the shore. This far away from the
city lights, the stars seemed to have multiplied one-hundred-fold,
and as I gazed up at the vibrant panorama of constellations I'd
never before seen, I realized that for the first time in two weeks,
I finally felt like everything was going to be okay.

Low tide approached, which meant that my journey to the
island would soon begin. There was a trick to getting to the
Hollow, according to one of the few websites I could find.
They'd never built a bridge from the mainland and the local
ferry stopped making trips there fifty years ago after they'd
shuttered the college. However, for one hour, twice a day, the
tide fell low enough to reveal a narrow sandbar between the
two shores.

My patience was soon rewarded. As the harbor waters receded, a beige line cut a direct path to Elderfield Hollow. I jumped the guardrail and sprinted across the thin smile of beach, unable to wait a second longer. Up close, I began to notice some of the island's more striking features. I had wondered before how visitors were expected to scale the Hollow's sheer cliff faces. Now I could see that someone had chiseled steps into the stone, which to anyone on mainland would appear flush with the cliffs.

At the top of the neolithic staircase, I passed under a wrought-iron gate that read "Elderfield" and onto the college grounds. The abandoned campus consisted of three white buildings and a greenhouse clustered around a quad. The buildings were modeled after Greek Revival plantations, with robust columns and black shutters. Under the gauzy light of the moon, I felt like I'd been transported back 150 years to the Antebellum South.

Beautiful as it was, something about the quad didn't sit right with me, and I couldn't put my finger on it. There was a vegetal scent in the air that smelled out of place.

I was suddenly overcome with the futility of what I was trying to do here. I'd found four journal pages so far, but those had all been with Atlas's help *and* with the full riddle at my disposal. This time, I was armed with only a few lines that Atlas had repeated to me in a drugged stupor. Without the rest, I could dig up all of Elderfield Hollow and still come away empty-handed.

I had to try. I refused to move from this island until the final journal page was in my possession. By morning, Atlas would have pulled through his detox. He could recite the riddle in its entirety to me then, using the phone I'd left with him.

Partway across the quad, I froze when I heard an unexpected sound: wooden chimes hidden in the trees, clanging dissonantly together. Disturbed by the noise, a cacophony of speckled seabirds erupted into the sky by the hundreds, all cawing in alarm. I watched in awe as they formed a monochrome vortex that circled the island.

I'd stepped on a latticework of nearly invisible wires that crisscrossed the lawn and disappeared into the trees. The chimes were some sort of rustic, cobbled-together "home security" system. No crazy squatter came out to greet me with a shotgun, so I prayed that whoever had rigged the alarm was long gone.

I watched my steps more carefully as I approached the largest of the three plantation houses. I unclipped the flashlight from my knapsack and shined it through the windows. My intention was to start combing through the classrooms and living quarters inside, searching for anything relevant to the myth Atlas had mentioned. I was reaching for the doorknob when the flashlight's beam illuminated an object lying next to one of the pillars.

It was an apple core. The exposed flesh had turned brown from contact with the air. The bite marks on it clearly belonged to human teeth.

And it had been eaten *very* recently.

All at once, I noticed the eerie details around the quad that I hadn't quite been able to digest before. The leafy odor I'd smelled was cut grass, which explained why the quad wasn't overgrown from years of neglect. The greenhouse's windows had all been washed. The plantation houses looked as pristine as they did because someone had applied a fresh coat of paint to each of them. In fact, a painter's ladder still lay in the grass next to the porch.

I suddenly felt like Goldilocks when she realized she'd stumbled into a den of bears.

This island had a human inhabitant after all.

From the skin remaining on the half-eaten apple, I could see that it was a golden varietal. According to the research I'd done on my phone while I waited for low tide, the trees in the mythical Garden of Hesperides all bore golden apples. If that wasn't a sign that I was on the right path ...

I also realized, as I swept my flashlight over the quad, that the freshly cut lawn consisted of two different shades of grass. Most of it was green, but a shade of vibrant blue ringed the quad's outer edge. It appeared to form a pattern, though it was impossible to say for sure without a higher vantage point.

I lifted the painter's ladder out of the grass and leaned it against the plantation house. I took the rungs two at a time, up to the roof. It only required a few seconds to recognize what I was staring down at.

The blue grass on the quad formed a serpent. Its reptilian body snaked in and out of the black walnut trees.

The Garden of Hesperides had been guarded by a hundred-headed dragon named Ladon, which Hera had placed there to keep intruders from stealing her immortality-granting apples.

The tail curled around the greenhouse and ended in a sharp tip that pointed due east. But where were the dragon's numerous heads? I traced the outline of the serpentine body around the edge of the island and found that it eventually disappeared behind the mansion. I scampered up the roof and when I popped up over the A-frame's summit, I drew in a sharp breath.

Whereas I had thought the island to be perfectly round before, a small peninsula protruded off the back, surrounded on three sides by the same imposing cliffs. It faced east, out to sea, where the earliest whispers of dawn were trickling over the horizon. The dragon's body ended there.

And where the peninsula began, so did a patch of golden apple trees.

I slid down the ladder and raced toward the grove, where I could hear the ocean swells crashing thunderously against the cliffs.

Only when I got closer did I see the blue glow emanating from the peninsula.

Because the golden apple trees were the least remarkable thing about the orchard.

Because from one end of the peninsula to the other, between the roots of the trees, grew a bed of vibrantly blue flowers that luminesced softly through the night.

The Serengeti Sapphire.

There must have been a hundred of them, all nearly uniform in shape and size. I knelt to examine one of the flowers more closely. The Sapphire was a blend of beauty and danger, seductively curling petals protected by crowns of thorns that spiraled around the husk.

Their unearthly glow illuminated something else as well. On one of the apple trees, a yellowed document had been nailed to the trunk and coated in a protective sheen—the twelfth journal page. I moved across the peninsula toward it, careful not to step on any of the priceless flowers.

When I reached the final page, I made a startling discovery: except for the number twelve in the corner, it had been left blank.

I shrugged off my knapsack and pressed my hand to the cold plastic laminate. "But where is the final riddle?" I whispered.

A voice behind me replied, "I am the final riddle."

I spun to find a man in paint-stained overalls leaning against a tree, a half-eaten apple in his hand. He was tall, trim, and black, and though it was hard to guess his age in the dim light, he couldn't have been much older than thirty. "Do you know who I am?" the caretaker asked.

This was a difficult question. The man standing before me looked too young to have stolen the journal four decades ago.

The more I thought about this crazy quest, the more certain I became that whoever penned those riddles had a personal investment in the story of Malaika and his son, in the Serengeti Sapphire. Atlas had destroyed Dr. Warwick's final entry before I could read it, but what if Jaro or his father had survived the slave quarters' fateful collapse? What if several generations later, one of his progeny had stolen Warwick's journal and planted the path of riddles, and to this day, his family watched over the miraculous flower?

If I truly believed in the Serengeti Sapphire, in this wild expedition I'd just risked my life to complete, only one answer made sense. "You're a descendant of Jaro, aren't you?"

Looking unimpressed, the man took a final bite out of his apple and pitched the core off the cliff, to be swallowed by the tidal waters below. "Try again. For someone who solved my riddles to find this island, this one should be easy."

My riddles, he'd said. And when I realized what he was suggesting, I struggled to string a full sentence together. "That's impossible. You can't be ..."

"You came here looking for the Serengeti Sapphire, yet you dare to use the word *impossible?*" The man emerged from the shadows beneath the apple tree, and his eyes gleamed an inhuman gold under the light of the moon. "Girl, I *am* Jaro."

I had put blind faith in a series of riddles written by a total stranger.

I had followed them to find a mystical plant that could restore my sister's health, where modern medicine had failed.

But now confronted with a living, breathing miracle, I found belief in short supply. "You're telling me that you're *the* Jaro from Cumberland Warwick's journal." I did the math in my head. "That would mean that you're a hundred and sixty years old."

"A hundred and sixty-two," he corrected me. "But I like to think I don't look a day over a hundred and sixty-one."

I felt woozy and braced myself against the nearest tree for support. There were only two options: Either the man standing before me was a lunatic and I'd fallen for one of the most elaborate hoaxes in the history of the modern world.

Or this was Jaro, the golden-eyed son of Malaika, who'd been stolen from his home in Africa and endured sickness and slavery. For years he had survived on the magic of the Serengeti Sapphire, calling on its restorative properties to cure whatever ills befell him and to even defy natural aging itself.

If that was true, then I was standing in a bed of flowers that could give my sister her life back. If that was true, then my long and painful journey was at an end.

Just like I had all along, I chose to believe.

That didn't mean I was without questions. "But why?" I asked. "If it's kept you in good health for over a century, at the peak of your life, why leave the riddles? Why invite strangers to come and take the flower from you? I don't know how to break it to you, but some really shitty people were looking for this."

Jaro chuckled. Despite his many years, I could see a little bit of boyhood left in him. "Immortality is a young man's dream— a fool's dream," he explained. "And for a time, I, too, was a fool. So I rationed the petals from the flower and clung to youth. I wandered the world and observed miracles and tragedies alike. I saw an industrial age rise and horses replaced by carriages that pulled themselves. Man joined the birds in the sky, then flew past them into space. I saw my people's place in this country evolve, but also watched how some things never changed. The wheel of time relentlessly turned and the friends around me came and went. Yet I remained."

"What changed, then?" I asked. "I don't care how much you saw. You don't just wake up one morning and give up everything because you're bored."

Jaro held up his hand. A golden wedding band glinted on his ring finger. "I fell in love. I planned to share the Sapphire with her, to share in eternity with her." His hand fell limply to his side. "But eternity is only a fragile illusion. Like anything in this world, the Sapphire has limits. It can cure the sick, it can speed up the healing process, but it can't bring back the dead. One winter's day, on her way to work at this very college, my wife's car hit a patch of ice. She lost control. They found her in the water at the base of a cliff not far from here." Jaro fixed his wistful eyes on the horizon. "One day taught me what one century had not. My father didn't cross the ocean and move the earth to give me an endless life. He only wanted to give me a *better* one."

Jaro wandered gingerly through the flower bed, closer to me, and he pressed a hand to the final journal page. "I stole the journal and created the riddles to ensure that whoever inherited the Sapphire had the same unbreakable resolve as my father. But I also decided to only bequeath the flower to someone who had undertaken a *selfless* odyssey, just as my father had—to save the life of another, not his or her own. So I ask you: Has your journey been a selfless one?"

I smiled, thinking to myself how disappointed he would have been if Nox had been the one to complete his quest. "My sister, Echo," I said. "She has cancer."

Jaro's stardust eyes, which had seemed to dull as he told the story about his wife, blazed with intensity. "And you swear on your soul you'd do anything for her? Without question, without hesitation?"

"Anything," I promised him, though his line of questioning was making me uneasy.

"Then there is one last test you must pass before my miracle becomes your sister's." He swept his arm out over the

279

flower bed. "Of the hundred flowers here, ninety-nine are impostors. Though they may all look alike, only one is the true Sapphire. See, away from its soil of origin, the flower will not accurately replicate. All attempts to clone the flower yielded only these doppelgängers. Rather than inheriting the Sapphire's curative properties, they produce a poison from their thorns that will slowly kill a man in twenty-four hours. Even worse, that poison is impervious to the medicinal powers of its parent. Do you understand what I'm telling you?"

A hollow cold spread through me. I had a feeling I knew where this conversation was headed.

"In the myth of Hercules," Jaro continued, "after he'd returned with an apple from the Garden of Hesperides, his twelfth and final test was to journey deep into the realm of Hades to capture Cerberus, the three-headed hellhound. To save Echo, you must make your own brave descent into the underworld."

"You're asking me to die," I said bluntly. After everything this past week had thrown my way, after beating all odds and surviving assassination attempts and outliving Horace Nox, I was doomed to never see my sister grow up after all, all on a technicality. Maybe old age really had driven Jaro mad.

But I knew that there was still no question about what would happen next. I would see this through to the end. "Guess I can't show you a picture of her from my wallet instead?" I joked. My voice sounded thinner than tissue paper.

"I'm afraid on this I will not budge—no journey ends without sacrifice," Jaro said solemnly. "But I promise you, once you have willingly taken the poison, then I will show you which of the flowers is the true Sapphire. From there, you will have twenty-four hours to return to your sister."

The more I studied Jaro, the more I knew that pleading with him to change his mind was a fool's errand. And with Echo as sick as she was, to delay at all was to risk her life.

I dropped to my knees, and with only a moment of hesitation, I wrapped my hand around the nearest flower and squeezed until the thorns pricked my flesh.

THE FINAL THORN
Elderfield Hollow, Maine

I WANTED TO FACE DEATH BRAVELY, BUT I COULDN'T help but draw in a shuddering breath as the barbs sank into my skin, nor could I stop the tears that welled in my eyes. I imagined the venom from the plant leaching into my bloodstream.

After a small eternity, I withdrew my hand and held it up for Jaro to see. Seven puncture wounds formed a constellation across my palm. Blood trickled out of them, painting the ground between us. Despite the fear that I felt, there was something else there: relief. My odyssey was finally at an end. Maybe it wouldn't conclude exactly the way I had dreamed, but I would at least get to go home, one last time.

Jaro was smiling at me with tears in his eyes. "The love of family is something to behold, a miracle far greater than any life-giving flower. I am now convinced that the riddles couldn't have produced a more worthy successor." His smile broadened into an Anansi grin. "That's why I feel so elated to tell you that the story about the poison was only a farce."

"Wait, you're telling me—"

Jaro put a hand on my shoulder. "You're going to be fine. While the children of the original Sapphire don't share its healing qualities, they won't kill you either."

I bent over, hands on my knees, and drew in several deep lungfuls of air. My heart galloped in my chest. "I'm so relieved that I might actually throw up. With pranks like that, you must be a real gas to have around on April Fool's day."

"I had to be sure of your virtuous heart—and now I am. Come." He beckoned me. "The Sapphire is yours."

Jaro led me toward the eastern cliff edge, where a peculiar object protruded from the trunk of an apple tree. It was a sword, plunged halfway to its hilt. I remembered back to the myth of the Garden of Hesperides. "Let me guess," I said. "A sword that indicates which of the dragon's hundred heads to slay—or which flower is the true Sapphire."

Jaro laughed. "I could have used more pupils like you when I still taught in the classroom." He knelt beneath the tree, next to a flower that looked no different than any of the others. Still, I felt awe ripple through me standing in its presence. Like its protector, this plant had been on a far longer journey than I could expect in my lifetime.

From the deep pocket of his overalls, Jaro produced a trowel and began to dig a wide swath of dirt around the flower.

"So how does this all work?" I asked him. "I mean, how much is the dosage you need to take?"

"One petal is always enough," Jaro explained. "I used one petal during a cholera outbreak at the turn of the century, one when I became infected with Spanish flu in 1917, and again in the 1950s for polio. The rest have merely been to sustain my youth, one decade at a time. Fetch that pot for me?" He pointed to a terra cotta urn that was tucked away among the roots of an apple tree.

I placed the pot beside him. "And you ... eat the petal?"

"Initially, I ingested it like that, yes," Jaro said. "But for each dosage throughout the last sixty years, I've found greater pleasure in drinking it as a tea."

Jaro had dug a moat halfway around the Sapphire when he abruptly paused. Slowly, he lifted his head to regard the sky over the island behind us. As I followed the line of his gaze, I saw what had troubled him. For the second time since my arrival, Elderfield Hollow's seabird colony had taken to the air en masse, a dense geyser of squawks and winged chaos.

Underneath their raucous frenzy, I could hear the peal of wooden chimes.

Jaro's face hardened. "Did you bring any friends with you?"

My initial instinct was that maybe Atlas had made an early departure from the hospital and followed me here. Worry wart that he was, though, he would have called at his first available opportunity to berate me for finishing the quest without him.

Jaro didn't wait for me to respond. He grabbed the hilt of the sword that was buried in the apple tree next to us. With a savage pull, he wrenched it free. "Be still," he whispered to me. "I will see if I need to revoke someone's invitation." Then he slipped into the shadowed glade between the trees, his gilded irises receding into the darkness.

The warning bells in my head told me to hide. But now that the Sapphire was within my reach, I couldn't just leave it here, half-dug out of the ground. The trench that Jaro had started carving around it would be a bull's-eye for anyone who'd come to the island seeking its magic.

I dropped to my knees, snatched Jaro's trowel, and resumed the quick yet delicate process of digging out the flower. After a while, I could feel the roots' grip on the soil slacken. I wrapped my fingers around the base of the Sapphire and with a gentle pull, the flower popped free of the earth. It had a dense nest of roots that filled the entire pot as I lowered it in. Eventually I'd want to plant it in a bed of soil, but this was no fragile flower. If it could survive a transatlantic voyage in a burlap sack, it could hopefully handle a short trip to Boston.

I had just started to pack soil around the Sapphire, when I was interrupted by the crunch of boots trampling flowers. From the darkness beyond, I watched a demon return from the dead.

Horace Nox sauntered toward me through the orchard in a methodical death march. The flesh on his face was puckered with burns. Several of his fingers were broken and jutted out at weird angles. Despite his corpse-like appearance, he was one hundred percent less dead than I had believed him to be until this very moment.

"You are very good at cheating death, Sabra Tides," he rasped. He withdrew a pistol from the waistband of his tattered trousers. "But I am better."

Jaro launched out of the shadows, the sword raised above his head. In three rapid steps, he crossed the distance between him and Nox and brought the weapon slashing down.

Nox saw the blow coming at the last second, and without time to step out of the way, he defensively raised his left arm to intercept the blade.

I expected a gruesome scene to unfold, but what happened next was in many ways much worse. Years of exposure to the elements had dulled the sword's edge, which Jaro had only ever intended to be a symbolic ornament marking the quest's end. Even with all of his might behind it, the blade only cut half an inch into the flesh of Nox's forearm, stopping at the bone.

The blow should have been excruciating for Nox—but he didn't even wince. He must have had enough Blyss in his veins to anesthetize an elephant.

Jaro faltered, confused. That moment of hesitation was all Nox needed to whip his gun hand around and fire two bullets at point blank range into Jaro's heart.

I screamed in futility as the one man who had seen more history than anyone else alive crumpled to the bed of flowers, his impossibly long life snuffed out before he hit the ground.

Vengeance urged me forward to make Nox pay for what he'd done, but to do so would be suicide. Already, the drug lord was swiveling his pistol toward me to finish the job.

I had never been so desperate. I prided myself on visualizing escape routes from every tight corner I found myself in, an instinct that had kept me alive for the last week. Now I'd reached a cul-de-sac. With no alternatives, I played the only bargaining chip I had left: the truth. I backed up until I could feel the rocky edge of the cliff beneath my heels and held the flower out over the sea. "Listen to me carefully, Horace: This is the *true* Serengeti Sapphire," I said. "The others around you are just powerless clones—only the original can save you."

"Then why don't you step away from the edge," Nox ordered, "and put my fucking flower down."

I shook my head. "Hear those waves crashing against the cliff? If you shoot me, this plant is going right into the surf. By the time you get down there, you'll be lucky if you can pick the Sapphire confetti out of the water with a spaghetti strainer. Now, this plant"—I hoisted the Sapphire—"has eight petals. All I want for Echo is one. Just one. I'm sure it will regrow before you even need it."

"This isn't the Oregon Trail—you don't get to barter." Nox beckoned impatiently for the plant with his free hand.

I tried one last Hail Mary, in hopes of playing to any shred of empathy he had left. "I don't care about avenging Jack anymore. I don't even care what becomes of me. I only care about Echo. Don't you remember what it was like to waste away your childhood, staring at the hospital door, waiting for someone to bring you a cure? The resignation that grew each day when that cure never came?"

"Enough!" Nox shrieked. The gun trembled in his mangled grip.

I extended the flower farther over the waves to remind him what was at stake. "While I can't begin to comprehend what that feels like," I said, "I do know exactly what your brother must have gone through. That has been my life for two miserable years. Every morning, I wake up in desperation, wishing I could trade places with her. Every day, I live in a constant state of anger, wondering what kind of unjust world would allow that disease to choose my sister over every other kid on the playground. And every night, I fall asleep with a cold hollow in my chest as I picture the possibility of a life without her. So when all this is over, you can chase me down to the ends of the earth and do your worst. There is no agony that you can submit me to, no hell that you could condemn me to, that would be even a fraction of the torture of losing Echo. All I ask is that you give me one petal and one day to change her life before you take mine." My voice broke as I added a soft, "Please."

My appeals to Nox's humanity had obviously made little impact on him, but it only took one look at his singed face to see the wave of logical calculations that his soulless inner CPU was crunching. He could shoot me and risk trying to fish the plant out of the water below, but the waves were still angrily slamming against the cliff wall. Even if he salvaged a leaf or two, that wouldn't help him twenty years down the line when he needed another for salvation from whatever vice or disease tried to kill him next. No, he needed the whole plant alive to secure his immortality.

In the interest of self-preservation, Nox's best option was to acknowledge our stalemate. "One leaf," he conceded. "Take it, but the rest of the Sapphire stays with me." I didn't budge— there was no way I was going to take him on his word without a show of faith. Nox flipped the pistol in his hand around and then chucked it in a high arc, off the side of the cliff and into the ocean.

While I still didn't trust him, I had to make my gamble now. I pulled the Sapphire back to safety, delicately plucked one of the petals from the top, and set the flower down on the ground. With our transaction complete, I edged across the orchard, back toward the main island, keeping my distance from Nox. My eyes never left him.

I'd only made it partway across the peninsula when Nox pensively scratched the stubble on his burned chin. "On second thought," he said, "what if I come down with a really bad cold one day? I guess I'm going to have to ask for that flower petal back after all."

He reached into his waistband, drew a second gun, and fired, as I simultaneously tried to lunge out of the way.

But I was too late.

I heard the gunshot at the same that I felt the slug hit my stomach. The round kicked me back a few steps, and I reflexively clutched my belly. I stared down, stunned, as blood blossomed out of the wound, pouring over my fingers. A heat seared through my abdomen, spreading through my torso. A ringing crescendoed in my ears and I dropped to my knees. My brain was struggling to catch up with the bullet that had just ripped apart my insides. And when I couldn't bear it any longer, I slumped over into the flower bed.

With glistening, tear-filled eyes, I stared up as Nox sauntered over to me. In one last stand of resistance, I closed my fist around the Sapphire petal. Nox smiled and drove his boot down hard on my wrist. I screamed out a dry, hoarse wail as the bone snapped. The bastard leaned down and pried the petal from my bloodstained fingers.

I was forced to watch as he pressed the glowing blue flower petal to his tongue and swallowed hard. He closed his eyes, reveling in this moment of salvation he'd waited so long for. "Of all the exotic game I've ever eaten," he said, "I like the taste of resurrection best."

Then he stood up and walked toward the cliff, leaving me to die.

As the darkness clawed at me, as hope drained from me, my bleary eyes spotted a familiar shape in the flowers only a few yards away.

It was my knapsack.

I remembered back to the events that had unfolded on Nox's compound and took inventory of all the Hydrobane I'd used.

One to set off that distraction fire in the fields.

One to cut down the giant sequoia while Nox was holding us hostage.

And one to rip a hole in the compound's perimeter wall during our escape.

Dec had given me four bricks.

I rolled over, fighting through the agony and unconsciousness that threatened to take me. On my elbows, I crawled through the flower bed. Thorns scratched at my face. My broken wrist screamed out every time it touched the dirt. Still, I kept moving until my good hand seized the strap of the knapsack. I unclasped the top.

At the cliff's edge, Nox picked up the Serengeti Sapphire, a difficult task given his bouquet of mangled fingers. Eventually he managed to cradle the flower between his hands. The blue glow washed over his face. "It's curious," he said, though I wasn't sure whether it was to me or to himself. "A plant nearly condemned me to death, yet years later, it was a plant that brought me resurrection."

With every last drop of adrenaline I had left, every will to survive for Echo's sake, I launched myself out of the garden bed and charged at Nox. He was so fixated on his prize that he took stock of me too late. I flung the knapsack so that the strap lassoed around his neck and I slammed my shoulder into his gut. "Resurrect this," I growled.

Strong as he was, Nox was no match for my legs, which all those long nights pedicabbing had transformed into two powerful pistons.

Four steps later, I shoved his body forcefully off the cliff, and he plummeted into the waves below.

He resurfaced immediately, one arm astoundingly still wrapped around the Serengeti Sapphire like a broken wing. He stared up the cliff at me with an incendiary gaze and screamed, "What? Did you think a little water was going to—?"

The ocean water filled the open knapsack, and after a deceivingly peaceful glow, the Hydrobane exploded.

I had half a second to watch the blast tear Nox apart in a tidal wave of red, transforming him into a magnificent crimson smear against the cliff, before the ensuing shockwave tossed me backward. I landed at the base of an apple tree, just far enough from the edge not to tumble into the ocean as a chunk of the cliff collapsed. It rained boulders down on whatever remained of Horace Nox.

I opened my hand reluctantly, expecting the worst. To my relief, a single petal of the Sapphire glowed in my palm.

I had grabbed for the flower, right as I gave Nox the final push over the edge.

My first instinct was to pull out my phone and call 9-1-1. Maybe there was still time for someone to rescue me.

But the longer I stared at the cerulean petal in my hand, the more I grew certain that it was the wrong thing to do. I needed to know for sure that the Sapphire would reach Echo. If I lost consciousness before the medics arrived, there were far too many ways for the petal to get damaged or misplaced in the evacuation. And I couldn't exactly explain over the phone to the emergency operator, "Now, when the rescue team comes, they have to make sure to keep track of my magical flower petal."

There was only one way to definitively know that Echo would receive the miracle I'd sacrificed everything to get for her.

It was the easiest decision I'd ever made.

I slipped the Sapphire petal into the pocket of my jeans. While I sat with my back against the trunk of the apple tree, I speed-dialed the phone I'd left with Atlas at the hospital. It went to voicemail after a few rings. He was probably still in treatment, or maybe being subjected to a lecture about the dangers of experimenting with drugs. When the phone beeped, I tried to keep it simple.

"Hey, handsome," I said. "I have a very long story, but very little time to tell it." I swallowed hard as pain lanced through my belly. "I'm hurt, pretty bad, but under no circumstances are you to call nine-one-one. I know that as you listen to this, you're probably already reaching for your bedside phone, but if you do, you will kill Echo. So here are the details you need to know: I am at Elderfield Hollow, leaning against a tree in the apple orchard. There is a single petal from the Serengeti Sapphire in my left jeans pocket. Come to the island as soon as you're able, take the petal from me, and *then* you can call anyone you want. But you have to promise to bring the Sapphire to Echo for me —I trust you, and only you. I wish I could do it myself, but ..." Another gut-wrenching pain. "Anyway, I guess this is the time when I'm supposed to make some grand gesture, some eloquent goodbye, but as you know, I'm not much of a softy, so I'll leave you with this: You saved my life. I know it might sound ironic given the reason I'm calling, but you did. Echo's going to live because of you, and without her, I am nothing. Look after her for me, will you? I love her so, so much. And for what it's worth, I think I sort of love you, too." Then I hung up.

Light was spilling over the horizon, but darkness was coming for me, so I called the second number immediately: the direct line to Echo's hospital room. In the age of cell phones, I still had that one phone number memorized, because honestly, it was the only one that ever really mattered.

To my surprise, given the early hour, Echo picked up after three rings. I had kept it together throughout my call with Atlas, but the second I heard her groggy little "Hello?" I started to quietly sob. I covered my eyes with my broken wrist.

I forced myself to find my voice again. "Hey, baby," I whispered. "It's your big sister."

Echo let loose an epic yawn. "Sabra? Why do you sound so weird?"

I massaged the bridge of my nose with my fingers. "I'm just tired, little one. Look, this is going to sound strange, but I've got a friend who's going to bring you something from me. I know Mom always told you not to take candy from strangers, but I need you to trust me and make an exception this time."

She huffed on the other end. "Why don't *you* bring it to me?"

"I have a little longer on my journey to go, but I'll be home soon." Of all the lies I ever told, this one really broke my heart. "The boy's name is Atlas. He's going to bring you a cool-looking flower petal that I hope is going to make you feel a whole lot better."

"What does this boy look like?" As always, her mood could shift from pouty to intrigued on a dime. "How will I know he's not an impostor?"

"Ask to see his tattoo of the sparrows," I instructed her. "And if he's not very, very good-looking, then he probably is an impostor."

Echo scoffed. "Who's to say that you and I even have the same type?"

"The same type?" I laughed breathlessly, even though it hurt. "I really have to stop watching reality TV with you. You're like a cougar in an eight-year-old's body."

A white numbness was spreading through me, starting in my stomach and fanning outward. I would hold onto Echo as long as I could. "Hey, kiddo, I have an idea—why don't you stay on the phone with me? I've been up all night, and maybe you can read me a story from that mythology book of yours, while I fall asleep. Just like Jack and I always read to you."

"The tides have turned, my friend!" she quipped excitedly. "Get it, since our last name is Tides? It's a pun." Again, I was forced to laugh. There was shuffling on the line and the flap of pages as she leafed through them. "I have the perfect story, a new favorite of mine about three siblings—two girls and one boy, just like us! There was Selene, goddess of the moon, and Helios, goddess of the sun, and each day and each night they'd race their chariots across the sky, only to plunge into the ocean. Their sister, Eos, was the dawn, and opened the gates in the morning to let Helios and his chariot out."

"That's the one," I whispered. The edge of the tangerine sun peeked its head out over the ocean. The colors on the horizon were bleeding together, a vivid watercolor of rose and blue and dusky indigo. "Start at the beginning. And don't stop 'til the very end."

Echo's voice sounded like it was getting further way, but I grasped onto every word she said, refusing to let go. "There once were three siblings," she began, "and together they controlled the sky and brought light to the world ..."

PYRRHIC VICTORY
10 DAYS LATER

SO MUCH HAD CHANGED IN BOSTON THROUGHOUT the course of one week.

The nightly roar from Fenway Park fell silent, after the Red Sox won the World Series. Halloween came and went, as the two hundred thousand college students who lived around the city emerged for one night of costumed debauchery, before tucking themselves back into their dorm rooms. On November 1, All Saints Day, winter descended early on Boston, blanketing the streets with six inches of snow. The autumn tides swept back out to sea without even a whimper.

Yet some things remained immovable. Gordon Atlas had been coming to this same park every day for the last week. At noon, he would sit down on a weathered park bench and wait for the miracle.

And for the seventh consecutive day, there it was: two childcare workers from the hospital leading a pack of children through the snow. It was easy to spot the miracle because she was taller than the other kids her age.

Echo was going to be strong and beautiful just like her older sister. That much Atlas could tell already.

Today, she had tucked her dark purple snow pants into her galoshes. She had been confined to her hospital bed for so long that she moved awkwardly, stiffly, at odds with a growing body that was a stranger to her now. In time she would mature into it and find the same powerful grace that had made Sabra Tides so formidable and alluring.

All because of a single petal from a single flower.

Nine days ago, Atlas had stolen a candy striper outfit from the hospital linen closet and used it to slip unnoticed through Echo's ward. His major concern had been formulating a plan to convince Echo to eat the Sapphire petal. He was a total stranger to her, after all. Should he tell her the truth about the wild journey he and her sister had been on to obtain the flower? Should he concoct a lie about being a doctor with an experimental treatment?

All of these options had sailed right out the window when he'd opened the door to Echo's room and found a miniature version of Sabra staring at him in sleepy wonder. She had the same olive complexion smattered with swatches of Irish freckles. The singular curl that dangled out from beneath her cap was the same untamable ruby red as Sabra's natural hair color. But more than anything, Atlas could see Sabra in the girl's emerald eyes.

Even more surprising were Echo's first words to him: "Let me see the tattoo."

Atlas had peeled back his sleeve and showed her Selene's name, with the sparrows rushing off the end. She'd smiled, satisfied, and drank in his whole body with her eyes. "I guess we do have the same type after all," she whispered.

Atlas watched anxiously as Echo chewed the petal, cringing at the bitter floral taste before swallowing it down. He didn't know what to expect, or how fast the Sapphire was supposed to work its magic. Would she immediately jump out of bed and start doing cartwheels? To his disappointment, she mumbled a weary "thank you," closed her eyes, and fell into a deep sleep. When it was clear she was out cold for the night, Atlas let himself out.

The rest of the story he later gathered from Calista Tides.

The morning after Atlas's visit, Calista had visited Echo's room to find her out of her bed, wide awake and standing in front of the television. She stood upright, no longer hunched over from pain and nausea. A half-eaten plate of syrupy pancakes occupied one of her hands, while she used the other to flip through the channels. "Clicker's broken," she explained to her mother through a mouthful of flapjack.

Overnight, her white blood cell counts had skyrocketed into healthier levels. The next day, when they took Echo in for an ultrasound, the mass that had metastasized on her liver—the one her doctors had just discovered a day earlier—had shrunk to a third of its previous size.

On the third day, the tumor had vanished completely.

After that, Echo was so supercharged with youthful energy that despite Calista's protective instincts, she couldn't bear to deny her a few hours outdoors between appointments to confirm that she had truly entered some sort of aggressive remission.

So Atlas continued to follow through with his silent, belated promise to Sabra to watch over her sister, the miracle child.

But if there was one lesson to be learned from Cumberland Warwick's journal, it was that even miracles came at a price.

And this one's had been far too high.

Ten days ago, after waking in a Vermont hospital bed to Sabra's bone-chilling voicemail, Atlas had suppressed the agonizing urge to dial 9-1-1, her final orders be damned. He'd raced to the rental car dealer across from the hospital and broke every speed limit to get to Elderfield Hollow before it was too late.

It had been high tide when he reached the coast. The sandbar was totally submerged, so he swam across the cold channel over to the stone-cut stairs. On his way through the apple orchard, he nearly tripped face-first over the corpse of a man he didn't recognize. The John Doe had a hole through his heart and a bloody sword beside him. Atlas had no time to puzzle over this, because just ten yards away, he spotted Sabra.

She was slumped against an apple tree, eyes shut, arms limp in the grass. There was blood everywhere, so much blood ...

As he cradled Sabra in his arms, he felt the flutter of her pulse beneath his fingers, weak and far too slow. Mad with grief, he pulled the Sapphire petal from her pocket and started to bring it up to her lips—if it was as powerful as they'd been lead to believe, surely Sabra's grave injuries weren't beyond repair.

In the end, he couldn't do it. She had offered up her life so that Echo could live. To feed Sabra the petal would be to make the last week for nothing. She would never forgive him if she pulled through. He'd never forgive himself either.

So he picked up the phone that had fallen from her hand and called 9-1-1.

A helicopter landed in the quad of the college an hour later. While he watched the chopper lift off and carry Sabra south to Maine Medical Center, Atlas tried to piece together a believable story for a suspicious detective, while begging them to let him follow the medevac. Between the voicemail Sabra had left him, confirmation from the hospital in Vermont that he'd been under supervised emergency treatment all night, and a severed wrist they found in the water with a Gaelic tattoo that matched the one on file for Horace Nox, they eventually cut Atlas loose, though they would call him in for questioning three times before the week was out.

Fortunately, Nox's reputation preceded him. When the police raided his mansion in Cohasset looking for answers, they found six riddles and a map in Nox's subterranean chamber that corroborated everything Atlas had told them. They'd also found another murder victim, a low-level Blyss dealer with two bullets in his head, who had been decomposing in the foyer.

Meanwhile, Sabra never woke up. Even after they stopped the internal bleeding and removed her ruptured spleen, she remained in a deep coma. When they talked to her, she showed only sporadic bursts of mental activity. Once her condition had been stabilized—whatever that meant—they transferred her by ambulance from Maine Medical to Children's Hospital in Boston, so she could be closer to her family.

When Atlas came to visit Sabra after her transfer, he inadvertently walked in on Calista Tides reading aloud at her bedside. They'd met twice before, when Atlas had tried to share with her the same patchwork story he'd given the police. It felt like a cheap, plastic version of the truth, but he wanted Sabra to fill in the gaps herself, if she would *just wake up*.

Mrs. Tides stopped mid-sentence when he entered the room. She sheepishly held up a book of Greek myths. "Echo's idea. She said it helped her get better, so maybe it would help Sabra, too. What's in the bag?"

Atlas pulled out a black hoodie. "In case she gets cold," he explained. "God forbid she wear something with color."

Calista patted him on the shoulder and offered to take a walk while he had a few minutes alone with Sabra. It was a lot more of a welcome than he'd anticipated.

For the past twenty-four hours, Atlas had been rehearsing what he would say to Sabra when he saw her, everything he didn't have a chance to tell her after her voicemail had wrenched his heart out of his chest. Yet as he sat beside her, taking in the awful details of the room—the plastic ventilation tube taped to her mouth, the IV in her arm, the endless rhythmic blip of the vital signs monitor—all those words evaporated.

What came out of his mouth instead was: "This is horse shit."

Even Atlas was surprised by the frustration that gushed out of him, but there was no stopping it once the floodgates

298

opened. "I am so, so furious with you. How many times?" he snapped. "How many times did you sneak away to do something dangerous without me there to protect you? Didn't you know it would eventually catch up with you? Twelve hours—all you had to do was wait twelve hours until morning, and then I would have happily escorted you to the Hollow as soon as I could stand on my own two feet. Hell, I would have crawled alongside you if you'd asked me. It didn't have to end this way."

Atlas picked up the book of Greek myths. "Do you know what a 'Pyrrhic victory' means? Twenty-five hundred years ago, the Greek king Pyrrhus defeated the Romans in battle, but his army's casualties numbered so many that he might as well have lost. That's what this is. Echo's alive, just like you wanted, but think of the devastating cost. She's already going to grow up without her brother, and now you're going to leave her without a sister, too? What kind of half-life is that?

"And what about me, Sabra? How am I supposed to go back to normalcy now? You can't carve out a niche in my life that huge, and then in only a few days' time, leave a hollow where you used to be. How dare you tell me that you 'think you sort of love me.' What kind of coward says that? What kind of coward doesn't even give me the chance to say it back?" He was crying now, for the first time since Selene's funeral. "I don't know what the hell love is or whether you can feel it for somebody you've only known a week. But dammit, I would give my life just for one more week to find out. That wouldn't be a Pyrrhic victory. It would be worth every single year that I lost."

Atlas stood up and leaned over Sabra. "I'm going tell you a secret. Back on the island, I knew you'd kill me if I fed you the Sapphire to try to save your life. But because I couldn't just watch the girl I'd fallen for die while I did nothing, I gave you a sliver, where the tip of the petal had ripped loose. So at the end of the day, you have no excuse not to come back to us. Stop being so selfish and wake the hell up. There are people who need you. You owe your mother the story of how you got here. You owe Echo a proper childhood. And dammit, you owe me another kiss." Because he was out of angry, passionate things to say and because he had a flashback to their last happy moment together on George's Island, right before Nox had blown up their rented Sunfish, he added, "Oh, and you owe me a boat, too."

After his diatribe, it felt like he should storm out of the room for proper dramatic effect. Instead, he lingered awkwardly by her bed. Eventually he sighed, dropped down into the chair, and read to her from the mythology book until Calista got back.

Now Atlas sat on a park bench, watching from a distance as Echo splashed about in the snow, making snow angels with the other kids. In the middle of a snowball fight, which the childcare workers were trying in futility to break up, Echo paused. While snowballs whizzed around her, she heartbreakingly tilted her head to the sky, searching for something, searching for someone.

Atlas followed her gaze upward. A ray of sunlight cut through the sullen clouds. *I failed you, Jack,* he thought. *I promised you I'd watch over Sabra, and I promised Sabra I'd watch over Echo, and I couldn't keep both promises.*

A snowball struck Atlas on the head. He searched through the gaggle of children for the perpetrator. One of them must have a wicked arm to have thrown so far.

When a second snowball pelted the back of his neck, he realized the cold projectile hadn't originated from the children after all. His eyes caught a flutter of paper on the bench beside him, a crumpled receipt that must have been packed into the snowball. On the back, hastily scrawled in smeared, blue ink, were the words:

IOU
1 *Boat.*
1 *Kiss.*

Atlas bolted upright like he'd stepped on a live wire. He looked frantically around the park. And then he saw her.

She limped barefoot through the snow, seemingly oblivious to the cold. A green hospital gown poked out the bottom of her black hoodie, which she'd drawn tight around her head. A cast covered one of her wrists.

Atlas moved to run to her, but stopped when he realized it wasn't him that she was walking toward. The girl in the hoodie was making a direct line for the group of children at the edge of the park, picking up speed with each passing moment.

Across the vast field, the little girl in the purple snowsuit stiffened when she noticed the newcomer who was limping toward her. Echo took off at a run, ignoring the shouts of her chaperones and dodging the snowballs that were falling around her like mortars.

Atlas had to hold onto the park bench to steady himself, suddenly short of breath.

Halfway across the park, when the pain in her stitched-up stomach finally overwhelmed her, Sabra dropped to her knees in the snow. But it was no matter—Echo closed the remaining distance between them in an unstoppable, meteoric blur. Sabra spread her arms wide just in time to let them envelop her baby sister, her miracle, and never again let go.

Notes on History and Gratitude

One of the perks of living in Boston: If you want to write a book about history, the city has spent the last four hundred years doing all the hard work for you.

I have done my best to remain faithful to the historical events and locales referenced throughout this book. However, I do not claim to be a historian, and this is foremost a work of fiction, so at times I have taken small liberties in the name of drama and entertainment. Some elements are entirely of my own fabrication, chiefly, the island of Elderfield Hollow, Cumberland Warwick's journal, and the story of the Serengeti Sapphire (though if only it were real).

I started working on *Nightingale, Sing* in 2012, and while many days it absolutely kicked my ass, I love this story so much that writing it has gotten me through some challenging, uncertain times, which is probably why Sabra's journey ping-pongs between darkness and hope.

So I want to begin by thanking my family—Mom, Dad, Erin, Kelsey, Ray, Logan, Victoria, and baby Brooke—for your love and support even when I'm being an insufferable grumble-face.

To the city of Boston, my home. You continue to teach me so much about hope, resilience, and what it means to pick yourself back up after you've fallen down.

To Ginger Clark, my wonderful agent, for your incisive big-picture revisions and your steadfast commitment to wombat advocacy.

To Dustin Martin, whose editorial feedback helped me trim my word count from a bloated 107k to a svelte 92k. You can take a red pen to my writing any day.

To Bernard and Lili Ozarowski for continuing to let me board at the Cat Hostel when I visit New York for "book stuff" or general shenanigans.

To Jenn Riopel and Jill Melnyk, since our trip to the Crane Estate back in the day inspired Jaro's first riddle.

To Steve Dicheck, Pat Alessi, Jenn Gilpin, Chris Keenan, Jessica Angotti, Amy McDonald Maranville, Lindsey Staniszeski, Justine Martin, Alexandra Mandzak, Meaghan Samere, and anyone else who had to listen to me ramble incessantly about writing, publishing, and researching obscure New England history over the last three years.

Oh, and to anyone who is good friends with Ben Affleck, my favorite director, feel free to casually mention to him what a kick-ass film adaptation this would make.

To my favorite restaurant, Masa. I firmly believe that every author needs a watering hole where he can stare off into space and grease the wheels of creativity with a margarita.

And because I am writing this the week before the AFC Championship Game, and because this is a book about Boston, it would be a grave injustice to end with anything other than:

Go Pats.

ABOUT THE AUTHOR

Karsten Knight is the author of the novels *Wildefire*, *Embers &*
Echoes, and *Afterglow* (Simon & Schuster), though some say his
writing career peaked at the age of six, when he completed a
picture book series about an adventurous worm. He is a
graduate of College of the Holy Cross and earned an MFA in
writing for children from Simmons College. Karsten resides in
Boston, where he lives for fall weather, bowling, and football
season. For more information on Karsten or his books, please
visit his cleverly titled website, www.karstenknightbooks.com.

89789492R00172

Made in the USA
Middletown, DE
18 September 2018